Eden Falls

Jane Sanderson

MIX
FSC
FSC® C104740

Sphere
An imprint of
Little, Brown Book Group
100 Victoria Embankment
London EC4Y 0DY

An Hachette UK Company
www.hachette.co.uk

sphere

SPHERE

First published in Great Britain as a paperback original in 2013 by Sphere

Copyright © Jane Sanderson 2013

The moral right of the author has been asserted.

*All characters and events in this publication, other than
those clearly in the public domain, are fictitious
and any resemblance to real persons,
living or dead, is purely coincidental.*

A CIP catalogue record for this book
is available from the British Library.

ISBN 978-0-7515-5022-1

Typeset in Sabon LT Std by Palimpsest Book Production Limited,
Falkirk, Stirlingshire
Printed and bound in Great Britain by Clays Ltd, St Ives plc

Papers used by Sphere are from well-managed forests
and other responsible sources.

For Eleanor, Joseph and Jacob – cool runnings

Acknowledgements

Thanks are due, as ever, to my wonderful parents Anne and Bob Sanderson, whose love and support is something I tend to take entirely for granted because it has always been there and continues to flow south-west from Yorkshire with steady dependability.

Thank you, too, to everyone at Sphere for transforming my words into books and particular thanks to Zoe Gullen, whose copy-editing leaves no comma unturned, no anachronism unquestioned. Like a good gardener she weeds my manuscripts and pulls out the words I don't need. My books are always the better for her diligence.

Thank you to my agent, Andrew Gordon, for his wise counsel and stoical support at times of need. And to my friend Mary Rose Gavin, thank you for giving me the word 'Pa' just when I needed it – on such small details is authenticity built.

Thank you to my daughter, Elly, for enjoying my books; I can't quite articulate how much that means to me. (To my boys, Joe and Jake, I hope you enjoy them when you do read them; there will be a short test on themes, plot lines and principal characters on our next holiday.) And to all three of you, thank you for the phenomenal frequent rushes of maternal pride that you give me without even realising it.

Finally, and crucially, thank you to Brian Viner for being a gold standard husband: loving, loyal, funny and calmly optimistic. I won't say I couldn't do it without you, but I'm profoundly happy that I don't have to.

Foreword

The following background is intended for those readers who are unfamiliar with *Netherwood* and *Ravenscliffe*.

When Arthur Williams is killed in a mining accident in 1903, Eve Williams has to find a way to support herself and her three young children, Seth, Eliza and Ellen. She does this by selling her home-cooked pies and pastries, supported in the venture by Anna Rabinovich, a young Russian widow who lodges in Eve's house with her baby daughter Maya.

Eve's enterprise attracts the attention of Teddy Hoyland, the Sixth Earl of Netherwood, who invests in her business, making it possible to move into new, large premises in Netherwood. Amos Sykes, a miner and union activist, and former colleague and friend of the late Arthur Williams, advises Eve not to accept help from the earl who, as the owner of Netherwood's collieries, is Amos's natural foe. However, Eve ignores his advice and the venture grows from strength to strength. Amos falls in love with Eve and proposes marriage, but is gently rebuffed. He throws himself into trade-union activity, and is sacked from the colliery for his efforts, but is promptly offered new employment with the Yorkshire Miners' Association.

Eve meets her future second husband when she works for

a short time for the Countess of Netherwood at their London home in Belgravia. Daniel McLeod is head gardener there, and he takes a position at Netherwood Hall in order to marry Eve. Her oldest child, Seth, initially resents Daniel, although gradually he comes to terms with his presence in the family.

With Anna and Maya, the increasingly prosperous family move to Ravenscliffe, a detached house on Netherwood Common. Eve's brother, Silas Whittam, has by now entered the story, having come back into her life after a sixteen-year absence, during which he made his fortune as an importer of bananas from Jamaica. Eve is delighted to see him, and makes him welcome, but Anna, Amos and Daniel find him abrasive and untrustworthy. Silas has little interest in their opinion, however; his priority is to rekindle the closeness that he and his sister shared during the years of their impoverished childhood. These days, he is an ambitious man. He buys a colliery near Netherwood to supply his own steam ships with coal, and he plans to build a hotel near Port Antonio in Jamaica, and expand his business interests into tourism.

When Teddy Hoyland, the earl, is killed in a freak accident in 1905, his elder son, Tobias, inherits the title. Tobias marries a lively American, Dorothea Stirling, whom everyone calls Thea, apart from Tobias's mother Clarissa Hoyland, the dowager countess, who disapproves vehemently of the match and always uses her daughter-in-law's full name. Thea is a sexually adventurous young woman, who embarks upon a passionate love affair with Tobias's sister, Lady Henrietta. Tobias doesn't know the extent of their intimacy, but is simply pleased that they are close. The affair cools of its own accord, and by the beginning of *Eden Falls* a new distance characterises their relationship. Lady Henrietta, meanwhile, has found another outlet for her energies; she has joined the campaign for women's suffrage, and her name is frequently in the newspapers as a spokeswoman for the Women's Social and Political Union.

Clarissa Hoyland, unwilling to embrace the role of dowager countess, accepts a marriage proposal from Archie Partington and becomes Duchess of Plymouth. With her youngest daughter Isabella, she leaves Netherwood, to live at Denbigh Court, the Partington family seat.

Amos Sykes, encouraged by Anna, runs for Parliament, and by the end of *Ravenscliffe* has been elected Labour MP for Ardington. He and Anna have fallen in love, and married. But their relationship is challenging. She, having discovered a talent for interior design, has painted a mural for Thea, the new Countess of Netherwood, and this leads to a great many enquiries from other aristocrats keen to commission Anna. Amos hates this idea; it compromises his principles, to work so closely with the people he regards as the enemy. Anna, however, loves her work, which is also an essential financial support for her husband's – unpaid – political career.

Ravenscliffe ends in 1906. *Eden Falls* opens in 1909.

Principal Characters

Jamaica

Silas Whittam	Millionaire shipping magnate and owner of the Whittam Hotel
Hugh Oliver	Second-in-command at Whittam & Co.
Seth Williams	Assistant manager at the Whittam Hotel, nephew of Silas Whittam
Ruby Donaldson	Cook at the Whittam Hotel
Roscoe Donaldson	Ruby's son
Scotty	Porter at the Whittam Hotel
Maxwell	Porter at the Whittam Hotel
Batista	Kitchen hand and waitress at the Whittam Hotel
Bernard	Gardener at the Whittam Hotel
Justine	Housekeeper at Sugar Hill, the home of Silas Whittam
Henri	Gardener and handyman at Sugar Hill

Netherwood

Daniel MacLeod	Head gardener at Netherwood Hall
Eve MacLeod	Businesswoman and wife of Daniel, sister of Silas Whittam
Angus MacLeod	Son of Eve and Daniel
Eliza Williams	Older daughter of Eve by her late first husband Arthur
Ellen Williams	Eve's younger daughter
Mademoiselle Evangeline	Eliza's ballet teacher
Lilly Pickering	Housekeeper and child minder at Ravenscliffe, Eve and Daniel's home on Netherwood Common

Bedford Square, London and Ardington, Yorkshire

Anna Sykes	Painter of interior murals, Russian émigrée
Amos Sykes	Labour MP for Ardington, Anna's huband
Maya Rabinovich-Sykes	Anna's daughter by her late first husband Leo
Norah Kelly	Housekeeper at Bedford Square
Miss Cargill	Maya's governess
Enoch Wadsworth	Labour Party activist, union organiser, Amos's friend and agent

Netherwood Hall, Yorkshire and Fulton House, London

Tobias Hoyland	The Seventh Earl of Netherwood

Thea Hoyland	The Countess of Netherwood
Eugene Stiller	American portrait artist
Lady Henrietta Hoyland	Older sister of Tobias
Parkinson	Butler at Netherwood Hall
Mrs Powell-Hughes	Housekeeper at Netherwood Hall
Sarah Pickersgill	Cook at Netherwood Hall
Ulrich von Hechingen	A young German man
Liese von Hechingen	Ulrich's aunt
Ballantyne	Butler at Fulton House
The Hon Dickie Hoyland	Younger brother of Tobias, living in Italy

Denbigh Court, Devon and Park Lane House, London

Archie Partington	The Duke of Plymouth
Clarissa Partington	The Duchess of Plymouth, formerly Dowager Countess of Netherwood
Lady Isabella Hoyland	Clarissa's younger daughter, sister of the Earl of Netherwood, debutante
Peregrine Partington	Marquess of Hampden, son and heir of the Duke of Plymouth
Amandine Partington	Wife of Peregrine
Padgett	Butler at Park Lane House

Others

Herbert Asquith	Prime Minister
David Lloyd George	Chancellor of the Exchequer

Emmeline, Christabel and Sylvia Pankhurst	Suffragettes
Mary Dixon	Suffragette
Marcia de Lisle	Client of Anna Sykes
Mr Arbuthnot	Magistrate at Bow Street Court
William Thorpe and Jennifer Hathersage	Students at the Slade School of Fine Art, employees of Anna Sykes

PART ONE

Chapter 1

~~~~

The charabanc laboured up the last stretch of the hill and then, where the road flattened out and swung left, took the corner with an air of quiet triumph, like a runner finding his stride. There was a break in the trees here which revealed, fleetingly, a glittering strip of sea; on cue, the English passengers exclaimed at the vivid turquoise, which was indeed an extraordinary sight, unless the slate-grey monotony of the Bristol Channel was unknown to you and Caribbean colours were commonplace. Certainly the driver, a local man, didn't even glance at the view; he only stared ahead, and his face remained shuttered.

They were here to see an old sugar estate, built in 1758 and abandoned some time in the middle of the nineteenth century, after emancipation had done for slave labour and the plantation could no longer meet its costs. There were many such places, and together they told the story of Jamaica. This is what Silas Whittam liked to tell his guests, the ones who politely enquired about the island's history.

'Jamaica's ruins,' he would say musingly, as if for the first time. 'They're everywhere, resonant with sorrow, redolent of disappointment and lost dreams.' Silas ran the tour from the

3

Whittam Hotel to the old sugar estate out near Hope Bay. He had had pamphlets printed, telling a potted, palatable version of plantation life, spiced up with a few distinctly less palatable details – all perfectly true: a slave whipped to death for looking the overseer in the eye; a Creole heiress, granddaughter of the original planter, who hanged herself when, after the Emancipation Act, her slaves simply set down their cane bills and walked away into the hills. The great house, the sugar mill, the boiling house, the slave huts: all of them stood in varying states of dereliction, and the guests from the Whittam Hotel picked their way in and out of them, imagining the goings on. The estate was on high land and the views were remarkable; it was comforting, said one of the visitors to her companion, to think that the slaves, in the midst of their travails, would at least have been able to enjoy this vista, the majesty of the Caribbean Sea, which winked in the sunshine in the near distance.

The driver always parked in the shade of a cotton tree, and took out his tobacco tin as the passengers disembarked. Once a week he made this trip, and his surliness was as steadily dependable as the heat of the sun. His name was Scotty, but he had nothing to say on that subject or any other. He brought them here; he waited; he took them back. While they explored the plantation he squatted against the trunk of the tree and chewed tobacco, and took very little care where he spat. Sometimes, as they came back towards the vehicle, he seemed to take aim.

It was unsettling for the guests. On their return one or two of them would always complain. Certainly no one ever took the trip more than once.

Ruby Donaldson followed the same coastal road as the chara-banc twice a day, with her boy, Roscoe. She was a cook at the

Whittam Hotel, he a pupil at Port Antonio School, and they had walked this route together for three years now, side by side, although he would no longer let her hold his hand. Sometimes, like today, they left home early and took a detour to Eden Falls, where Roscoe liked to swim in the lagoon, while Ruby watched him from the bank, as patient and still as the hill behind her. Ruby never swam: even as a child she had always preferred to be dry rather than wet. But Roscoe – he was half boy, half fish. Sometimes she checked him for fins and gills.

Today he carefully folded his school clothes and placed them on a rock, to keep the red ants out of his shorts.

'Count until I come up again,' he said to her. 'See how long I can stay under.' Then he swallow-dived into the blue water with no more of a splash than if he were an arrow fired from a bow. For a little while she could see the shape of him, a skinny shadow moving down into the darker depths of the lagoon. Then, too quickly, she lost him, his shadow blending with other shadows, his shape swallowed by the water. On this side of the lagoon, far away from the falls, the water was as still as glass.

Unease came stealthily upon her and her placid, clear-eyed face grew troubled. Roscoe was gone and here was she, sitting on the bank in the early morning, counting aloud like a fool-fool. So she stopped counting and stood, brushing dry grass from the seat of her green print dress, trying to dispel her fear with busyness. She turned her back on the water, told herself that when she turned again to face it he would be there, bobbing like a cork, droplets of water hanging like crystals in his black hair. And she kept herself from turning too soon. If she did, she told herself, he wouldn't be there; and if he wasn't there when she turned, he would be drowned.

Something delicious had woven itself into the breeze and carried itself down the mountain, and instinctively Ruby sniffed the air. Someone was cooking up fish for breakfast; herring sprats, blackening over hot coals. She imagined the cook at the barbecue pit, flipping the fish onto a platter with a stick, pulling away the hot flesh, avoiding the pesky pin bones, burning her fingers. She hated her, this unknown woman, for her trivial concerns. Envied her too. Then Ruby turned and the thread of hope she had carefully spun snapped at the sight of the untroubled water. You would think to look at it that no living thing moved beneath its surface, least of all a strong and beautiful boy. She walked to the rock that he'd dived from and picked up the small, tidy pile of clothes. She buried her face in his shirt and inhaled; the smell of him was of warm cornbread. She put the clothes back on their rock, cupped her hands to her mouth and called for her son, summoning him from the depths, demanding that he return to her.

'Roscoe!'

Her voice came out shrill with panic and her chest heaved with the beginnings of grief. Poised, ready to shout again, she waited. Nothing. The pool returned her gaze with a glassy stare. He was dead then, claimed by the water. This she knew for a fact. Still, though, she shouted again.

'Roscoe!'

And then, on the very far side, where the lagoon boiled and foamed as the falls hit the water, the boy rushed upwards like a newborn child expelled from the womb into the world, gulping at the air. Warm relief flooded Ruby's body then, hard on its heels, fury. She sat down again, made lightheaded by the swift exit of fear. Roscoe, oblivious, trod water and grinned at her from a distance, and his teeth flashed in the sunshine. He began to swim away from the falls with the ease and skill of a water-dweller, until he was close enough to be heard.

'How long?' he shouted when he stopped, as if that was

all that mattered. She didn't answer because she couldn't; she had thought she had lost him to the pool's bottomless depths, and so she watched him swim back to her across the water, haul himself out of the shallows and step up towards her onto the bank. Then she seized him by his bony shoulders. Her fingers dug into his skin and it hurt. He writhed to get free, but she had him pinned.

'Lord, chile,' she said then, not gently.

'How long?' he said again, though he knew she hadn't counted at all, and it was a shame, because he'd almost burst his lungs under there and he knew it must have been four minutes, maybe five. She released one hand, cuffed him on the side of the head and said, 'Cu ya! Me thought you a dead.'

Roscoe thought, If she caught me talking in that way she'd smack me for that too. He was eight now and since the day he first opened his mouth to speak – early, Ruby said, taking the credit – he'd had standard English rammed down his throat and when he drifted into patois she fell on him like the wrath of God. The king's English was the way to raise yourself on this island of Jamaica, she always told him; the king's English showed your brains and your breeding. So when Ruby lapsed into the language of her childhood it was a desperate measure, a signal to Roscoe that his mother had moved beyond anger and into the realm of distress. He felt resentful, not sorry, but he swallowed the temptation to talk back at her, choosing instead the useful device of artful meekness.

'Sorry, Ruby,' he said. He called her by her first name because, although she was his mother, there were just fourteen years separating them and she seemed to the world, and to him, more like an older sister. His face was the image of abject contrition: large brown eyes full of pain; mouth downturned, full of sadness. It was an act, but he hated it when she was like this; the sooner he brought her back to him the better. She hesitated, and some of the tension left her face. She let go of his shoulder. He could feel the place on his skin where her nails had dug in and he raised a hand and rubbed, and Ruby capitulated. She pulled him to her and rubbed his head where she had struck him.

'Come,' she said. 'Dry yourself off and get dressed. You're making me late, and you know what a terror Mr Silas is about tardiness.'

She rolled her eyes and grinned, and Roscoe grinned back at her.

'I wish you'd counted though, Ruby,' he said, risking a complaint. 'I was under a long, long time.'

'Did you see the water dragon?'

He laughed. 'Yes I did. He sends his regards.'

'And did you touch the bottom?'

'There is no bottom, Ruby.' He'd always heard this, but now he believed it. 'I swam and swam, but it never came.'

'I thought I'd lost you,' she said, suddenly serious again. 'Don't do that again. Stay away from the water.'

'No. You stay away,' he said. 'You stay away.'

He was right, she thought. He shouldn't be fettered by her fears for his safety. He should test himself, find his limits, explore life's possibilities: and he should do it unobserved by her.

There was a path from Eden Falls, a narrow strip of vegetation trodden flat leading first up the mountain, through a tunnel of green, and then down again, to Port Antonio. Ruby and Roscoe, single file, picked their way along it and at the top, where it met the road, they fell in beside each other again. In due course, Ruby turned for the hotel and Roscoe continued on to school.

The Whittam Hotel was a fine building, the finest in Port Antonio, although there were plenty of locals who thought the town had done very well without it. Built in the style of a plantation house, it occupied the higher reaches of Eden Hill, which rose to the west of the town in a series of natural terraces. The hotel was a perfect distance from the port: close enough to afford a view of all its colour and bustle but far enough that its less edifying characteristics – the pungent smells, the ripe profanities – stayed where they belonged.

Beyond the port lay the Caribbean Sea, and Silas Whittam, hotelier and shipping magnate, could never look upon it without emotion. These peerless waters reminded him of his younger self: a ship's lad, seeing the tropics for the first time and believing this to be an enchanted place. The years had passed and the fates had singled him out for special treatment. The fates, that is, and Sir Walter Hollis. His former boss at the Global Steamship Company had been so entirely won over by his protégé's judicious mix of hard work and sycophancy that he had gifted to Silas a small fleet of refrigerated ships. With these, Silas had prospered and grown, wealth coming swiftly and easily as he sailed between Bristol and Port Antonio. He'd bought an old sugar plantation – they were going for a song by the time he was in a position to cast an acquisitive eye across Jamaican soil – and replaced the cane with bananas. In this way he had truly made his fortune, for the fruit he shipped was now his own, and the powerful growers no longer his concern. The hotel had come later, when he realised that his cargo ships could be equipped for passengers; or, rather, that luxury passenger liners could be equipped for cargo. He bought Eden Hill and, with machetes and manpower, had vanquished the jungle. The hotel had been built to Silas's precise specifications and its grounds meticulously landscaped; now, where ferns and vines had once romped in unchecked abundance, there were lawns and herbaceous borders immaculately planted with English flowers. It was the garden of a proud colonialist, not the garden of a plantsman. The indigenous blooms – the poincianas, the alamandas, the trusty plumbago – were cast aside in favour of hollyhocks, delphiniums and Michaelmas daisies, whose pale hues seemed paler still in the unrelenting yellow light of the Jamaican sun, or the periodic onslaughts of warm tropical wind and rain.

A long path zigzagged down the terraces to the wrought-iron gateway at the road and as Ruby approached it from one direction a man was coming towards it from the other. He carried a great wooden box of provisions on his head and moved lethargically, like a soul burdened not with vegetables but with all the cares of the world. His face, when he saw Ruby, bloomed into a wide smile.

'Good morning Maxwell,' Ruby said, her words clipped and bright.

'Miss Ruby,' Maxwell replied, talking in the same way that he walked: slowly, lazily, taking all the time in the world. 'How de pickney?'

'Roscoe is very well, thank you.'

She smiled at the porter and waited with him while he leaned his lanky frame against the gate and lifted the box from his head. He placed it on the road at his feet and they both looked down at it: asparagus, carrots, celery, mushrooms – English vegetables shipped over from Bristol's costermongers as if nothing grew in the fertile soil of Jamaica. Maxwell gave Ruby a look: a languid, disdainful roll of the eyes. The twisted cotton cotta looked ludicrous with the box gone, but he left it on his head anyway, and dipped into the pocket of his baggy trousers for a tin of Red Man. Ruby said, 'Maxwell, that tobacco is turning your teeth the colour of wet mud,' but he chuckled and with gracious irony held out the open tin to her as if she might be tempted to nip out a portion, as he had done, and pop it into her pink and white mouth.

10

'It rots your body from the top down,' she said sternly, and he laughed again, a full-throated, drawn-out, Jamaican laugh. He liked Ruby. She was full of advice that he hadn't asked for, but she wasn't as prim and proper as she made out. She was built for love, was Ruby, with her wide, slanting eyes like a cat and her beautiful round backside. When, like this morning, providence brought them to the hotel path together Maxwell always let Ruby go in front, waving her on in a gentlemanly manner then feasting at his leisure on the sight of her lovely buttocks, which moved against the fabric of her dress like two ripe mangoes in a bag.

'Shall we?' she said now, indicating the gate and the upward path.

Maxwell bent down, his long body folding itself in two, then, with a fluid, seamless movement, unfolding again to lift the box up and onto his head. 'After you, Miss Ruby,' he said and she nodded approval at him, pleased by his manners.

Halfway up the path, where it diverged so that kitchen staff and tradesmen could make their final ascent to the hotel's back door out of sight of the guests, Silas Whittam was waiting, a scowl darkening his handsome features. He held a fine gold fob in one hand and he shook it at them as Ruby and Maxwell approached.

'Here de harbour shark to wish us good day,' said Maxwell none too quietly, and Ruby laughed. It was this insolence, as much as their lateness, which now provoked their employer.

'God damn it! You were due here thirty minutes ago and you have the brass neck to mutter and smirk at me.'

They couldn't deny it so they said nothing at all, and continued their measured pace up the path.

'I should sack you here and now,' Silas said. His face was

11

hard with resentment. 'I should send you packing, you useless, feckless, no-good pair. Thirty staff, and not a good one among you. Can you actually tell the time? Or do you just stroll along to work when the cock stops crowing or when the mango drops from the tree?'

Maxwell whistled through his teeth and Ruby nodded slowly as if to say, I hear you and I see you, but I don't heed you. He had built himself a great house but it didn't make them slaves, and the plain fact was he needed them more than they needed him. A hundred and forty-six arrivals today, the Whittam liner due in at midday; without Ruby in the kitchen they'd all go hungry, and without Maxwell and Scotty they'd all be carrying their own valises. All of this she expressed with her eyes, cutting the boss a cold, bold look as she passed. Ruby Donaldson had a friendly word for almost everyone, but not for Silas Whittam, no. He was a waste of good breath.

Chapter 2

⤜⤜⤜⤜∾∾∾

'**M**ust the dogs be in the painting?'

'Why? Can't you paint dogs?'

Eugene Stiller laid down his brush.

'I can paint dogs, yes. But what I can paint and what I choose to paint are quite different matters.'

'But Eugene,' said Thea Hoyland, who knew the artist well and as a result had scant regard for either his professionalism or his personal dignity, 'you don't actually choose to paint anything, do you? You paint what you're paid to paint. Or at least that's what I understood.'

She smiled at him to temper her rudeness, which was apparent even to her. He'd placed her on a cushioned window seat at such an angle that her face was on one side washed in natural light, and on the other almost wholly in shade. This, thought Eugene Stiller, was nicely symbolic, a representation of the good and bad in her, the sweet and the sour. It was how he entertained himself through the long hours of any commission: revealing, by the tilt of a chin or the glint of an eye, a facet of his sitter's personality that other artists – perhaps less well tutored than he in the school of realism – would be unable to depict satisfactorily through the medium of oil on canvas.

Selfishness, cruelty, kindness, avarice, loyalty: Eugene Stiller saw these traits as physical characteristics which, like a mole on the cheek or a missing finger, must be faithfully represented.

'To a point,' he said now, tartly. 'Though I have been known to say no.'

'But you won't say no to my spaniels, I hope?'

'Jittery creatures, spaniels.'

'Well so am I, for that matter. If it's jitteriness you object to, better paint that bowl of fruit over there.'

Eugene laughed. He'd forgotten how relentlessly sassy Thea Hoyland was; or, at least, he remembered the sassiness, but had expected it to be replaced with something more mellow and soberly aristocratic now that she was – of all things – a countess. Eugene and Thea were friends of the type whose shared history was of more significance than their shared interests. For twelve consecutive years their respective parents had rented neighbouring beach houses on Long Island, and every summer vacation of their childhoods had been spent in enforced proximity to each other; they would bicker tirelessly on the sand as they toiled, summer after summer, on the same joint projects – a hole, a castle, a pool for a captive lobster, a channel to the sea. When, one summer, Eugene's parents came to the beach house without him, Thea's first emotion had been relief that the holes, castles and channels would this year be done entirely her way. She had been disappointed to discover that, without Eugene, none of it was much fun: the bickering, she realised, was the part she most enjoyed. Now here they were, in the drawing room of Netherwood Hall, she the Countess of Netherwood, he a significant young painter with a gold medal for portraiture from the New York School of Art, and still they bickered. And yet the back-and-forth snippiness, the trading of snipes, possessed an excluding, confidential quality, as if, far from being an obstacle to friendship, it was absolute proof of it.

'If you tip your head downwards a little, and look directly

14

at the canvas, you'll find we see more of your lovely eyes,' Eugene said. He waited a beat before continuing. 'And at the same time, the weakness of your chin is disguised.'

'Beast,' she said. She pulled the spaniels closer as if for comfort, one on her left side, one on her right. They gazed up at her adoringly, resting their muzzles on her lap.

'They should at least face me,' Eugene said. He felt the need to assert his authority; she had treated the whole exercise as something of a joke ever since his arrival. 'I'll sketch them in and see how they look. I'm absolutely not convinced.'

Behind them, the door opened and immediately both dogs sprang down to the floor, further proving their unsuitability for the project. Eugene shot Thea a look of smug justification, which she ignored. Instead she stood up and stretched extravagantly, as if all her joints were stiff, although their session had really only just begun. Her husband wandered in – another aggravation for Eugene, these constant and casual interruptions – and stooped to fondle the silken ears of the dogs at his feet. He then said, rather flatly and as if they were already mid-conversation, 'I'm going to see a man about a yacht.'

'A yacht?' Thea said. 'For sailing?'

'Of course for sailing.' The earl answered his wife but looked at Eugene, who said, 'Kinda landlocked for that caper, aren't you?'

Tobias smiled at him. 'I don't propose to sail through Yorkshire. The yacht's moored at Portsmouth.'

'You don't sail. Buy another car if you need a diversion.'

This was Thea, and her voice seemed altered, Eugene thought: not cold exactly, but bored. He had noticed this, living, as he currently did, with the earl and countess. Sometimes Tobias and Thea spoke to each other like a couple with no expectation of mutual amusement.

Tobias looked at her now, and said, 'I'm quite sure, when you're fully apprised of the facts, that you'll take a different view,' and then he turned and left the room, leaving the door open so that the spaniels trailed out after him, until Thea called them back in a petulant voice that reminded Eugene very much of his contrary little playmate on the Long Island beach. He raised his eyebrows at her.

'Hmm, chilly in here,' he said.

And Thea, who was now thoroughly put out by her husband's cryptic announcement, said, 'Oh button it, Eugene,' and walked from the room too, leaving the artist alone with the spaniels. They sat side by side in front of his canvas, as if waiting for direction, watching him closely. Eugene pushed the hair out of his eyes – he grew it long, because he was an artist – and blew a low whistle of exasperation. 'What a madhouse,' he said to the dogs.

With Toby gone, it was hardly worth setting the table for dinner. This, at least, is what Thea told Parkinson, the butler. And although he did as instructed and prepared to serve the evening meal in the morning room, it was with profound misgiving bordering on reluctance. In his view, the morning room was so named for a very good reason; east facing, it caught the best of the early sun and held on to it until midday, after which the natural light travelled westward through the house, concluding its daily duties by alighting on the crystal and silver plate in the dining room. These long early-summer evenings meant that candles need not be lit nor chandeliers switched on until almost nine o'clock. The morning room, however, was another matter: gloomy by evening, and the table barely big enough for the tureens.

'It's not as if it's any less trouble,' he said to Sarah Pickersgill, the cook. 'If anything, it's more so. All the glasses to be moved, all the china, all the silver; and it's that bit further from the back stairs.'

She nodded. The best way, with Mr Parkinson, was to agree. At least then there was a possibility that the conversation might move towards something more interesting than the countess's unreasonable requests. Sarah regarded him across the top of her cup of tea. He had aged in the three years following the terrible death of the sixth earl and his son's succession. Mr Parkinson's preternaturally blond curls had, at last, lost their youthfulness and turned a peppery grey; his once unlined skin had succumbed to wrinkles, which gathered at the corners of his mouth and eyes, and ran in spidery lines across his brow. It was ironic, thought Sarah, that the more grave and dignified Mr Parkinson's appearance had become, the less like a butler he behaved. Eight years ago, when Sarah had first come to Netherwood Hall as kitchen maid, he had been a perfect living template for the job – discreet, efficient, unswervingly loyal – yet in appearance he had resembled nothing so much as an overgrown choirboy. Now, when the cherubic twinkle had at last been replaced by something more apt for his age and position, Mr Parkinson had turned into an inveterate grumbler. It had happened by degrees: a tart comment here, a disapproving remark there, until his occasional pique had grown into a permanent state of disgruntlement which was quite unlike his old self and, truth be told, entirely inappropriate in an elderly family retainer. At least he confined his outbursts to a limited audience; Mrs Powell-Hughes, the housekeeper, was his preferred confidante but, in her absence, Sarah Pickersgill would do. She was a placid listener, rarely interjecting or contradicting. Now she sipped at her tea and ran through the evening's menu in her head while appearing to share his troubles. There was little need to concentrate; his was a one-note song. His criticisms and complaints were always directed at the countess, at whose feet he placed all perceived ills: lapsed standards, dismantled traditions, flouted moral codes.

'I can't imagine,' he said now, 'what Lady Henrietta will have to say about it. Even when she's alone in the house it wouldn't enter her head to dine anywhere other than the dining room. And quite right too. But you see, there's the difference between being born to this life and stumbling into it by chance.'

'Oh, well,' said Sarah neutrally. She made a mental note to remove the chicken terrine from the cold store before tackling the rainbow trout. Parkinson grumbled on.

'English traditions have always been upheld in this house, not to say revered. Why upset the applecart? There's nothing to be gained from it, and very much indeed to be lost.'

'I expect Her Ladyship just fancied a change,' Sarah said, meaning to soothe. The butler snapped his mouth into a firm line of disapproval. Her Ladyship's capricious nature, her deliberate breaking of the unwritten rules was, in his opinion, chipping away at the dignity of the household. Sometimes he felt quite alone in the battle to preserve it. Across the table, Sarah smiled. She felt a little sorry for the butler, so thoroughly out of kilter with the new order. If he could but forget how life used to be and embrace – or at least accept – how it now was, he would be a good deal happier, she thought.

'I should get on,' she said. 'Them fish won't fillet themselves.' She stood, expecting Mr Parkinson to do the same. Instead he stayed in his chair, holding his teacup in both hands and staring hard into the dregs as though he was reading his future in the leaves.

In spite of Parkinson's concerns, the morning-room table was quite large enough for three diners and, being oval, it seemed somehow more convivial.

'Good idea, Thea,' Henrietta said when she tracked down the countess and Eugene after finding the dining room empty. 'We should do this more often.'

'Tell Parkinson that,' Thea replied. 'But do it quickly, because I think he might be taking his own life in the silver safe.'

'Oh dear, poor Parkinson.' Henrietta glanced at the footmen, who stared blankly ahead. 'He does seem down in the dumps these days, doesn't he? Do be kind, Thea.' She took up her knife and fork and sliced a neat corner from her perfect square of chicken terrine, then said, 'What do you think about the yacht?'

'I *am* kind. That is, I'm not unkind.'

'A little impetuous sometimes, perhaps.' Henrietta spoke with a calm authority, feeling entitled to her opinions since she and Thea had once indulged in a short love affair of considerable intensity. There was no longer the warmth of desire in Henrietta's eyes when she looked at Thea, however, just a calm cordiality, a sisterly affection, but certainly she was in a position to gently judge.

'Toby's yacht,' she said again now. 'What do you think of the scheme?'

Thea took a sip of the Meursault that Parkinson had chosen to accompany the course; she had yet to show an interest in the terrine. Henrietta watched her, waiting for an answer, but it was Eugene who broke the silence.

'Sailing's terrific fun,' he said. 'Do you remember Pop's boat, Thea? The little sloop at Oyster Bay? Some laughs, huh?'

'Gosh, Thea, do you sail?'

'Does she sail? I'll say she sails. They used to call her Pocahontas at the Seawanhaka Yacht Club – though it may have been on account of the braids rather than the expertise.' Eugene laughed, and Thea watched him, unsmilingly, with cool green eyes. She picked up a fork and glanced briefly at her plate, then looked at Henrietta.

'He told me he was buying a yacht, yes,' she said.

'And? What do you think?' Henrietta was a dogged conversationalist, rarely discouraged by reluctance on the part of another. She was also used to Thea's intermittent sulks, which in the hot vortex of her infatuation with her sister-in-law, had had the power to wound. Now, however, Henrietta was happily impervious. Having discovered, with Thea's help, her sexual preferences, she had learned how to read the signs in others. She was currently exchanging letters with a plucky little suffragette in Guildford, whose trenchant views were matched in their vigour by a fierce devotion to Henrietta. It wasn't entirely mutual, but it was diverting and better than nothing.

'We can take the yacht to Cowes in August,' she said cheerfully. 'You too, Eugene, if you're still with us.'

'Oh,' said Thea, 'do you mean to abandon the cause for the high life, Henry?' She carried a sliver of terrine up to her mouth, placed it in and chewed. The combination of chicken, tarragon and aspic was curious: the meat dry, the herb pungent, the jelly cold and wet on her tongue. She took another, larger mouthful of wine to wash away the taste.

'No,' Henrietta said with great and exaggerated patience, 'I shall go to Cowes a suffragette and I shall doubtless return a suffragette. I don't believe I am obliged to eschew all merriment in the name of votes for women.'

'You're talking about the Cowes regatta, right?' said Eugene, keen to move the conversation on from this uncomfortable bout of restrained bickering.

'Are we?' said Thea, and in spite of herself she looked a little brighter.

'Mmm,' said Henrietta, through her food. Unlike her sister-in-law, she ate with gusto – always had. She was tall and strong and hungry, and made no apology for her appetite. Also, since her mother's marriage to the Duke of Plymouth there had been no one at home to upbraid her about it. 'You're being fearfully slow, Thea. This year the Russian emperor is to sail to the Isle of Wight on the imperial yacht to visit the king. Absolutely everyone will be there.' She paused and laughed, including both Eugene and Thea in the joke. 'There's not an aristocrat in England, nor a royal in Europe, who isn't all of a sudden a passionate sailor.'

'Gee,' Eugene said. 'Don't throw eggs at the tsar, Henrietta.' She humoured him with a small smile.

Thea replaced her knife and fork on her plate to indicate that she had finished. Her face had the glow that came and went with her moods; Eugene regarded her through his painter's eyes and thought how lovely she could look, and how unlovely: how to capture that in oils?

'Toby didn't tell me all that,' she said. 'It sounds fun.'

'Oh good, you've cheered up,' Henrietta said.

'Well, Toby didn't tell me the best part.'

'You didn't exactly encourage him, did you?' Eugene said. 'You told him to buy another car instead. You were very disagreeable.'

'Well. He started it.'

She sounded like a five-year-old, thought Henrietta. She looked at Eugene, who was licking his knife. He winked at her and she almost wished her mother were with them; she would have so detested this evening. Thea raised an arm and snapped her fingers at a footman.

'More wine, Thomas,' she said, and then: 'So, Henry, what do we wear?'

'The art at Cowes,' Henrietta said, 'is to dress very simply, at huge expense.'

'Like Marie Antoinette's shepherdess period, but nautical?'

'Exactly.'

Thea sighed contentedly. How pleasant to have a scheme. She wished now that Tobias were still here, so that she could be pleased with him. Still, at least she had Eugene at her beck and call, and he was much better than nothing at all.

Chapter 3

༺☙ ❧༻

There was a garden for the residents of Bedford Square and, though it was small, it was green and peaceful, at least until the city roused itself and began to bustle and roar. Today had dawned like a blessing: soft sun, gauzy mist and the trees blurry at their edges in the half light. Anna Sykes had woken just before dawn and left the sleeping house to walk under the canopy of fresh spring leaves and look back at her lone footsteps in the dew. Once, not so long ago, she'd lived in a house on the edge of Netherwood Common and had grown accustomed to stepping out of the door and onto grass; here, in the heart of the city, she could almost do that still.

She loved this London home and the square in which it sat. She could think and paint steadily here, rarely lacking ideas or inspiration, and the sober flat-fronted house they rented seemed possessed of a steady creative influence, unusual and precious. In Ardington, at their constituency home, people knocked on the door and made demands, and were quite within their rights since Amos was their Member of Parliament and she his wife. She never tried to sketch there or try out her ideas on canvas, or even think, much. In Ardington her sense of self was informed entirely by her husband's success

22

rather than her own. Here, in London, Anna Sykes was someone else, with a successful business and an income that supported Amos's life at Westminster as well as paying the rent and the wages of a housemaid and a governess. These two different Annas weren't contradictory or incompatible: they rubbed along with each other very well, as long as each had space to breathe.

Now, alone in the sleeping square, she strolled through the grass for a while then took up a stick and wielded it like a golf club to strike the dead, dried head of a late daffodil, watching with some satisfaction as it leapt from the stem and into the air. Another, then another, and then she stopped, thinking that if this were Maya's game instead of her own she would certainly forbid it. She sat down on a convenient bench and tucked her hands under her legs, as if to keep them from further mischief. She was small and slight and colourfully clad in a blue frock and an Indian shawl that depicted exotic flowers in yellow, crimson and white: gaudy flowers she doubted existed, even in India. She was hatless; her preferred condition at a time of day when she knew there would be no passers-by to judge her unrespectable. Her hair – blonde, cropped to just below the jawline – looked tousled, as if she had yet to brush it, which was indeed the case.

On her bench, watching the day begin, Anna considered the light; the way it filtered through the haze of early morning and the leaves of the trees, and fell across the grass in a dappled, lacy carpet. There was no warmth in this dawn sunshine, merely the suggestion of it. Why not, she thought, depict exactly this on the walls of Marcia de Lisle's summer-house? Or perhaps each wall of the hexagonal building could show another phase of the day: dawn through to dusk, the light waxing and waning on its progress. The idea excited her and she stood abruptly, startling a pair of pigeons that had ventured too close, lulled into complacency by her stillness. The birds erupted into ungainly flight and alighted on a gas lamp, from where they watched her with beady, mistrustful eyes. Galvanised by her thoughts, anxious to commit them to paper, Anna walked briskly through the garden and across the road to the elegant Georgian house. She pushed open the door and entered the hallway, and the grandfather clock struck six, as if in greeting. Norah, the maid of all work, heard the latch click shut and stuck her head around the door of the parlour.

'Morning missus,' she said cheerfully. 'Beat me to it again?'

Anna smiled, but abstractedly, and without pausing to pass the time of day she took the stairs, two at a time, all the way up to the top floor of the house where once there would have been a nursery and servants' bedrooms, but which was now furnished with desks, easels and shelf after shelf of artists' materials. She took up a paintbrush and a palette of water-colours and, at a draughtsman's board on which a large sheet of paper had been attached, ready for just such a moment as this, she started to duplicate the images in her head.

An hour later she was still there and so absorbed in her work that she didn't hear her husband's footsteps on the stairs, clomping upwards from the first-floor landing. Amos Sykes might be an MP these days, but he still dressed like a miner, and on the occasions when even he deemed it proper to wear a suit he refused to put anything on his feet other than sturdy boots better suited to a pit yard than the House of Commons. Rightly or wrongly, Amos judged a man by his footwear as much as by his principles. A fellow in two-tone calfskin spectators with a sole no thicker than a rasher of back bacon was not a man to be trusted. For a reasonable man, Amos was unreasonably stubborn in this regard.

'Morning, Rembrandt,' he said now.

His wife looked at him and rolled her eyes, then returned to her work. He laughed at his own joke, since she wouldn't, and then he came up behind her, lifted her hair and kissed the soft nape of her neck.

'Can you see what I'm getting at?' Anna said, stepping back into the circle of his arms. He tilted his head left and then right.

'Dawn, I'd say. Sunrise over Bedford Square.'

She was pleased. 'For that,' she said, 'you get this,' and she turned around and kissed him on the mouth, lingeringly, as if all she had to do today was this, and she was committed to doing it well. When at last she broke away they held each other's gaze for a beat, then she said, 'I'll be down soon.'

He groaned. 'Do you mean you're sending me away?'

She nodded and adopted a stern expression. 'I need to finish this.' She turned back to the painting with that firmness of resolve which, generally speaking, was one of the qualities Amos admired in his wife but at this moment would have happily exchanged for something else: helpless desire perhaps; wanton lust. But he knew his Anna well. Nothing would be gained by pestering so he left her to it, resigned to breakfast for one and the relentlessly perky chatter of Norah Kelly.

Anna Rabinovich hadn't been looking for a safe harbour, but she had found one anyway. Since childhood she had embraced the principle of change and adventure, had always known that there was more than one life to be lived in the allotted span of one's existence. But there was probably a limit, and these days she assumed that for her it had been reached. For now, at least, she wanted no more than she already had, and when her previous lives impinged on her present – when the memories barged in, unbidden – she felt a small wave of anxiety at the possibility that everything might change again. She was twenty-eight years old, and she had already known so many different ways to live. She had been the cosseted child of a merchant in Kiev; she had been the young wife of a Russian Jew reviled by her parents; she had been an immigrant, fleeing the pogroms and leaving Russia for England in search of sanctuary; she had become a mother and then a widow, and had known abject poverty; she had found peace and friendship in Netherwood, and forged relationships that would always sustain her; and now she was Anna Sykes, and she hoped this fundamental fact would never change, or anyway, not soon. She cherished the present because she understood how different it could be from what was to come.

A woman can't be permanently grateful, however. When she came downstairs to find Amos already gone and the table in disarray she felt a flash of annoyance: with him, with herself and with Norah. There was a pot of stewed tea, a silver rack bearing one slice of brittle toast and a dish that, judging by the unappealing traces of cold fat inside it, had once borne bacon or sausages but was now quite empty. There were crumbs on the tablecloth, lids off the preserves and no clean cutlery or china anywhere in evidence. The morning sun was unforgiving; it streamed through the windows, highlighting the sorry scene.

'Norah!'

Anna waited. Really, the girl had very little to accomplish in the mornings. They were such a small household, especially with Maya away. The child was in Lyme Regis with her governess, Miss Cargill, who had studied Greats at Cambridge and was now funding further academic study by tutoring Maya in all of her own enthusiasms. She took a lively, itinerant approach to teaching: at the moment they were fossil hunting at Church Cliffs, and would be gone for two weeks.

'Norah!'

Maid of no work, Amos called her, which would have been funny if it hadn't been so depressingly true. Footsteps from the kitchen signalled her approach and then there she was, smiling all over her freckled face as if she couldn't be more delighted to have been summoned.

'Mrs Sykes,' she said. 'We'd given you up for lost, me and the mister.'

Norah was from Limerick, where, she was fond of recalling, the pace of life was slow and what work there was to be done got done in its own sweet time. This interesting life philosophy hadn't emerged until after she had been appointed.

'Norah, do you think it might have been an idea to clear away Mr Sykes's breakfast things? Do you think it might have been nicer for me to find table looking spick and span?'

Anna's Russian accent grew stronger when she was cross. Ordinarily, her command of English was near faultless; she had made a hobby of it, collecting idioms and correct pronunciations like other people collected stamps or china thimbles. Annoy her, however, and suddenly her Ws were all Vs and her As were all Es and the definite article – often elusive – disappeared entirely. Norah, reading the signs, flushed a little, though her smile barely faded.

'Well sure, missus, now you're here I'll be clearing that table and putting some fresh toast out, so I will. Will you be wanting tea? Or should I put a pot of coffee out, it being nearly half past nine?'

This sounded like a reproach, even to Norah. 'Either way, it's no trouble missus,' she added judiciously.

'I'll have tea, thank you Norah. I'm going to leave room now and come back in ten minutes, and I expect to see everything as it should be. Do you understand?'

Norah flashed her a baffled, injured look.

'Sure, what do you take me for? An eejit?'

This was something else that Norah's interview hadn't revealed: a tendency towards lippyness when a simple 'yes' would serve. Her manner was altogether too casual and familiar, and in many other households she would have been dismissed within a week of starting. But she was young and Irish and – Amos had said – vulnerable. They had hired her and now they had a moral responsibility to keep her, flaws and all. She was good with Maya, minding her when the two of them were working and Miss Cargill's lessons had finished for the day, and in any case Amos couldn't spend his working day trying to protect the poor and oppressed, then come home in the evening and sack the maid, could he? Anna supposed not, though there had been many a time in the past two years when she would have liked to do exactly that.

'Norah,' she said now, 'please, just do as I asked.'

'I shall, missus.'

Anna made to leave, but before she was out of the door Norah said, 'Ah bejesus, I'll be forgetting my head one day,' and produced a folded piece of paper from the pocket of her pinafore. 'The master asked me to give this to you, missus. It's a few lines to say sorry he missed you and would you like to take a stroll by the river at dinner time?'

'You mean you've read it?' Anna's voice was cold.

'Well of course I have. Sure, what's the point of being able to read if you don't from time to time exercise the talent? He didn't say I wasn't to.'

Anna held out her hand for the note. 'In future, please leave any messages from Mr Sykes on the hall table. Unread, preferably.'

'Oh,' said Norah, diverted from the possibility of contrition by a sudden new thought. 'There's a letter for you, missus, on the hall table, since you mention it. A big fat one. Probably from Mrs MacLeod because it looks to be from Barnsley, although the postmark's a bit blurred and it could be Burnley, so it could, although I thought to myself, But who does the missus know in Burnley?'

As she prattled she handed over Amos's note to Anna and smiled, quite oblivious to the irony of her situation. Anna considered pointing it out – postmarks should not be scrutinised, just as private notes should not be read – then thought again. There was a letter from Yorkshire, and it might be from Eve. Norah's incorrigible nosiness was, by comparison, of no account at all. She left the room and Norah burst immediately into song. She couldn't work if she wasn't allowed to sing; another idiosyncrasy that had revealed itself after her appointment, naturally.

Chapter 4

❦

The docks in Port Antonio were seething with ships, fruit and people, and at the eye of the storm was the stately bulk of the Whittam liner, the *Cassiopeia*. She was a fine vessel, one of three luxury passenger ships owned by the company, and noticeably more spruce than any of the other vessels moored in the greasy blue-green waters of the harbour. The gangplank was down and the first passengers, hesitant and unsteady after three weeks at sea, were beginning to pick their way towards terra firma.

Scotty, watching them, drew on what was left of his cigarette, pinching the inch of stub between thumb and forefinger and pulling the acrid smoke through his teeth. He squinted across at the new arrivals, looking for trouble; he could tell, from their face and bearing, which of these newly hatched Englishmen and women would end up on his wrong side before they had even reached the hotel. He was a connoisseur of the multifarious forms of disdain employed by whites in their dealings with blacks: the curled lip and up-tilting nose, the click of the fingers in place of a 'please'. Scotty had seen it all, and so often that it didn't rattle him any more: it wasn't personal, he knew, and it wasn't even their fault. These highborn English folk had simply lost their way when it came to manners and mutual respect. Scotty didn't care. He relished the prospect of engaging them in battle.

Down on the dockside Mr Silas was running back and forth like a man with bees in his pants, and two steps behind him was young Master Seth, who took his lead, always, from his uncle. Mr Silas in a stew, Master Seth in a stew. Mr Silas happy, Master Seth happy. It was as if the boy had no ideas of his own about how he could be. Neither of them had learned that the way to go in Jamaica was slow: you get there anyway, but you don't break sweat. There were four charabancs belonging to the Whittam Hotel, but they were late – forced to wait, more than likely, for the congested harbour road to clear – and the bewildered gaggle of English passengers milled by the luggage, sticking close together for safety. They looked, thought Scotty, as though they fully expected to be robbed. He laughed aloud at their imagined predicament, and Edna, the mule, shot him a sideways look of reprimand.

'Beg pardon, Your Ladyship,' Scotty said with a small bow. He sucked the last scrap of flavour from the stub of his cigarette, dropped it and ground out its glowing end with his heel. He was barefoot as usual, but the skin on his soles was as good as boot leather. He could strike a match on the balls of his feet; he could walk over hot embers in a barbecue pit.

'Scotty!'

This was Mr Silas, shouting as usual. He dressed cool and casual, thought Scotty, yet he burned up with anger all the time. Today his face, beneath his panama hat, was taut with irritation.

'Scotty, move your idle backside and get this luggage up the hill. Where the devil is Maxwell? And the charabancs?'

Scotty gave no indication that he'd heard and stood where he was for a few comfortable moments longer, before

31

moving in his rangy way towards the trunks and valises that were forming a sizeable obstruction on the quay.

'Seth, you'll have to help him load up the cart or we'll be here all day.' Silas spoke sharply, even to Seth, who had done nothing but oblige him all morning. The boy jumped to it and scowled at Scotty, a reflex he'd learned from his uncle.

'Where's Maxwell?' Silas said again, and then, 'Hands clean?'

Scotty raised his brows and his broad, smooth forehead erupted into furrows. He didn't answer either question, and he certainly didn't hold out his palms for inspection. Instead he hauled a leather trunk up and onto his shoulder, and loped towards the cart that he'd left in the shade cast by the offices of United Exotic Fruits. This had been strategic, calculated to irritate.

'What in God's name are you doing, tethering the mule there?' Silas had followed Scotty; he hissed at him under his breath, keen to disguise his discomposure.

'Shadier shade,' Scotty said. He smiled as he walked along, though to himself, not at Silas.

'Tie the damn beast by the Whittam buildings in future,' Silas said, trotting beside him. Behind, Seth staggered under the weight of two suitcases. His young face was set in a grimace of effort and rivulets of perspiration ran into his eyes. Scotty and Maxwell should deal with all the luggage, he thought; it reflected badly on him to be compelled to do their job. These episodes were frequent, and he found them undermining. It was hard for him to introduce himself as anyone who mattered when all the guests had seen him labouring like a porter at the docks, sweating like a pig. Ahead he could see his Uncle Silas berating Scotty, though his words were inaudible. Scotty, even from behind, exuded unconcern.

'Young man! I say, young man!'

The crisply imperious tones sliced through the hubbub

and commanded attention. Seth turned. A large woman in cerise chiffon – high-necked, long-sleeved, tight-cuffed – was bearing down on him with steely purpose. Seth, immediately anxious at the prospect of a confrontation, felt his ears flush red and his heart beat a little faster, but suddenly there was his uncle, his voice and manner quite altered by a seamless transition to mellifluous cordiality.

'Lady Millbank,' he said, all charm and smiles. 'May I assist you in some way?'

She laughed, hollow and humourless.

'Mr Whittam,' she said stridently. 'We are being jostled by negroes in atrocious heat on a vile-smelling dock where bananas and pineapples appear to take priority over people so, yes, I should imagine you can assist in some way, and I sincerely hope you can do it swiftly.'

There was a brief silence and then Scotty laughed again, mouth wide, showing brown teeth and a wet pink tongue. Lady Millbank took a step backwards in distaste and alarm, and Silas, thin-lipped with fury, ordered him about his business. Scotty gave an insolent shrug and loped off towards the luggage.

Silas shuddered inwardly. In all the time he'd been running this luxury service from Bristol to Jamaica, he still hadn't quite managed to overcome the difficulties encountered after mooring in Port Antonio harbour. An atmosphere of cheerful chaos presided here, always. Crates of bananas, pineapples, mangoes and coconuts blocked the thoroughfares while cargo ships were loaded and unloaded; farmers and peddlers came daily to hawk their paltry produce; old men with rotten teeth and addled minds smiled inanely at visitors and sang strange, tuneless songs, holding out straw hats in expectation of coins; mules brayed, dogs barked, children ran through the mêlée looking for easy pickings from unguarded pockets. Lady Millbank, who had paid for her passage to paradise, was sorely disillusioned. Furthermore, the bones of her corset dug into her damp flesh and beneath her flamboyantly beribboned bonnet her hair – she alone knew – was steaming gently in the absurd heat, spelling certain disaster for her curls. She glowered at Silas, purveyor of false promises. Silas turned on Seth.

'Why are you still here?' he said. 'Lady Millbank needs assistance. Please deposit those suitcases,' – because Seth was still holding them, legs braced and arms tensed, like a strongman demonstrating his prowess – 'then make it your business to accompany Her Ladyship to the charabancs.'

Seth looked at his uncle, appalled. The charabancs hadn't arrived, and both of them knew it, but Silas's eyes were cold and Seth recognised the challenge. The crisis had been handed to him in its entirety, and to fail now would be unmanly, unacceptable, unprofessional; this was familiar territory. Lady Millbank swivelled her head like an owl, turning her hostile gaze upon him.

The charabancs came, of course. They finally processed in stately fashion towards the variously stupefied, hostile and wilting huddle of English guests. Relieved beyond words to see the vehicles, Seth made flamboyant movements with his arms, waving the charabancs to a standstill as if without him they might have merely rolled on by. No one was fooled. His only small success had been to find a chair for Lady Millbank. She had accepted it ungraciously and sat like an angry monarch, waiting impatiently for a further improvement in her circumstances. At last – ushering, coaxing, apologising – Seth had them on board, and while it was perhaps in less comfort than they were accustomed to – the seats were wooden, and the long upward sweep of Eden Hill rutted – the journey was swiftly accomplished, at least once the crowded harbour was behind them.

At the hotel, the atmosphere of the group lightened. The elegant porticoed entrance and polished wooden floors of the foyer did much to lift flagging spirits and the great flat blades of the ceiling fans stirred the damp air, bringing a modicum of relief to the suffering souls in their suits, gowns and hats. Ruby, in a loose cotton frock and with bare feet, circulated with a tray of lemonade, pitying them. Lady Millbank stood with her brother Charles. They had little to say to each other, and nothing to say to anyone else. Charles took a glass from the tray offered by Ruby and raised it at her in a salute of silent thanks. Lady Millbank took another and peered into it with an expression of profound distaste, as if it were full of frogspawn.

'Odd colour,' she remarked without looking up.

'It's lemon-colour,' Ruby said, not being facetious but simply stating a fact. 'If you taste it, you'll find it very refreshing.' She smiled, because unlike Scotty, Ruby always tried to give the guests the benefit of the doubt: she was minded to like them, or at any rate to speak with them, noting as she did the nuances of pronunciation that would raise her own English to the standard to which she aspired.

'I would like a glass of water,' Lady Millbank said, replacing her drink, untasted, on the tray. She had set her gaze just above Ruby's head, for optimum *froideur*.

Ruby said, 'Very well, but first I shall offer around what is on my tray.' She was pleased with the way she sounded, pleased particularly with her 'my', which was full and rounded and quite unlike the short, lazy 'ma' she had grown up using.

Now Lady Millbank was forced to look upon the young woman who stood before her. Ruby smiled again, though she was beginning to realise that her attempt at pleasantness was falling on stony ground; there was no warmth in the woman's expression.

'Insolent creature,' Lady Millbank said, raising her voice so that conversations stopped and people turned to stare. 'In future you will address me as "Your Ladyship". In the meantime, you will do as I ask, and you will do it at once.'

Ruby pursed her lips. The Englishwoman, stout and overheated, glared at her with prominent, angry eyes. If she would but take off her bonnet and sip her lemonade she'd feel a deal less botheration, thought Ruby. She sighed and said, 'If you ask me again, but nicely, I might oblige.' Her tone was weary, like a mother teaching manners to a child. She waited for a long moment, head cocked in expectation, quite undaunted by Lady Millbank's horrified gasp, and then, when it became apparent that no progress was to be made, she shook her head almost sadly, but not quite, and sashayed away. There were, here and there, a few sympathetic tuts, but Lady Millbank, whose face was now a study in shades of purple, had made few friends on the Atlantic crossing, so there was very little interest in her plight. She turned for support to her brother who, standing beside her, lifted his own glass of lemonade, which was already half finished.

'It's very good, Mildred,' he said.

She glared at him. 'That's hardly the point, Charles.'

'Isn't it?'

'No! The point is, that girl just addressed me in the most offensive manner.'

'Mmm.' He took another deep drink and lemonade splashed from the glass on to his nose and chin. He whipped a silk handkerchief from his top pocket to dab at his face, and though he wasn't trying to further annoy her, he did.

'After all, Mildred, we were tipped the wink about the natives, remember? Brunswick's been more than once to Jamaica and he's never yet found a man willing – not to mention able – to dress him.'

'I'm not looking for a valet, I'm looking for a glass of water,' Lady Millbank said coldly. Her brother was a fool; she'd always known it, but three weeks on the *Cassiopeia* had revealed new heights of ineptitude and now here he was, dribbling lemonade and failing, once again, to defend her position. She cast her gimlet eyes around the room, looking for prey. The boy who'd accompanied them to the hotel on those dreadful bone-shaking contraptions was occupied, still, with the luggage, which had now been piled up just inside the hotel entrance. Lady Millbank was able to count one, two, three – no – *four* unoccupied negroes in the boy's vicinity, and yet he strove alone to organise the trunks and suitcases into manageable lots. And there was the rude young woman with the lemonade. Her tray was empty now, and she beat it gently against her hip as she walked, like a percussion instrument. Something about her – her casual, swaying gait, her long, exposed neck, her bare, brown feet – made Lady Millbank look away with a new flush of anger. Where was the owner? He and his pitiful sidekick presided over a shambles. She was beginning to rue the day that Charles – ever the enthusiast for new experiences – had burst into her drawing room, flapping in her face a printed advertisement extolling the beauties and benefits of Jamaica, courtesy of Whittam and Co.'s bespoke holiday service. Well. Mr Whittam must be sought out, she decided now. Sought out, and called to account.

Chapter 5

~~~~~~~~

If he was entirely honest, Tobias was no more at home at Portsmouth docks than he was in one of his colliery yards. He felt the same sense of dislocation, the same fundamental lack of interest, as he did when he stood in the shadow of the winding gear, feigning interest in a safety report or the monthly productivity figures from one or another of his pit deputies. It rattled him considerably that Thea was right: a new motorcar would have set his pulse racing, be there ever so many – and most of them still in mint condition – already parked in the garages of Netherwood Hall. It rattled him, too, that Thea could still rattle him. He was trying to achieve immunity from her repertoire of chilly barbs; she was sharper than he was: funnier, cleverer. He felt like the underdog in a sparring contest. Outclassed, unable to equal her in mental acuity, he aspired instead to indifference. Thus far, he hadn't attained it.

'Watch your back, guvnor. Coming through.'

Behind him a burly stevedore, bearing an implausible load of timber on each shoulder, wove a path around the earl and along the crowded wharf. There was such purpose and industry here that Tobias felt like an obstruction. He tried to look as though he belonged, and gazed out past the crowded docks

38

to the harbour mouth itself, the passage of water beyond which lay the open sea and the rest of the world. The sight, Tobias was sure, would stir many a man's imagination, but he remained unmoved. He had not the slightest interest in seamanship; he possessed none, and believed he had no urge to acquire it. The sea, through his eyes, looked grey and uninviting, and in his experience, the greater the expanse of it, the smaller and lonelier one felt.

'And again, sir.' It was the same docker, walking towards him now, with great loops of thick rope adorning his person. It was as if he intended to taunt. Tobias held his ground, affecting a nonchalant stance. He groped for his cigarette case; a man who was smoking always looked more comfortable, more gainfully occupied, than a man who wasn't. He took a drag, blew the smoke out through his nostrils, checked his fob: half past two, give or take. Where the devil was this Carruthers fellow, then? Just behind him, as it happened. He spoke, startling Tobias, who jumped in alarm and dropped his cigarette.

'Lord Netherwood, Gordon Carruthers – oh, I do apologise . . .' He bent down to retrieve the cigarette from the cobbles, then, handling it gingerly, passed it to Tobias. It had suffered on its journey, but it seemed rude to discard it when the chap had taken the trouble to pick it up, so Tobias took it, thinking all the while what a frightful hash they were making of things, the Earl of Netherwood and Gordon Carruthers, master boat builder. They shook hands.

'Had a good look about?' asked Mr Carruthers brightly. He was a spruce little man in a jaunty nautical get-up: all navy blue serge and brass buttons.

'Not really,' said Tobias. 'Not at all, actually. Not entirely my thing, boats.'

Only after he'd spoken did he realise the insensitivity of his remark, but Carruthers turned out to be one of those fellows who asked a question but didn't hear the answer. He smiled broadly and said, 'Splendid. HMS *Warrior* across the water there, poor old thing; not what she used to be. Top of the range warship middle of last century, then obsolete before ten years was up, y'know.'

He set off at almost a canter as he talked, and Tobias sauntered behind him, smoking the damp cigarette and looking – he hoped – moderately interested.

'That's the trouble with shipbuilding. Advancements all the time. Not so bad for us, but the poor old Royal Navy's always on the hop, keeping one step ahead of the kaiser.' He looked round at Tobias. 'Have you seen *Dreadnought*?'

Tobias looked at him, baffled.

'I beg your pardon?' he said.

'HMS *Dreadnought*. Battleship. Fastest in the world on account of her steam turbines. Have you seen her?'

'No, why – have you lost her?' Tobias said, and laughed.

'Ha!' said Mr Carruthers, a little uncertainly. He fell silent for a moment, and Tobias said, 'Do you drive a motorcar, Mr Carruthers? I used to favour a Daimler, but the new one's a Rolls-Royce. Silver Ghost. Best car in the world, bar none.'

He smiled. A taste of his own medicine, he thought. Then Mr Carruthers stopped by the long, sleek navy blue hull of a two-hundred-foot yacht whose masts towered majestically in the blue Portsmouth sky and said, 'Here we are. Isn't she a beauty?' and Tobias was silenced. Silenced, and humbled.

Tobias was spending that night at Denbigh Court, and he desperately underestimated the length of the journey, turning up so late that there was a sense of crisis about his arrival, like a doctor called in the night or an intruder caught red-handed. He had pulled on the bell rope fully five hours after the time he had given them; everyone had long retired, assuming that his plans had changed. His mother's husband, the Duke of Plymouth, received him in pyjamas and a paisley dressing gown, but the duchess had been hastily buttoned back into her gown by Flytton – the maid having been dragged, herself, from deep sleep – and was now torn between joy at seeing her best beloved eldest son and profound irritation at the disruption. Tobias was characteristically oblivious. He was all animation as he drank his glass of claret and wolfed his Welsh rarebit, and all he could talk of was his new yacht.

'You should have sailed here, darling,' said his mother. She stifled a yawn, conspicuously. 'Perhaps, then, you might have arrived at a more sociable hour.'

He grinned at her. 'Sail? Not I,' he said. 'Don't know my anchor from my elbow.'

'Can't trust the water if you haven't grown up by it,' said the duke. He wagged a knowing forefinger at Tobias. 'Can't always trust the damn crew, either. I come from a long line of naval men, of course, but I'm a cavalryman myself. Put me in the saddle and I'll give anyone a run for their money.'

'Once upon a time, perhaps, Archie,' said the duchess. He was older than her by fifteen years and she never let him forget it. 'Now, I should say you're more of a steady plodder.'

He smiled vaguely, but Tobias thought the old boy looked a little sad.

'Egypt, wasn't it, Archie? The last campaign?'

The duke's face brightened. 'Tel-el-Kebir,' he said, sitting up in his wing chair. 'Dawn attack on Arabi Pasha's lot, then a thirty-nine-mile dash back to Cairo to put the Khedive back on the throne. More claret?'

'Oh, let's not meander back to Egypt, Archie,' said the duchess. 'So pointless, and so dull. What news of Henrietta, Toby? Is she still bringing the family name into disrepute? Throwing eggs at Mr Asquith? Mining for coal?'

Tobias laughed. 'She's a brick, Ma. Steady hand on the tiller, that's Henry. She keeps an eye on the bailiff's accounts and walks the estate twice a week with Mr Arkwright. If she occasionally disrupts public order . . . well, everyone needs diversion of one kind or another.'

'Dickie wrote,' his mother said. 'From Verona this time, though he's based on the Italian Riviera, I believe. I do think it odd, don't you?'

'What, the Italian Riviera?'

'No. Well, yes. I mean the fact that your brother seems to prefer Italy to England.'

She said this as if he preferred cold tripe to hot buttered toast.

'Climate's marvellous, of course,' said the duke, venturing an opinion. His wife glared at him and he shrank back in his seat.

'I think Dickie feels at a bit of a loss in England,' Tobias said. Dickie Hoyland, Tobias's younger brother, had bravely borne the disadvantage of being a second son until a proposal of marriage had been coldly rejected for lack of a title. The resulting bout of heartbreak had sent him to the Continent three years previously and he was yet to return. 'In Italy, he has cachet.'

His mother wrinkled her small nose, as if she doubted this were possible. 'And Dorothea?' she asked. 'Didn't she want to travel with you? Such a pity.'

This was disingenuousness of the highest degree, thought Tobias. His mother's loathing of his wife was immutable, and the one thing that made him feel protective towards Thea these days.

'Thea's in Yorkshire, having her portrait painted,' Tobias said, and regretted it at once. His mother arched a brow.

'By whom?'

'American chap, Eugene Stiller. Comes highly recommended.'

She smiled ruefully.

'One worries for her,' she said. 'That chin.'

'Oh tosh, Ma. Thea's considered very beautiful among our set. She has the modern look.'

'Really? I would have thought a recessive chin could never be in vogue.'

'Cracking filly,' said the duke recklessly. 'Can't half dance.'

The icy silence following his remark was broken by the sound of someone rushing pell-mell along the first floor landing and down the stairs. The door of the drawing room burst open and there stood Isabella. Her face was flushed from sleep and she was barefoot. The ribbons of her nightdress were untied, and her charming décolletage artlessly exposed. She had blue cotton rags tied and twisted all over her head, performing – no doubt – some mysterious feminine function, the effects of which would only be seen tomorrow. She was seventeen years old and as lovely as her mother had once been, but kinder. Her mother's face and her father's heart, thought Tobias. He stood and she hurled herself across the room at him.

'Tobes,' she said. 'Tobes.' She hugged him, hanging about his neck, and it struck him that it was a long time since Thea had greeted him with anything approaching this sort of warmth; Thea, or anyone else for that matter. The love in his life these days was the kind he had to pay for, in one way or another.

'Isabella!' said the duchess, speaking sharply. 'Put Toby down and fasten your nightgown. You're behaving like a child.'

Isabella stepped away from her brother, though she still held his hands in hers. He saw her so rarely since their mother had remarried; she had gone away to Devon three years ago, and each time he had seen her since some improvement in her appearance seemed to have taken place, so that his pretty little sister was now possessed of the sort of head-turning,

43

show-stopping looks that blessed only a handful of girls in each successive generation. She was coming out this summer. London had better brace itself.

'Izzy,' he said. 'Look at you.'

She widened her eyes at him.

'How's the boat?'

'Magnificent. It's a yacht, y'know, not a rowing boat.'

'What's it called?'

'She. You have to say she, not it. Not sure. Undecided.'

'Call it Dorothea,' said Isabella. 'Or Thea. But that seems a bit short.'

'I say,' said the duke, suddenly seeing a way out of the dog house, 'what about Clarissa, after your mother?'

The duchess gave a coy squeak of protest, but looked immensely pleased. Tobias thought what an almighty nail it would be in the coffin of his marriage if he named the yacht for his mother. Dorothea wouldn't do, though. Only his mother ever used it, and then only to wound. And yet, he was in no mood to be painting 'Thea' on the side of his yacht either; these honours had to be earned. He felt backed into a corner.

'Lady Isabella,' he said, suddenly inspired. 'How would that be?'

The duchess never rose for breakfast – never had, even when the king had been a guest at Netherwood – and the duke was with his nurse, who came three times a week to manipulate his leg joints, so Isabella and Tobias had the dining room to themselves. He was dissecting a kipper; she was dipping fingers of toast into a soft-boiled egg and pleading with her brother to take her to Cowes. He would see, he said, but it would be up to Mama in the end.

'Oh Tobes, that's such a tedious, adult response,' she said.

'I am, I'm sorry to say, a tedious adult.'

'No, you're not. You're an irresponsible gadabout. Everyone says so.'

'Do they? Splendid. I was concerned that my reputation was on the wane.'

'I should so love to come, though.' She cupped her charming chin in her hands and fixed her wide blue eyes upon him. Last night's rags had produced a mass of soft curls that dropped on to her shoulders and made her look very beguiling. She'd done it for fun, she said; for something to do. This evening she would straighten them out again. 'It's what passes for entertainment at Denbigh Court,' she had said, affecting resignation to her dismal fate.

'Archie and Mama will be going to Cowes, darling. Archie's from a long line of naval men. He told me so himself.'

'Yes, but with you and Thea I might actually enjoy myself,' she said, and Tobias grinned. 'When do you go to Park Lane?' he asked.

She set about her egg again, mining the shell with a tiny spoon for the remains of the white. 'We're obliged to wait until Perry and Amandine return from Marienbad,' she said. 'I don't know why. Everyone'll be up by the time we trickle along.'

'Is Perry as fat as ever?'

'Fatter. It's blamed on his thyroid gland, but I've tried to share afternoon tea with him at the Savoy, so I know better. Marienbad's waters are miraculous, I hear, but there's nothing they could possibly do for Perry.'

Tobias laughed. Peregrine Partington, the Marquess of Hampden, heir to the dukedom and the Plymouth estate, was the sort of man who blamed his ailments on everything but his own behaviour. Amandine, his wife, was a vapid creature whose name, Isabella assured Tobias, was absolutely the most interesting thing about her. It meant 'she who must be loved', and Isabella said it was just as well she came with the instruction.

'Poor you. Not much company, is it?'

Isabella grimaced and rolled her eyes in answer.

'End's in sight,' Tobias said. 'You'll be fighting off dashing young men with a stick by the end of June, let alone the end of the Season.'

'I wish Daddy was alive,' Isabella said out of the blue, and to his absolute shock Toby's eyes filled with tears. His sister regarded him gravely across the table.

'Could I come with you, to Cowes?'

Tobias felt, suddenly, the benign and interested presence of his father. Isabella had always been Teddy Hoyland's darling; of all of them, she had felt his loss the most keenly. She had lost her greatest admirer, and the safe and steady flow of unconditional paternal affection. Now, thought Tobias, she had the Duke of Plymouth on one side and on the other the fat and foolish Perry Partington. Small wonder that Teddy felt a visitation was in order: he only ever returned – in Toby's experience, at least – to prod his son into the correct course of action. Now, thinking of their father, imagining him listening, he said, 'Of course, you can, Izzy. And I'll tell you what . . .' – he paused and smiled; she was all eager attention – '. . . I'll take you back up to Netherwood with me when I leave tomorrow. How would that be? You can travel down to London with us in May.'

Ah, the joy of giving true pleasure. Isabella pushed back her chair and danced around the table to where Tobias sat, and then she pulled him to his feet and made him dance too, an awkward polka from which he immediately tried to extract himself. After all, the butler was watching, as well as their father.

Chapter 6

~~~~~~~~~~~~~~~~

There were visitors in the grounds of Netherwood Hall: two men in dark suits and black Homburgs, holding measuring wheels and Box Brownies. They paced up and down the outside of the old glasshouses, and in and out, with expressions of grim satisfaction, as if what they saw was disappointing, but no more so than they had expected. Daniel MacLeod, head gardener, watched from a distance as the men performed their cogitations and calculations. He had told them what he wanted, and now Messrs MacAlpine and Moncur were deciding what was possible. Behind him he heard the click of the gate from the kitchen garden, and he turned. His wife, Eve, was crossing the grass with their little son, Angus. The boy had a bucket in one hand and he talked as he walked. He talked much of the time, in fact; there weren't enough hours in the day for all that Angus MacLeod had to say.

'Found this urchin in among t'vegetables,' Eve called to Daniel across the lawn. She'd been away for two days and he feasted his eyes on the sight of her: small, slight, effortlessly lovely. When he'd first met her she didn't seem to know she was beautiful. She had no mirror at home, she'd said, and wouldn't have time to look in it anyway.

They reached his side and Daniel bent to kiss her. 'Aye,' he said. 'He came with me to work today. Been out on snail patrol, isn't that right, son?'

The child nodded sagely. 'It's 'portant to pick 'em off t'plants, because, Mam, if you don't they just eat your cabbages and that. You can sprinkle lime on slugs and snails, can't you Pa? I pick 'em off and put 'em in my pail though. I'm not to touch lime.' He held up the bucket to Daniel. 'See? They look right fed up, don't they?'

Daniel studied the snails: five of them, in shock in the bottom of the metal pail. 'Good work, Angus,' he said, and pointed at the largest. 'See? You've caught the ringleader.' He smiled warmly at his son and then at Eve, and kissed her again. 'Welcome home, my darling. How was Harrogate?'

'Very grand. A cut above.' She nodded in the direction of the men by the glasshouses. 'They look miserable.'

'Aye,' Daniel said. 'It's a necessary prelude to the estimate of costs.'

'Well, if you will hire Scotsmen . . .'

He winked at her, a Montrose man himself. 'They'll not bamboozle me, don't you fret. They're crafty buggers, but it takes one to know one.'

The men seemed to have finished. They snapped the lids back onto their pens and crunched morosely across the gravel. Daniel's proposal was typically ambitious: the demolition of all but the finest of the existing plant houses, and the erection of one enormous glasshouse, comprising a wide central palm corridor, two hundred feet long, with subsidiary houses branching off to its north and south sides. All manner of exotics would be grown, but the countess – concentrating, finally, on the new scheme and flicking through a selection of colour plates – had pointed at gardenias, orchids, camellias and ferns. There would also have to be a stove house and another for propagation, but these technical details bored her. She was content, on

48

the whole, to leave Daniel to his own devices; she barely glanced at his plans, meticulously drafted on sheets of paper, before approving them. He found he rather missed his regular skirmishes with her predecessor. The previous Lady Netherwood had always questioned everything he suggested, believing herself a horticultural visionary. She demanded the same from her gardens as she did from her gowns: flounce and flair, dash and glamour. What tended to happen, after each long negotiation, was that he would have his way, and she would take the credit: this was their unacknowledged arrangement. The present countess, whose home before she had come to Netherwood Hall had been a New York brownstone, took a different view. What was a head gardener for, if not for making all the decisions? All she knew was that she had a garden that was bigger than Central Park, and a capable fellow whose job it was to tend it. He could do as he wished. Demolish six plant houses and build a new one? Sure! The cost was never a consideration. Thea Hoyland might have grown up on a limited allowance, but she had quickly adapted to an unlimited one.

However, the Edinburgh hothouse engineers Mr MacAlpine and Mr Moncur appeared to think they might have to fund the project themselves and were walking towards Daniel like a pair of pallbearers in search of a funeral. Angus and his snails hid behind his mother's skirts at their approach.

'Gentlemen?' said Daniel.

'Aye, quite an undertaking,' said Mr Moncur sadly.

'You'll be needing a rain-water cistern in every one of the houses,' said Mr MacAlpine.

'Aye. Welsh slate, sixty gallons apiece,' said Mr Moncur.

'And eight rows of six-inch pipes all down the central corridor, four rows in your side houses, six rows in your stove house.'

'And ventilation sashes throughout.'

'Aye. And a new boiler house. Your existing one's entirely inadequate.'

'Aye. Three, maybe four, boilers in a new brick building away out of sight.'

All of this they intoned as if breaking the worst possible news.

'And when could you start?'

This was Daniel, defiantly cheerful in the face of their gloom. The two engineers exchanged doleful looks.

'You'd like to proceed?' said Mr Moncur.

'Of course,' Daniel said. 'We're none of us here just for the good of our health.'

'Only, you'll be looking at something over four thousand pounds for a scheme of this magnitude,' said Mr MacAlpine.

'Not far short of five thousand, possibly,' said Mr Moncur.

'Well,' said Daniel. 'Let's not stand here waiting for it to reach six. Put it in writing, gentlemen, and we'll take it from there.'

They nodded, then tipped their hats at Eve and made for their motorcar.

'You'd think, wouldn't you, that they're being charged a guinea a smile,' Eve said, watching them. She turned to Daniel. 'It sounds like a proper upheaval, though. All that knocking down and building up again. Can't you manage with what you 'ave?'

He gave her a reproving look. 'That's rich coming from you, with your ever-expanding pork pie empire.'

'Can I 'ave a pork pie?' Angus asked.

'Not right now, Gussy,' said Eve. 'I don't carry them under my 'at.'

The child's face fell. Now he knew there were no pies, he felt hungry.

'C'mon,' Daniel said, holding out a hand. 'Come and see my fruit wall. Peach now, pie later.'

50

The Harrogate branch of Eve's Puddings & Pies was the fourth in the chain: the fourth and probably the finest, housed in an elegant Regency building near the Pump Rooms. Like the other branches – in Netherwood, Barnsley and Sheffield – it had a café for the leisured shopper and a counter for the hurried and the harried, and the bill of fare was the same too: pork pies, meat pies, steak puddings, fruit pies and a small, surprising range of Russian specialities, the legacy of Anna's involvement in Eve's life back when it all began. Six years ago, now. Six years and three months since Arthur Williams was killed at New Mill Colliery and Eve had had to find a way to keep herself and the children from the workhouse. It seemed like another life, another time. Anna – Russian, widowed, homeless – had pitched up at the little house in Beaumont Lane and had placed herself like a lucky charm at the centre of Eve's existence. She had been Eve's prop then: stronger and indefatigably optimistic. They had made an unconventional family group – Anna and Maya, Eve and her three – but those days, which began dark with sorrow, were also golden in Eve's memory. Eve Williams and Anna Rabinovich, a force to be reckoned with, a winning team. Now, amid the trappings of their respective success, despite everything each of them had gained, Eve still sometimes felt a jolt of loss. On her dressing table she had a small inlaid jewellery box, the tiny key of which had long ago been mislaid. She didn't need the key because the box was always open, but still, she felt the lack of it. That was how she felt about Anna.

Certainly she would have been an asset in Harrogate. Not just as company, though the solitary train journey had been long and dull, but for her unassailable confidence. Anna was a stranger to inferiority; she had an air of Russian imperialism about her, Daniel always said: a touch of the tsarina. In Harrogate, Eve could have wished herself similarly equipped; the town's mineral springs and noble connections had given it a very high opinion of itself. There she had been, representing meat pies and suet puddings in a town blessed by the patronage of princes and dukes. Of course, Eve had once cooked for the king; she told herself this as she stood by the railway station, feeling humble. But the driver of the hansom cab that took her to Crown Place had evidently held himself in high esteem, looking down his nose at Eve even as he took her business. She had over-tipped him to make a point, and then had immediately felt like a fool.

The day had improved, though, and her shop had looked very fine. She had been before, of course: chosen it, supervised its renovation, appointed the staff. But this was her first visit for some weeks, and she'd forgotten what an imposing building it was: double-fronted, with an elegant iron porch at the entrance and a tiled floor pristine in black and white. Eve had stood a little distance away and watched as an arresting pyramid of produce in the windows and the irresistible aroma of hot pastry had lured customers through the door. It was early days, but the signs were promising. She had been thinking of this and smiling to herself on the train home when the ticket collector had accused her of looking happy.

'Pies,' Eve had said. 'I was thinking of pies, and how far they've brought me.'

'Is that so?' He had taken her ticket, stamped it, handed it back. 'Change at Leeds,' he said.

Lilly Pickering, a former neighbour and a miner's widow, had known Eve since the days when a tin bath and a brick-built privy had seemed like a step up. Lilly held the fort at Ravenscliffe every day, to one extent or another. She was there when Eve and Angus arrived at their house on the common.

'Oh,' she said. 'I expected you sooner.'

It was Lilly's habit to scold. She didn't always mean anything by it.

'Ah well, 'ere I am now,' Eve said. She took off her coat and hat and hung it on the stand in the front hall, and by the time she'd accomplished this Angus had gone: straight through the house and out of the back door to the hutch in the garden, from where his new rabbit Timothy gazed balefully at the world. Angus was trying hard, but failing, to love Timothy. The creature's pink eyes were unsettling, and he shrank from human contact. Angus squatted in front of the hutch for a while and stared at his pet. Timothy, unblinking, stared back. In a box by the hutch were some carrots, and Angus considered them now, trying to decide if his rabbit deserved the treat. No, he decided. He shook his head firmly at Timothy and stood, then took two carrots anyway and went looking, instead, for pit ponies. They grazed on the common after retirement and they were so accustomed to human contact that Angus had once persuaded one to follow him into the kitchen. By the time it was discovered he was feeding the pony Cox's Orange Pippins from the fruit bowl. Lilly had hit the roof, Angus had cried and the pony had bolted, smashing two tureens and a milk jug on its way out. Now he understood that ponies were strictly an outdoor diversion, but he knew their haunts and they knew his.

'Don't go too far, Gussy.' This was Eve, who had followed him through the back door and now watched him opening the gate to go onto the common. 'Tea time soon.' He smiled at her and waved a carrot, and Eve went back into the kitchen.

'Where are the girls?' She could tell from the quiet that her daughters weren't in the house.

'Eliza's at that Evangeline's again,' Lilly said. 'She'll end up with rickets at this rate.'

'I doubt it, Lilly,' said Eve. 'It's not caused by ballet dancing.'

'Mary Sylvester 'as bow legs from rickets.'

53

Eve looked at her. 'From rickets, yes, not from ballet. And it's because she's half-starved, not because she likes dancing.'

'Aye, well.'

Lilly snapped out the tea towel she'd been using and it cracked like a pistol. She folded it twice and hung it on the brass rail in front of the range. 'That's me done then.'

'Is Ellen in?' Eve said.

'Outside wi' mine. Doubtless black bright by now, though that pinafore was clean on this morning.'

'It'll wash.' Eve walked to the back door and looked out. Four children squatted in a circle at the back of the garden where the grass met the hawthorn hedge. Ellen, true to her reputation, had mud on her frock and a headdress of leaves and fern. Her face was flushed with the effects of recent exertion and fresh air. She was talking: issuing instructions, no doubt. She had a long stick in one hand, and she stood suddenly, wielding it like a spear and making a fearsome, ululating war cry, which her gang immediately, obediently, imitated. Eve called her name, shouting over the racket, and Ellen, sensing rather than hearing her, scowled.

'Mam! We're busy.' She looked like Seth had at the same age: plain as a pikestaff, with her dad's ears jutting out like the handles on a sugar bowl and a pugnacious little face to match her hard-boiled personality. She kept her hair as short as she was allowed, and if she could have worn shorts in place of her pinafore, she would have done.

'Come on, Sitting Bull. Time for tea.'

Lilly materialised beside Eve on the back doorstep. 'Cheerio then,' she said. She'd hung her housecoat on a peg in Eve's kitchen and was shrugging herself into a lumpy green cardigan, which at least had the advantage of making her look plumper. She was skin and bone, always had been. Even now, when she had her own weekly pay packet from Eve and two of her boys had jobs at Long Martley Colliery, she still looked as if she lived on potato water. She stepped out onto the path and without raising her voice said, 'Right,' and her children, responding at once to the higher authority, stood up and cut shamefaced looks of apology at Ellen.

'That parkin's all gone,' Lilly said to Eve. 'And you've no milk.'

She walked off, her dishevelled posse trailing behind her. Ellen flung her spear over the hedge and onto the common. She had a good arm and a good eye; in a skirmish or a siege she would have been an asset.

'Are you going to say 'ello, then?' Eve said.

Ellen crossed the garden and gave her mother a stiff-armed hug, but Eve caught her and held on, kissing the top of her head, then, with one arm still around the child's shoulders, she tried to pick out the dried leaves from her tousled brown hair. Ellen submitted to the attention, but only briefly. She pulled away and bared her teeth dramatically, to show Eve a new gap in the top row.

'Another one gone?'

Ellen nodded. 'Feels nasty,' she said, poking her tongue into the space. 'What's for tea?'

'Eggs and bacon, I expect. But run on to t'Co-op for me first, fetch some milk.'

'Can I get some sherbet?' She held out her hand for money. Just seven years old, but she'd been driving a bargain since she learned how to talk.

'No. Oh, go on then. And find Angus on your way back; bring 'im 'ome with you.'

The child turned and ran. Ellen Williams never walked unless there was absolutely no avoiding it. She went through life at full tilt.

'Be careful,' Eve said, thinking of glass bottles and milk, but she spoke to an empty garden.

Chapter 7

The letter on the hall table hadn't been from Eve, though Norah had been right about the Barnsley postmark.

'Alderman Simpson,' Anna said to Amos, handing him the folded writing paper. 'He wonders whether I might stand for Ardington town council.'

They were sitting on the Victoria Embankment, a short stroll from Westminster Bridge. The bench was one that they had used so often they considered it their own. Amos had been sitting there when Anna arrived, and had already sent away three other perfectly entitled citizens, begging their pardon but making it plain that the bench could not be shared. It amused Anna that her husband always managed to get away with this: it was the element of surprise, Amos told her. No one expected to be moved on from a public bench, and therefore they always obliged.

From the wicker basket on her lap from which she had produced the letter, Anna now brought out a sandwich wrapped in waxed paper. This, too, she handed to her husband.

'Bread and dripping?' he asked, and she laughed.

'Bad luck. Cheese and tomato.'

He placed the package on his knee and opened the letter,

scanning its contents and smirking at Greville Simpson's copperplate handwriting. 'You'd never know 'e were dragged up in a Grangely slum,' he said.

Anna, who liked the alderman, tutted. 'Nothing wrong with an elegant hand,' she said. 'And we can all improve our lot.'

This was true, and Amos conceded the point with a nod of his head. But Alderman Simpson's cursive was the least of his affectations, in Amos's view. There was a rumour that since being elected to the council, he had spent a few bob on elocution lessons and, certainly, when he addressed committee meetings in the town hall his aitches were these days very much in evidence, though not always in the right place. *Halderman* Simpson, Enoch Wadsworth called him, pillar *hof* the community. Enoch was Amos's agent, friend, adviser and confidant: Enoch was the reason Amos was an MP. And if he couldn't laugh at Greville Simpson with Anna, whose Russian ear, Amos was convinced, prevented her from hearing the comedy in the alderman's voice, he knew he would be able to laugh with Enoch later.

'Will you stand, then?' he asked Anna now, because that, after all, was the purpose of the letter and the reason she had shown him. 'They could use you on that education committee.'

'Of course not.' She took the letter back, suddenly irritated. How did he imagine she had time to run for the council? As it was, she barely had time to play the MP's wife in Amos's Yorkshire constituency.

'What?' Amos said.

She looked at him. 'How do you think I can be councillor, when so much of my life is in London? I'd have to be always in Ardington.'

'Well, would that be so terrible? There's plenty to be done up there.'

She laughed, astonished. 'But I have commissions until the end of summer, and new enquiries almost every day.'

He was looking straight ahead, at the grey-brown Thames.

It moved sluggishly, as if it were made of something thicker than water, as if it were weary of its journey. 'Right, then,' he said. 'In that case I suppose it's out of t'question.'

Anna heard his words, but was certain his true meaning lay beneath their surface. For a while, she considered his profile; he was a handsome man, but there was a stubborn set to his expression that did him no favours. And she knew exactly what was on his mind.

'You think I should run for Ardington Council, don't you?'

He turned to look at her again. 'I think you'd be a cracking councillor. I think with you on t'Labour benches, they'd 'ave a much better chance of getting summat done.'

'And Anna Sykes Interiors? We just close door and say, sorry, all finished?'

He looked away again. 'I think,' he said carefully, 'that there are more worthwhile ways for you to spend your days than painting murals for pampered aristocrats.'

It wasn't, by any means, the first time Amos had said this, but it was the first time in a while. Anna's spirits plummeted. It was such a familiar refrain; He can never mention aristocrats without calling them pampered, she thought now.

'I love what I do,' she said. She kept her voice quiet and steady, because they were just a stone's throw from the House of Commons and who knew who might overhear if she truly gave vent to her feelings?

'I don't,' he said, as if she didn't already know this. 'I don't love what you do.'

This was what happened, from time to time. The catalyst would arrive by stealth and suddenly everything would be spoiled. And now, Anna thought, I should point out how my income supports his unpaid position as Labour MP for Ardington. She didn't, though.

'I'm your wife and Maya's mother, and those things will always be so,' she said instead. 'But also, I'm an artist.'

'Artist to the privileged few. Artist to them as 'as a bare ballroom wall they want painting, or a billiard room that wants cheering up.'

'You make me sound so trivial.'

'You're not. The people you work for are.'

'But if it makes me happy?'

His face was set: grim and unrelenting. On his lap, the waxed-paper parcel lay untouched. Too cross to eat a sandwich, she thought: how like Maya he could be. She knew from experience that, short of pledging right now to shun every illustrious name in her order book, there was nothing she could do to unravel this tangle of resentment. Time, and a little distance, would free them, as it had done before.

'I'm going to Slade,' she said, standing. 'I need to see Clara and William; ask them to come with me on Friday to Marcia de Lisle's place in Sussex.'

He didn't answer, and she hadn't really expected him to. But she was damned if she would pander to his prejudices. Anna was all for equality: not least her own, with him.

He was sorry, when she walked away, that he hadn't said goodbye. He felt mean-minded and petulant and then, when he stood, the forgotten, wrapped sandwich fell to the ground and he felt even worse. By the time he reached the Socialist Club he was mired in a profound gloom, made all the deeper by the knowledge that it was of his own making. Enoch, early as usual, had already stood him a drink; he and the pint waited at a carefully selected corner table, from where the members' bar was in full view and the red plush curtains at an adjacent window would help muffle their voices; he was nothing if not cautious.

'What's up?' he asked. 'You've a right face on.'

Amos sat down.

'Nowt new,' he said. 'Bit of a barney with Anna.'

Enoch grimaced and pushed his round, wire-framed spectacles back up his nose. 'Not this again? For God's sake man, will you let 'er be?'

Amos, struck dumb by his friend's vehemence, stared at him.

'She's making a living, and a good one at that,' Enoch said, more calmly. 'Let 'er get on wi' it. You can't use sheer force o' will on a woman like Anna.'

Amos raised an eyebrow and Enoch immediately took his meaning; could hardly miss it. Unmarried, scholarly, dedicated to the party, Enoch was meant to confine his expertise to politics. What did he know about the fairer sex? Bugger all, said Amos's expression.

'Aye,' Enoch said. 'Well, 'appen I'm no authority on women in general. But any fool can see Anna's 'er own woman. You knew that three years ago, when you wed.'

She was a grand lass too, he thought: bonny and clever, and younger than Amos by nearly twenty years. He should think himself lucky. If he, Enoch, had been given a chance – even half of one – with a woman like Anna, he wouldn't have spent any time grousing about her. He stared into his pint for a moment, thinking about loneliness, and the lot of the political agitator. He was younger than Amos by a couple of years, but he looked older. His lungs were bad after twenty years in the pits, and the frequent struggles for breath gave him a strained, stooped appearance and a sickly pallor. He no longer thought of romance, though he'd once exchanged letters with a fellow Fabian from Lytham; for a time, he had imagined himself attached. But then she had written with news of an engagement, which, she said, 'made further correspondence impossible' and he had turned back to his books and pamphlets with something resembling relief. The episode, while it had lasted, had made him feel vulnerable: waiting for her next letter, worrying that he'd replied too promptly to her last. These anxieties had distracted him from his true path, he had told himself; a solitary life suited him best, and was necessary to his particular brand of political commitment. That was fifteen years ago and, for the most part, he believed it. He knew, though, that if fate had delivered him an Anna Rabinovich, he would have felt himself blessed.

He looked up at Amos, who was looking down. 'Anyroad,' Enoch said, returning to the theme, 'she's not doing any o' them lords and ladies a favour, is she? They're all paying through t'nose, from what I've 'eard.'

'It's talked about, then,' Amos said, as if Enoch had just delivered a terminal diagnosis.

Enoch made a gesture of irritation. 'Not so you'd notice. Believe it or not, t'Labour Party 'as more to worry about than where your money comes from.'

This was blindingly obvious. From within and without, the party was under attack. Victor Grayson, a young firebrand MP from the Colne Valley, seemed hell-bent on bringing down the old guard with public denunciations of their class treachery and lily-livered policies. Meanwhile, the new Liberals were stealing all Labour's best lines; last year they'd announced an old-age pension provision and this year Lloyd George had gone for the jugular of the landed aristocracy in his People's Budget, proposing taxes on the rich that even Robin Hood might think a bit steep. It was hard for Labour to hang on to its identity when the Liberals were redistributing wealth and taking on the House of Lords, so Amos knew well enough that the source of his wife's wealth was the last of his party's problems, but still.

'Anyroad,' Enoch said, 'Ramsay MacDonald makes no secret that it's 'is wife's money they live off.'

Amos gave a grim laugh. 'Margaret MacDonald does more Good Works than your average saint. She 'as no time to rub shoulders wi' aristocracy. There's trade schools to set up, and t'Women's Labour League to run. If she paid for MacDonald to bathe in champagne, nob'dy would call her to account.'

Enoch made a discreet shushing motion: a brush of his finger against his lips. Walls had ears, and there was Amos, detracting in public from the irreproachable wife of Ramsay MacDonald; like sitting in a chapel and heckling the minister, it just wasn't done. He lowered his voice to not much more than a whisper.

'Do you want to know your problem?'

'No.'

'Your problem is, you let a bit of personal strife cloud your professional 'orizons.'

'Nice one; put it in a pamphlet,' Amos said, but he knew it, really, and he didn't need lessons in psychology from Enoch. He was out of sorts with Anna, and therefore out of sorts with the world – Enoch Wadsworth and Margaret MacDonald included. His opposition to Anna's chosen career, his resentment of her clientele, had the power to make blue skies grey. It wasn't a permanently debilitating condition; rather, like heartburn or gout, it would flare up at some outside provocation, which, today, had been the letter from the alderman. If she would just consider how it looked to the wider world when the wife of a Labour MP counted earls and countesses, dukes and duchesses among her friends. Clients, Anna would say. Clients and acquaintances, not friends. And yet every Christmas, cards, in red velvet lavishly embossed with gold foil, dropped onto their doormat, bearing festive good wishes from one or another titled family. Maya would cut them up for collages: Amos would rather they went on the fire.

'When Keir 'ardie 'ad 'is appendix out,' Enoch said now, 'King Edward sent 'im a letter of sympathy.'

'And what's that got to do wi' t'price of fish?'

'I'm just saying,' said Enoch. He drained his pale ale, wiped his mouth with his cuff and exhaled with pleasure at the simple satisfaction of a good pint. 'And, as far as I know, it was accepted with good grace.' He gave Amos one of his pointed, piercing looks. 'So think on.'

Chapter 8

ᏙᏙᎡᏗᎨᏙᏙ

Everything in the Whittam Hotel had been shipped from England; even the pink roses, which blushed, palely English, in the guest·drawing room. To encourage British entrepreneurs in this colonial outpost, the government at home had lifted all duty on imported goods, which had saved Silas a small fortune, as the rigorously upheld aesthetic in his Jamaican hotel was that of a large country house in the South Downs, perhaps, or the Cotswolds.

It was a veritable haven of Chippendale and Chesterfields, of chintz, silk and damask. Paintings played a key role in the deception: a Gainsborough, *Conversation in a Park*, which hung in the entrance hall, was of course a reproduction of the original, but it hit precisely the note of nostalgic elegance for which Silas strived. In the dining room a trio of Constables evoked rural English summers. On the walls of the wide first-floor landing pale-faced English heiresses gazed soulfully from verdant gardens and sumptuous boudoirs, and in the billiard room gun dogs held dead birds in their soft mouths while men in Norfolk jackets aimed their rifles at the sky. No English traveller could arrive at the hotel and feel displaced. True, the ceiling fans and mosquito nets were quite out of step with the theme, but they could not be done without, and in any case, they were so comprehensively eclipsed by rose bowls, ottomans and Wedgwood vases that their incongruity was minimal.

However, if the *objets* were reassuringly English, the staff most certainly were not. The duty on imports had been lifted, certainly, but there was a proviso: if Silas Whittam was to benefit from the British government's tax exemptions, he must also hire all his staff from the local population. And none of them, Silas had fast discovered, would cooperate with guests who believed themselves vastly superior to the servant class. It was an unhappy chemistry: the Jamaicans demanded basic courtesy before they'd stir themselves to action, while the English demanded instant service at the most peremptory signal. And any number of interior trappings, be they ever so authentic, could not obscure or remedy the fact that a coddled egg had just taken fifty-four minutes from the moment of ordering to its arrival at the table. Lady Millbank – for it was she who had waited, in a state of mounting disbelief – knew very little about the culinary arts, but she did know that an egg, carefully placed in simmering water, took six minutes to reach perfection. Her brother's grilled kipper had come quite promptly, and although he had refused to eat it until the egg was brought, Lady Millbank suspected that she had been singled out by the hotel staff for special ill treatment. The waitress, a large elderly woman with a lumbering gait, had taken the order with a palpable lack of interest. There had followed a long period of inactivity, during which Lady Millbank and her brother had quite run out of conversation. Then the kipper arrived, delivered by a boy who appeared to be dressed for school, in grey shorts and socks. The kipper had grown stone cold while a further stretch of time was endured in suffering silence. When the original waitress had finally wandered back into the dining room with Lady Millbank's breakfast, she had carried the egg on a plate, holding it out at arm's length as if it were a small bomb. She had placed it rather fiercely on the table and looked Lady Millbank directly in the eye.

'An egg, missus,' she had said. 'That all?'

Really, her insolence was quite threatening.

'I'm not at all sure that we're safe in our beds,' Lady Millbank said to Charles when the waitress was out of earshot. 'That woman gave me my egg with an attitude of naked loathing.'

Charles laughed, and his sister regarded him icily.

'Sorry Mildred,' he said. 'Bone in the throat.' He made a short pantomime of expelling the phantom obstruction.

'How can you laugh, Charles? Is my life of so little importance to you that the idea of my throat being slashed as I sleep is comical?' Her chin wobbled and her voice cracked.

'Oh, I say,' said her brother. 'Steady on.'

'Truly, the negroes look daggers at me and I'm quite sure I've done nothing to offend.'

Charles considered his options. He could tell his sister the truth, which was that she had not yet herself shown a scrap of courtesy to anyone, for anything; that she was rude, imperious, ungrateful, querulous and universally disliked. Or he could finish his kipper. He tucked in.

In the kitchen, Ruby had finished the breakfast service and was making lunch for the hotel staff. Roscoe had been and gone. Today, Ruby's shift had started two hours before school, so her boy had come with her and had been put to good use. He had sat at the table folding linen napkins into sailing boats, the way the white boss liked. He had spared Batista's swollen feet by carrying some of the food through to the diners. He had helped Ruby chop scallions, and had stirred a slick, sharp butter and vinegar sauce that the English poured over their eggs. It looked like yellow grease, he had told his mother: it is, Ruby had said. She kept to hand a great tome of a cookbook, to which she was forced to refer many times a day as she picked her way through the obstacle course of English classics. Roscoe – a reader, even before he started school – liked to open it at random and laugh at the names of the dishes and their ingredients, reading them aloud to the kitchen in the solemn voice of a scholar: jugged hare, bubble-and-squeak, eel pie, plum pudding. Mrs Beeton sounded interesting, Roscoe thought; she added thoughtful, informative notes. This morning he had read about the barberry, a fruit so sour that even birds refuse to eat it.

'Like the tamarind, Ruby,' he had said to his mother. 'Mrs Beeton says so. Listen.' He adopted his reading voice. '"In this respect, it nearly approaches the tamarind. When boiled with sugar it makes a very agreeable preserve."'

Ruby had smiled at the words. Very agreeable preserve: such elegant English. She had little time or respect for the recipes, which to her were inextricable from the demands of Mr Silas, but she did like the way Mrs Beeton wrote. She wasn't confident enough of her own skills to read to an audience, but sometimes, if Ruby was alone in the kitchen, she would read aloud as Roscoe did, practising the vowels, memorising the phrases for future use. She found them mysterious and lyrical: 'The Ayrshire is peculiarly adapted for the dairy. In this, it stands unrivalled' and 'the philosophy of frying consists in this, that liquids subjected to the action of fire do not all receive the same quantity of heat'. Marvellous. Marvellous.

But it was later in the day now, and she no longer had need of Mrs Beeton because she was cooking from the heart for her own people. The smells of her childhood filled the room: green bananas, salted mackerel, Scotch Bonnets, coconut milk. She stirred and sang, and let the vapours from the pots envelop her face. The peppers had bite; she breathed in their heat.

'Girl, that a fine, fine sight.'

Scotty stood at the kitchen door, watching her. She waved her spoon at him.

'Boiled bananas and mackerel rundown,' she said. 'But it won't be ready a while yet.'

'I no talkin' 'bout da food, girl,' he said, and winked. He smiled at her with his loose, lascivious mouth, and she sucked her teeth at him disapprovingly and turned away.

'Ah Ruby, why you so hitey-titey? You breakin' ma heart, girl.' He walked through the kitchen and over to the range. Ruby cut him a look, the one she reserved exclusively for impertinent men.

'If you stand there panting and drooling don't be surprised if I treat you like a dog,' she said. He roared with laughter and shook his head, as if amazed by her. He was as thick-skinned as a calabash, thought Ruby. There was just no insulting him.

Batista came into the kitchen carrying the last of the crockery from the dining room. On an island where no one seemed to hurry, she was slower than most; she rested from time to time on every journey, whatever its length. She stood now and blew four long breaths, as if she'd run through the hotel to get here. She was padded all over with soft flesh, which in the three years Ruby had known her had swelled and spread, and it was strange, because Ruby had never seen Batista eat. She always declined staff lunch and dinner, and would sit instead with her Bible: feeding her soul, she said.

'Bakra, 'im want see you,' she said to Ruby. She meant Silas, whom she held in the deepest contempt. Batista was descended from Maroon warriors; rebellion ran through her veins. When she looked at Silas Whittam she saw a white slave master and untold suffering; the fires of hell were awaiting him.

Scotty whistled, a long, flat note. 'Cu ya, Little Miss Badness, what you been an' done now?'

Ruby shrugged.

'She slow-slow,' Batista said, moving again. She hauled herself over to the sink with her pile of plates, and dropped them heavily in the sudsy water. 'Trouble wid an egg, nuh?' She looked at Ruby and smiled knowingly; a wide, slow smile that fattened her cheeks and closed her eyes. 'Bakra, 'im waiting in 'is office.'

'If he wishes to see me, he knows where to find me,' Ruby said.

'Good girl.'

Batista puffed and sucked at the air again, in and out, standing with her hands on her huge hips, catching her breath. 'Mi too bufu-bufu for dis life,' she said. 'Mi fit only to sit an' talk to de Lord.'

Later, Ruby sat beneath the frangipani tree on the road home, her meeting place with Roscoe. Its branches formed a wide, shady parasol and the ground beneath was soft and fragrant with fallen flowers. A hot breeze blew and Ruby pulled the red cotton scarf away from her head and leaned back, letting the tree support her and the canopy of leaves cool her head. Mr Silas, catching her as she left, had been nasty, tearing into her with the language of the docks. She had told him, if he cared so deeply about Lady Millbank's coddled egg he should prepare it himself. Perhaps he wasn't aware of the manner in which Lady Millbank had addressed her on more than one occasion. Mr Silas had put his angry face too close to her own and had spoken through bared teeth: 'Who the hell do you think you are?'

'Ruby Marie Donaldson,' she had said, 'as you well

know,' and she had walked away, though he all but screamed for her to come back. Now she let the wind in the leaves and the smell of crushed flowers soothe her agitated spirit. Roscoe would be along soon. She closed her eyes and, presently, she slept.

Seth had rooms at the hotel, a bedroom and a bathroom above his uncle's office. A private staircase – small and wooden, enclosed by doors top and bottom, like his early childhood home in Netherwood – led from the office directly into Seth's bedroom. It was an odd arrangement, but he was glad of it. He shouldn't have liked to descend the guest staircase each morning, placing himself in the line of fire the moment he stepped out of his quarters. Silas's office, a large, airy room with shuttered windows, was off-limits for hostile guests: like a buffer zone between warring nations, it was a neutral space, free of conflict. Unless his uncle was on the warpath, of course, and by the end of this trying day he was.

'They play me for a fucking idiot,' Silas said. He brought his fist down on the desk and every object upon it bounced or rattled. Seth, pink and speechless, nodded.

'I give them respectable, paid employment, the chance to better their miserable fucking lot, and they repay me with insolence and disrespect. Do you know how my own reputation stands as a result? Do you?'

This was the worst thing about Silas's rages; he peppered his rants with questions that lay like rabbit traps, waiting to snap at the wrong answer.

'Compromised, sir?'

It was a worthy effort: frank, yet diplomatic. But the jaws of the trap sprang shut anyway.

'Compromised? *Compromised*? Do you see or hear

anything as you go about your business? Or does your funda-mental idiocy preserve you from the harsher facts of life? My reputation on this island is in tatters. My reputation, painstak-ingly built over years of hard work and investment, has been ground into the dirt by the filthy fucking heels of the savages I am forced to employ by a Colonial Office staffed by fools who sit on their complacent arses, congratulating themselves on solving the Jamaica Problem.'

He flung himself back in his chair, depleted by the torrent of words. Seth shifted uncomfortably on his own seat, wishing himself elsewhere: wishing, too, that Hugh Oliver were here. Hugh, second in command at Whittam & Co., was as calm as Silas was volatile. His presence was a balm. Even the guests were happier when Hugh was on the premises. But he was back in Bristol, where the banana warehouses were and, thought Seth, since he himself didn't have the excuse of being on the wrong side of the Atlantic, he'd better try to offer a solution. So he ventured a thought that he'd had yesterday evening, when every single one of the diners who had chosen beef en croute had sent it back with the pastry – flaccid, damp, pale – completely untouched.

'Why don't you write to Mam,' he said. 'She could come over, show them kitchen staff 'ow to go on.'

Silas winced. He had told Seth to lose his Yorkshire accent; it had been all very well when his only prospect had been to follow his late father down a coalmine, but was entirely inap-propriate now that he was under Silas's wing. One day the ships, the bananas and – God help him – the hotel would be his, and yet he still sometimes lapsed, and when he did he sounded like a pit lad with a lamp in his hand and clogs on his feet. However, Silas was interested in the suggestion, and when he spoke he didn't shout.

'Good God, Seth, that's actually not a bad idea.'

'Thank you, sir.' To his irritation, he felt himself redden, and he wondered how old he would be before his emotions stopped advertising themselves in his face.

'It's a brilliant idea. Eve MacLeod, pastry queen of the North of England, riding to our rescue at the Whittam Hotel.' He gave a bark of delighted laughter. 'Evie. Brilliant.' He looked at Seth. 'You write the letter, though.'

'Me?'

'You. Pull on the maternal heartstrings. My sister can possibly resist me, but she won't be able to resist you.'

Now it sounded like subterfuge, and Seth felt uncomfortable. He didn't want to be the lure that brought his mam all the way to Jamaica. He wanted her to come, of course, but only if she knew the truth and thought it a good idea.

'Don't worry, Seth,' said Silas, and for a moment Seth thought his uncle had softened. He hadn't. 'I'll write the letter. All you have to do is copy it out and sign.'

Chapter 9

It was most out of the ordinary for the cook, the house-keeper and the butler all to be summoned at once to the morning room by the countess, and yet, increasingly, the extraordinary was becoming rather routine. What would actually be extraordinary, grumbled Parkinson to himself, was if nothing extraordinary happened: if one day – just one, that was all he asked – could come and go in a dreary, comfortable, conventional manner. He exaggerated, of course; this was becoming a habit, particularly when his arthritis played up, as it did today, the pain seeping down his left hip towards the thigh from somewhere deep inside the bone. He rubbed it surreptitiously as he climbed the servants' stairs, following Sarah Pickersgill and Mrs Powell-Hughes. The housekeeper – who was possessed, Parkinson was certain, of a sixth sense – turned and said, 'I hope you tried my remedies for that, Mr Parkinson. Sooner you do, sooner you'll find relief.'

'I have, Mrs Powell-Hughes, I have,' said the butler, though in fact he hadn't; the preparation of Epsom salts, cream of tartar and ground rhubarb root was not his idea of a bedtime drink. Nor did he consider it feasible to rub the afflicted joint twice a day with hot vinegar. He took pride in his high standards of personal grooming, and did not wish to go about his duties smelling like a pickled onion. It had been kind of her to think of him, though. Kind of her to take the trouble to grind the root. He winced at the top of the flight of stairs and paused, rubbing again at the place from where the pain seemed to emanate. It really was a drain on the spirits, he thought: like a permanent toothache, but worse, since nothing could be pulled. Then he let the green baize door swing back into place and he followed his colleagues into the morning room, where Lady Netherwood greeted them with characteristic informality. Oddly, she was standing by the window with her arms raised, bending at the waist like a sapling in a strong wind.

'Come in, troops, come in, and do forgive the gymnastics. I've been stuck in the drawing room with Eugene for an age, and he's very cruel to me if I so much as twitch an eyelid. Such a relief to be released.'

None of them knew what to say. You see, thought Parkinson, this familiarity was all very well, but it resulted in awkwardness in the end.

'So.' The countess righted herself and clapped her hands, indicating excitement. 'You've heard that the earl has bought a yacht?' She paused, looking at them for confirmation. Again, the trio was stumped. They had indeed heard: yacht-talk gleaned in the dining and drawing rooms had been carried below stairs and discussed at length. But there were carefully constructed codes of discretion, learned and handed down through generations of household staff. To admit to knowledge that could only have come from overheard conversations was contrary to everything the butler, the housekeeper and the cook held dear.

'Really, Your Ladyship?' Parkinson said, taking control. 'That *is* exciting news. Congratulations.'

The countess beamed. 'Thank you, Parkinson. She's docked

at Portsmouth, and that's where she'll stay until we travel down there in August and pick her up for Cowes Week.'

'I see, Your Ladyship,' Parkinson said, as if newly informed. It was a commendable performance in disingenuousness. Beside him, Mrs Powell-Hughes held on to her half-smile of polite interest and Sarah Pickersgill, younger than the others and less practised in pretence, looked confused.

'Now, how are your sea legs?' the countess said, addressing all three with a bright smile. They stared. She laughed.

'What is it you English say when you're flummoxed? Puddled? Muddled?'

'Baffled, Your Ladyship?'

This was Sarah, relieved to be able to admit that indeed she was.

'That's it, Sarah! I've baffled you all. But I put it to you again, how are your sea legs?'

Mrs Powell-Hughes had once taken a trip on a paddle steamer at Filey, but that was all; still, it made her the most experienced sailor of the three. She said – to fill the anxious pause – 'I quite like the sensation, so long as it isn't too choppy,' and the countess gave a small chirrup of laughter and said: 'Good, because I'd like all three of you to join us on the *Lady Isabella* in August.'

Later, back in the kitchen, Sarah Pickersgill told Mr Parkinson that his mouth had dropped open at this point. He resented the suggestion. He would never stand open-mouthed in front of anyone, let alone the countess. And yet he had been wholly taken aback: for an intuitive man – those were his words – he had failed utterly to predict the outcome of the conversation.

'I suppose if you think about it,' Sarah said, 'it makes sense. They'll be living on that yacht for a few days. And if we don't go, who'll cook, who'll buttle?'

'Well, what about the Fulton House lot?' Mrs Powell-Hughes

said. 'They're that much closer to Portsmouth than we are. I'm surprised they weren't asked.'

'Mrs Carmichael's too fat for a galley kitchen,' Sarah said and, to her great surprise, Parkinson laughed.

'I must say Mr Parkinson, you look happy enough about the situation,' said the housekeeper a little peevishly. In truth she really didn't want to go. She had a morbid fear of small spaces, and she had never learned how to swim. The butler considered for a moment, and then said, 'Do you know, Mrs Powell-Hughes, I believe I am.'

'And I am,' Sarah said. 'It'll be a lark. It'll get me out of this kitchen.'

'Aye, and into another one the size of your cold store,' the housekeeper said.

'It's our privilege to be asked,' Parkinson said piously, 'and our privilege to oblige.' Mrs Powell-Hughes bridled. She needed no reminders about honour and duty, thank you very much.

'We'll see how you go on with a salver of champagne flutes in a force-nine gale, then,' she said. She had no idea what a force-nine gale was: it was something she'd read in one of her gothic novels. But it wiped the smile off the butler's face, so it served its purpose. Sarah laughed.

'Like I said, a lark,' she said, picturing sailors in white suits with blue trim and a twinkle in their eyes. Mrs Powell-Hughes, who could only picture a watery grave, took herself off to the stillroom where there were lavender bags to be filled for the linen press. And Parkinson, busy now in the candle cupboard, wondered if he might somehow practise carrying crystal glasses on an unsteady surface, in a high wind.

Isabella's presence at Netherwood Hall altered the mood of the household, subtly shifting the dynamic just as a pawn, carefully placed, can adjust the balance in a game of chess. Tobias had kept her a secret, driving home without wiring ahead to announce his cargo. It was a long and rather arduous journey. They had broken it by making overnight stops in old coaching inns, which thrilled Isabella, who had revelled in the novelty of discomfort: lumpy mattresses, chipped chamber pots, greasy eggs served by surly landladies. She enjoyed it so much that Tobias began looking for patently unsuitable hostelries, so that as they drove away the next day they could scream with laughter at what they'd seen. This shared adventure had only increased their mutual affection, and by the time they rolled into Netherwood they were the greatest of friends as well as the fondest of siblings.

Isabella fell quiet as Tobias steered the motor past the lodge at the bottom of Oak Avenue, where old Bartholomew Parkin held open the gate, though it was a long time now since his milky eyes had been able to see to whom he was granting admittance. The drive from the gate to the house was exactly one mile, and the details of it rushed at Isabella, assailing her with their familiarity: the staddle stones mottled with lichen, the pinkish gravel raked into stripes, the rise and swell of the parkland, the towering oaks. The grass appeared greener than the grass anywhere else, the deer prettier, the late spring flowers pinker, bluer, more abundant. The place seemed flooded by light and colour. She hadn't been back in three years: she had forgotten how much of herself she had left behind.

Isabella was discovered first by Parkinson. He stepped outside to greet the earl and there she was, and he smiled with such heartfelt pleasure to see her that she burst into tears.

'I'm so glad to see you, Parkinson,' she said through the sobs. 'I'm so happy to be here.'

'Goose,' said Tobias and gave her a little shove, but the butler was touched beyond words. Lady Isabella belonged at

Netherwood Hall; this was Parkinson's belief, though he did understand that when her mother remarried and went to Denbigh Court a duchess, the child had to go too. But it was just one sad and sorry outcome of a sadder, sorrier event: the premature death of the sixth earl. His fatal accident, so freakish as to seem like an act of cruelty by a bored and spiteful God, had dealt a devastating blow to the rhythms and cycles of family life, and the departure of Lady Isabella, baby of the clan, darling of her father, had seemed, to the butler, to be a further rent in the fabric that held them all close. Parkinson loved this family. It wasn't his place to love them, he knew this, but nevertheless, he did. And in his private rooms, his inner sanctum, he had wept more than once over the frailty and impermanence of human life and happiness. Now, though, here was Lady Isabella restored, albeit temporarily, to the house in which she had been born and raised. Quite grown up, but weeping joyfully in the entrance hall where she had once played hopscotch on the marble. Parkinson's eyes were damp as he carried her modest trunk: a footman's task, in truth, but at this moment he considered it an honour.

'Isabella! Goodness me.'

Henrietta, fresh out of the saddle, strode in through the front door. She slotted her crop into the umbrella stand and held her little sister at arm's length, looking her up and down.

'I'm not a filly at the horse fair, Henry,' said Isabella.

'No indeed, but you're a sight for sore eyes. There simply aren't enough of us since Mama stole you away and Dickie ran off to Italy. I won't hug you because I'm covered in Marley's hair.'

She released her sister and Isabella wondered if the horse-hair was just an excuse. They had never been particularly close: too much of an age gap, too many differences in personality. As a child, younger by twelve years, Isabella had found Henrietta aloof and a little austere, and had always considered her a rival for their father's affections. Teddy Hoyland had adored Isabella, of course, but he had depended on Henrietta; they had had shared interests, odd things such as coal prices, mining equipment, septic tanks and silage – things that no one else in the family cared two hoots about. Everyone called her Henry and it was apt, thought Isabella; even now, her sister's preoccupations were masculine in nature and she ran the estate – not only in Tobias's absence, but also when he was in residence – with authority and expertise. She was a brick, Toby had said in the motorcar, a godsend. She could also be rather cool and extremely high-handed, thought Isabella, although she had kept this opinion to herself.

'How long are you with us?' Henrietta asked.

'Ages. Until you all go to Fulton House, then I'm to come with you. Mama and Archie will be late to Park Lane. They're waiting—'

'For Perry and Amandine to get home from Marienbad,' said Tobias, striding through the hall and, with one arm, sweeping Isabella away from Henrietta and towards the stairs. 'Never mind all that. Let's go and find Thea. She'll be ecstatic. She loves a surprise and she loves a guest, and here we are with a surprise guest!'

He laughed, pleased with his wit. He was – and this was, from an objective point of view, remarkable – looking forward to seeing his wife. Time away, perhaps: distance between. But also the four days he had spent with Isabella had done him the power of good. She had, without trying, without knowing, restocked for him some depleted store of self-worth, a corner of his being that had languished since . . . Here he paused in his thoughts, for he was never entirely sure whether it was his father's death or his own marriage that had signalled the start of it. Either way, he felt he had not, for some time, been quite the man he once was. Not the man, certainly, who had pursued and won Thea Stirling, the liveliest girl in London in that carefree spring and summer of 1904. If he met such a girl now, he sometimes thought, he would more than likely watch from the sidelines while some other fellow danced her up the aisle. But in the car with Isabella – rescuing her, entertaining her, driving her safely back to Netherwood – he had begun to recognise himself again. Their mother had been livid. Manoeuvred into agreement with a scheme that didn't please her, her objections batted away easily like drowsy bees, she had watched them go with a face like stone, while beside her Archie had waved his stick merrily and wished them bon voyage. Isabella had said Clarissa was jealous. 'Pure envy, green with it. She married Archie to become a duchess, you know. To trump Thea.' This Toby knew. They all did.

'He's a nice old cove, though,' Toby had said.

'Nice enough, but stubborn as a mule and when we don't have company he reverts to barrack-room behaviour. Belches, passes wind, shouts "There she blows!" whenever he does.'

'Poor Mama,' said Toby, but he was laughing.

'She's made her bed, as they say. And, anyway, he's terribly well connected. There was a Partington in the Tudor court, apparently, or at the Battle of Bosworth Field, or somewhere. I forget.'

'Oh, well then. Who cares if he farts like a trooper?'

They had looked at each other and howled, and the tone had been set for the entire journey. Now they bounded up the marble stairs together, arm in arm, and Henrietta, trailing slightly, wondered if there was anyone at all to whom she could confess that she didn't always like Isabella, and who wouldn't judge her harshly for it.

Chapter 10

～ ～ ～

Mademoiselle Evangeline's School of Dance was housed in a former cotton mill, a wide, tall, many-windowed building with four hundred looms still in place, though it was ten years now since any linens or fancy drill had been sent out from there. Eliza thought it was haunted. That is, she hoped it was, although no evidence had yet presented itself. The girls had to pass through the old weaving room on their way to the studio and they all did it at a clip, since Eliza told them that, once, she saw one of the machines moving, as if worked by a ghostly foot. Mademoiselle, hearing the story, had seized on it as an opportunity to galvanise the half-hearted among her girls.

'*Mais oui, mes chéries,*' she said to them, her face a study in sincerity. 'It is the ghost of Dolly Treddle, the lady of the loom, and she only appears when lazy girls are in the building. She was lazy herself, you see. She was flogged to death for her laziness. She comes to warn you of the perils of *la paresse*!'

Eliza, the originator of the myth, was impressed at the way her teacher had smoothly embellished it. Mademoiselle Evangeline, sending them all to the barre with Dolly nipping at their heels, had winked at her.

'*Merci, ma petite,*' she had said confidingly, then, in her usual, commanding voice, ordered them all into first position.

These moments of complicity helped to inspire a level of devotion in Eliza that she had never felt for anyone, and she was a child who gave her heart quite readily. Mademoiselle, sparing with praise, lavish with criticism, was Eliza's great obsession. She was easily the most beautiful creature in her world, and quite how she had ended up in Barnsley no one really knew. But here she was, with her long neck and perfect poise, and as she moved gracefully through the crush of the market or up the sweep of Peel Street people fell away and stared, as if a gazelle was in their midst. She was luminous in Eliza's eyes, a higher being. An approving nod or a kind word from her dance teacher was worth more to Eliza than the most heartfelt acclaim from anyone else. Three times a week she caught the train from Netherwood to Barnsley, for dance classes after school. She wished it were more. '*Mon petit papillon,*' Mademoiselle called her when she was pleased: light and graceful, like a butterfly. Eliza longed for her teacher's attention, yearned for the moments when, scanning her small ensemble of ballerinas, Mademoiselle's eyes would alight on Eliza and she would say: '*Alors, le papillon va nous montrer. Eliza, show us your arabesque, s'il te plaît.*' This happened perhaps only once a month, because Mademoiselle detested favouritism, but Eliza knew what she knew. She had seen the way her teacher watched her, and each discreet nod of approval elevated her soul. They were moments of glory, and though few and far between, they sustained and encouraged. And then today, as she prepared to leave the studio, glancing one last time in the wall mirror at her face, flushed with exertion and all the prettier for it, Eliza had been called back by Mademoiselle, who had said she wished to speak with Eliza's mother and stepfather as, at fourteen, she believed Eliza was ready to accompany her to France, to the Ballet de l'Opéra de Paris.

'Ask your mother, first of all, if she would come and speak with me. I can explain all.' She had smiled at Eliza's instant torrent of questions, and answered none of them.

'*Silence, ma petite, c'est tout*,' was all she had said. 'Run away, shoo, shoo.'

So Eliza had left, and in her mind was a frenzy of possibilities. She was a fanciful girl, even without the promise of Parisian adventure; awake or asleep, her imagination ran riot, and at night her dreams were so crammed with incident that sometimes, when she woke, she had to lie stock still for five minutes to give the scenes in her mind time to fade and retreat. On the thrice-weekly train journeys to and from Barnsley she would rest her head on the window, close her eyes and let her thoughts carry her away – to centre stage, more often than not: Coppélia, Giselle, Odette on the London stage, before a rapt audience. Sometimes, if Eve had been working in the Barnsley shop, she would catch the same train home and Eliza would have to forgo the adulation of hundreds of ardent fans in order to answer her mam's questions about school and what she'd had for dinner. This always felt like a sacrifice, though she bore it stoically.

This evening, though, she travelled alone. It was half past six by the time she got off the train at Netherwood Station, a quarter to seven when she walked into the house. Ellen was sitting on the bottom step of the stairs, as if she'd been waiting for her sister to arrive, although she didn't look up at Eliza but stared down at her own bare feet.

'What's up?' Eliza said, because clearly something was. This was how Ellen communicated anxiety; she would place herself in the certain path of whomever she wished to confide in, and then let the truth be coaxed out of her.

'Nowt,' she said. She wiggled her toes. They were filthy, thought Eliza, mud stained.

'Where's Mam? She'll flatten you when she sees your feet.'

Ellen shrugged. Eliza took off her hat and coat, and hung them on the hall stand. 'Where's Mam?' she said again. It was quiet, at a time of day when ordinarily the house was full of activity. 'What's for tea?'

'There is no tea,' Ellen said, looking up now. Her eyes implored Eliza to share the burden she carried. 'They've 'ad a barney.'

'Who? Mam and Daniel?'

Ellen nodded. 'Mam went upstairs and Daniel went outside. 'e banged t'door.'

Daniel didn't bang doors. He didn't shout or play merry hell like some of Eliza's friends' dads. She sat down next to Ellen.

'It'll be all right,' she said. 'What was it about, anyway?'

Ellen shrugged again. 'A letter, or summat. I was sent out, then got told off for listenin' at t'door.'

'Is Angus in?'

Ellen nodded. 'Upstairs, playin' trains.'

'Well, what a carry on,' said Eliza, feeling protected from these petty tribulations by her own glorious news. Ellen sniffed and looked doleful.

'Come on,' Eliza said. 'I'll make some toast and a pot o' tea and take some up for Mam. It'll all be right as rain by bedtime.'

Ellen, who had heard the worst of it, doubted this very much. But she followed Eliza, because there would be some semblance of normality if the kitchen smelled of toast and the kettle was whistling on the range.

A letter had come, from Seth:

Dear Mam,

I hope this finds you all well. I have been in Port Antonio now for nearly two months of the six that Uncle Silas intends for me, and already I have forgotten what it is to be cold. Even the wind and the rain here are warm.

However, the reason for my letter is not a happy one. Indeed, it is a matter of grave concern. The success of the Whittam Hotel is being jeopardised by the lazy, good-for-nothing staff that Uncle Silas is obliged to hire. Our English guests expect the standard of service that they enjoy in their own homes, and they find us sorely lacking. Our housekeeping staff are slapdash and lackadaisical, and our kitchen staff are idle and stupid. As a result our reputation is suffering, and the rival hotels – all of them American and all of them staffed by Americans – laugh openly at our difficulties. Often our guests leave the Whittam and go instead to the Mountain Spring or some such alternative. It is frustrating and humiliating, and it vexes me to see Uncle Silas, who has been so very good to me, being thwarted in all his efforts to succeed. For my part, I feel something akin to despair with each new day.

Mam, do you think you might come? I believe you could be the answer to all our difficulties. You have made such a wonderful success of your own business and I'm sure you could guide and inspire the Jamaican staff here to adopt your own rigorous professionalism.

I should add, of course, how much it would gladden my heart to see you again. I feel very far from my family. And this is a wonderful island, as abundant in fruit and blooms as one of Daniel's hothouses at Netherwood Hall. You would be enchanted by it, I am sure.

I shall anxiously await your reply, and pray that it will be the one I long for.

Your loving son,

Seth

'Silas wrote that,' Daniel had said the moment Eve had finished reading it out loud to him. He had his arms folded and a look on his face that Eve recognised. It was the look he often wore when Silas was mentioned: sceptical and a little stony.

'Now, why would you say that? It's Seth's hand, Seth's signature.'

'But not Seth's words. Pass it here.'

Daniel reached for the letter and Eve hesitated, then gave it to him. Always she felt pushed into the role of sole defender of her brother's honour. She had wondered herself, when she first read its content, whether the letter was entirely Seth's work. He was a clever lad but unsophisticated, and some of the language seemed – what was the word? Ornate, perhaps: flowery. But Daniel had ignored that.

'Listen,' he had said. '"Lazy, good-for-nothing staff" – well that's not like Seth. And, "our kitchen staff are idle and stupid" – that's not like Seth either.' He had put the letter down on the table and pushed it back at Eve. 'He wouldn't speak in those terms about people. Silas would, though. I've heard it often enough.'

'So what're you saying?'

'As I said, Seth penned it, certainly, but I'd bet the shirt on my back that Silas dictated it to him.'

Eve looked at the letter again. She read it to herself, her lips moving silently. *Mam, do you think you might come . . . I feel very far from my family.* These phrases leapt out at her. She said, 'You're very quick to think the worst,' and Daniel, who in truth was filled with panic at the thought she might go, replied, 'I've learned that it's the shortest route to the truth where your brother's concerned.'

She looked at him. 'That's uncalled for.' Angus, sitting on the floor with a tin train, looked up at the sharpness in her voice. "e's my brother.'

'Just because he's kin doesn't mean he's kind. You have a blind spot where he's concerned, Eve. You see him differently from the rest of the world.'

He hadn't raised his voice in the least. He spoke in reasonable tones. But nevertheless she felt under attack. She looked down at the letter rather than meet his eyes. *I feel something akin to despair with each new day*, she read. Angus stood and came to the table, holding the train. He rolled it along the surface hissing and puffing in his own approximation of a steam engine leaving a station.

'Move your 'and, Pa, t'train's coming,' he said, and Daniel took his hand from the table and sat back in his chair, though he was still watching Eve.

'If Seth needs me, I must go,' she said.

'It's Silas who needs you. Will you cross the world for him?' There was anger in his voice now. The tin train halted, and Angus stared at his pa.

'If I write back with a refusal, what kind of mother does that make me?'

'Eve, it's not your mothering that's in question. It's Silas's dubious morals, and not for the first time.'

'Pa?'

'Away upstairs, son,' Daniel said. 'Your mother and I need to talk.'

'But I don't want—'

'Upstairs, Angus.' This was Eve, and the boy stuck out his bottom lip, snatched up the train and cast each parent a reproachful look, but he went. He'd heard that note of warning in his mam's voice before, and it was best heeded. He walked out of the kitchen, wilfully slowly, running the sharp, thin wheels of the train along the walls as he went. Anna had painted them blue when they had first moved in to Ravenscliffe, before Angus was born, before his mam and his pa were even married. Not bright blue or dark blue, but nice blue: his favourite colour of all the colours she'd put in this house. But he saw now that his train was leaving fine grey trails with its wheels, like the tracks that a real steam engine ran on. He risked a furtive glance at his mam; she hadn't seen, or if she had she wasn't interested. He slipped the train into the pocket of his shorts and left the room.

Chapter 11

There were slogans chalked on the streets leading to Caxton Hall, and posters on the walls. Outside the hall a toothy young woman in a WPSU sash had rushed at Amos with a 'Votes for Women' badge. He'd said, 'No thanks, flower,' and earned himself a sharp poke in the back from Anna, who had taken the proffered badge and worn it herself. Amos was in a facetious frame of mind; had declared himself disappointed to have seen no one chained to a railing, had rolled his eyes derisively at the distinctive yellow Daimler – the Hoyland livery – parked outside the hall, and, finally inside, had pulled his cap down low, turned up the collar of his coat and arranged his features into an expression of sceptical amusement, in case anyone should spot him and mistake him for an acolyte.

The walls and balconies of the packed hall were hung with calico banners exhorting the faithful to action: 'Deeds not Words', and 'Arise! Go Forth and Conquer!' On the stage, a stern body of some fifty women sat in close rank.

'Jury looks 'ard as nails,' Amos said to Anna. 'Wouldn't fancy my chances there.'

She smirked. 'They'd make mincemeat of you,' she said, and then she nodded to a side door, through which three

88

more women had just appeared. 'Look,' she said. 'Stars of the show.'

Emmeline and Christabel Pankhurst and Lady Henrietta Hoyland took their place on the stage, front and centre. Behind them the seated ranks rose and applauded, and the audience clapped too, though the detractors among them made themselves heard, whistling and catcalling, turning the tumultuous welcome into a discordant racket. Then Emmeline stepped forwards and, in a quiet and oddly religious gesture, raised her right arm, holding it horizontally before her with her palm down and fingers outstretched. Immediately, remarkably, the room fell silent, and without recourse to notes she began to speak. Christabel followed, then Henrietta, and with each change of speaker came an increase in moral outrage, a hotter, fiercer, bolder call to arms. Henrietta – golden, somehow, glowing with purpose – was the apotheosis of a steady climb in tempo and emotion as intentional and choreographed as an opera.

'We wish to make the law, not break the law,' she said, emphasising each phrase with a small punch in the air. 'But break it we shall, if we must. There is no obstacle so great, no politician so implacable, no magistrate so harsh that our conviction will falter. We shall prevail, and our legacy will be a fairer, more democratic society. But we do not ask, as supplicants, humbly petitioning for favours. Instead, like warriors for justice, we demand!'

She paused here, basking in frenzied applause. Anna said, 'She's good, isn't she?'

'Too soon to tell,' Amos replied. But he watched and listened to this daughter of the aristocracy, this sister of the Earl of Netherwood, and he could see that she knew how to win a crowd and, having won it, knew how to keep hold. There were plenty of men in the House of Commons who couldn't do as much. He didn't like her voice, though; those upper-class vowels stood for injustice, in Amos's view. Nothing would alter that.

It confounded all Amos's most cherished prejudices and preconceptions that Lady Henrietta Hoyland was a rabble-rousing, egg-throwing suffragette. Anna enjoyed his discomfiture and took every opportunity to make him face facts.

'Lady Henrietta was apprehended again last night,' she would say from behind her newspaper. 'Another night in a Bow Street cell.' Or, 'Lady Henrietta addressed a rally in Hyde Park, it says here, and your Mr Hardie was on the platform with her.'

Amos took the point well enough: not all aristocrats were complacent ninnies. But most of them were, of this he was sure. And just because Lady Henrietta had made a name for herself in the WPSU, which counted Keir Hardie among its supporters, it didn't make Amos a fan, nor did it make her a socialist. Just this week the papers had reported that she'd donated nearly five hundred pounds to buy a new car for the cause, and a further two hundred and fifty for a chauffeur and running costs. Amos was disparaging.

'What kind of cockeyed logic is that?' he said to Anna. 'Cars and chauffeurs! Is that Lady 'enrietta's contribution to social justice – luxury trappings for t'Pankhursts?'

'It's just one of Lady Henrietta's contributions to the Women's Political and Social Union,' said Anna. 'And it's the least of them, as you well know.'

He did, too: could hardly fail to, since her activities were followed slavishly by the newspapermen, intrigued by this highborn combatant in the fight for women's suffrage. Her presence on a platform with the Pankhursts was a draw to the crowds and to the journalists, although her novelty value was nothing compared to the passion of her rhetoric and her devastating way with hecklers. Anna knew her, of course. Henrietta was sister-in-law to Thea Hoyland, and Thea Hoyland had given Anna her first professional commission three years previously. It was Thea who had begun the flow of enquiries from her titled friends; a flow of enquiries that had yet to cease, and that Amos, try as he might to accept it, would have dearly loved to staunch.

But Anna, who would only judge as she found, liked Lady Henrietta, and she was sure that if Amos would but take off his blinkers, he would like her too. This was why she had coaxed him into accompanying her to Caxton Hall and he'd agreed, though only in the interests of domestic harmony. He had no intention of taking off his blinkers, in fact. His blinkers, he told Anna, had got him elected as a Labour MP; his blinkers kept his eyes on the goal and prevented him being distracted by other, marginal issues. He knew very well what the demands of the suffragists and suffragettes were, and while he could absolutely see their point, there were many other higher priorities on Amos's list of matters pending than whether a select group of educated, wealthy women won the right to vote.

But then the speakers took to the platform, and they were clever. Their rhetoric was well honed, their styles of communication practised and artful. Christabel Pankhurst was all animation, a vigorous speaker: brilliant and daring, active and lively. Her mother Emmeline was quieter by far, and less physical; she stood very still as she spoke, only occasionally reaching her hands out to the audience in a beseeching gesture. Henrietta was bold. And she was funny. She banged the same drum as the Pankhursts, but did it with an underlying humour, so that when the hecklers tried to throw her off course she was always ready for them, never caught out. Rather, she seemed to relish the interruption, striking like a cobra at her foe, though her venom was cloaked in comedy and courtesy.

'Do you wish you were a man, madam?'

This was a fellow with a brolly and bowler hat, who looked as though he'd dropped by on his way home from the bank. Disapproval twisted his features and he called his question from a spot near the door, as if for a quick getaway when things turned ugly.

Henrietta, interrupted mid-flow, looked in his direction and said, 'Forgive me, sir, what was that you said?' so that the crowd turned their heads too, and the man in the bowler had the floor. He rose to the moment and raised his voice.

'I said, madam, do you wish you were a man?'

'Yes, sir, sometimes I wish I were a man,' Henrietta said. 'Do you?'

There was temporary uproar. Amos, caught in the act of laughing, said, 'All right, she's good,' and Anna kissed him on the cheek for being generous. If they'd left then all would have been well; better than well. But they stayed, and by the time they left Caxton Hall there was barely a shred of goodwill between them.

Henrietta's theme was the urgent need for increased action. Passive protest was useless, she said. No gains would be made waiting for the eternally disappointing Mr Asquith to do the right thing. It was essential to keep the WPSU in the public eye, to be ever more inventive and daring in the strategies they employed.

'Our commitment to this cause cannot be called into question,' she said. 'Yes, we have been dogged; yes, we have been consistent; but what have we ever done to truly shock the establishment out of its complacency?'

At this Amos laughed, and quite loudly; heads turned towards him and Henrietta, some distance away from him but blessed – or cursed – with a preternatural sense for a dissenting presence, immediately homed in on him and said, 'You are amused by us, sir? If you find comedy in rank injustice, do you go through life with a permanently happy countenance?'

Amos felt Anna's hand on his arm: a tight, restraining pressure. But his head boiled with anger – startling, how very quickly this happened – and he moved forwards through the crowd, his eyes fixed on the haughty countenance of the tall young woman centre stage. Then he stopped and spoke in a voice that dripped with bitterness and contempt. It was his MP's voice, his House of Commons voice: polished and potentially devastating.

'You speak to me of injustice? You lecture this audience on the complacency of the establishment? And outside in Caxton Street, a liveried chauffeur waits to whisk you to a house – one of your houses, I should add – that was built on the profits from the ceaseless labour of underpaid, underprivileged, underrepresented miners. You are the establishment, *Your Ladyship*. Look to yourself, if you wish to address injustice and complacency.'

All around him the crowd was quiet, stilled by a collective awareness of being witnesses to a momentous drama. Henrietta, recognising, now, her opponent, said, 'Ah, the honourable member for Ardington,' in a collected manner, which belied the fact that her heart pounded and her throat had begun to constrict. Amos had had the advantage of a surprise attack, but she stood her ground, literally and figuratively. 'Mr Sykes,' she said, wearily patient, 'on this platform, we do not attempt to address all injustice. We are modest in our aims, and seek only the right to have our say in the electoral process of this country.'

'Indeed. With all the many privileges you already 'ave, you'd like to add one more.' Amos sneered as he spoke. He made no attempt to disguise his distaste.

Henrietta faced him like a latter-day Boadicea, all internal fire and fury; it was as well, thought Amos, that she didn't hold a spear, because there would surely then be bloodshed. He returned her glare, and it held all the loathing that, for decades, he had felt for her family: the Hoylands of Netherwood, coal millionaires who had never needed to get their own hands dirty, let alone risk their lives. Amos himself, man and boy, had toiled in their pits and mined the coal that kept this young woman in ermine and diamonds. Now here she stood, demanding the vote. Well, if it were up to him, she could bloody whistle for it.

'What are you afraid of, Mr Sykes? That the women of Ardington might vote you out of office?' She sounded shrill and disparaging: a little of the control had left her voice. For all her articulacy and quick wit, Amos was simply more practised in gladiatorial debate. He had her on the run; he felt it.

'My only real concern is that parasites like you and your ilk continue to leech the lifeblood from the working classes. I'm not against women having the vote. I'm against women like you demanding it when there are still working men who're not entitled to an opinion on polling day.'

On the platform, Christabel Pankhurst stepped forwards and whispered something to Henrietta, who cast a final, filthy look in Amos's direction then stepped back, leaving Christabel to pick up her abandoned theme and carry it through to conclusion. She strove valiantly to reclaim the moral high ground, but Amos had beaten her to it and, in any case, the gentlemen of the press, who surged out of the hall behind him, had their own clear idea about what the story for tomorrow's morning editions would be.

Amos gave the journalists short shrift – 'My position is t'Labour Party's position, and those views have already been widely aired' – then waited outside for Anna, who took her time. When she did appear, she was with Henrietta. Amos stared at the pair of them, walking together out of Caxton Hall like bosom pals. Perhaps they would part company before they reached him, he thought. But no.

'Mr Sykes,' Henrietta said, extending a gloved hand, which he took, but without enthusiasm. 'Thank you for coming this evening, and I'm sorry we led each other into so public a disagreement.' Her face wore a gracious smile, and he felt like a churl by comparison. Still, he thought, no Swiss finishing school for the likes of me, so what does she expect?

'Don't be sorry. I'm not,' he said. 'Those things needed saying, and I can't speak for you, but I feel better for it.'

'Amos,' Anna said. That was all, but it was filled with meaning. He didn't catch her eye, but looked steadily at Henrietta and said, 'I shall never be able to hear you speak of injustice without bile rising in my throat. This is just the way it is; the way I am.'

'There are many forms of injustice, Mr Sykes. I can't address them all at once, and neither can you. May we at least part on friendly terms?'

He laughed. 'We're natural foes, you and I. Prefer to keep it that way, if it's all t'same to you.'

'Very well,' said Henrietta. She turned to Anna, who had stepped away from Amos, putting a little distance between them. 'Sylvia sends her good wishes, and asked me to thank you. She'll need the canvas a day or two before the exhibition, if that's possible?'

'Of course,' Anna said. 'Tell her, it'll be my pleasure.'

Henrietta nodded silently at Amos, and said a warm goodbye to Anna. They watched her go.

'What was that about?' Amos said. 'What canvas?'

'You,' she said, 'are a pig.'

He stared.

'A pig and a bigot. I am embarrassed for you and by you.'

He bridled at this. 'I speak my mind, that's all. You should know that by now.' He did, truly, feel wronged by his wife. He'd said nothing to Henrietta Hoyland that he wouldn't say again, given the chance. 'Come on,' he said, softening, holding out a hand. 'I never meant to fall out with you an' all.'

She folded her arms. A cold, insidious rain had started to fall; these were poor conditions for a stand-off. Behind them, the yellow Daimler slid by, slowly enough for Henrietta to say, as she passed, 'Can I offer you a lift back to Bedford Square?'

As Amos said no, Anna said yes. The motorcar drew to a halt and she got in, without even a glance of farewell. Amos turned up his coat collar and began to walk towards home. The rain, needle-sharp where it found bare skin, fell from a dark cloud that seemed to hang over him alone.

Chapter 12

❧❧❧

There were still bargains to be had in Jamaica, for someone with vision. Silas had tried to talk Hugh Oliver into buying a property here, but his second-in-command lacked an adventurous spirit, or rather, a speculative one. Hugh's interest in property began and ended in Bristol; his money was safe there, he believed. He didn't trust Jamaica. He'd once been forced to sit out a hurricane, and had seen an entire house and its contents lifted and carried through the air. At least when he returned to his Clifton townhouse, he knew it would still be there, anchored to the earth by its foundations.

In any case, since Silas had a house and a hotel on the island, there was always somewhere for Hugh to stay. Unlike the boss, who had never yet spent a night at the Whittam, Hugh preferred to lodge at the hotel. He was possessed of greater natural charm and sociability than Silas; guests – even dissatisfied ones – seemed drawn to him. Also, Silas's house, though beautiful, was isolated: the jungle, and its creatures, felt too close. Hugh liked an establishment with a well-stocked bar and the likelihood of company. He liked to know that the people around him outnumbered the lizards.

When Silas had bought the plantation fifteen years ago,

the house that had stood at the heart of it was all but derelict. The agent who'd shown him the property seemed to be trying to talk Silas out of the sale and himself out of the commission: you'd need a small fortune to restore it, he said; that, and a failsafe plan for the future. Silas, as it happened, came with both.

He sat now on the veranda of his own great house, and it was immaculate: white-painted, pristine. The jalousies were new this year, and the porch furniture too; oiled teak, with white and green cushions. It had replaced the cane pieces with which Silas had grown bored, and which now stood, incongruously chic, on the rudimentary wooden platform outside the low bungalow where Justine and Henri lived. His housekeeper and handyman had come as a pair – a matching set, Silas said – from Martinique: refugees, in 1902, fleeing the destruction of St Pierre, a city swollen with people and swallowed whole by the eruption of Mount Pelée. People always said there were just two survivors of the disaster, but Justine and Henri knew this to be untrue, for they were not the only ones who had walked away almost unharmed from the fringes of the devastation. Their provenance – their strange patois, their Catholic ways, their manner of dress – set them apart from the locals, and kept them tight-knit, bound together by shared differences and the memories of shared horror. They had not been a couple in Martinique; indeed, they had been strangers, flung together only by fate and the urgency of their escape. But now, in Jamaica, they were inseparable, though as brother and sister, not husband and wife. Silas had found them on the wharf in Port Antonio and something in their faces showed a predisposition to servility, easily recognisable here, where it was such a rare commodity. He had brought them home and kept them to himself, teaching them what he required from them and no more. Their gratitude, and their self-imposed isolation, kept them loyal. As far as Silas knew, they spoke only to each other, and to him, though the latter only when it was unavoidable. The day he gave them the cane furniture, Justine had looked at the floor and bobbed a curtsey, and Henri had said, 'Mercy, Masser,' which was his version of a French thank you; at least, Silas assumed so.

Where once there had been acres of sugar cane, there now were banana plants, but Silas's house was still called Sugar Hill, the name given to it a hundred and fifty years ago, when it was first built. He liked it: liked the sense of history and continuity, and also the hint of a hidden meaning – Sugar Hill, where life is sweet. Like most growers on the island, he cultivated Gros Michel bananas: they were vigorous and thick-skinned, a little like himself. They grew well, travelled well, sold well, and he could ask nothing more of them. So far, the hurricane season had come and gone fourteen times and left his banana plants in the earth, to which he attributed his own lucky streak rather than the blessing of the Lord. It was a long time since Silas had prayed for anything. Look to your own resources, was his philosophy. Or, put another way, every man for himself. In any case, he knew planters whose entire crops had been obliterated by winds, and who had been back in business two seasons later, so obliging was the crop, so fertile the soil.

He had his feet up and his eyes closed, but he was thinking, not sleeping. Hugh had written to him from Bristol, suggesting, not for the first time, that they bail out of the hospitality trade, and concentrate on what they did best. The American-run Mountain Spring Hotel, which was owned by the mighty United Exotic Fruits, had made another offer.

'They want the Whittam, Silas. They'd take it lock, stock and barrel, and the price they offer is excellent,' Hugh had written. 'Enough, in fact, to build another ship for the fleet and increase our banana export capacity in a controlled and profitable manner. The figures speak for themselves. Let's not fall victim to that old, colonial trap of believing that an Englishman should never admit defeat.'

'Masser?'

Justine stood before him, and she spoke tentatively, almost fearfully, as if he was convalescing from a long illness, there on the porch. He opened one eye. Her sad face was fixed on him, waiting for an answer. She would never simply state her business. He closed the eye again, then said, 'Mmm?'

'Masser, dayj'nay ready.'

'Well I'm not, quite,' he said. 'Leave it on the table, under a cover. I'll take some punch first.'

She nodded, and walked backwards away from him, as if in the presence of the monarch. He hadn't taught her this behaviour: he seemed simply to inspire it, and had done nothing to correct it. He liked it, in fact. He pushed the footstool a little further away, the better to stretch his legs. He opened his eyes, and even that fractional movement felt like an effort in the late afternoon heat, which pressed against him like a physical weight. He had acquired the native way with it: acceptance, indolence. The usual insect cacophony rose from the grass and the shrubs around his veranda, and an iridescent cloud of doctor birds weaved and darted about the hibiscus; it grew abundantly from a large stone pot on the porch and its mass of flowers flopped like a soft magenta bedspread over the balustrade.

Truly, this is a remarkable place, thought Silas. He thought about Evie, his sister, thought about bringing her here, plucking her from the granite-grey North of England and dropping her into paradise. He thought about Hugh, bleating from Bristol about cutting their losses and bailing out. He thought about United Exotic Fruits and how he would sooner gouge out his own eyes than let them have the Whittam. Hugh was a decent man, but limited, hampered by his own narrow horizons. Silas, if anything, suffered from the reverse condition. He could see a day when the Whittam Hotel would rise to glory, in direct proportion to the Mountain Spring's fall from grace. Indeed, he saw Whittam Hotels throughout the island, from Montego Bay to Spanish Town, offering sea views and casting elegant shadows across landscaped gardens while pouring profits into the company coffers. Granted, this image was hazy and distant, but the difficulty of achieving a goal had always increased its appeal to Silas rather than diminished it. He had begun life with no material advantages; he was his own living proof that anything was possible.

The screen door swung open and Justine edged out on to the porch once more. She carried a tray bearing a tumbler, a bucket of ice and a jug of her Martinique punch: white rum, cane syrup and lime – an infinitely superior cocktail, in Silas's view, to the fruit-filled concoction the Jamaicans liked. She poured, and as she did so he watched her face, which was serious and steady, as if she dispensed communion wine. Her skin was a burnished blue-black and she wore a white scarf in her hair, tied with a flourish at the front, not at the back. She was young, still; that is, she wasn't old. Henri was lined, and his hair was turning grey at the temples. But Justine had the soft, dewy skin of a purple plum. Silas wondered if she tasted as sweet, wondered if Henri had ever taken a bite.

'Justine,' he said.

She looked up, though her eyes settled just below his. You might think she was a blind woman, following sound, not sight. She had hoops in her ears: brass, Silas assumed, not gold.

'Masser?' she said, and immediately looked down again, at the tray.

Silas sat up, leaned forwards and cradled her chin in his

hand, lifting it so that their eyes met. 'Look at me, when you speak to me,' he said. His hand remained there, cupping her chin and he wondered how it would go if he pulled her to him and took a taste for himself. But he shifted his hand and, with a quick flick of his fingers, dismissed her.

He would sip the punch to the music of the cicadas, he thought, then drive to Port Antonio and find himself a whore.

He saw Ruby and the boy as he weaved recklessly down Eden Hill in the gentleman's roadster he'd recently had shipped from America. Silas was new to driving. At home in Bristol he shunned the motorcar as the root of all idleness, and whenever he travelled to Netherwood – he had a colliery there, as well as a sister – he took the train, since the rail network in industrial Yorkshire delivered him almost to the doorstep of the inn at which he liked to stay. But here, in Jamaica, he needed a vehicle. It was an hour's walk from Sugar Hill to the Whittam, and an hour and a half's uphill trudge back. At first, Henri had driven him about, and this had suited Silas's vanity, as well as neatly sidestepping the small issue of his inability to handle a motorcar. But on occasions such as this one, when his destination was a harbour-front brothel, Silas had found it demeaning to have the car parked outside and the patient bulk of Henri waiting motionless at the wheel. Nothing was ever said when he returned, but the silence was thick with meaning: at least, Silas felt this, especially if he was back within the quarter-hour.

So, instructed by Henri and on the private tracks of his own land – if indeed they could be called private, with all his banana-pickers surreptitiously watching the show from under the brims of their straw hats – he had picked up the rudiments of driving, and was beginning to look ever more comfortable at the task. This hill, though, this precipitate slope, which must be navigated between his home and his destination, seemed often to fox him; between braking speed and changing gear, he sometimes forgot to steer, and with four tumblers of Martinique punch inside him, he always did. Ruby watched his progress, and all her face was a sneer.

'Cha! Drunk,' she said.

'Pie-eyed,' said Roscoe, who listened closely to the English guests at the Whittam Hotel. He laughed. 'Drunk as a skunk.'

The motorcar wended its way towards them, filling the road with its meanderings. In the driving seat Silas reclined like a man in a deck chair, and he held the wheel with one hand only. He was yawning, and his eyes were closed.

'Roscoe!' Ruby shouted as the Ford Model K seemed to pick up speed just as it ought to have been slowing. She saw them both, mother and son, flattened in the road by this fool-fool Englishman; she seized Roscoe's arm and pulled him backwards, so that the boy fell smack on his backside in a patch of ram-goat roses. Silas, eyes open again, saw at last that he didn't have the road to himself, and to Ruby's utter dismay he came to an untidy halt and clambered out.

'Well I never,' he said. The roadster was skewed at an angle across the lane, and he leaned on it with one hand, to steady himself. 'Ruby Donaldson and her fine young son.'

She set her mouth into a hard line and walked on, saying, 'Come along Roscoe,' though he was still sprawled among the flowers and in no position to follow her. Silas picked an unsteady path over to the boy and held out his hand. Roscoe took it.

'There,' Silas said, pulling him up. 'A helping hand. Who doesn't need one from time to time?'

He turned to look at Ruby, but slowly, because his head felt heavy with the effects of the rum. 'Mmm? Don't all of us need a helping hand?'

'Roscoe. Come.'

There was something like fear in her eyes and Roscoe didn't know why, since his mother was afraid of no one. He said, 'Thank you Mr Silas,' and moved away from him, towards Ruby.

'How's school, boy? How's your studies?'

'Very good, thank you, Mr Silas.'

'You a bright boy?'

Roscoe, puzzled at the attention, nodded his head very minimally, torn between truthfulness and humility.

'I say, Ruby,' Silas said, in a pointed way that was hard to ignore. They were already walking away from him, but she stopped and turned. 'He's very light, isn't he?' His smile called to mind a crocodile, she thought. She let his question hang in the humid air, took Roscoe by the hand, and marched away. She was so brisk that the boy struggled to keep pace.

'Ruby,' he said, 'did he mean I'm not very heavy, or did he mean I'm not very dark?'

'Hush, child,' Ruby said.

'But which?'

She knew he would demand an answer, would keep asking until one came. 'I expect, as he'd just pulled you to your feet, he meant light as a feather.' She was just ahead of him still so he couldn't see her eyes, which was a shame, because they always told the truth.

'I am light-skinned, though Ruby, aren't I? Because my daddy was a white man.'

Ruby stopped and turned to her son. Silas was out of earshot and, anyway, he was cursing his starting handle.

'You are who you are,' she said. 'You are Roscoe Donaldson, and there's no one else in the wide world like you.'

'And you're Ruby Donaldson, and there's no one in the wide world like you either.'

'Exactly so.'

'But it's a good thing, Ruby? That I'm light brown?'

She crouched, now, so that their faces were level. He waited with serious eyes for her answer.

'It's of no account whatsoever,' she said evenly. 'All that matters is what you feel here,' – she touched his chest – 'and what you know here,' and she laid a hand on his head. 'Fill your heart and your head with good things, and the colour of your skin will be the very least important thing about you.'

Behind them, the gleaming red roadster sprang noisily into life. Ruby and Roscoe, smiling at each other, barely heard it.

Chapter 13

It was a curious phenomenon, but in England, one felt
lonelier in a crowded place than a quiet one. This was
Eugene Stiller's theory, and he was currently feeling the truth
of it, sitting alone at a table for two in the midst of the chat-
tering customers at the Lyons Corner House on Coventry
Street. He had been there for the best part of an hour, and
apart from the waitress – who didn't count, since she was
obliged to speak to him – no one, not a soul, had so much
as nodded at him. The English leisured classes were a very
buttoned-up lot, he thought. If he'd been in New York, in a
similar establishment, he would have made enough new friends
by now to hold a party. Here, however, it was impossible to
catch anyone's eye.

Eugene had always been uneasy in his own company. He
needed the stimulation of other people to keep him jolly; alone,
he tended to brood. He blamed this weakness on his artistic
temperament – a certain insecurity that was part and parcel
of his sensitive nature. It had ever been thus. An only child, he
had, early in life, fallen into the habit of always making friends,
and he had found this easy as he was pleasant-looking without
being actually handsome, amiable without being overbearing.

But he wished he were more self-sufficient. Even now, as a young man of some account in the world, he craved the attentions of others; indeed, he almost seemed to dwindle with the lack of it, growing paler and somehow less substantial, like a sun-loving plant placed in the wrong part of the garden. So, two months after the Cunard liner had deposited him in Southampton, he was missing the easy familiarity of New York, where strangers in the street might pass the time of day without fear of overstepping an invisible social mark. For it was snobbery, he was convinced of this, that dictated the terms here; the famous rigid social hierarchy, which prevented one fellow speaking to another for fear that encouragement might be given to the wrong sort of person. He missed the democracy of America in general, and the specifics of New York in particular. He missed Central Park and pastrami sandwiches, Broadway and Brooklyn Bridge; the longer he was away, the rosier and more perfect were his recollections.

He should, in truth, be making plans to return. The portrait was finished. He could, perhaps, add a scrap here, a dab there, but he had left it on its easel in the drawing room of Netherwood Hall, and if he didn't return, it wouldn't suffer for it. It was a fine piece and, in the end, he'd been glad to have the spaniels. Thea was throwing a challenging stare directly out of the canvas and the dogs were gazing up at her, their liquid brown eyes fixed on their mistress's face; it was a neat composition, and symbolic – Eugene liked to think – of Thea's place in the world. Plumb centre, with an audience. She had loved it. She wanted him to paint another one, of the earl standing by his new Rolls-Royce. 'I don't work with motorcars,' Eugene had said, and she had laughed, not as if he'd made a joke, but as if *he* were the joke; she mocked him most of the time.

Yet here he was, still, in England; and if it wasn't work that held him here, what was it? He couldn't say for sure. A relationship, of sorts, but not a courtship, certainly; not even a love affair. Rather, it was a monstrous physical urge: a consuming obsession that he once naively believed only true love could inspire. It had turned out that, within Eugene's pure and idealistic soul, there was a seam of rather filthy-minded lust, which had him completely enslaved. It thrilled and intoxicated him, but also it disappointed him. He had thought himself a higher being; not superior to other men, exactly, but driven by an artistic imperative, not a physical one. He was compelled to adapt and accept this new self, since he seemed powerless to escape it.

He looked at his watch. She was late, by half an hour. The waitress, three times now, had passed his table, glancing at him meaningfully, and it was true that a line of people stood at the entrance to the restaurant, waiting to be seated. Perhaps he should order more coffee to justify his presence? But then, if he drank more coffee, he feared he might drown in it. Five more minutes, and then he would leave. Ten, perhaps. But he mustn't be played for an utter chump. These thoughts ran seamlessly through his mind, while all about him the mêlée of conversation and laughter ebbed and flowed, reminding him of his solitude and making him feel miserable. Absently, he picked up a starched white napkin and spread it flat on the table, then began to fold, roll and tuck. It was a trick his father had taught him: a few deft twists of the cloth produced a little oblong body and a long tail. Frank Stiller used to make little Eugene laugh by resting the mouse on the flat of his hand and offering it to his son to stroke. Gently now, he would say; he's a timid little fellow. Then, with an imperceptible flick of his fingers, he would send it shooting up the length of his arm. Eugene smiled at the memory. He was almost done. He tugged at the tail to secure it.

'Busy?'

Thea – for it was she for whom he was waiting – had appeared at last and now regarded him with a look of arch amusement, as if she'd caught him in the act of something faintly embarrassing; which, in fact, she had.

'It's a mouse,' he said, a little too defensively, and regretted it instantly. He sounded absurd. He looked at her, feeling thoroughly disadvantaged. Not only was he holding a linen mouse by the tail, he was also seated while she was standing. Plus, with her back to the window, her gauzy silk dress was quite transparent. He could see the outline of the lace edging on her underclothes, and he knew that she was probably aware of this, and its riveting effect. So, then: here was the reason he had not yet left English shores. The Countess of Netherwood, famously irresistible, had, in the course of their interminable sittings, decided to seduce the artist. She had done this casually, with an emotional detachment that was, in an odd way, part of her charm: this is of no consequence, her eyes had said as she peeled off her blouse the first time, and lifted her chemise over her head. This is something and nothing. She'd done it before, with others; that had been very clear. Eugene, not entirely inexperienced, but no Casanova, had felt himself in expert hands. Thea had reeled him in like a bass and now, to continue the analogy, he was flapping at her feet, waiting to know his fate. Actually, he thought, a bass would've put up more of a fight. Eugene had capitulated the moment Thea cast the line. He was not without conscience; he liked Tobias, and by nature Eugene wasn't a deceitful person. But any qualms he had were as chaff in the wind against the power and pull of Thea Hoyland.

He unfolded the mouse and shook out the napkin, then, because he felt foolish, he said, 'I was thinking I'd like to be back in the States,' and he was pleased to see Thea look not exactly affronted, but certainly a little put out. She sat down next to him.

'But I'm not finished with you yet,' she said. She smelled of jasmine, or of hyacinth: something heavy and floral, and very possibly narcotic. 'And you're not finished with me, are you?'

'I believe I am,' he said, deliberately obtuse. He raised his voice, and said, 'I formally declare *The Countess with Spaniels* complete,' and a wary hush descended on the neighbouring tables.

'I wasn't talking about the portrait,' she said, lowering her voice to a seductive drawl. She leaned close to him, so that her lips brushed his ear, and she whispered, 'I don't want a cup of tea. Let's go home and fuck.'

This was how she operated, he thought wretchedly. This was how he fell, every time. Embarrassment and desire had him in their clutches and rendered him temporarily speechless. Furtively, he pulled the napkin onto his lap and, staring ahead, tried hard to think of something unpleasant, but Thea had unnatural powers and she used them now to occupy his mind with the erotic details of their previous couplings. She laughed, and wormed a hand under the napkin. He pushed it away in alarm. She only wanted him because she was bored, he knew this; he was her toy, and only for the present. Part of him – a small corner of his mind, too small a corner to influence his actions – disapproved very severely of her wanton appetites. He wouldn't want such a woman for a wife, he knew that much.

Beside him, Thea waggled her fingers at the waitress, who came to the table with the air of a woman showing immense forbearance. There should be a law against taking up residence, she thought; the gentleman must be putting down roots by now.

'Is it the bill, madam?' she said, without hope.

'Nope. Earl Grey for me, and a macaroon for my friend. Thank you.'

Eugene waited until the waitress had gone, then managed to say, 'I don't want anything to eat.'

'I know. But you look so sour, I thought it might sweeten you up.'

'This is all an almighty joke to you, isn't it?' He sounded pained, which merely provoked Thea to more mischief. She shrugged.

'I thought we were both having fun. Sex, with no obligations.'

She spoke, now, at a perfectly audible pitch, and Eugene looked stricken. 'For God's sake Thea!'

'Well, let's say making love then, for the sake of your feelings. Don't you want to do it?'

He moaned, almost imperceptibly, but she caught it.

'Good,' she said. 'So do I. Look, here comes your cake, so polish it off and let's get going.'

He was as a lamb to the slaughter, he thought gloomily: there could be no happy ending, for him or the lamb.

At Fulton House, Isabella was crossing the hall when the front door opened to admit Thea and Eugene. He was a few steps behind, as usual, and looked sheepish. Really, he was such a sap, thought Isabella; she had seen the portrait of Thea and admired it, but still it was hard to believe he was capable of such a feat.

'Thea, there you are,' she said, stopping abruptly. 'And Eugene too. What a pity.'

'What's a pity?' Thea tossed her hat towards the hat stand as if it were a hoopla ring. She missed, and it skittered across the marble tiles, swiftly followed by a footman.

'Tobes was looking for you.'

'For me?' Eugene said, and his craven heart skipped a beat.

'Well, for Thea really. And then, when he couldn't find her, for you. He's at White's now.'

'Why did he want me?' Eugene said, and Thea shot him a look which lay somewhere between pity and contempt.

'Oh, nothing urgent,' Isabella said, entirely unaware of the drama playing out in Eugene's breast. 'That is, he didn't look very hard for either of you.'

Unwittingly, she had restored calm to Eugene's ragged spirits and he smiled at her warmly. She was a very beautiful girl, he thought: classically beautiful. Not like Thea, whose appeal was less apparent on first meeting, but who stole your heart insidiously, like a thief in the night.

'He left a message, though,' Isabella went on. 'You're all dining at the Ritz this evening, and he wondered if you'd remembered. He'll meet you there, he said.'

Thea said, 'Are we? How dull,' which Eugene thought unkind. Isabella just smiled, however.

'Yes, poor you,' she said. 'I, on the other hand, am expected at Park Lane in just over an hour. Mama and Archie have arrived, with Perry and Amandine. So, you see, I'll be having so much more fun than you.' She pulled a face to underline the irony, and Thea took both Isabella's hands in hers and looked earnestly into her face. 'Oh my poor darling,' she said. '*Courage, mon brave.*' She meant to be amusing, and, indeed, Isabella laughed, but Eugene had never met the Duke of Plymouth, or his son, and he didn't see the joke. He felt suddenly gauche: superfluous and uncomfortable. He wondered, too – now that the panic had subsided – how he and Thea could possibly move from this imposing, and very public, front hall to the privacy of her rooms without it being perfectly obvious what they were up to.

'Actually, I don't really mind,' Isabella said. 'My gowns are ready and Archie bought me diamonds, and Perry and Amandine will have to defer to me for a change, as it's my Season.'

'It doesn't alter the fact that you're still only seventeen.'

The voice arrived before the person came into view, but it could only be Henrietta, who did indeed appear at the top of the staircase to look down at Isabella. 'You sound rather brattish,' she said. 'That's all.' She descended the stairs as she spoke and now she said, 'Eugene, do you have a moment?'

He opened his mouth to say yes, but it was Thea who spoke. 'Henry, what can you possibly need him for?' she said, and then, to Eugene, 'In fact, you don't have a moment, at the moment, do you?'

Poor Eugene. He stared at Thea, helpless as a kitten, a man with no self-determination, a subordinate.

'Later, then,' Henrietta said affably. 'But Thea, I'm sure Eugene can speak for himself.'

'You'd think so, wouldn't you?' Thea said. 'Come, Eugene.'

She started to spring up the stairs. He gave an apologetic smile to Henrietta, then followed. Isabella and Henrietta watched him go.

'Do you suppose they're . . .' said Isabella, a new consternation suddenly clouding her face.

'Certainly they are,' said Henrietta.

Isabella looked aghast. 'But what about Tobes?'

'It won't last, Isabella. These things never do with Thea. And, to be frank, Toby's just as bad.'

Isabella looked about to cry. 'Oh, how horrid! I can't understand why you're so calm and cold about it, Henry. I can't possibly love Thea as I ought, now. Not if she doesn't love Toby.'

'Oh, Isabella, she never loved Toby, not really. Do grow up.'

Isabella stared. Henrietta, who hadn't really intended to be brutal, said, 'It's just their way – it's not the same for everyone. Don't think any more of it. Truly. They quite understand each other, and that's all that counts.'

'But they're so indiscreet,' Isabella said, with a sort of helpless despair. She glanced up the stairs, trying to imagine what they were up to and failing.

'Thea is,' Henrietta said. 'Eugene just does as he's told.'

Chapter 14

❧❧❧

Stepping off the train at Netherwood Station always felt to Anna like stepping back in time. Not that there was anything quaint or old-fashioned here. Indeed, it was just like any other railway station: busy with engines and people, grey with smoke and soot. But the familiarity to Anna ran deep, so that arriving here always had a sense not so much of coming home but of going back, of revisiting her past.

On the platform Harry Beddle, the stationmaster, was watering baskets of pelargoniums. They had been foisted on him by the rail company and were hanging from the ironwork in an effort to prettify the – frankly – grim outlook that greeted alighting passengers. Harry Beddle thought them a blessed nuisance. When he watered them he did it grudgingly.

'Hello Mr Beddle,' Anna said.

'Ey up,' he said, to the plants.

He hadn't seen Anna for the best part of a year, but if she'd been away for a decade the greeting would have been the same.

'Maya, say hello to Mr Beddle.'

'Hello Mr Beddle.'

The child held out a gloved hand. Really, her manners

were very becoming, thought Anna. Two weeks in Lyme Regis, in the sole company of the governess, and her daughter had returned equipped with a whole new set of disarming niceties. Miss Cargill was evidently a dark horse. First impressions had been of hearty enthusiasm rather than polish and poise, and she'd been appointed as Maya's governess for her kind face, excellent qualifications and boundless energy for exploration and investigation; but it seemed she numbered the teaching of etiquette among her responsibilities too, and some light elocution. Maya had started calling Anna Mama instead of Mam. 'One small additional vowel,' Miss Cargill had said, 'makes a whole world of difference.' Mr Beddle, however, whose sixty-two years at the school of life had taught him nothing about manners, gave Maya a nod but stuck to the job in hand. The little girl withdrew her hand gracefully and Anna winked at her, approving of her daughter's discretion. Water had now begun to stream haphazardly through the moss that lined the baskets, splashing down onto the platform, and Anna and Maya started to move on.

'No Mr Sykes, then?' Mr Beddle said, to the plants.

'Busy in London,' Anna said. 'He wasn't able to join us.'

Rum do, thought Mr Beddle; Amos Sykes, busy in London – she might as well have said he was busy on Mars – it couldn't have sounded stranger or less appealing. Speaking for himself, Mr Beddle had never found any reason pressing enough for him to leave Netherwood, let alone Yorkshire. He put folk on trains to all corners of the country, but he never felt the smallest urge to climb on board himself. He did, at least, recognise that if everyone felt the same way as him he'd be out of a job. But it didn't alter the fact that there was far too much to-ing and fro-ing. Mrs Sykes and the bairn here in Netherwood, Mr Sykes there in London. A rum do.

Anna and Maya, hand in hand, each holding a small bag of belongings, emerged onto Station Road, and began the walk up to Netherwood Common, and Ravenscliffe. When she'd married Amos and they'd left for their new home in Ardington, Anna had promised Eve that she'd be back often. 'All the time,' she'd said. 'If Maya has any say in it.' But Maya was a child; she lived in the present and never hankered for anything she couldn't actually see. If she was taken to Netherwood she was happy; if she spent half a year in London she was happy too, especially now that she had Miss Cargill as an additional distraction, filling each new day with discovery. So Anna and Eve, whose friendship had once been as necessary and natural as the air they breathed, had found that life had filled and swelled to occupy the distance between them. While their thoughts often wandered from one to the other, they themselves rarely did. And yet, thought Anna, here she was, bolting to Netherwood, because even now it was her port in a storm. Amos, torn between his feelings and her happiness, had given no ground at all since the evening of their argument. He could be stubborn as a mule and today, when she and Maya travelled north, he had left early for the House of Commons, so that when the hansom cab came to take them to King's Cross, there had only been Norah on the doorstep waving them off. Always, Amos relied on Anna's more amenable nature to ease their passage back to friendship after a disagreement. This time, she thought, he could wait a little longer than was usual.

'Look,' Maya said now, stopping dead and releasing her mother's hand to point. 'Dad's allotment.'

This was still a novelty, and if Amos had been with them it would have lifted him out of the doldrums. He had become Dad only recently ('Not Papa though,' he had said when Mama got its first airing. 'I'm definitely not a Papa.') and while what she called him seemed to hold no significance for Maya, to Amos it meant the world. There had been no debate, no fanfare, no announcement. She had simply said, at the table one morning, 'Please could you pass the salt, Dad?' and Amos, overcome, had had to pretend he had something in his eye. Anna had said, 'That was nice, Maya,' and the little girl had looked puzzled and said, 'But I always say please.' This was like her, though; she had, at six ('and three-quarters,' she would always add) a naturally literal, matter-of-fact manner: a way of dealing smartly with complexities and thereby simplifying them. Grasping the nettle, Amos called it. It was an admirable trait, he said: there was many a government minister would do well to observe Maya's style and adopt it.

Anna stopped by Maya's side. There was a low, dry stone wall and, behind it, a patchwork of allotment plots showcasing varying degrees of expertise and commitment. Maya pointed.

'That one's Dad's.'

It was roughly central in the run of plots, and distinguishable by its raised vegetable beds, which Amos had made from old railway sleepers. When the sun was hot the children had been forbidden to sit on them because they seeped tar. There were canes up for sweet peas and runner beans, and young broad bean and potato plants stood in rows, shoulder to shoulder.

'It was Seth's, really,' Anna said. 'Dad helped him. Not theirs now, though, is it? Somebody else must be gardening there.'

'It's a shame,' Maya said. She had been very young when this town was home, but she remembered rootling around in the soil for potatoes, which emerged like precious stones in her hands, and picking fat green caterpillars off the cabbages and sprouts. She remembered, too, the guilty pleasure of eating the peas that they'd harvested for Eve, then chewing on the empty pods, extracting every last drop of pea flavour. Anna laughed.

'It's not a shame. It'd be a shame if they did still have it and it was all gone to weeds, with Seth in Jamaica and Dad in London.'

'Who has it now, then?'

'You'll have to look for Mr Medlicott or Mr Waterdine. They'll tell you.'

It was like balm for her chafed soul, being here, thought Anna: invoking these familiar names, certain of the fact that Clem Waterdine and Percy Medlicott would still know everyone's business. These were names she never heard in London, or even in Ardington, which was really very close. They were Netherwood names, Netherwood people, as much part of the scenery as the towering headstocks of the collieries or the rows of terraced houses with front doors that were never used and back doors which were rarely closed.

She took Maya's hand again and they moved on, checking off the familiar landmarks as they walked. The Hare and Hounds, where Amos used to keep a tankard all of his own; the cinder track to New Mill Colliery, where Amos worked for nearly thirty years – an impossible length of time, in Maya's eyes; the little sweetshop where Maya had tasted her first sugar mouse; the school where Seth and Eliza had gone, and where Ellen went, after that last summer here. Then they reached the lane on to the common where the pony had kicked the Sixth Earl of Netherwood in the head and killed him, and then they passed the grassy hollow where Seth had fixed a rope swing on the bough of an elm (and there it was, still). After that, a short upward climb on rough grass peppered with cowslips and buttercups, and then the house was suddenly before them, its solid stone bulk as reassuring and inviting as ever it had been. If it was possible to truly love a building, Anna loved this one. She had lost her heart the moment she first saw it. Leaving it, for Amos and Ardington, had been a sadness that she'd hidden from everyone – even, to an extent, from herself – and nowhere that she had subsequently lived had come close to stirring in her the affection and esteem in which she held Ravenscliffe.

'It's sooty,' said Maya.

'Yes, well,' Anna said. 'If you stood in the same place year in, year out, you'd be covered in coal dust too. Come on, I think I can smell drop scones.' She sniffed the air. 'And straw-berry jam.'

Maya, laughing, began to run, and Anna followed her across the final flat expanse of grass and flowers, and through the gate into the garden. When they reached the house they walked straight in, as if it were home.

Eve was there, and Ellen: a small reception committee, standing in the square hallway where the grandfather clock tocked as it always had, and Anna's ochre walls still held their promise of warmth and comfort. The women felt a jolt of pure relief at the sight of one another, and they hugged with a silent intensity that, for a few moments, made the girls feel awkwardly superfluous. They eyed each other silently, honouring the wariness they both felt, put together again after so long an absence. They'd grown, but Ellen more so. She had on an old pair of Seth's shorts – she had finally prevailed – and she'd talked Eve into cropping her hair. She was barefoot, and her feet were filthy. She had a sharpened twig pushed behind one ear, like a carpenter's pencil, and from the pocket of the shorts dangled the elastic sling of a catapult. Her arms were folded and this gave her a belligerent air, on top of which her face bore an expression of disdain. Maya, in her blue travelling coat and cotton gloves, with her black patent buttoned boots and her white straw boater, looked like a different species.

Eve released Anna and bent down to take Maya's face between her hands.

'Look at you!' she said. 'What an elegant young lady you are these days.'

This sounded to Ellen dangerously like a reproach. She and her mother had already had a long, heated discussion about her appearance, which had ended with Ellen running

119

away for an hour to punish her mother for trying to get her into a frock. She glared at Maya as at a traitor, and Anna, surmising in an instant what might have gone before, whipped off her daughter's hat and coat, and tugged off her gloves, so that the impression of Sunday best was at least diminished.

'Shall we go to our room?' Maya said to Ellen. It was a brave gambit, under the circumstances; a fainter heart would have baulked under Ellen's baleful gaze. But when they were little they had been inseparable: shared a room, shared a bed, even shared a chair at the kitchen table. They might have been glued together, and though everything had changed now, and Ellen seemed set on being a boy (and an unfriendly one at that), Maya stood firm, armed with and bolstered by all her happy memories. Her strategy paid off. Ellen nodded; together, and in silence, they went up the stairs, and when the bedroom door clicked shut behind them, Eve made a rueful face at Anna. 'Sorry about that,' she said. 'She's awkward these days. I just 'ave to mention a pinafore dress and she's all black looks.'

Anna shrugged and smiled. 'Then don't mention pinafore dresses.'

'But she looks like a boy!'

'She looks like a tough little girl. No harm in that.'

It was so good to hear her again, thought Eve. So good to have her back in the house. They were in the kitchen now, called in at the insistence of the kettle on the range. Eve spooned tea into the pot, then poured in the boiling water, holding the kettle high so that the water hit the leaves with a flourish. This was how it was done here, where the rules and rituals of making tea were observed with the same fastidious devotion to duty as that of a priest preparing holy communion. Tea was offered as comfort for whatever ailed you: liquid nourishment for the soul. So the pot must be warmed; the tea must be loose – not caught up for convenience in muslin or mesh; the water must be actually boiling on impact with the leaves and poured from a certain height; the milk must follow the tea into the cup and never, ever, the other way round. In Russia Anna had drunk it strong and black, and heavily sweetened. Here, sugar was never offered, though there was always a cake or some other sweetmeat to counter the bitterness. Anna watched the process now, wondering how many pots of tea she had shared with Eve. Four a day, for three years? In any case, here was one more.

'So,' Eve said, stirring the brew in the teapot – the final ritual before pouring. 'What's gone on?' Something had, she knew that much. This unplanned arrival, narrowly preceded by a telegram, suggested a small crisis in the Sykes household. Anna sighed and looked woebegone. 'Amos doesn't like any of my clients,' she said. 'He wants me to stand for Ardington council.'

It didn't sound like the end of the world. Eve looked at her with mild amusement. 'Really? As well as everything else?'

'Instead of.'

'Oh.' This, Eve could see, was a difficulty.

'He was so angry,' Anna said. 'So was I. We had a terrible row.'

'Snap.'

'You had a row with Amos?' Anna, round-eyed, bewildered: still, sometimes, confused by the language.

Eve laughed. 'Don't be soft. Seth's asked me to go to Jamaica, and Daniel won't 'ave it.' She poured tea into mugs through a metal strainer and when she added milk, the liquid turned dark terracotta, the colour of a house brick. She looked up at her friend, who stared back, suddenly quite distracted from her own woes. 'Close your mouth,' Eve said, 'or you'll catch a fly.'

'Jamaica? He wants you to go to Jamaica?' Anna was – in her Netherwood circle at least – the acknowledged world

121

traveller, but it was beyond even her experience, this island in the distant Indies. Added to which, she had thought Seth safely ensconced in Bristol, at Whittam & Co., in an office, behind a desk. Truly, she was astonished.

Eve nodded. 'Aye. And Daniel thinks it's folly. So we're at logger'eads, like you an' Amos.'

'And shall you go?' Anna asked, ignoring the whys and wherefores and cutting straight to the chase.

Eve considered her answer. Daniel had asked her something similar, just this morning, and she hadn't been able to answer because, between them, the subject was so clouded by recrimination that she couldn't see the way forward. But now Anna's simple enquiry had the effect of clearing Eve's mind. Would she go to Jamaica? There was only one answer.

'I shall,' she said.

There. It was decided. She smiled at Anna, who smiled back, though a little uncertainly.

'And you,' Eve said. 'Shall you stand for Ardington Council?'

Anna took a sip of hot tea, and looked at Eve over the top of the mug. 'Not on your nelly,' she said.

They both began to laugh; neither of them knew quite why, but there it was. They were helpless with it, and the release was exquisite.

Chapter 15

'Your problem,' said Hugh Oliver, 'is that you came to this colony believing yourself to be the new messiah.'

Silas regarded him unsmilingly. He didn't reply. He tilted his face upwards, to feel the breeze from the ceiling fan. Hugh continued.

'You believed you could raise Jamaica from economic ruin single-handed. You imagined yourself fêted by the Colonial Office for restoring the island to the Imperial firmament: Jamaica, brightest star of the British Empire.'

His arm spanned the sky in an arc, and he spoke a little louder than was necessary, drawing attention. They were perched on bamboo stools at the bar of the Mountain Spring Hotel – Hugh's idea: keep an eye on the competition, he said – and around them American guests turned affable, enquiring faces in their direction. Hugh, who had arrived yesterday on the latest liner so that Silas might return to Bristol for a fortnight, was one of only two people in the world who could speak to Silas in this manner, but now, frankly, he was pushing his luck. They had worked together for ten years, and Hugh was, in truth, the firmer, steadier hand on the company tiller. And yet, thought Silas, he was not unsackable.

'Interesting analysis, Hugh, but vastly wide of the mark. And if you don't pipe down I'll dismiss you, just as publicly as you're trying to humiliate me now.'

'Oh, steady on,' Hugh said mildly. He'd felt the cold wind of Silas's disapproval too many times to be much exercised by it. His barks were always worse than his bites. 'I'm merely pointing out that even you can't make a silk purse out of a sow's ear.'

Silas looked away. Beyond the veranda lay the hotel gardens – implausibly, garishly abundant – and they, in turn, gave way to a wild tumble of jungle flora, through which an enchanting narrow pathway had been hewn, leading guests to a sea-water swimming pool where steamer chairs and parasols had been set on the grassy surround, and a weathered, wooden jetty enabled the intrepid and the uninhibited to take the plunge into the salty, health-giving depths. The pool was just visible from here: a glittering rectangle of blue, barely distinguishable from the sky. And this was merely one small, tamed piece of paradise on a paradise island.

Silas looked back at Hugh. 'Sow's ear?'

Hugh smiled patiently. 'What I mean is, we can't shape the Whittam into something it isn't. Another year like the last one and we'll be selling ships to keep us afloat, if you'll forgive the pun.'

Silas laughed harshly. 'No spine, that's your problem,' he said. 'No backbone.'

Hugh took a deep draught of scotch and soda. Silas was a handsome fellow, but by God he could be an ugly drunk. His smile, now, was twisted with contempt. Hugh's own head was beginning to spin. This was his third drink, and they'd yet to ask for a menu. He signalled to a waiter on the other side of the bar, who in an instant was by Hugh's side.

'Yes sir, how can I help you?' the waiter said in tones that suggested nothing would be too much trouble. On his perch, Silas growled.

'May we see a menu?' Hugh said.

'Certainly. Both of you, sir?' He flashed a cautious, sidelong glance at Silas, who glowered back at him.

'Yes, please,' Hugh said. The torrent, he thought, would commence when the waiter retreated. It did.

'Why, in the name of all that's holy, are we stuck with the fucking natives, while the Yanks here are free to staff their hotels with impeccably trained waiters, fresh from Boston? How can we compete? What's the value of tax-free fixtures and fittings if our hands are tied when it comes to hiring? Hmm?'

He wasn't shouting – instead, he seemed to hiss – but he was bolt upright in his chair, and his eyes were hot, dark pools. A vein throbbed like a warning at his throat, and the muscles at his jaw were coiled and tight. He looked like a madman. Hugh leaned across the table.

'Then let's sell,' he said, deliberately calm, and enunciating carefully as if Silas were hard of hearing. 'Sell the Whittam to United Exotics, invest the profit in a new cargo ship, concentrate on what we do best.'

Silas was shaking his head before Hugh had finished speaking. 'Never. I won't gift my hotel to these smarmy bastards. Wouldn't give 'em the satisfaction.'

Hugh sat back in his chair. 'Then we're ruined,' he said, pleasantly. He meant it too; he had a closer understanding than the boss of the accounts. The banana-export side of the operation was in fine fettle, but its future would surely be in jeopardy if Silas insisted on keeping this millstone of a hotel – albeit a luxurious one – around their necks.

'The menus, gentlemen.'

The waiter made a small bow. He was young and clean-cut, and he wore the Mountain Spring livery of white and green. A red hibiscus was embroidered on the pocket of his jacket, and also on the front of the heavy, bound menus that

125

he handed over with discernible pride. He smiled as he spoke, which Hugh found ingratiating and a little unnerving. 'Today's special entrée is sole *bonne femme*,' he said, 'and we have a wonderful consommé on the hors d'oeuvres menu, as well as a spinach and Monterey Jack soufflé. Please take your time, and if I can be of any further assistance in your choices, I'll be only too happy to oblige.'

He slid away. Hugh laughed.

'What?' said Silas crossly.

'I'm just thinking about Batista. I don't think she went to the same finishing school as that fellow.'

Silas grimaced. 'Glad you can find something to laugh about.'

Hugh sighed. 'I really don't understand why you're being so stubborn. The answer to our difficulty is staring us in the face.' He had the soft lilt of a true Bristolian and this made him sound peaceable, even when he was feeling rattled. Sometimes people made the mistake of thinking him a bumpkin; in fact, he was sharper than Silas, and less driven by pride. He had a finely tuned instinct for business, which right now was telling him to bail out. 'We have a failing hotel and an eager buyer. Let's jettison the hotel and cut our losses.'

Silas ran his hand over his face, the gesture of a weary man. He hadn't told Hugh about the letter to Evie. Until she replied, he saw no reason to reveal his plan. There was an outside chance that she might decline, in which unfortunate case he would look foolish and perhaps a little vulnerable. The truth was that, having set the scheme in motion, he was rather desperate for her to come. He was proud of his sister – of her beauty and her business acumen – and his faith in her capability was immense. He liked to think of them as a team. He liked to think that, together, they would be invincible. But he didn't say any of this to Hugh, only made a moody, visual orbit of the room, observing the contented diners on the wide veranda, dipping their heads towards each other in genteel conversation, acknowledging with small smiles the services of the waiters, who refilled their glasses without being asked and, between tasks, stood like sentries until they could again be useful. There was no faulting the staff, thought Silas – unless their ever-presence could be deemed an intrusion. Speaking personally, he preferred to be in charge of his own bottle of claret; he liked it always within reach.

Hugh followed the line of Silas's gaze, to where their waiter was engaged in the task of replenishing the glasses of a group of hearty men in golfing garb.

'Ghastly get-ups,' Hugh said.

He meant the plus fours and jaunty stockings. In the Whittam dining room, a chap might not be able to find a waiter for love nor money, but he'd never sit down to dinner in tweed.

'Americans,' said Silas bleakly.

'Have you chosen?' Hugh said. 'I might try the trout.' He flicked through the pages of the menu, which was as thick as a periodical. 'How do they manage to offer so much, and do it so well?'

Silas's menu lay untouched on the table. He ignored Hugh's question – again – and instead skewered him with a hard stare.

'Now I understand,' he said. 'Professional espionage my eye. You got me here in order to strengthen your argument. To hasten my progress towards what you consider to be the inevitable.'

Hugh arranged his face into a mask of innocence, then looked up.

'Not at all,' he said evenly. 'I simply think we need to keep an eye on what the opposition is up to.'

'You thought you'd rub my nose in their slick operation: make me see what a hopeless case we have in the Whittam Hotel.'

Hugh shrugged, conceding the point. 'Well all right, yes, I suppose there was an element of that in my calculation. But you have to admit, they have polish.'

'And we,' said Silas, standing up, 'have a potential gold mine. If you're unable to see that, you're not the second-in-command I thought you were.' He placed pointed emphasis on 'second' – as if, thought Hugh, he could ever forget who was in charge. Silas stalked to the door and the heels of his glossy shoes clipped crisply on the parquet, an audible accompaniment to his extreme displeasure. Hugh was clearly expected to follow; they had driven here in the Model K and it was a long walk back without it. But it seemed, to Hugh, of the utmost importance to stay put, and when the young waiter appeared at his side, all anxious concern and enquiry, Hugh simply flashed his charming smile and ordered not just the trout but also a half-bottle of champagne. He liked it here. There was a pleasant atmosphere – now that Silas had gone – and the clientele seemed, for the most part, urbane and potentially interesting. Certainly, if he were a traveller to this island and had to choose between the Mountain Spring and the Whittam, he knew where he'd be resting his head.

At Musgrave Market the heat of the day was starting to roast the tomatoes on the cart, and even before the sun came up they'd been past their best. Ruby picked one up, sniffed it, squeezed it gently and rejected it: too soft, on the turn. The stall-holder, an old man with a long, thin face and a wiry puff of grey hair, sat on a stool beside his produce and picked his yellow teeth with the sharp end of a curved knife. He watched Ruby's every move as if, she thought derisively, she might be about to make a run for it with his inferior wares. He had yams too, and okra, and they looked better than the tomatoes, but Ruby was affronted now so she walked on. Everyone sold the same vegetables, anyway; she didn't need to buy them from someone who didn't know the difference between a common thief and a respectable woman. She moved along purposefully, browsing the stalls, lost in her task.

She was a single-minded shopper and her determination sometimes gave an impression of unfriendliness, though this was misleading. There were plenty of people who came to the market to be sociable, and Ruby didn't begrudge them, not at all. But who knew what treasures might be snapped up by others while no-account nonsense was swapped with a neighbour? No, the market was a serious place, intended for a serious purpose, and Ruby was only willing to part with her money when she was sure there wasn't better to be had elsewhere. It made a slow business of shopping, though, and so far she had only a calabash, pimentos and a pound of salted codfish; there was plenty she still needed. She glanced up at the courthouse clock and then down again at the contents of the straw basket, which she carried not on her head but in the crook of her arm in the manner of an Englishwoman. Tomatoes, cassava, sweet potatoes, okra and, if they were good and fresh, some sprats for Saturday breakfast: these were all still to be purchased. She continued on, a small line of concentration creasing her brow.

A commotion ahead, a small scream followed by a hubbub of mingled exclamation and laughter, drew Ruby's eye away from the produce. She craned her neck slightly to see the source of the disturbance, which sounded, to her, more threatening than the usual verbal jostling that periodically erupted in the crowded marketplace. A woman appeared to be on the floor, on her hands and knees, though it was hard to see what she was at because the crowd around her had closed in, forming a ragged circle. Ruby moved a little closer, propelled by a protective instinct, alarmed by the crowd and what felt like menace behind their catcalls and whistles. She could see better now, and the woman was scrabbling at yams and green bananas in the dust, but two young men in the circle around her were kicking the produce, rolling the yams like footballs and flicking the bananas up into the air. The laughter and jeering that accompanied their antics had an uncomfortable quality, a recognition of its own inappropriate cruelty, but still it continued.

Ruby was seized by fury, and she rushed at the crowd like a small tornado, barging through its ranks with a kind of howling admonishment that had the immediate effect of splintering the cordon and silencing its noise. The basket on her arm became a weapon, and she swung it wildly at one of the young men, bringing its calabash-weight hard against his ear.

'You shameful creatures! Leave her be! Leave her be!'

Ruby's voice possessed authority and this, together with the basket whirling about her like a medieval flail, caused the crowd to fall back, not resentfully but almost with relief, as if they'd merely been waiting for someone to end it. What laughter there was now, was directed at the fellow with the swollen ear, who clutched it with tender concern and wailed a self-pitying lament.

'Me ear ripped off,' he moaned with a rising pitch of hysteria. 'Me kyaan hear. You done ripped off me ear and me kyaan hear.'

Ruby cut her eyes at him contemptuously and then dropped to her knees beside the woman on the ground. Unimpeded by her tormentors, she had now regained most of her goods, which she was piling hastily into the big rush bankra by her side. She said not a word to Ruby, nor caught her eye, and when Ruby retrieved the last of the yams the woman took it from her silently and rammed it into the basket with the rest. But then, when she made to stand, she gave a pitiful cry and placed herself gingerly back on the ground.

'What is it?' Ruby said. 'Are you hurt?'

Finally the woman looked at Ruby directly, and at once she recognised her. It was Mr Silas's live-in help, the Martiniquan, and this made some small sense of the ruckus that had ended with her and her vegetables on the dusty ground of the market place.

'Justine,' said Ruby. 'Is that correct?'

The woman nodded. She was very dark, with beautiful eyes that registered hurt and her lips, full and the colour of cherries, were down-turned like an unhappy child's.

'Here,' Ruby said, standing. 'Take my arm.'

Though she looked profoundly reluctant, Justine reached up and used Ruby's strong, supporting arm to get awkwardly to her feet. She staggered, seemed somewhat faint and, evidently, was in considerable pain. At the same moment she and Ruby both looked down to see an ugly, reproachful bloom of fresh blood on the vibrant yellow fabric of Justine's dress. Wordlessly, Ruby reached down for the loaded bankra and placed it expertly on top of her own head. Then she slung her shopping basket back on to one arm and gave the other arm to Justine. Together they made their way slowly through the market place and people fell away from them in mingled fear and respect, clearing a path.

Chapter 16

Ruby took Justine home; that is, Scotty did. He had the donkey cart and was on his way back out of town with nothing on it but linens from the washerwoman, and because he had a soft spot for Ruby he agreed to let the silent Martiniquan ride beside him. Ruby sat on the cart, on a tied bundle of pillowcases, and she wedged the shopping beside her so that, if Scotty hit a rut in the road, those yams wouldn't be back rolling in the dust.

'You know she obeah woman,' Scotty had muttered to her after Justine had been helped up on to the seat, by now with blood trailing in lines from her knee to her shin. 'What she done hide in dat bankra? Chicken feet? Dead man's fingers?'

'Cho!' Ruby hissed back at him. 'Hush your nonsense. You know no such thing.'

'I just sayin' what ever'body say.' Scotty made a stirrup with his linked hands and hoiked Ruby up onto the back of the cart, efficiently, if inelegantly.

'Then you're a fool,' Ruby said. 'Or a parrot, repeating what you hear.'

He rolled his eyes at her and grinned.

'Miss Hitey-Titey,' he said. If he'd dared, he would have

132

kissed her rump, which for an enticing moment was level with his face. 'You de finest piece o' goods I ever carried on me cart.'

'Get on,' Ruby said, though not crossly, 'before the poor woman expires.'

He loped to the front of the cart and climbed up, sliding his body on to the seat next to Justine, who didn't register his presence but sat rigid and straight, even when he shook the reins and the mule lurched forwards with a violent jerk.

'Where we headin'?' Scotty said, twisting round so that Ruby could hear him over the rattle of the wheels.

'To my house,' she said. 'I need to fix up that bleeding. Then on to Sugar Hill.'

They exchanged a strange, guarded look before Scotty turned round again, to keep the mule in a straight line. Nobody went to Sugar Hill who didn't live or work there. If it were up to Scotty he'd be dropping this woman at the end of Sugar Hill Lane. Correction: if it were up to Scotty she wouldn't be on the cart at all. Ruby Donaldson didn't know trouble when she looked it in the face.

Ruby and Roscoe lived in the wooden house that her great-grandfather had built with his bare hands nearly ninety years ago. Here and there were amendments and additions, made necessary usually either by the weather or the expanding family: a replacement roof when a hurricane stole the original one; an extra room, tacked on to the side of the house; a new chimney, when the brick oven went in. There were two rooms upstairs and three down, but the staircase was outside because Great-Gran'daddy Donaldson forgot to build one within the walls. It was only when he moved in with his wife and children that he realised there was no means to access the upper floor, of which, until that point, he had been immensely proud. But the outdoor staircase did the job well enough: at least, it did when he'd knocked out a hole for the door at the top. Great-Gran'daddy and Great-Gran'mammy Donaldson had been freed even before the Emancipation Act made it compulsory. According to family legend, he had earned their liberty by being a hero; when the overseer's house went up in a blaze Great-Gran'daddy had climbed the walls and pulled out every one of the five little white children sleeping upstairs. He had thrown them from the window and Great-Gran'mammy had caught them in her apron. This last detail sounded unlikely to Ruby, but still, she'd passed the story on to Roscoe, who would doubtless do the same, come the time. Whatever the truth of it, the Donaldsons – who had been given their name by their Scottish owner and, out of gratitude for their freedom, kept it for ever – had been set up with a hand cart, a sack of flour, a crate of cassavas and a hessian bag of tools, including their old cane bills. The telling of the legend always went that they felt like the king and queen of Jamaica, not because of their possessions but because they went hand in hand away from the sugar plantation and nobody set the dogs on them. They walked for two weeks before they finally stopped and built a house. They were grateful to their old master, but they didn't want him for a neighbour.

For a while after Roscoe was born, Ruby had lived here with her mammy and daddy, but they were both dead now, and for just the two of them Great-Gran'daddy's house was really quite spacious. Ruby cherished and cared for it. She'd painted the outside blue and yellow, and every year, before the rains, she painstakingly applied a fresh coat of paint. Great-Gran'daddy had grown vegetables, and Great-Gran'mammy had been a higgler, selling at the market whatever she couldn't use herself. They had fended well for themselves, improved their lot, handed on to their sons the ability to take pleasure in a long day's work and an appreciation of the joy of a free man's wage. Now their original plot was tended by Ruby; she grew small quantities of breadfruit, callaloo, sweet peppers and plantain. She had an ackee bush, which had sprung up of its own accord like a gift from heaven, and Bombay mangoes lolled heavy on their branches just by the small porch, close enough that you could reach out and pick the fruit without leaving your chair.

But what she loved best was her medicine garden: fever grass, vervine, wild sage, cow's foot, cerassee, aloe vera, pulsey, toona, sage, jack-in-the-bush – all of them had their place and their calling. They fascinated her, their particular strengths and properties, and sometimes people came to her for her apothecary's skill with them. Ruby could make a treatment for any ailment, and while she couldn't promise that the poultice wouldn't smart or that the infusion would taste pleasant – the boiled leaves of the cerassee plant made a particularly disagreeable drink – she believed ardently in their healing powers. When they didn't work she was apt to blame the patient for their lack of faith.

'Sit,' she said now, not wishing to sound peremptory, but nevertheless slightly out of patience and sympathy with the silent, suffering Justine, who lowered herself onto the broad porch step. Scotty watched from a distance, with a vague but persistent sense of foreboding. Whether or not she was an obeah woman, she was certainly from Martinique, and that was enough, in Scotty's book, to make a man wary. He squatted under a cashew tree and took out his tobacco tin, but he had the women in range. Edna, released from the cart, joined him under the tree to escape the flies, and, feeling companionable, he passed her a plug of tobacco, which she took from the palm of his hand with her whiskery lips.

Ruby knelt at Justine's feet, and with a cloth and a bowl of boiled water she swabbed the bloody wound, a jagged gash of about two inches long, just below her right knee.

'What happened?' she asked Justine now, looking up into the woman's face, which was taut with the effort of not yelping in pain. 'Did someone push you to the ground?'

Justine shook her head. She opened her mouth to speak at last, then seemed to think better of it and closed it again. She stuck out her good leg and mimed a small sideways lurch, then gave Ruby a nod of encouragement, inviting her to guess the charade.

'They tripped you up? Is that it?'

Justine nodded energetically and smiled, a brief, beautiful smile that appeared and was gone, like a moment of sunshine in a sky heavy with clouds. Ruby took up a small sharp knife and sliced a spiny-edged leaf from the aloe vera plant. She pared back the edges of the cut end, revealing as much as possible of the pale jelly inside. Of all her healing plants, this was the one she most revered: the workhorse of her medicine cabinet, the cure-all. She applied the jelly directly to the wound and Justine winced, though she held her leg steady. Ruby sliced again, further along the leaf, and again applied the sap.

'There.' Ruby sat back on her heels. 'I'll bandage that, then we'll drive you up to Sugar Hill.'

She made to stand, but Justine suddenly reached for her and held her by the wrist, holding her so that their faces were level. Scotty stood and stepped out from under the arching canopy of the cashew tree, but Ruby knew the woman meant no harm: it was evident in her face.

'Mercy, Madam,' she seemed to say. 'Mercy.'

Ruby, a little perplexed, said, 'Mercy?' and Justine smiled again, but shyly.

'Thank you. Very kind.'

Her voice was faltering and a little hoarse, as though she wasn't at all accustomed to conversation. Perhaps, thought Ruby, the world was a quiet place when your neighbours took you for a voodoo priestess, and when your native patois wasn't much use on the island you called home. She pitied Justine: pitied her isolation, her situation, up there on the Sugar Hill plantation. There was a man, of course, a husband, Ruby assumed, or perhaps a brother; she didn't know. He was much older than Justine and far less exotically attractive: lined and just a little stoop-shouldered, though perhaps he was blessed with a beautiful character, which in Ruby's opinion was a far rarer and more valuable quality. She mistrusted physical beauty in a man: she had learned that it counted for nothing.

Down by the tree, Scotty watched as Ruby fetched a strip of clean, white cotton and wound it around the gash in the Martiniquan's leg. She was brisk and tender at the same time, and the sight of her provoked in him a queasy nostalgia, whisking him back thirty years to a scene from his childhood: his mammy fixing up a cut on his forearm with the same expression of concentrated kindness. He looked away, and shook his head to dispel the picture, because memories of his mammy always led to memories of his daddy, an inveterate, rum-soaked wife beater.

'Ruby, come,' he said now, his voice edged with impatience. 'I don't got all de laang day to sit waiting for you.'

She turned to look at him in surprise. She couldn't ever remember being ticked off by Scotty. Beside her Justine hauled herself upright. She was taller than Ruby, and the white cotton headscarf twisted into its front knot gave her another couple of inches still. She said, 'Sorry, sir,' in her unpractised voice, and began to make her way down the path towards the cart, carrying herself with great dignity despite the pronounced limp. Scotty, feeling a little ashamed, brought Edna out of the shade and backed her into position. Ruby reached the cart and gave him a subtle nudge, undetected by Justine, who was stoically levering herself back into the seat.

'Mr Hitey-Titey,' she said, and he bestowed his easy smile on her, enjoying the joke.

The cart bumped on, and though Justine was again entirely still and quiet beside Scotty, the mood had somehow loosened and lifted, so that when Ruby began to hum an old tune, a plantation song, Justine joined in, though with a shy backward glance, as if permission might be needed. Then Scotty pitched in too, supplying the lyrics in a surprising baritone, and they travelled for a while in this holiday spirit, until Sugar Hill drew closer and, as if by prior agreement, everyone fell silent.

The track took them in a curve through the banana fields, the broad flat leaves towering above and around them like glossy green parasols, and the workers, the pickers and the carriers, stared with frank curiosity at the passing cart. Ruby had spent her days here as a girl, working in the lee of her mother, bearing on her head a towering pile of bananas and walking in stately procession to the Rio Grande where boats waited to carry the fruit to Port Antonio. For a while she had been content enough. By the end, she hated every square inch of the Sugar Hill plantation. Now, although she fought it, a knot of hard anxiety had formed in the pit of her belly; how odd, she thought, that a tract of land could have such an effect, as if she'd come face to face with Silas Whittam himself, on an empty lane, in the dead of night.

The bungalow that Justine shared with Henri occupied a corner of flattened land at the foot of the final sweep of the track to Silas's residence. The two of them walked back and forth to the house so often that ruts marked out their path on the shingled track. Outside their own dwelling there was no garden, but two dusty chickens scratched half-heartedly at the baked earth and a pot of Scotch Bonnet peppers brought a splash of colour to the drab porch steps. Scotty brought Edna to a halt and Ruby clambered off the cart, dragging Justine's basket of vegetables with her. Justine lowered herself gingerly from the seat. Up the hill, the great house could just be glimpsed through the trees that surrounded it: a small corner of the western end of the house, its long sash windows glinting wickedly in the afternoon sun.

'You'll be all right now,' Ruby said to Justine, and it was a statement, not a question. She was anxious to be on her way. Justine nodded.

'*Vous êtes très gentille,*' she said. 'Very kind.'

Ruby shook her head. 'It was nothing. Be careful next time you come to the market.' This made it sound as though Justine's own carelessness was to blame for her injury, so Ruby added, 'I mean, be wary.'

Justine nodded.

'Do you have friends here?' Ruby said, finding herself unable to simply spring up into the cart and be gone. The pickers nearest to them moved about their business, keeping their distance. Somewhere, someone was singing. Justine laughed sadly.

'No friends, only Henri.'

Ruby looked about her. Everywhere there were people. 'No one?'

Justine shrugged. 'They fear me,' she said in her faltering voice. 'And they believe I am . . .' She paused here, reluctant to help spread the rumour by repeating it now. 'Quimbois woman. Obeah woman. *Mais pas vrai,*' she added. 'A lie.'

There was a pause. Ruby wondered if Justine had given them cause for mistrust. There was, however, nothing sinister about her appearance, apart from the blood on her dress, and that had been spilled at the hands of ordinary rogues in the market place.

'They don' like masser,' Justine said. '*Mais* they think masser like me.'

Ruby nodded, understanding at once. There were no advantages to being a favourite of the boss, especially this particular one, who was known to value his banana plants above the people who grew, picked and carried them.

'And does he? Like you, I mean?'

Again, Justine shrugged. 'Sometimes, *oui. Et quelquefois non.* I mean, sometimes, no.'

She spoke without self-pity and gave Ruby a rueful half-smile.

'Well,' Ruby said. 'You know where I live. You have a friend now.'

Behind her, Scotty sucked his teeth and gave a low hiss of disapproval. Justine glanced uncertainly at him then she seized Ruby's hands and squeezed them hard in a wordless gesture of gratitude, before stooping to pick up her basket and turning towards her house.

Up on the cart, with Ruby now beside him, Scotty said, 'You be careful, Ruby Donaldson. You make friends with dat woman, you make trouble fo' yourself.'

She cut him a withering look. 'Superstition and prejudice is the bane of this island,' she said grandly.

He laughed his long, slow wheeze of a laugh. 'Superstition and prejudice,' he said, imitating Ruby's hauteur then shaking his head, as though the words were hilarious. 'You mighty fine, Lady Donaldson. You mighty fine.'

He clicked his tongue at Edna and the old mule threw back her head and split the air with a jagged, doleful bray, before hauling the cart into motion and heading for home.

Chapter 17

The debutante curtsey was by no means a simple, perfunctory bob, nor was it a lavishly theatrical flourish. Rather, it was a slow, graceful descent, left foot positioned behind the right, back straight, head erect, arms and hands motionless by one's side. As the curtsey reached its lowest point the head must then be very slightly bowed, in grateful obeisance to Their Majesties.

'The greater part of the weight must be on the right foot when descending, on the left when ascending,' Isabella said, quoting from an old, yellowing manual that her mother had retrieved from a casket of precious things: dance cards, invitations, a pressed rose, a bundle of letters. Isabella had been surprised at the existence of the box. Clarissa was not the keeping type, she had thought. 'Perform this action repeatedly,' she continued, 'slowly, and with great care, until it may be accomplished in one fluid movement.'

She dropped the book, a little carelessly given its great age, on to a side table and demonstrated a perfectly steady, perfectly elegant, perfectly restrained curtsey. Tobias clapped. Rising, Isabella took up her manual voice again, reciting now from memory.

'In a Court curtsey, the young lady must take care never to stoop from the waist, but only to make the smallest inclination of the head at the deepest point of the curtsey,' she said.

'And did you manage that?' said Tobias.

'I did. Alicia Treaves-Desmond fell to one side and had to put out a hand to support herself.'

'Oh Lord. Off to the Tower?'

'She was graciously ignored, until she righted herself. Utterly shaming.'

'I'll say,' said Tobias. 'It's hardly a task, is it?'

'Easy for you to say,' said Isabella. 'I'd like to see you curtsey before the king and queen without making an ass of yourself.'

'And I'm perfectly sure I could,' he said. 'It's one of those things that sounds desperately complicated when written down, but in reality is quite simple, like trying to give someone instructions for getting out of bed.' He adopted the same scholarly tones that Isabella had used and said: 'Pull back the counterpane with the left hand in a sweeping motion towards the centre of the bed and, at the same moment, raise the upper body and swing the right leg towards the floor, being sure to allow the left leg to follow swiftly after.'

'Very amusing, darling,' said Clarissa, glancing up from her embroidery, which was only ever a device for listening to other people's conversations while affecting not to. 'Of course, the joke is that a manual to help you out of bed might actually be rather useful.'

Isabella laughed. Her mother was very rarely intentionally funny; it was important to appreciate her wit if you should chance to encounter it. Tobias said, 'Unfair, Mama. Isabella, what time did we ride this morning?'

'Up with the lark, as a matter of fact,' his sister said. 'We were out before the Household Cavalry.'

Clarissa looked up again. 'When I had my Season I attended

fifty balls, forty parties and twenty-five dinner parties,' she said, in the way she had of appearing not to have registered the previous comment. But then she added, 'And every morning I rode out before ten o'clock, to keep the colour in my cheeks.'

'All those parties, but you met Daddy on Rotten Row,' Isabella said, taking up her favourite family legend. 'He cantered up alongside you . . .'

'. . . spooking my grey mare as he did so,' said Clarissa, supplying – as she always did – the sour to the sweet.

'. . . and you rode together for a whole hour . . .'

'. . . well, I couldn't shake him off.'

'. . . at the end of which, he said, "I would ride to the ends of the earth, simply to see your face one more time."'

'To which I said, "No need, we're both expected at the Abberley's tomorrow evening."' Clarissa was pink and pert, remembering her heyday.

'I wish I'd been there to see you,' Isabella said, with a dreamy face. She was determined that romance should blossom for her in a similarly heroic, all-obliterating way.

'I know what you mean, Iz,' Tobias said. 'You were a famous beauty, Mama.' It was a pretty compliment, but rather spoiled by the past tense. 'Suitors galore.'

'Mmm,' Clarissa said in a dampening way, returning to her needlework. Tobias and Isabella exchanged a grimace that said, Let no one hint at the passing of the years, nor make any reference to Mama's fading looks.

The three white ostrich feathers that Isabella had worn in her hair the previous day, at her presentation at Court, were now in a slender vase on the card table. She had looked exquisite in a white gown by Worth, long kid gloves and a beaded Alençon veil, but had felt utterly cooped-up and frustrated, waiting for almost two hours in a cold anteroom at the Palace, with dozens of other debutantes and their mothers, for her turn to be called. They twittered and squawked like captive birds, and any sense of the honour about to be conferred was quite lost in the crush and the tedium. Some people hid hot-water bottles under their furs, and others sipped hot soup from of flasks, as if they were waiting at the roadside, having lost a wheel from their carriage. Isabella had borne the ordeal stoically enough, but all the time nurturing the mutinous feeling – which she strove to keep from showing in her face – that this custom had deteriorated into a silly panto-mime, as pointless for the debutantes as for Their Majesties. There were so many girls! And anyone seemed to be able to come along; indeed, there were peeresses for hire these days, to present those girls whose own families didn't qualify. Clarissa, with stony indifference, cut those she knew to be guilty of malpractice and murmured a bitter commentary, a litany of disapproval, to Isabella. By the time they were summoned to the Throne Room they were both as tightly wound as watch springs. Granted, thought Isabella, the great state room, decorated in a glorious red, white and gold, was worth a look, and the Yeomen of the Guard, who lined corri-dors and staircases, brought a proper sense of order and ceremony to the occasion. But it hadn't been fun; it hadn't even been especially interesting.

Afterwards, Isabella had had a champagne supper in the Palace, served by powdered footmen. Then the Plymouths' motorcar was announced and she was brought home. Some of the girls were going on to parties at the Savoy or Claridge's, but Clarissa had developed a nervous headache and Isabella, who knew well enough that the rest of the Season was packed with engagements, had decided to be docile. She did wonder, though, how soon the lovely Worth gown could have another airing. The tulle ballerina dress, adorned at the bodice with silk camellias, deserved a proper outing, a spin around a dance floor in the arms of a handsome beau.

The drawing room door opened and Padgett, the butler,

said, 'The Countess of Netherwood,' stepping back as Thea stepped forwards. She smiled, though at the room rather than the people in it. Her legs, startlingly slender, were clad in miraculous stockings that seemed to shine as if silver-plated, and this effect only emphasised the boldness of the hemline of her pewter silk dress. The fabric looked slight and expensive. Below the hips, it was pleated; above them, it clung like a second skin. With a small shrug Thea discarded the Arctic fox tippet from her shoulders directly into Padgett's waiting hands.

'Darling,' she said to Isabella. 'How were the Royals?'

'Oh, we've done all that,' said Isabella with a dismissive wave. She was chilly and discouraging, and had been since her discovery. Clarissa looked up, and smiled at her daughter.

'Funny little thing,' Thea said, simultaneously condescending and maddeningly, sweetly affectionate. 'Oh well. Let me tell you what I've been up to.'

Isabella looked startled, and glanced across the room at Tobias. He was draped crosswise on a button-backed armchair, watching his wife with an idle smile. As he was here, he might as well watch the show.

'Eugene took me to the Slade,' she said, all alight. 'The art school, right? He has a friend there, studying life drawing under the most terrifying man I have ever met. Eyes like a shark and a great beaky nose, and a withering disdain for his fellow man, especially if she's a woman.'

Clarissa leaned forwards and pulled the brass bell pull for Padgett, or anyone else whose entrance would disrupt Thea's flow. She said to Tobias, 'The Maharaja of Jaipur is in town, I hear.'

Thea laughed, a short bark of amusement and pity; Clarissa's tactics were so clumsy. 'So,' Thea went on blithely, 'this awful fellow was stalking about the studio growling and sneering at the students, and in the middle of them all was a young man, absolutely bare. Imagine!'

Tobias gave a snort of laughter.

'I know,' said Thea. 'Classic. Anyway, the beaky tutor threw me out. Girls and boys don't mix at the Slade, especially nude ones.'

Isabella, leaning against the mantelpiece, arms folded, was miffed. She'd had all the attention, and she could have kept it, but she had handed it on a plate to Thea. Now she was torn between fascination with the story and sheer bewilderment at the ease between her brother and his faithless wife. Her own frostiness, liberally doled out, seemed to be having no effect at all; Thea shone in the centre of the room, glowing with style and charisma and supreme confidence. She was invincible, thought Isabella with grudging admiration; she was a life force. Small wonder Mama's manners had deserted her; with Thea in the room, every other woman was at a disadvantage.

Behind them all, the door opened and the solemn figure of Padgett stepped back into the drawing room.

'Your Grace?' he said. It was almost time for luncheon, and his duties were manifold, but nevertheless he was the duchess's eternal servant and nothing was too much trouble: all this was somehow conveyed in his voice and bearing. 'You rang.'

Clarissa, casting about for a job for him, caught sight of the empty grate and said, 'Thank you Padgett. It's a little chilly in here, and I thought it would be nice to have a fire after all.'

'Mama, do you think so?' said Tobias. He panted and pulled at his collar comically, and his mother said, 'You think only of yourself, Toby. Archie, as you ought to know, mustn't be in a draught.'

'You make him sound like that tortoise Izzy used to have,' Tobias said, and Isabella, drawn into better humour by the aptness of the analogy and the memory of her pet, said, 'Sir Terence – how I miss him still,' and Tobias laughed.

'Sir Terence, that's right. From a street market in Alexandria all the way to Netherwood in Great-Uncle Richard's carpet bag.'

'What became of Sir Terence?' Thea asked. 'I would've liked to meet him.'

In perfect unison, Isabella and Tobias said: 'Being a creature native to a strip of coastal desert in the south-east Mediterranean basin, Sir Terence was constitutionally unsuited to the draughty conditions of a box in the scullery of Netherwood Hall,' and then they both hooted with delighted laughter at their double act, still word-perfect after ten years. Thea, excluded from the joke but still smiling good-naturedly, said, 'What's that?'

'The post-mortem,' Tobias said. 'It was magnificent. Papa sent dead Sir T to one of his old Cambridge tutors. We all gathered in the drawing room to hear the professor's diagnosis. Somehow it made up for Sir Terence's demise that his autopsy was so dignified. They kept hold of him, I believe. Pickled him, or stuffed him, I suppose.'

The Duke of Plymouth suddenly materialised, sticking his head and long neck round the door of the room in a manner that could certainly be seen as tortoise-like, now that the seed of that idea had been planted. In their joint effort to remain straight-faced, Thea, Isabella and Tobias felt uncommonly fond of each other. Sensing this, Clarissa stalked out of the room just as her husband came in, leaving him with the sad impression that he had offended her simply by existing.

Henrietta was supposed to be joining them for luncheon at the Park Lane mansion, but in the end they sat down without her. She was increasingly unreliable. Thea said she'd seen Anna Sykes at the Slade and, according to her, Henrietta was terribly involved with the Women's Exhibition at Prince's Skating Rink in Knightsbridge. Anna herself had painted a life-size canvas of women sowing grain; it was up with Sylvia Pankhurst's work at the exhibition.

'The theme is, "They who sow in tears shall reap in joy" and there are suffrage plays and a suffragette drum-and-pipe band.' Thea had a look of someone trying to give a serious account of something she thought fundamentally ridiculous.

'Good Lord,' said Archie. Increasingly, he found the modern world upsetting. 'Gels playing fife and drum. Good Lord.'

'I'm going to have a look tomorrow,' Thea said. 'I'll take you if you like, Archie. They have a soda fountain, Anna says, paid for by an American suffragist.'

Clarissa said, 'Anna this, Anna that. Do we know her?'

'Anna Sykes. Rabinovich, as was,' said Thea. 'She painted my rooms at Netherwood Hall.'

'Oh, the little Russian,' said Clarissa, as if this was the dullest possible answer. 'Henry mixes with the oddest people.'

'Anna Sykes has a waiting list of extremely distinguished clients, Clarissa,' said Thea with a patient smile. 'If you don't have an Anna Sykes wall, you simply haven't arrived.'

Clarissa lifted a finely drawn eyebrow. 'Oh, speak for yourself,' she said. 'The rest of us can justify our place in society without the help of a Russian émigrée, thank you very much.'

'Soda fountain, you say?' said Archie, still one topic behind.

'Mmm.' Thea pushed a piece of salmon around her plate. She looked up from the fish and at the duke, of whom she grew fonder each day – in direct proportion to her dislike of his wife. 'You don't have them here. Where I come from, you find them in drugstores. They're fun. Delicious.'

He nodded as she spoke, eagerly trying to decipher what she said. His hearing was letting him down, added to which Thea, with her American drawl and odd vocabulary, very often had him stumped. Currently, he was wondering what a drugstore was, and it irritated Clarissa to see him gazing like a milksop across the table, his pale blue eyes shining with a sort of baffled devotion.

'Toby,' she said, turning to her son in a determined manner. 'I'd like you to speak to Henry. I fear she's being exploited by those horrid people. She imagines herself indispensible to the cause, when in actual fact all they want from her is her money.'

'I'd like to know where you got the idea she might listen to me,' Tobias replied. He nodded at Padgett, who refilled his glass with some of the duke's excellent hock.

'Have you ever heard Henry speak?' Thea, directing her question at Clarissa, knew the answer to it, but asked anyway.

Clarissa said, 'Well, of course not!' and she smirked around the table, looking for someone to share her incredulity.

'Then, with all due respect,' said Thea, 'I don't think you're qualified to pass judgement. Henry is magnificent on a podium. If anyone can shame Mr Asquith into making concessions, it'll be her.'

'I think I know my own daughter, thank you.'

'And yet, I think you don't, if you imagine she'd let anyone take her for a ride.' She rose, suddenly and unexpectedly, and the footman stepped smartly forwards, reaching for her chair just a few seconds late. 'Will you all excuse me?' she said. 'I feel a little nauseous.'

Thea trailed away and out of the door, seeming not so much ill as weary or, perhaps, bored. Tobias let his eyes follow her until she left the room. He didn't seem particularly concerned, thought Isabella, but neither did he seem entirely indifferent. For a moment no one spoke, and then Clarissa said, 'She's terribly cold, I think, your wife.'

Tobias gave a strange, secret smile, looking not at his mother but down into his glass of wine. Opposite him, Isabella felt the onset of tears. Her Season would be spoiled by this selfish family of hers, with its horrible, internal battles and stubborn preoccupations with private interests. She stood too, and her mother snapped out a brittle command to sit down.

'I shan't,' Isabella said. 'Why should I oblige, when everyone else is being perfectly beastly?' And she exited the dining room, leaving the duke, the duchess and Tobias gazing gloomily at each other, like the last, unwelcome guests at a party, marooned together not by choice but by circumstance, long after the band has packed up and gone home.

Chapter 18

Just as the poached salmon was being served in the Duke of Plymouth's gilded Park Lane dining room, Lady Henrietta Hoyland was being escorted by two constables from the foyer of the Women's Exhibition to the lowlier confines of Sloane Street police station, where she was made to wait on a hard bench in a small holding cell for four hours before being released without charge. Someone had daubed a slogan on the wall of St Stephen's Hall in the Houses of Parliament, and the trail had led to Henrietta on the flimsy pretext that the culprit had been glimpsed darting into a waiting motorcar after committing the outrage. The same person, it was presumed, had tied a jaunty 'Votes for Women' flag to the statue of William Pitt the Younger, whose stony expression only served to increase the poignancy of his helplessness. Instead of proclaiming her innocence, Henrietta had said as little as possible, leaving it to the police to work out that she had a copper-bottomed alibi, having been on the programmes and pamphlets stall at Prince's Skating Rink in the company of Sylvia Pankhurst and Eva Gore-Booth from eight in the morning until the moment of glory when she was marched from the building. There was nothing quite so effective at lending weight to a cause than for one of the organisers to be wrongly accused in so public a manner.

It wasn't the first time Henrietta had been hauled away from a gathering by police officers, and it always amused her to see them struggle between duty and inclination. Taking her details at the station, she had given Fulton House, Belgravia and Netherwood Hall, Yorkshire as her places of residence, and the young constable had blushed furiously as he completed the formalities, then apologised as he showed her to the holding cell. Here was a titled lady, to whom he would doff his cap if their paths crossed on a Sunday afternoon in Hyde Park, and yet he had to log her presence in the book and lock the door on her, just as he had with every other sneak thief and chancer they'd collared in the course of the day. In deference to her class she was offered a cushion, which she declined with a cursory shake of the head.

The truth was, every time she was apprehended it gave Henrietta a frisson of satisfaction and excitement: a sense that she was in the vanguard of the struggle, where 'deeds, not words' truly was the credo. As she sat on her bench, gazing at the obscenities and witticisms that others had left on the walls before her, she found herself wishing not for freedom but for sterner treatment: something that would propel her to the forefront of the campaign. She knew she would be released in due course, shown out of the station with all the courtesy at their disposal when the police realised their mistake. She knew, too, that this episode might be no more than a single lost paragraph in the papers – and perhaps not even that, if the actual St Stephen's artist made herself known. Henrietta, in her darker moments, worried that what her sisters in the struggle valued most about her were her wealth and her title; Clarissa's view, in fact, and a theory which, in the company of her mother, Henrietta would laugh off, but in the privacy of her own thoughts found harder to contradict.

The problem was, she decided, in the Sloane Street cell, that she was too well bred to behave sufficiently badly. Christabel and Emmeline – though perhaps not Sylvia – could spit in the faces of policemen or strike them across the face with a clenched fist, and with such actions guarantee arrest and a good long spell behind bars. Henrietta couldn't spit and she couldn't hit, no more than she could hoist her skirts and dance the can-can in the street. Spitting, in particular, was out of the question. She considered it now, as an amiable young police constable led her out of the cell and back to the freedom of the Sloane Street sunshine. She looked at his pleasant face and considered spitting into it in order to be marched back whence she'd come, but though she knew what she was meant to do she simply couldn't bring herself to do it. The very worst she could manage was to return neither his smile nor his farewell, and to rudely ignore his offer of a lift back to the Women's Exhibition. She felt his eyes on her as she walked away; it was all she could do not to turn round and thank him for his kindness and hospitality. At that moment, she despised her impeccable manners: they threatened, she felt, to expose her.

However, this dissatisfaction with the apparent limits of her militancy, while temporarily dispiriting, proved productive. Henrietta was, fundamentally, the sort of person who found solutions rather than problems, and her train of thought ran very naturally from the inherent difficulties of her aristocratic heritage to the inherent advantages of the same. At home in Netherwood, she reminded herself, she managed (to all intents and purposes) a twenty-five-thousand-acre estate with three collieries and the largest private house in England. The land agent, the bailiff, the butler, the housekeeper – all of them deferred to her when she was in residence, as indeed did her brother, the Earl of Netherwood, who would be the first to concede that Henrietta was much better equipped than he to grapple with the myriad practical matters that arose in the course of a single day at Netherwood Hall. Thus bolstered by her own stern talking-to, Henrietta slipped into a state of mind more conducive to decisive action: a practical, plan-hatching condition in which she was able to think quite logically about how to progress. By the time she swept back through the doors of Prince's Skating Rink she was so full of vim and vigour for the cause that she clambered immediately onto the trestle table – from which this morning she had merely been selling programmes – and issued a rousing, forthright and entirely unexpected call to arms. It was a brave thing to do, and very possibly foolhardy; there was every chance she might have looked foolish, if – say – she hadn't managed to be heard above the hubbub. But as well as irreproachable good manners and a characteristically high complexion, Henrietta had also inherited the carrying voice of the true aristocrat, and she employed it now to exhort her fellow campaigners to take, once more, to the streets of London.

'Let us present ourselves, en masse, at the House of Commons and demand of Mr Asquith our ancient and inviolable right to petition the king,' she shouted. Beneath her, at floor level, Sylvia Pankhurst murmured, 'Now, dear?'

'The prime minister is accountable to the king,' continued Henrietta, from her lofty platform. 'And as such he is duty and honour bound to receive our deputation, and to hear our petition.'

Christabel Pankhurst, torn between admiration at Henrietta's initiative and her own irritation at this impromptu rallying cry, said to her sister, 'I suppose we could. We're all assembled, after all.'

'If Mr Asquith refuses to hear us, if Mr Asquith sets the police on us as if we were common criminals, if Mr Asquith prevents us from deploying our right to petition the king, then it is he who will be guilty of illegality.'

Henrietta was flushed with zeal, and her enthusiasm was catching. Someone tore down a banner and shouted 'Votes for Women'; a cheer went up through the hall.

'So,' Henrietta said, still on the table. 'Those of you who wish to force Mr Asquith's hand, we shall march to the House of Commons in' – she glanced down, now, at Christabel, who raised her eyebrows as if to say, 'Now you consult me?' so that Henrietta, to maintain the mood and momentum, had to look away again, and lay down her own terms – 'in thirty minutes' time. Ladies of the pipe and drum band' – she waved at them, in their corner of the exhibition hall – 'bring your instruments, and take us to Westminster on a tide of glory!'

She clambered down, but the buzz of excitement she had created continued on about her. Christabel said: 'Tide of glory? What does that mean?' but Eva Gore-Booth flung her arms round Henrietta and said, 'Brilliant! You're brilliant!' and this, Henrietta found, made up for any coolness from other quarters.

In the event, there were almost a hundred women in Henrietta's deputation. They formed themselves into an almost-disciplined regiment and walked four abreast to Westminster, parting and stopping only for the most insistent of motorists. The pipe and drum band played marching songs and on the pavements people stood and either jeered, cheered or simply stared. On Millbank the police caught up with them, among them the young constable from Sloane Street, who had been pulled off the front desk to maintain order on the streets; he greeted Henrietta with a look of pleasant surprise, as if it was a co-incidence at a cocktail party, and to her abiding annoyance, Henrietta automatically smiled back and nodded a gracious acknowledgement.

The police joined the procession to Parliament, walking on either side of the column of women with expressions of weary forbearance. They knew, of course, what would happen. At the entrance to the House of Commons the ringleaders would hand their written request to the duty police officer, who would then disappear inside, returning after a period of time with a written refusal from the prime minister's private secretary. In fact, Mr Asquith's opinion would probably not even be sought, being already well enough known by everyone involved.

All of this was predictable, and all of it came to pass. What no one had expected was that when the private secretary handed the exquisitely worded rebuttal to Henrietta with an apology of almost palpable disingenuousness, she snatched it from the functionary's hand, screwed it into a tight ball and threw it directly into his left eye.

'Oh I say, good shot,' someone said in the massed ranks, and there was laughter and scattered applause. A police officer stepped forward and took hold of Henrietta's elbow, in case the prime minister's man should cry foul play, and the Sloane Street constable said, 'It's Lady Henrietta Hoyland, sir. I'm sure she intended no harm,' at which point, Henrietta saw red. Was she always to be excused on the grounds of her title and breeding? It was intolerable.

She began to run – in itself, a shocking sight. Her hat flew off in her haste and she didn't stop to retrieve it but barrelled on, up towards Parliament Square, into Parliament Street and down into Whitehall. Behind her, a small pack of women followed, unsure of her intention but carried along by the thrill of the moment. Behind them, a couple of constables, dispatched by a senior officer, jogged along with vaguely bashful expressions as if this unforeseen duty was an assault on their dignity and a certain distance – both actual and emotional – had to be maintained.

Up ahead Henrietta had swung left into Downing Street and here, she stopped. She clutched her right side and took great gulps of air, and while she caught her breath she cast about with her eyes, as if she'd lost something and was desperate to find it.

'What's the plan?'

This was Mary Dixon, Henrietta's ardent admirer from the Guildford branch of the WSPU, dressed as she always was in white, green and purple, like a walking pennant. She had followed Henrietta to Downing Street, just as she would follow her to the ends of the earth. Henrietta didn't answer her question, but lurched suddenly to a small pile of house bricks stacked tidily against a wall, awaiting the moment at which they might be useful. It was only when Henrietta seized one of them and ran with it towards the prime minister's residence that her intention – and the scale of her frustration – became clear. She was fast, though, and while she might not have been a spitter or a puncher she was a first-rate flinger: a childhood at the wicket with Toby and Dickie had given her an eye for a target and an arm for distance. As the two constables rounded the corner from Whitehall into Downing Street, and as the startled officer positioned outside Number 10 stepped forwards into her path, Henrietta launched her missile at the fan light above the door and had the satisfaction of hearing the ugly fracture and splinter of glass and wood before she was pinioned in the unforgiving grip of the constables. She threw her head back and shouted, 'Votes for women!', and as she was led away, Mary Dixon and the other women with her took up the cry, chanting the slogan again and again so that their voices accompanied Henrietta as she was shoved and bundled away from the scene of her crime.

At Park Lane, Isabella had found Thea in the drawing room, which pleased and surprised her, as she was sure her sister-in-law would have other things to do than wait for her husband. Instead, Thea looked extravagantly content and comfortable, nestling among a heap of cushions on a couch, leafing idly through the fashion plates of the *Tatler* and smoking a slim, dark cigarette in an elegant silver holder. Clarissa detested the smell, so it struck Isabella as a provocative act until she said, 'Mama hates cigarette smoke,' and Thea, looking up from her magazine, said, 'Oh Lord, yes, I forgot,' and immediately stubbed it out. She smiled at Isabella and patted the seat next to her.

'I thought I was at home, in Fulton House,' she said. 'Silly me.'

Isabella sat.

'Thea?' she said.

'Mmm?' Thea was back at the fashion plates again, her fingers stroking the pages as if she could feel the folds of silk and satin.

'Do you have a pash for Eugene Stiller?' Her heart pounded at her audacity.

Thea tilted her head and flashed a sharp, sidelong glance at Isabella. 'Oh, I see. That's why you've been so snippy.'

'Never mind that. Do you?'

'No, not overly, although I did at first. Do you like him?'

'Since you ask, no,' Isabella said, feeling calmer since her question had clearly caused neither consternation nor anger. 'He's not half so handsome as Toby.'

Thea laughed lightly. 'Agreed.'

'But you spend so much time with him. And you take him up to your rooms.' At this Isabella coloured, and again her heart pattered; how she would love, she thought, to possess just a fraction of Thea's sangfroid. Thea closed her magazine and placed it on the lamp table. She turned to Isabella.

'You mustn't worry about Tobes,' she said. 'He has his fun and I have mine, but we are the Earl and Countess of Netherwood and ever shall be, until fate decides our number's up.'

Isabella looked troubled. 'Doesn't Toby mind?'

'Not really,' Thea said. Then, 'Sometimes,' she added, more truthfully.

'I thought when one married it was to the exclusion of all others,' Isabella said. She knew at once that she sounded silly, and that Thea would laugh; she did.

'No, dearest, not necessarily. Monogamy isn't compulsory, and it's certainly not something Tobes and I have ever suffered from.'

'Well I intend to honour and obey my husband when the time comes.' She sounded like a prig, she knew she did, and her face felt foolishly warm and pink.

'Good for you,' Thea said almost kindly. 'Do let me know how you get on with that.'

There was something in Thea's tone that she didn't quite like, but Isabella was prevented from speaking further because the drawing-room door opened and Padgett entered, with the demeanour of a man bearing bad news.

'Padgett?' said Thea. 'Are we to worry about something?'

'Thomas is at the door, Your Ladyship,' said the butler.

'The Fulton House footman?'

'Indeed, Your Ladyship. It seems Lady Henrietta has' – he hesitated, choosing his words with care – 'orchestrated an incident.'

Thea heaved a sigh. 'Oh what now? Eggs at Mr Churchill? Flour at Mr Lloyd George?'

'A brick, Your Ladyship, through a window of the prime minister's residence in Downing Street,' he said, and then – in a moment of dramatic spontaneity – he added, 'It's uncertain whether anyone was injured by her action.' This last detail was neither a truth nor an untruth, he told himself: therefore, it was permissible.

Isabella gasped and Thea stood at once, shaken into seriousness. And Padgett, though he assumed an attitude of sympathetic concern, drew some considerable private satisfaction at the effect of his words.

Chapter 19

The parlour at Ravenscliffe was full of clothes, organised in piles according to function. Two empty leather trunks stood in the middle of the room, their lids yawning open. They smelled of horses, Angus said. Eliza said, 'Saddles, do you mean, Gussy?' and the little boy said, 'No, 'orses,' as if his big sister were simple not to understand the distinction. She picked him up and blew a wet raspberry into his hot, soft neck, and he squirmed in her arms, laughing and protesting. Eliza helped herself to Angus like other people helped themselves to buns from a tin – she just took him up, whenever the urge came upon her, and feasted on his unique deliciousness. The prospect of his absence loomed like the threat of icy rain: she could prepare for it, but it wouldn't make it any more pleasant, or any easier to bear. For his part, Angus had no real sense of time and distance, and even the knowledge that he and his mother were going together to see Seth was an abstract idea that he was perfectly capable of forgetting when something more interesting turned his head.

'Oh, my little bear,' Eliza said. He held her face between his two sticky palms and kissed her on the nose in a final, authoritative way that he clearly intended to signal his release. 'Who'll I cuddle when you're not with me?' she said.

'Timothy,' Angus said in a helpful voice, but pushing at her now with stiff arms so that even she couldn't ignore his desire to be set down. 'I shan't be taking Timothy.'

Eliza placed him down on the couch and he clambered off awkwardly, then looked up at her with a magnanimous smile.

'Timothy?' she said. 'Not likely. He bites.' He had mean pink eyes, too, and a pair of back legs that could punch the wind out of you if you held him wrongly.

'Oh well,' Angus said, waving his little hand in a funny, dismissive gesture, as if he thought Eliza impossible to please. He climbed into one of the trunks and sat down. 'Close it,' he said in the peremptory way of a small child.

'Please,' Eliza said.

'Close it, please.'

'Well, just for a mo', then. We don't want you suffocating.'

She lowered the lid and he ducked his head, shunting his body lower. He liked this game, although it was bizarre to Eliza, who couldn't bear to be confined.

'Knock and shout if you want to come out,' she said, feeling anxious at the very thought of it in there, dark and airless. He began to sing, a sea shanty that his pa had taught him, so that he could join in with the sailors when they swabbed the decks. Daniel came into the parlour now and looked at the trunk, from where his son's muffled voice was telling a lilting tale of gentle nor'westers blowing the sloop o'er the seas.

'In the box again, is he?' Daniel said. 'Och well, good practice for the cabin.'

Eliza shuddered. 'Don't. That's not funny.'

He smiled. 'Sorry. You do know they're going first class, right? Captain's table, quoits on deck, all that malarkey?'

162

She nodded. 'I wish we all were going,' she said, and then, because she thought that sounded petulant, added, 'But we'll be just fine, won't we?'

Daniel ruffled her hair and pulled her to him for a reassuring hug. Eliza warmed and melted his heart: she always had, from the day he met her. She was effortlessly good and kind, and full of a blessed, innate happiness that she shared indiscriminately. She had her mother's lovely face too, and it was tilted up at him now.

'They'll be back in no time, won't they?' she said, though they both knew this was nonsense. Eve and Angus would be gone for at least three months, and without them the house and their lives would be entirely out of kilter.

'Aye, sweetheart, they will,' Daniel said, and for a moment they stood together thinking about tomorrow's goodbyes. Then, inside the trunk, the shanty ended and Angus, with a mighty heave, flung open the lid and shouted, 'Land ahoy, cap'n!'

They all laughed, although Eliza could just as easily have cried.

Later, after they'd eaten and the dishes were cleared, after they'd drifted to their different corners of the house and garden and Eve, finally, had begun to fill the trunks with clothes for Angus and herself – worrying, all the while, that nothing they owned was suitable for the tropics – there was a rap at the door. Eve had been thinking about Anna – wishing she were here, being brisk and practical – so when she heard the clatter of the brass knocker the impossible thought that it might be her friend flashed through Eve's mind, then was immediately dismissed, not because Anna was in London – although she was – but because Anna would never knock first. For a moment

Eve hesitated, waiting, listening for the sound of someone else going to the door. Then, when no one did, she left the room, huffing a little with irritation, and crossed the hall, still holding, in the crook of one arm, a little heap of Angus's woolly combinations, which she knew she probably shouldn't pack but couldn't quite give up, because a place where it didn't get cold at night was simply unimaginable. So, thus encumbered, she opened the door to find a young woman, certainly familiar to her but not quite known. She wore a striking skirt of red velvet, a black bombazine jacket and a little black boater trimmed with red ribbon. Her hair, also black, was smoothed over her ears and pinned into a twist at the nape of her neck. She had bright eyes, like a squirrel's, and she smiled in a swift, pragmatic way before speaking.

'Good evening, Mrs MacLeod,' she said. 'I am so sorry to arrive like this, out of the blue, as it were.' The accent was barely discernible, but still there was something distinct and unusual about her perfect diction. She held out a pale, slim hand and Eve took it, noting its cool softness, but she still couldn't place the visitor, and it showed in her expression of mild bewilderment.

'Evangeline Durand,' said the woman. 'Eliza's—'

'Dance teacher, of course, of course.' Eve was all confusion, feeling somehow caught out though in fact they had met only twice before, and then only at the dance school. There followed an awkward silence, broken by Evangeline, who said, 'May I come in?' and Eve answered, 'Oh, yes!' as if she'd entirely forgotten the simple protocol of admitting a visitor to one's home. She held the door a little wider and the dance teacher stepped inside, delicately, precisely. Her patent-leather boots made pleasing clicks on the tiled floor. She looked about her appreciatively.

'What a beautiful house,' she said.

'Thank you.'

'No, it's beautiful. The light is magnificent, and this colour . . .' She reached out a hand and grazed it on the wall, then looked at Eve. 'Like a field of wheat.'

'Mademoiselle!'

This was Eliza, who had clattered out of her bedroom and along the landing, but whose descent of the stairs was abruptly halted by the extraordinary sight of her dance teacher standing in the hall, her dainty feet in third position, which was where they always seemed naturally to settle. Evangeline looked up at the girl and said, 'Eliza, you must forgive me, but I thought it best to speak with your mother.'

'Why? What's 'appened,' said Eve, alarmed now.

On the stairs Eliza opened her mouth, but nothing came out. Evangeline said to Eve, 'I wanted to impress upon you the value to your daughter of my proposed trip to Paris, and to urge you to reconsider your decision.' Her voice was a little stern and teacherly. Eve turned to Eliza, still frozen on the stairs, and raised her eyebrows.

'Down you come, young lady,' she said. 'I think we need to have a talk.'

France, the Ballet de l'Opéra, the glories of Paris: it was all news to Eve and Daniel. Eliza had simply never mentioned it, though she'd gone back to Mademoiselle Evangeline and said she wasn't allowed to accept her offer because her mam and stepdad thought her too young. There was a brief, kindly inquisition at the kitchen table and Eliza grew tearful, though no one was angry with her. On the contrary, it was evident that she'd acted from the sweetest motives, believing her presence at Ravenscliffe essential during Eve's absence.

'You said you'd be relying on me,' Eliza said to Daniel, her cheeks wet and her eyes sorrowful. 'I just thought I shouldn't even ask.' She didn't add that on the evening she'd come home bursting with the news, riding high on a sense of her own thrilling future, Eve and Daniel had been at loggerheads, and there had been no speaking to either of them, really; not about something like this.

'Whisht, child, dry your eyes,' Daniel said, and he passed her his handkerchief. Eve asked Evangeline when she'd planned to travel and for how long, and it dawned on Eliza that a trip to Paris was, after all, a simple and perfectly possible thing, not the shattered dream she had believed it to be.

'Two weeks,' said the dance teacher, holding up two fingers as if to clarify. 'And we would leave, perhaps, June the nineteenth? Or a little later, if it suits you better. We would visit the Ballet de l'Opéra, but also the Ballets Russes, which has arrived in Paris and will be simply . . .' – she hesitated, summoning a suitable English word, then turned instead to her native language – '. . . *stupéfiant, incroyable.*' She was looking, now, at Eliza, who in turn looked at Eve. Eve cleared her throat. Everything seemed to be moving a little quickly, and the woman was now speaking in French. She liked her: liked her brisk manner, her lively face, her obvious affection for Eliza. But still.

'Thank you, you're very kind,' she said. 'But there are lots of things to consider. Can we let you know?'

A small spasm of alarm crossed Eliza's face, but Daniel, spotting it, winked at her and she took heart once more. Evangeline nodded, stood and clapped her hands smartly, twice, just as she did in class when she required silence.

'*Bon,*' she said. '*Alors, c'est très bien.* I am so pleased that I came and got to the bottom of the mystery.' Her voice dropped to a lower register and she widened her eyes at Eliza, who blushed and looked down into her lap, then up again, before saying, 'I'm sorry I lied to you, Mademoiselle.' Evangeline placed a cool hand on the girl's cheek.

'It was not a lie, merely a different version of the truth,' she said. 'And it shows us what a good girl you are, and so thoughtful.' Eve and Daniel, both slightly mesmerised by the Frenchwoman, watched as she stooped to bestow two darting kisses, one on each of Eliza's cheeks. '*A bientôt, petit papillon*,' she said. When she straightened up again, she said to Eve, 'How proud you must be.'

'I am, yes. We are.'

'One day you will be prouder still,' said Evangeline. Then she turned on her heel, and before anyone had the wit to stand and show her out, she was gone.

'Papeeyon?' Eve said.

'French for butterfly,' said Eliza. 'It's what she calls me.'

'I see,' Eve said. 'You've a fan there, then.'

Eliza dipped her lashes modestly, then peeped up again at her mother and at Daniel. 'Can I go?' she asked. 'Will you manage?'

'What do you think?' Eve said to Daniel. 'We hardly know 'er.'

'But I know 'er,' Eliza said. 'That's t'main thing.'

'And you want to go, do you?'

'With all my 'eart and soul,' Eliza said, so passionately that Eve laughed.

'Well,' Eve said to Daniel. 'As I shall be away, it should be your decision, really.'

He considered Eliza with pursed lips and narrow eyes, as if weighing up the pros and the cons, and then, 'Ah, get on with you, wee butterfly,' he said. 'Away and spread your wings.'

Eliza squealed and hugged herself and Eve said, 'Three down, two to go, then. Somebody best talk to Ellen, let 'er know she's in charge.'

'Och,' said Daniel. 'I reckon she knows that already.'

Chapter 20

When the Sykes entourage left London for Ardington, Norah Kelly went with them. In Yorkshire they didn't keep an equivalent of Norah – not that there was one; they broke the mould, said Amos – for although they had the income for more domestic staff, they didn't have the inclination. That is to say, Amos didn't. Anna would happily have hired an army of maids to facilitate the smooth running of their two homes, but his unease with questions of deference and – perish the thought – exploitation meant that Norah was where the comfort and convenience of domestic help began and ended. One capable girl was ample for all their needs, Amos maintained. One capable girl might well have been ample, Anna said, but they had Norah.

They all travelled by train from King's Cross and the maid shared their carriage, because – irritating though she was, with her near-constant observational prattle – neither Amos nor Anna could countenance sending her down the train to third class, while they journeyed in greater comfort with Maya and Miss Cargill. However, being Norah, she displayed neither grace nor gratitude; she pushed herself forwards in the group, eager to settle herself into a window seat that faced the direction of travel, while Anna, Amos and Miss Cargill arranged their sundry cases and a wicker picnic hamper on the overhead luggage rack and organised their coats into a tidy pile. By the time they too were able to sit down, Norah had already begun her observations on the comings and goings on the platform.

'Sure that fellow looks fit to pop, all red and out of puff like that. If he did but think to set off five minutes sooner, he'd be doing himself a favour. My word, look at the size of that lady. You'd think someone fat as a barrel would dress modest, but no, she thinks well of herself, so she does, all dolled up to the nines just to catch a train. She'll be needing an extra seat with a rear that wide . . .'

On she went, and as the train moved out through the suburbs and into the dreary farmland of Hertfordshire, she found the view no less remarkable and was able to comment on the condition of the crops, the likely weather pattern indicated by the clouds, the cosy appeal of the clustered rooftops and Norman church towers of rural villages, and, more than once, the comical expressions on the faces of the Friesian cows. Miss Cargill was absorbed in Herodotus, Maya had a book of conundrums and Amos had taken the precaution of bringing enough newspapers to last the journey. Currently, he was hidden by *The Times*, but the *Daily Chronicle* and the *Labour Leader* were waiting in the wings to perform the same function.

It was Anna, then, who sat by Norah and made a credible job of pretending to listen to her, though her mind was on Eve, who was sailing tomorrow, and on Daniel, who was being left behind. She felt for him; felt for them both, in fact. If Maya was across the seas and needed her she would go in a heartbeat; and yet, the influence of Silas – self-serving, arrogant, manipulative – seemed to colour the picture. For everyone, that is, but Eve. Norah's monologue washed over and around her as she let these thoughts turn in her mind until suddenly, like the snuffing of a candle, the maid fell asleep, overcome by the effort of passing comment on everything she saw. Her head was against the window, squashing the brim of her green felt hat, and she whistled quite distinctly on each exhalation of breath.

'You can come out now,' Anna said to Amos. 'You'll be quite safe.'

He lowered the newspaper. 'Even when she sleeps she makes a racket,' he said.

Maya laughed and Miss Cargill looked up from her page with a distracted expression, as though she wasn't sure exactly where she was, then looked back down again. She was reading *The Histories*, in the original Greek: Miss Cargill shunned translations. Thanks to her tutor's classical leanings, Maya already had the Greek alphabet off pat, and Anna had noticed that when her little daughter doodled she drew dumpy little sigmas and omegas, long rows of them marching across the page.

Amos said, 'Your friend looks like she's done it this time,' and folded the paper into a manageable square before turning it round so that Anna could see the headline. EARL'S SISTER ARRESTED IN DOWNING STREET FRACAS. 'It'll not be two nights in a Bow Street cell then off 'ome wi' nowt but a caution.'

'No, well, that's what Henrietta's hoping for,' Anna said mildly. 'That's exactly why she threw a brick – so they wouldn't just caution her and set her free. She got what she wanted.'

'Who threw a brick?' Maya's dark eyes were round with the scandal of such a thing.

'Lady Henrietta Hoyland threw a brick at the prime minister's house,' Miss Cargill said, putting down her book again and addressing Maya in a matter-of-fact voice. 'She wants Mr Asquith to give women the vote.'

'What a naughty thing to do,' Maya said.

'Aye,' said Amos. 'Good job we don't all throw bricks when we want summat.'

'Will she go to prison, Dad?'

'More 'n likely.'

'You see, Maya,' said Miss Cargill, seizing the opportunity for a short lesson. 'Lady Henrietta feels that the only way she can make Mr Asquith listen is by breaking the law. The newspapers have all reported what she's done, and the court case will be in the newspapers too. Perhaps as a result someone in the government will think, I say, this lady has a point, and then throwing the brick will seem like exactly the right thing to have done.'

Amos gave her a hard look. 'Thank you for that, Miss Cargill. I think it's clear which side of t'fence you're on.'

'Well it's no secret, Mr Sykes. I'm all for grasping the nettle.'

'And throwing t'brick an' all.'

Miss Cargill was a true scholar: she loved a debate and took no offence at Amos's sardonic tone, but merely smiled in a thoughtful way. 'I doubt I'd actually throw a brick, myself,' she said. 'And I certainly wouldn't condone brick-throwing per se—'

'Well that's nice to 'ear,' Amos said grumpily.

'However, the suffrage movement is being constantly provoked into more extreme action through the government's implacability. As ever, we should look to the Ancient Greeks for guidance. They understood democracy to mean "administration in the hands of the many, not the few", and "equal justice, to all alike, in their private disputes". I quote Pericles, of course.'

Miss Cargill possessed a naturally smug expression – solemn, a little purse-lipped, calmly self-satisfied – which she now adopted, having finished her point, and Amos felt rather than saw the warning in his wife's eyes. She needn't have worried; he had no particular appetite for a scene. In any case, Maya piped up with a question, which did more than Amos could have done to puncture the moment.

'So, were Ancient Greek women allowed to vote, Miss Cargill?'

The governess looked at her charge. 'Well done, Maya, for asking such an interesting question,' she said in a bright voice.

'And?' said Amos.

'Well, no, as I'm sure you're aware, Mr Sykes, Athenian democracy did not extend to women.'

Amos picked up his newspaper again. He smirked as he did so. On the facing seat Norah opened one eye. 'Might we be having that picnic, missus? Sure, I can't sleep sound on an empty stomach.'

The MacLeods had travelled by train too, south-west to Bristol's Temple Meads station, from where a hansom cab took them through teeming city streets to the docks at Avonmouth.

Angus could barely contain his excitement; the world, to date, had been a small place, with Netherwood, Ardington and Barnsley forming the three points of a very familiar triangle. Here, though, were tugs, boats and ships crowding the dark, oily waters of the harbour and rough men staggering with crates down creaking gangplanks, making towering piles of them on the wharf. Eve held his hand very tight. A small boy might be knocked into that water and nobody would even hear the splash. For the first time she felt the stirrings of fear at this undertaking. The smells were appalling: oil, salt, smoke, fish, rotting fruit. And the dockers called to each other using words she didn't recognise, in an accent she'd never heard. There were folk who considered a colliery the closest thing on earth to hell, but Eve knew already that she'd take a pit over this heaving, stinking, watery mayhem. She glanced across at Daniel, but he was turned away from her, scanning the vast warehouses, looking for Whittam & Co. In any case, she thought, she couldn't tell him that she thought she might not want this. It was all far too late for that. It had taken all her persuasive energy to win him round to this plan; she would look an utter fool if she changed her mind now.

'There it is,' said Daniel, pointing out the bold, painted fascia of Silas's company, and now they could see it, it was impossible to understand how it could have been missed, so fine was the sign and so relatively close to them. Then Silas was walking towards them, striding along the wharf with a beaming smile and a patrician air. He held out his arms in general welcome but Eve was anchored on one side by Angus and Daniel on the other, so she just smiled at her brother, a little wanly, and he let his arms drop, since no one seemed inclined to run into them.

'Well here you all are,' he said. 'And I have to say, you look a little stunned.'

'Landlubbers,' said Daniel. 'Fish out of water, if you'll forgive the pun.'

Silas laughed in the way that Daniel had forgotten but now remembered: a short, derisory snigger, which always seemed to be inspired more by pity than amusement. 'Evie, darling girl – beautiful as ever,' Silas said. 'And Angus, you're a little one, aren't you? The image of your father, but in miniature.'

Angus, abashed and confused, looked at his boots. This Uncle Silas of his was a bit of a puzzle: warmish words and a wide smile, but eyes that flicked away as soon as he'd spoken, as if he didn't much care about an answer. Silas hardly ever came to Netherwood these days, content to leave the running of his Yorkshire colliery to the managers he had installed there when he bought it, so Angus tended to forget him between visits. The little boy felt shy; he drew closer into his mother's skirt and, feeling this, she put an arm around his shoulders and kept him tight against her side as they followed Silas through the crush and into the most extraordinary place any of them had ever seen.

'*Voilà*,' he said, laughing at their expressions. 'The secret to eternal wealth.'

It was a cavernous room, filled floor to ceiling with bananas. They hung in hands of ten or twelve from iron hooks attached at close intervals to wooden poles, which were each some forty feet high. Thousands of bananas, ranging in colour from a hard, unappealing green to soft, edible yellow. Men in overalls patrolled the aisles and there were ladders on retractable wheels, placed at intervals through the room. Silas reached out and plucked a banana from the nearest bunch, opened it, and handed it to Angus, who took it not because he wanted it but because he didn't know how to say no. He'd tried banana before, in his pa's hothouse at Netherwood Hall, and he didn't like the way the flesh turned to slop in his mouth. When Silas turned his back to lead them through the warehouse, Daniel took the banana from Angus and stuffed it in his pocket, and they shared a small smile of complicity.

'So,' Silas said, striding on ahead and up a spiral staircase, 'Jamaica awaits, and I know you're going to adore it, Evie. There's work to be done, but there'll be plenty of time for relaxation too. I think my letter explained the essential problem, but we can talk about the nuts and bolts en route.'

'Seth's letter,' Eve said.

'Say again?' Silas glanced back at her.

'Seth's letter. Seth wrote to me.'

She couldn't see his face now, because they were single file on the stairs, and he had turned away again to continue the climb. 'Yes, of course,' he said smoothly. 'Dear boy – he's longing to see you. So, the *Cassiopeia* sails at three, and you'll find your trunks are in your cabin. I'll be sailing with you, of course.' He spun on his heels, forcing everyone to stop, and he smiled down at Eve. 'Three weeks at sea for the two of us,' he said. 'What a treat.'

Eve took Angus by the hand and raised his arm, waggling it to remind Silas of the boy's existence. 'Three of us, you mean,' she said with a reproving smile, and Silas frowned a little, as if he didn't quite follow. Then, 'Ah yes,' he said, and marched on up the stairs to his office, where tea and scones awaited on a silver tray.

Bringing up the rear, Daniel considered the extent to which

he disliked and mistrusted his brother-in-law; very considerably, he concluded. And yet, the two individuals most precious to him on God's earth were about to be placed in Silas Whittam's care. If there had been a time in Daniel's life when he had felt more wretched, he couldn't now remember it. He should never have capitulated, should never have consented to the trip, although the reality was that he'd caved in because she was set on going, with or without his say so. She missed Seth, he knew that, and understood it. But also, she was stubborn about Silas. There was a doggedness about her love for her brother: an implacable loyalty founded in shared poverty twenty years ago. There was no competing with that. Silas was lodged in her heart, and no attempt to shift him ended well. As he followed them into the office, Daniel's fists were clenched in two tight balls; fear and frustration raged in his breast. He fought hard to disguise his feelings, however; it seemed a poor thing, to send off your loved ones under a cloud.

He watched the *Cassiopeia* sail. There were others on the dockside, family and friends of passengers, waving cheerful handkerchiefs and calling out messages of farewell. In their midst, Daniel stood and waved too, but fiercely, desperately, already aching with loss. They had held on to each other on the ship, Angus wedged between them with his arms round his pa's hips, and Daniel had breathed her in. Then he had released Eve and stooped to pick up Angus, covering his hot face with kisses and telling him, over and over again, that he would be right here on the dock, in this harbour, when they came home in three months' time. He had had to leave then, and he still didn't know by what impulse he had got himself down the gangplank, because every part of him wanted to stay with them there on deck; or, better, bring them back with him to the harbourside.

The liner heaved into life surprisingly quickly, considering its noble bulk. It carved a confident path through the water, heading out into the Bristol Channel. Very soon – too soon – Eve and Angus were tiny, indistinct figures at the rail, but they didn't move, and neither did Daniel, until there was nothing at all to be seen. Silas stayed away from the goodbyes. At the top of the gangplank, as they boarded the ship, Daniel had gripped his arm, holding him back for a brief moment.

'If they come to harm, I shall hold you responsible, and call you to account,' he had said. 'They are in your care. Return them to me, or you'll rue the day we ever met.'

Shocked by Daniel's intensity, Silas had wrenched his arm free and rubbed it resentfully. 'Calm yourself, man,' he had said. 'They're not sailing to war.'

Now, staring at the place where his wife and child had been, Daniel forced himself to turn and walk away from the docks. Inwardly he cursed himself for antagonising Silas at that moment of departure, in case it should, in some small but significant way, compromise the safety of Eve and Angus. He wanted to roar with the pain of their leaving, but he didn't wish to be taken for a madman on this crowded wharf. Instead, he told himself that each passing day would bring them closer: that now their dreaded departure was accomplished, their return must, by dint of logic, be ever more imminent. It was a comfort of sorts, although for days afterwards he was periodically afflicted with bouts of raw panic and a sense that something irreplaceable had been mislaid, or forgotten, or lost for ever.

PART TWO

PART TWO

Chapter 21

Seth would have liked to have been down at the harbour when the *Cassiopeia* sailed in. He had thought about the moment for some weeks before his mam's arrival: had thought, even, about what he might wear. He had never given much consideration to clothes back in Netherwood, but these days he was proud of his garments. Uncle Silas, with half an eye to his own reputation, kept his nephew well dressed, ordering lightweight linen suits and debonair flannels from his own tailor in Savile Row, and Seth, a few months short of seventeen, felt older and wiser in them. He could picture himself on the wharf, a calm, still point in the mêlée, his flannels pressed, his shirt fresh, his panama at just the right angle, greeting his mam and little Angus with the urbane manner of a man of the world: charming, composed, entirely at ease in the utter strangeness of Port Antonio.

However, it was not to be. He had woken on the day of their arrival to a foul smell – sulphurous and unmistakable. He had followed his nose to the first-floor bathrooms, where two lavatories had spilled effluent on to the black-and-white tiled floor, and two others were brim-full of the same. Neither Scotty nor Maxwell were anywhere to be found – they were

179

both skilled at evasion – so Seth had waded in with a rubber plunger and a box of caustic soda, and waged valiant battle for the best part of the morning. When Eve and Angus were shepherded through the door by Silas later that day Seth had been forced to greet them in damp, soiled overalls, and it was plain from the way everyone recoiled that the smell of the drains and their contents lingered around him. It hadn't been the reunion he had envisaged; not at all.

'Good God man, don't think much of that new cologne,' Silas had said with a snigger, and Seth, mortified, had turned a shade of beetroot so entirely familiar and beloved to Eve that she had rushed to him in spite of the stink, and hugged him as if he were a child.

'You've grown!' she had said, keeping hold of him but stepping back. 'Look at you, taller than I am now, and t'spitting image of your dad.'

'Especially in those filthy overalls,' Silas had said. 'Sixty-four new arrivals are following us up from the harbour, and we have a besmirched handyman front of house.' He smiled, though Seth knew he wasn't amused. 'Off you pop. Sluice off the smell of the privies. We'll be in the bar.'

Eve had smiled and said, 'See you soon, sweetheart.' Seth, feeling like a twelve-year-old, had sloped away to his quarters while Silas showed Eve the residents' lounge, the dining room, the shady veranda, the bar. Occasionally, from his room, Seth could hear his mam exclaiming with pleasure at the unusual beauty and elegance of the place, and it made him feel sullen and resentful, that he had no part in these first delighted impressions. Also, no one had thanked him for unblocking the drains.

Later, scrubbed clean and sweet smelling, clad in a casual linen two-piece and a soft cotton shirt, his dignity took the first steps on the road to recovery. New arrivals drank fruit punch and fresh lemonade in the bar, and Seth made his way through them towards Eve, stopping here and there to exchange the sort of small talk that he knew he must practise. He felt her eyes on him as he moved among the guests, and because of this he made rather more than he might have done of each new encounter: overdoing it slightly, like a ham actor playing an urbane party host. Seth had his father's features – vivid blue eyes, soft brown hair with the same unruly cowlick, ears that jutted out like wing nuts, a tendency to scowl even when he was perfectly happy – and they were the sort of looks that no one ever coveted for themselves. But there's more to a man than his face and, just as Arthur Williams had done, Seth now presented a pleasing whole to the world, in the way he carried himself, the things he said, the careful way he listened to what people had to say. The Jamaican sun had given his naturally pale complexion a honeyed glow. He looked well, and he knew this.

Now and again he glanced across the room at his mam as if to say, I'll be with you just as soon as I can, and each time she smiled at him with evident pride. It was odd to see her here at the Whittam: odd, and a little unsettling, like witnessing a friendly apparition. She was beautiful, his mam, and he was glad of it now. In this room full of fashionable English folk she would not be found lacking. It worried him a little that her Yorkshire accent was undiminished, though he could hardly have expected otherwise. His own accent was more neutral these days, the result of a concerted effort to sound less like himself. Only rarely did he drop an aitch. He hoped he wouldn't lapse under his mam's influence. And he must remember to call her mother. Uncle Silas had made it clear that while mam was all very well in the kitchen of Ravenscliffe, it was unprofessional in the context of the Whittam Hotel. Seth had agreed, although he wasn't absolutely sure that it could be managed.

He reached Eve's side and she gave him her lovely smile, which made him entirely glad that she had come.

'Look at you,' she said.

He glanced down, as if to remind himself what he looked like.

'You're taller now than your dad was,' she went on. 'You've shot up.'

'Everything does in Jamaica,' he said, and she laughed fondly, filled with pleasure at seeing him, her first boy, her first born. Already she felt an ease between them that was new, and she supposed it must have emerged from the distance between them: that and, she hoped, some personal contentment. When Silas had offered to take him on at Whittam & Co. – out of the blue, with his usual certainty of success – Eve had baulked at the idea. Seth had been in his second year at a college for young men in Sheffield, a quietly conscientious student, cleverer than any of them had realised. An academic life seemed to beckon; Cambridge had been mentioned. But Seth had very often chosen whichever path seemed least appealing to his mother, and he had done so again, accepting his uncle's offer with alacrity, turning his back on his books. Yet, thought Eve, here he was in Port Antonio, as comfortable in his own skin as she had ever seen him.

'It's so beautiful, Seth,' she said now. 'I've many a time tried to think what it might be like, but I didn't have enough imagination for it. It's so . . . so . . .'

'Lush, verdant, tropical,' said Silas, slipping into place beside her and laying claim with the palm of his hand in the small of her back. 'Fertile, hot, wet, green, pink, purple, blue. It's everything you could possibly imagine, then more so.'

'When I first came I thought I'd landed in paradise,' Seth said. Eve noticed the alteration in the way he spoke: more like Silas, less like her. Perhaps this was a good thing, she thought.

'A paradise within reach of sinners,' said Silas. 'Well

– sinners who can pay their passage on my ships. Do you like your room?'

She was billeted in the hotel, of course, the better to accomplish her mission.

'Lovely,' she said. 'I shall feel like a princess under them muslin swags.'

'Mosquito nets,' said Silas. 'Close them, won't you? Make sure there are no gaps, or they'll eat you alive.'

Across the room a man whose pallid, newly arrived complexion bore a sheen of perspiration said, 'I say, boy!' in exasperated, carrying tones and Silas, ever alert to imminent discord, hurried over to nip it in the bud. A lanky Jamaican porter seemed to be the source of the problem; he leaned against the wall, picking his teeth and feigning deafness, and Eve watched as Silas spoke first to the guest and then to the porter, whose expression remained a study in boredom. He flicked his brown eyes in Eve's direction and grinned in a louche manner; she looked away quickly. Seth said: 'You see, this is what happens.'

'What?'

'The Jamaicans won't lift a finger if they're not spoken to nicely.'

'Well, and do we blame them?'

'We pay them to fetch and carry,' Seth said, not answering her question. 'We shouldn't be required to stand on ceremony.'

'Is that you talking, or Uncle Silas?'

He ignored her again. 'But they don't like it. They don't have the temperament. They look at us and see white slave masters.'

'I 'ope they don't see a slave master in me. I shan't get on very well in that kitchen if that's t'case.'

Seth looked uncomfortable, but Eve wasn't paying attention; instead she gazed about, taking in her surroundings. A fancy room, a little overdressed. Fancy folk, ditto. It was done up in the English style, which surprised her. She would not, if the place were her own, bother with chintz and Chippendale. The ceiling fans were nice, though: like the paddles on a pleasure boat. The blades silently stirred the humid afternoon air and made it tolerable. A small brown boy in grey shorts and shirt wove a path through the gathering, carefully dispensing lemonade with an endearing expression of great concentration. Eve watched him for a moment, charmed. He looked about the same age as Ellen, she thought, though it was hard to imagine the little girl being half as obliging as this child. As he passed he looked at her quite suddenly, as if she'd spoken to him, and he smiled broadly, offering up the frosted jug.

'More lemonade, lady?' he said brightly. Eve laughed and let him refill her glass.

'Thank you,' she said. 'And who are you?'

'My name is Roscoe Donaldson.' He spoke with a sweet formality and held out his free hand for Eve to shake.

'Thank you, Roscoe,' Seth said. 'Move along.'

'Sorry, Mr Seth.'

He dipped his head and slipped away, and Eve shot Seth a reproachful look. 'He was just answering me, you know. There was no need to be unkind.'

'If the adult staff were more reliable and efficient he wouldn't be here at all.'

'Oh, listen to yourself.'

'I'm just saying.'

'Aye, well I think that bairn's doing a smashing job, and look . . .' – she pointed at the boy, who was now standing uncertainly on the fringes of the gathering – '. . . you've taken t'wind right out of 'is sails. Somebody should tell 'im well done.'

Seth regarded her a little coolly. He hadn't expected to be

reprimanded, and so soon after her arrival; he had only expected to be admired. He looked away and saw that Roscoe was now leaving the room, draining, as he went, the last of the lemonade directly from the jug into his mouth, and it struck him how little his mother knew about the Whittam Hotel: how very much she had to learn. He could try to explain, or he could let her discover for herself the problems inherent in trying to bend the will of uncooperative Jamaicans. He thought, perhaps, the latter course held more appeal.

'Would you like to see the kitchens?' he said now, but she shook her head.

'I'll get to work tomorrow. I'd like a stroll, though. Will you come with me, outside?'

So they left, arm in arm, through the French windows, out on to the veranda and down the steps into the English garden that Silas had insisted upon. Here and there Eve smiled and nodded at other guests, people she'd become acquainted with on the ship, and she said to Seth, 'Everybody looks content, broadly speaking. I can't see that things are as bad as you think.'

Seth thought of Ruby in the kitchen and Batista waiting on, and merely smiled in a non-committal sort of way. He led her down a herringbone path that was shady and almost comfortable, and which opened out onto a bed of unhappy pink peonies, whose pale-hued petals belonged in the garden of a Cotswold vicarage. Overhead, a great white and black frigatebird wheeled and cried and swept off towards the sea. The heat pressed down from the sky and up from the earth, and the cicadas' incessant racket filled the air.

'You're a long way from home,' Seth said. She was like the peonies, he thought: transplanted into tropical soil. He hoped she'd fare better than they had.

'That letter,' Eve said. 'Daniel was certain you hadn't written it.'

185

Seth blushed. He had never yet successfully fooled his mam, and he wasn't about to try now.

'They were Uncle Silas's words, but it was my idea that you come,' he said. 'Are you sorry you did?'

She reached up and placed a tender hand on the back of his head, drawing it down on to his neck and holding it there for a moment. 'No,' she said, and she meant it. She wasn't sorry, she was glad: more than glad, and not just for Seth, but for herself. Easier, much easier, to be the traveller than the one left behind. She felt almost ashamed to admit it, but already, merely hours after docking, she was feeling the intoxicating effects of this island: the mixed and unfamiliar fragrances on the wind; the strange calls of birds the like of which she had never seen; the vast, dense, glossy greenness of the mountains beyond the town; the startling, infinite, changing blues of the sky and the sea. All these things stirred in her an excitement at the unfamiliar, a curiosity she was impatient to sate. She was in a hurry to become properly acquainted, aware, suddenly, not how long a time she would be away from Netherwood, but how short. She had never in her life felt confined or dissatisfied at home, but she felt now that she had sailed from the mundane to the extraordinary. Angus was upstairs in their room, in a deep sleep on a soft mattress under a tent of netting, but Eve felt wide awake, all her senses alive to this extraordinary new place.

'Evie!'

Silas had come looking for them, and he stood now on an upper terrace of the garden, his hands in the pockets of his loose, linen trousers, a baffled smile upon his face as if he couldn't for the life of him understand why she wasn't where he'd left her.

'Don't be outside without a hat,' he called. And Seth, feeling a pang of anxiety at his uncle's tone, took his mam

– his mother – by the arm and led her back up the path to the hotel.

In the kitchen, Ruby said to Scotty, 'Well? Does she have her brother's crocodile smile?'

'She certainly fell from de same tree,' he said. He snuck a finger into a bowl of custard and sucked it lasciviously. She slapped his wrist, but it was a half-hearted gesture because her mind was on this sister of the boss, whose imminent – and now actual – arrival filled her with apprehension. A female version of Mr Silas at her shoulder by the stove; she shivered, though her skin was delicately laced with beads of sweat and the kitchen shimmered with heat.

Ruby turned back to the haunch of roast venison, which she regarded with distaste: the colour and texture of a coconut husk, and just as dry. She wouldn't feed it to a stray dog.

'Carve this, Scotty,' she said. 'Then send it up.'

Chapter 22

Lady Henrietta Hoyland, denied bail by a magistrate who detested suffragists in general and suffragettes in particular, was being held at Holloway Prison until her trial at Bow Street Court at the end of June. This harsh decision was, of course, the very thing she had craved, bringing as it did increased notoriety for herself and yet more publicity for the cause.

She had baulked, though, at the sullen grey crenellations of the jail; its alarming resemblance to the Tower of London gave her pause for thought as she was driven through the portals. However, thus far she had borne her incarceration stoically, and her situation had been somewhat eased by the fact that Tobias had arranged for a meal to be sent to her from the Ritz Hotel at seven o'clock each evening. Toby was with her now; they faced each other across a scarred wooden table, cheek by jowl with their near neighbours; privacy was a privilege of the innocent and the free, Henrietta had learned. Toby, in his crisp new lounge suit and spotted silk necktie, was out of context in this harshly dreary institution. He was sleek and groomed, his reddish hair grown longer than usual, his face clean-shaven; women, the other prisoners, stared.

Henrietta, unadorned, felt a small pang for her rooms, her clothes, her jewellery, her maid, but it came and went unremarked upon and from their expressions, he might have been taken for the prisoner.

'Cheer up, can't you?' Henrietta said. 'You have a face like a wet weekend.'

'I can hardly bear it,' he said.

'Well if I can, you certainly ought to be able to.'

'There's a permanent stink of old sprouts and piss pots.'

She grimaced. 'I know, and it's odd, because sprouts aren't even in season. Perhaps the smell lingers from last Christmas.'

He looked around the room dolefully. The other prisoners – all clad, like Henrietta, in dowdy frocks of grey striped ticking – looked more at home here than she did; their visitors too. He looked at their pale, plain faces, their lank hair, their dull, lightless eyes, and he thought that their presence here must surely be less of a shock, less of a disaster, for them and their families than Henry's presence here was for him. He looked back at her, and though he had never thought her beautiful – no one did, generally: Isabella was the beauty, Henrietta the brains – she looked finely made by contrast with her surroundings.

'Do you have companionship?' he asked, and his voice was so soulful that Henrietta laughed.

'Oh Tobes,' she said.

'Well, they all look so beastly.'

'I'm not here to add to my social circle. In any case, no one's being actively unpleasant, apart from a couple of the warders. I'm left alone for the most part. The Ritz dinners inspire some hostility, mind you. Mixed grill yesterday, with the most delicious lamb-loin chops.'

He managed a watery smile.

'Monsieur Reynard sends his special regards,' he said. The French chef had left Netherwood Hall three years ago to take up a position in Cesar Ritz's new hotel on Piccadilly. Tobias had gone to him on the day of Henrietta's arrest and commissioned his services – at considerable expense – for the duration of her ordeal. It had surprised Henrietta that such concessions were allowed in Holloway. Toby, however, felt it was the very least they might allow for the sister of an earl; if he had his way, she would be held prisoner at the Ritz too. 'He prepares your meals himself, you know. Doesn't let the underlings anywhere near.'

'Sweet of him,' Henrietta said. 'Look, can we talk about something other than my plight? I find my spirits are flagging. Tell me something interesting.'

He nodded, and heroically rearranged his features into something less tragic.

'Well,' he said, 'Isabella's Season continues apace. Hectic schedule, every day, from lunchtime onwards. Mama sends Thea in the evenings from time to time. She's terribly choosy.'

'Who is?'

'Mama. She sends Thea to the functions she doesn't want.'

Henrietta raised a brow at this news. 'Thea as chaperone: novel idea.'

'She enjoys it.'

'I'm quite sure she does. Anyhow, go on.'

'It's Izzy's dance in three weeks. They're preparing the ballroom at Fulton House because the proportions are better than Park Lane.'

'Why not Denbigh Court?'

'Too far, and from what I gather, Archie's household isn't geared up for big flings. So Mama is treating Fulton House as her own and has quite taken over. Absolute mayhem, ladders everywhere.'

'Not repainting it I hope?'

'No fear. But the chandeliers are being cleaned, and some of the gilt needs touching up on the plasterwork. It's to be transformed, on the night, into a flowery bower. Isabella wants garlands of jasmine or some such.'

'Does she indeed?'

'Every time she attends a dance she comes home with another scheme. Last night she and Thea drove to Farnham Park for Minty Harrington's ball. Mama jibbed because they're new money.'

'Parvenus throw the best parties. Was it lavish?'

'Of course. Excess was the order of the evening, apparently. The house dripping with lights and flowers, urns sculpted out of ice and filled with strawberries, that kind of thing. The grounds were lit with hundreds of blazing torches and they brought extra deer into the park to make majestic silhouettes for the benefit of departing guests. You could see the house for miles, Izzy said. Plus there were swing boats on the gravel at the front.'

'Golly. Do tell her it's vulgar to compete, though.'

'Oh, well, Mama makes all the decisions anyway, and she's constitutionally unimpressed by anything the Harringtons do.'

'And Thea?' Henrietta said. 'How does she amuse herself on these occasions?'

'Oh, well, she has to take a back seat, naturally.'

'Not easy for her.'

'I'll say not. Positively painful, to play bridge with the oldsters while the youngsters frolic in the next room.'

Bridge my Aunt Fanny, thought Henrietta; if I know Thea, she'd be plucking the young men – and, perhaps, the occasional young woman – from the ballroom like sugared plums from a silver bowl. She was disappointed in Thea: two weeks in prison, and her sister-in-law was yet to visit. Granted, it was a long time since their mutual passion had cooled, but still, Henrietta had fully expected an appearance by now, if only inspired by curiosity. Not that she had been short of visitors in general: Sylvia and Emmeline had been, Eva too.

Mary Dixon – released without charge that day in Downing Street – had come every day, with the result that they were beginning to run out of conversation. Henrietta had started to wonder how to shake her off. There was something dogged and desperate about the way she clutched Henrietta's hand and kissed her on leaving; it gave Henrietta the urge, sometimes, to treat her unkindly, and at the last visit she had asked Mary to come a little less, to give them both time to think of something to say. Yesterday, out of the blue, Anna Sykes had visited – down from Yorkshire for two busy days, but still finding time to look in. She had talked brightly about her commission for the de Lisles and her waiting list of notables, and just how considerable their wait was to be as she was actually trying to spend the summer in Ardington in order to help her grumpy husband with his constituency business. Anna had not, of course, called Amos Sykes grumpy; Henrietta supplied that adjective now, as she related the encounter to Tobias.

'Anna Sykes,' he said. 'Oh, yes. Pretty blonde?'

'Well there's rather more to Anna than the colour of her hair, but yes. She married Amos Sykes – used to be one of our miners, now MP for Ardington. Loathes me.'

'Does she? Then why did she come?'

'Idiot. He loathes me, not she. He's against inherited wealth and privilege. I'm just the sort of person he most dislikes in life, and it maddens him that Anna and I get on rather well. Very cross man generally, in fact.'

'Never met a socialist who wasn't.'

'Tobes, you've never met a socialist full stop.'

'Have, in fact. Lloyd George, at the club. Week last Wednesday.'

'He's Liberal, dear boy.'

'Same difference these days. Have you heard his views? Pretty rum, I'd say.'

'Not rum enough, in my opinion. His ideas for reform certainly don't extend to enfranchising women.'

There was a pause in their conversation, a natural break, a perfectly comfortable hiatus, yet because of it, the sounds around them became suddenly evident: here a raucous laugh, there a hawking, phlegmy cough; at the back of the room a harsh bark of command from a warder, a snarl of assent from a prisoner and, underneath all of it, a constant, quiet, desperate sobbing from the young woman nearest to them, whose head was low to the table and whose visitor stared at her with impassive eyes. This little tableau in particular seemed to augur a hopeless, helpless immediate future, and Henrietta and Tobias suddenly and simultaneously became aware of the intrusion of awfulness, pushing its way into this innocent break in their own cheerful dialogue. It was as if they had each, for a short while, forgotten where they were, and had now reluctantly remembered: as if, waking from a pleasant dream, they found themselves back in a dire reality. And at this very moment a bell rang out, shrill and startling, telling them that the visit must end; telling them that Tobias would now return to the considerable comfort of Fulton House and that Henrietta must stay within the walls, and behind the bars, of Holloway Prison.

'Oh God, Henry,' Tobias said. His voice cracked and his face was once again stricken.

She hesitated on the brink of misery, collected herself, stood up. 'It won't be much longer, Toby,' she said, speaking quickly and low because, after the bell, further conversation was forbidden. 'By the time the case comes to court I shall have had four weeks in here, and the lawyers say there'll be no further custodial sentence.'

He leaned across the table and took her face in his hands. It was a gesture of pure tenderness and concern, such as their father might have made, back in that other, simpler time when he presided over their lives. Again Henrietta fought tears;

again, she conquered them. She was glad, in fact, that her father wasn't here to witness her imprisonment. Before he'd died, she had been in the process of modernising him, thinking to bring him in line with her world and away from his own. She'd made some considerable progress; this, though, would certainly have been too much.

'So,' Tobias said, releasing her. 'No Ascot, but at least you'll be out for Cowes,' and his voice, face and entire manner had lightened with relief.

This was so like her brother, thought Henrietta; he saw time not as a series of days or weeks, but of social milestones, events to be attended. She smiled encouragingly, although she was moving now into the stream of inmates heading through a door into the body of the prison.

'Thea sends her love!' he called at the last moment, just as Henrietta disappeared from view. Kind of her, she thought. Shame it isn't true.

Tobias wasn't sure if his sister had heard. He thought, on balance, that she probably hadn't, which was just as well because it was a spur-of-the-moment fabrication, a well-intentioned impulse to supply the compassion that his wife seemed entirely to lack. Her unconcern troubled him more than he liked to admit, even to himself. Thea seemed to be turning the pursuit of pleasure into a vocation; her dedication to this cause was unwavering, formidable and excluding. She had always been free of care, and this cavalier spirit had once been, to Tobias, the most attractive and endearing of her qualities, for in marrying Thea, he had lost none of the privileges of bachelorhood: she made few demands of him and he made few of her. They each had liaisons, because he was not a hypocrite who expected his wife to turn a blind eye to his own affairs while indulging in none of her own. And yet, he had begun to wonder if the pair of them weren't going too far with this freedom business; he wondered if they might have a go, instead, at mutual obligation and respect. He wondered if they might try conventionality. He wondered if they might make an heir.

He stepped through the final wooden door of the prison, out into the June sunshine, and stood for a moment, a frown of concentration on his face. How to tackle this? No point laying down the law. Thea had never warmed to instructions or edicts: quite the reverse, in fact. Perhaps she could be wooed? Once upon a time he had wooed her. He was expert at wooing: he did it all the time. Yes, he decided, he would woo his wife. And, having wooed her, he would tame their relationship into something more respectable, something less avant-garde. The thought of this, the mere idea, made the day seem brighter and more productive. There was a new spring in his step as he put Holloway Prison behind him.

His car was waiting for him on the Holloway Road.

'Home, Your Lordship?' said the driver.

'Yes, Wilkinson, but via Hampstead please. There's a flower seller on Heath Street, I think.'

'Righto, Lord Netherwood. Who's the lucky lady?'

Wilkinson was prone to this kind of jaunty informality. Also, he happened to know that the recipients of the earl's floral tributes were manifold. Bouquets for actresses, nosegays for society hostesses, impromptu single roses for a beautiful girl in Regent's Park, Hyde Park, Green Park: Wilkinson had seen it all. This did not, however, give him the right to be impertinent.

'Drive on, Wilkinson,' said Tobias.

Thea was at home. What's more, she was at home alone. The Eugene phase had passed: gone almost a week, now. His oils and brushes had been snapped back into place in their wooden travelling cases and a lingering smell of turpentine was all that remained of him at Fulton House. It had been a pleasurable seduction, but ultimately pointless and though Eugene had wept for love for her, Thea had merrily tutted at his misplaced devotion. He looked like one of her spaniels, she had said, with his sad brown eyes turned upon her in that way. This had been as effective a cure for his ardour as a bucket of cold water, which is exactly what Thea had intended. She was shallow and callous, he had said. The scales had fallen from his eyes. Excellent, she had replied: so pleased you've wised up, now shut the door on your way out and have a good trip. She had meant it kindly. She wished him only well, though she wished him gone.

Now she was in the garden of Fulton House, on a wrought-iron kissing seat with no one to kiss. Already, she felt the lack; not of Eugene, but of the idea of him, or someone, anyone. She sighed in the sunshine, thinking of lust and its splendid capacity to banish ennui. She had found that deadheading the rose garden only exacerbated the tedium of an empty day. She knew it was the sort of pottering activity countesses were meant to enjoy, but the trug and the secateurs lay beside her, barely used. She appreciated the garden, of course; she just had no instinct for it as an activity. In any case, they had staff for that. She gazed about her and saw perfection. This was where Daniel MacLeod used to garden before he went to Netherwood Hall, and she could see that this long narrow portion of London land bore all his hallmarks: a parterre, clipped box, borders of entirely white or entirely blue, a small canal endlessly refilling itself by means of an electric pump. Barney and Fred, protégés of Daniel, busied themselves in front of Thea, snipping at the lawn edges with long-handled shears. They kept it exactly as Daniel had, and they worked as if he was still here watching them. Thea, however, was barely aware of them. She wore a straw hat but her face was tilted up to the sun, rendering the wide brim quite pointless. Clarissa, her mother-in-law, treated sunshine the way she treated beggars and urchins: she shunned it, hid from it, turned her back on it. But Thea was a child of the great American outdoors and she preferred a light honey glow to Pierrot pallor.

She heard Tobias before she saw him. First, the ruckus of arrival through the *porte cochère*, the dying of the engine, the slamming of the motorcar doors. Next, the cheerful exchange of manly small talk, an indecipherable conversation between the earl, the chauffeur and Samuel Stallibrass, the family's elderly coachman who had never learned to drive a motorcar but was kept on out of fondness and because, once in a blue moon, the horses and carriage were called for. Then the clip on the courtyard stones of Tobias's new calfskin shoes – Italian, parcelled up and sent by Dickie from Italy. The footsteps were coming around the side of the house and without turning Thea called, 'In the garden,' and then she did turn to see Tobias, his arms spread wide with their burden of flowers, his face and torso entirely hidden by them.

'Delivery, Countess of Netherwood,' he said, his voice muffled by blooms.

'What on earth . . .?' She laughed, incredulous.

'I couldn't choose.' He lowered the flowers so that his face appeared above them. 'Roses, lilies, gladioli, irises, dahlias. So I bought the lot.'

She stood and walked up the path towards him. Barney and Fred leaned on their shears and gawped. Their borders were crammed with colour and the cutting garden full to bursting. They were a little offended.

'Are you trying to make an impression, Toby?' Thea said, her voice creamy with approval.

'Am I making one?'

'I do love a flamboyant gesture.'

'I went to see Henry.' He was still holding the flowers, but his voice was serious now. 'Then I came out into this lovely day and I thought of you.'

'Henry. Silly girl, how is she?'

'Stoical, but unwashed. Expects to be out soon, thank goodness. Will you go?'

Thea winced. 'Rather not, to be frank. Hospitals, prisons – I shudder at the thought. Look . . .' she scratched at his lapel with a fingernail 'you have pollen on your jacket.' They gazed into each other's green eyes for a moment, saying nothing.

The French windows at the back of the house opened behind them, and Mrs Devine emerged onto the terrace. The new housekeeper had been Thea's first appointment as Countess of Netherwood and she took daily satisfaction and personal credit for the excellence of her choice: the divine Mrs Devine, housekeeper extraordinaire, famous for predicting one's needs almost before they arose.

'May I take those flowers, Your Lordship?' she said now, in a distinctly rhetorical manner, easing the burden from the earl even as she spoke. 'Quite beautiful,' she added. 'I shall arrange them myself. Lady Isabella wishes to speak to you, Your Ladyship. She's in the ballroom.'

Thea said, 'The earl and I have some rather urgent business. Half an hour should do it, if Isabella can bear to wait.' She grinned impishly. Mrs Devine, poker-faced, said, 'Very good, Your Ladyship,' and backed into the house. Tobias, never slow on the uptake, winked at his wife.

'My rooms, or yours?' he said. He hadn't expected it to be quite this easy.

Thea said, 'The summerhouse,' and he almost moaned out loud at the look on her face. She took him by the hand and led him past the two gardeners, who pretended to be occupied though they knew perfectly well what the earl was in for.

Tobias, who had forgotten the particular joy of being prey to Thea's carnal appetites, was light-headed with longing, and his heart and loins rejoiced. If she had trodden this path to the summerhouse before, with someone other than himself, he didn't wish to know, and – for now, at least – he didn't much care.

Chapter 23

Early dawn, half-light. Outside, a cacophony of birdsong. Eve stirred in her bed and opened her eyes, and was confused, as she had been every morning, by the muslin canopy above and around her. It was like waking in mist. She propped herself up on one elbow and peered through the curtain at the blurred shape of Angus, sleeping on his own little bed beneath his own swathe of netting. There he was, lying face down as he always did, knees tucked under, bottom in the air. Eve lay down again, satisfied that he hadn't been stolen in the night. She closed her eyes just for a moment, but knew at once that she might as well get up as lie here, listening to the birds. There was a mockingbird, a lonely bachelor living among the creepers outside her window; Eve could swear she'd fallen asleep to his song and there he was, still at it.

She parted the curtains of the mosquito net and climbed out of bed, then went to the window and folded back the shutters. The view demanded a moment of quiet awe, though she had by now gazed on it every morning for seven days. To the right the high, dark peaks of the Blue Mountains, towering over a tree canopy so densely packed you might reasonably expect to be able to simply stroll across it; to the left, the gardens of the hotel and the dusty, downward trajectory of Eden Hill, winding towards the town; ahead, the sea, flashing in the early sun like a perfectly set jewel. It would be pleasant, she thought, to dress quickly and step outside before the rigour of the day began. She would take Angus with her – he would hate to wake and find her gone. She turned from the window, then started and smiled, because he was sitting up in bed, watching her.

'Morning Gussy,' she said.

'Morning.' He yawned and screwed his little fists into his eyes.

'Fancy a walk?'

'Can we take a picnic?' Even at three, the child had learned that a walk was more worthwhile if it involved food.

Eve laughed. 'Are you 'ungry again?'

He nodded. He had one pink cheek, flushed from being flattened against the pillow, and his hair stuck up and out, hedgehog-fashion. People often said he looked more like Eve these days than Daniel, but this morning he looked to his mother like a woodland creature just out from under a pile of leaves.

'Come on,' she said, crossing the room and hauling his warm body into her arms. 'Let's get you dressed. We can sneak out through t'kitchen and take some food with us.'

He clapped his hands together, thrilled at waking up on the very brink of an adventure, then stood obligingly, lifting an arm here and a leg there while she helped him into shorts and a soft, loose shirt that Anna had sent him for the trip. He had a small pile of them in different colours: collarless, with full sleeves. They gave him a flamboyant, piratical air, and he knew it, so he aimed to wear one of them every day. Today's was a chalky shade of red, which in Netherwood would have attracted attention but here in Port Antonio was just another splash of colour.

They tiptoed through the sleeping hotel like a pair of pantomime thieves, pulling faces at each other when the stairs creaked, shushing each other's sniggers. Angus led the way to the kitchens, already familiar with the short cut across the dining room to the discreet door at the back. He darted on, enjoying his own expertise among the twists and turns of this temporary home in which he had found himself. Through the door, down the plain wooden stairs, along a short passage and then into the kitchen through a final door which had no knob, but swung wide open with one push, before continuing to swing, back and forth, until it settled into place again. Every door should be like this one, Angus had thought, the first time he had used it. It had a covering on the inside of soft baize, the colour of grass. He bundled into the kitchen – no need now, for quiet – and then stopped short so suddenly that Eve stepped on his heels and made him yelp. The big, slow, insolent waitress Batista was sitting at the table pulling feathers off a dead bird. On one side of her was a pile of carcasses she had already plucked, on the other, a pile still awaiting her attention. Eve glanced at the wall clock. It was half past four. Batista met Eve's eyes with a dull challenge.

'Oh,' said Eve, uncertainly. She hadn't been here long enough to know the routines of the kitchen, and in any case Batista had barely spoken to her, and then, only in riddles. 'You're plucking t'ducks already.'

The rip of feathers leaving flesh broke the silence between them. Batista worked steadily, looking all the while at Eve. The birds on the table looked obscenely dead, as if they never could have lived; the innards were congealing in a basin, on the edge of which a fly squatted proprietorially.

'So,' Eve said, as if the conversation was following a perfectly conventional course, as if Batista had shown an interest. 'We're going out, Angus and I. We won't be long. We can talk then about t'duck – I mean, t'recipe for t'duck.'

Batista emitted a throaty chuckle. 'Me no cook, bakra sister,' she said. 'Me pluck de duck, dat's all.'

It was the most Batista had said to Eve so far, and she barely understood a word.

'They'll need a good wash,' Eve said, thinking of the fly.

'You tink me hands dirty, bakra sister?' Batista held up two palms, fiercely.

'No, no,' Eve shook her head. 'I only meant – oh, never mind.'

It was no good, she thought, being cornered into a defensive position, and it was too early to do battle. She reached for Angus's hand but, mesmerised by the grim still life, the boy had crept up to the table and was poking experimentally at the inert mound of dead birds. Batista cut him a glance and chuckled. At least, thought Eve, the woman spared the child her hostility. As she watched, Batista picked a large, blue-green wing feather and passed it to Angus. He held it respectfully and looked at Eve for permission to keep it. She nodded at him.

'Come on, then,' she said. 'Let's be off.'

'I'm 'ungry, Mam.'

Batista chuckled again. The sound seemed to brew and bubble in her throat before emerging. 'Is 'im bong belly pickney?' she said, but to herself, and then, to Eve, she said: 'Ruby done put batch a bammy cakes yaander.' She pointed towards the stone-floored pantry. 'Pickney kyan 'elp 'imself.'

Eve, not following, ignored her. Instead, she picked up a ceramic jar from the worktop, opened it, and took out two rolls of yesterday's bread. She passed them to Angus, who pushed the feather into his pocket and took them doubtfully. Eve smiled brightly at Batista, who stared. Then they left, taking the tradesman's exit from the kitchen.

'Dem rolls not for pickney,' Batista told the dead ducks. 'Dem rolls for Ruby chickens.'

Her deep-throated laughter filled the room and followed Eve as she hurried Angus away, past dustbins and empty fruit crates and on along the path to where it joined the main terraced walkway down to Eden Hill.

Eve wanted to strike out, away from the Whittam Hotel. At this time of day the heat was manageable, the sun still low in the sky, and it took them just ten minutes to find a likely looking track, leading off the road and down into the gloaming of a tunnel of trees. Angus clutched the bread rolls, one in each hand. He'd licked one, but that was as far as he was prepared to go, even though his stomach grumbled for food. He didn't want to be awkward, but the picnic his mam had provided was a poor business. He was happy, though: happy to be out and about, following her down a path of flattened grass and ferns. He walked carefully, noticing how the cicadas' noise stopped where he trod, then started up again as he moved on. The noise of the birds, however, never ceased and from time to time a gorgeous flash of green or gold would dart from one hiding place to another.

'All t'birds on Netherwood Common are brown, aren't they?' Eve said. 'But 'ere they're all colours. I don't think I've seen a brown one yet.'

'We do get robins,' Angus said patriotically. 'Robin redbreast.'

'Oh, so we do.' She turned and smiled at him, then carried on.

'And woodpeckers are green.'

'They are. I'm talking nonsense,' she said. 'Don't know what I'm thinking of.' He was one of those children, she thought, who would soon be questioning the logic of everything she said.

The path was leading downhill now, and soon Eve could see that the crush of vegetation was lessening, the path widening.

'Listen,' she said, stopping. 'Can you 'ear summat?'

Both of them stood still and listened. Underneath the constant caw and chirrup of the birds was another sound, and it made Angus think of the rush of water from the dolly tub, when Lily Pickering dragged it outside and tipped it upside down.

'I think it's water,' Eve said. 'A river, maybe.'

They crept on, Eve setting a slower pace now, made cautious by the idea that ahead might lie a torrent, waiting to sweep them off like a pair of dried leaves in the wind. This footpath was well trodden, thought Eve; it had been made by, and intended for, visitors to this place. This was how she reassured herself as they progressed. Still, though, she wondered if Jamaica had bears.

Immediately ahead lay a wide, low oval of sunlight, the end of the tunnel, and Eve reached back for Angus in case they should find themselves on the edge of a precipice. Furtively, he dropped one of the bread rolls and took her hand. Then, together, they emerged and saw what hadn't been visible before: a long, broad band of water, streaming and bouncing down a wall of pale grey rock into a pool of the deepest, most startling blue imaginable: bluer than blue, infinite blue, bottomless blue.

'Look!' Angus said, pointing, as if she might have missed it, and he pushed in front of his mother and began to rush onwards, towards the water. Eve followed quickly behind, so that when the ground finally flattened out into a soft green mossy carpet leading to a strip of shingle at the water's edge, they were side by side again.

'Oh, I wish t'others were with us,' Eve said. 'I wish your pa could see this, and Eliza and Ellen. It's magical.' She looked up, following the waterfall to find its beginnings. It poured over a flat ridge, perhaps forty feet high, and above it, descending from yet another plateau of rock, was a further stream of water, feeding the other.

'Two waterfalls, see?' she said. But Angus was on all fours, gazing down at his reflection in the pool, which was as still as glass on this, the opposite side to the falls. She crouched down next to him and peered in too. She could see stones and ribbons of weed, so it couldn't be too deep here, unless it was an illusion. She dipped a hand in, and reached down, and before her elbow was wet she was touching the bottom, so she sat back on her heels, relaxing now: no raging current, no perilous drop, no bears.

Then a boy shot up out of the water, and she almost died of fright.

He stood and stared, as shocked to see them as they were him. For an absurd moment Eve thought he was a water sprite – though she had no idea what such a thing might be – but then she realised who she was looking at: Roscoe Donaldson, the boy with the lemonade. His mother, Eve knew after these first few days of observation, ran the hotel kitchen, in the same languid, incompetent manner shared by all the Whittam staff. She had almond-shaped eyes and a beautiful smile, though she saved it for a select few. Eve was not among them.

The pounding of her heart began to calm, and Eve said, 'It's Roscoe, isn't it?'

The boy nodded. 'Roscoe Donaldson.'

'I'm Eve MacLeod, and this is Angus.'

'I know,' said Roscoe. He had his hands on his skinny hips, and water dripped from his black curls and ran in silvery trails down his skin. His expression was pleasant and open. Beside Eve, Angus stepped forwards and tried to look more impressive: taller and older. He stared at Roscoe with unalloyed admiration. Angus couldn't swim at all, and here was this brown-skinned boy who looked as if he might live in the pool.

Roscoe backed away, into deeper water, and floated on his back. He watched Eve and Angus over the top of his toes, which poked up out of the water.

'Would he like to come in?' he asked.

'He can't swim,' Eve replied.

'And he never will, if he stays on the bank.'

Eve laughed at the boy's reasoning. He spoke as his mother did: carefully, with rounded vowels.

'Well, perhaps a paddle, if you'd like to, Angus?'

Angus nodded solemnly and dropped the remaining bread roll. Off came the shoes and socks, the shorts and the Russian shirt, until he stood on the shingle shore of the pool in his baggy undergarments, looking pale and exposed alongside Roscoe, who had come out to hold his hand and help him into the water. Eve was standing now, the better to plunge in after him if he sank like a stone, but Roscoe kept a tight hold and took him no further than knee-deep, then sat down on the rocky bottom and put Angus in his lap so that the water swelled and washed around their chests as if they were taking a bath.

'Mam!' Angus shouted. 'It's warm!' He smacked the water with his palms and made sun-filled droplets, which danced up and then down again, all around them. Roscoe turned so that they were facing Eve, and she could enjoy the delight in her little boy's face. Roscoe was laughing too, bouncing up and down a little to make Angus squeal, and this was how Ruby found them all when she came down to the pool to collect her son: all three of them laughing in the early sunshine as if they were the best of friends.

Chapter 24

❧❧❧

Roscoe saw her first and his smile faded into uncertainty, which alerted Eve to the new presence. She turned, and there was Ruby, standing a few paces away from the water's edge looking as if she'd been sucking a lemon.

'Good morning lady, look at me,' sang Angus, who saw in Ruby merely a new and welcome person to admire his exploits.

Ruby, whose heart was too kind to rebuff a child, said, 'What a clever boy you are,' and managed a smile, although she was evidently displeased. Roscoe, knowing this, adjusted Angus so that the smaller boy was once again standing and then stood up too, all the while keeping hold of his charge. Angus gazed up at him with adoring eyes.

'There are mosquitoes by the water at this time of day,' Ruby said.

'Oh dear, yes, I never thought of that,' Eve said. She looked about her anxiously.

'And Pity-Me-Likls,' Ruby said. 'They'll be in his clothes by now.'

Eve looked blank.

'Red ants,' said Ruby with a hint of satisfaction. 'Their

bite can be nastier than the mosquito, although at least they don't carry disease.'

Roscoe began to feel cross with his mother, who he could see was trying her best to be unkind. He knew who Eve MacLeod was, of course, knew she was Mr Silas's sister and here to boss everyone about. But she was very pretty, and seemed very kind, and in Roscoe's world there were few enough interesting newcomers: why shun them when they chanced along? This was his view, and he demonstrated it now by scooping Angus up and backing further into the water until the child, to his obvious delight, was submerged up to his shoulders.

'They can't bite him now,' he said to his mother reasonably, and then, to Eve, he added, 'Give his clothes a good shake, Mrs MacLeod, then put them with mine on the rock.' He indicated the spot with his head because both his arms were around Angus's chest.

'Time to go, Roscoe,' said Ruby.

'Is it?' His voice was full of doubt and Ruby, who felt a stirring of shame at her own bad manners – which were, after all, in such stark contrast to the gracious courtesy of her boy – conceded with a small gesture of her arm that, in fact, it wasn't.

'Five more minutes, then,' she said, then looked at the ground and wondered how slowly the time would pass with the sister of Silas Whittam standing awkwardly beside her.

''e's a grand lad,' Eve said in a voice full of warmth. Ruby looked at her, and Eve smiled. 'Such a credit to you. 'ow old is 'e?'

'Roscoe is eight, soon to be nine.'

There was a small silence, until Ruby's conscience stirred her into doing the right thing. 'And your boy? How old is he?'

'He was three in April.'

'Tall, for his age.'

'Mmm, well, his pa's tall. Your Roscoe's a fine-looking boy, too.'

Again, silence. Ruby gave a tight smile and turned away. Eve, puzzled, went on, ''e looks a lot like you. Folk say Angus looks like me an' all, but you can never see it in your own bairns, can you?'

Ruby turned her head slowly and Eve noticed her long and lovely neck. 'Forgive me,' Ruby said, 'but I don't know what you're saying. Are you speaking the king's English?'

This made Eve laugh out loud. 'No,' she said. 'Sorry. I was just saying, you can't see a resemblance to other people in your own child. They're just themselves, aren't they?'

'They are,' Ruby said, inviting no further discussion on the subject.

For a while the two women watched the boys in the water. Angus had his plump arms around Roscoe's neck, while the older boy swam in wide circles on his back. 'Kick your legs, Angus,' he was saying. 'Don't make me do all the work.'

'This water's so blue,' Eve said, and felt immediately foolish. 'I mean, we 'ave a pond on Netherwood Common, but it's always grey, even in t'sun.'

'Grey water,' Ruby said, as if she couldn't imagine such a thing.

'Where are we?' Eve said. 'What is this place?'

'Eden Falls.'

'Eden Falls,' Eve repeated. 'Eden Falls. That's beautiful. You're fortunate, to call this 'ome. Home, I mean,' she added helpfully.

Ruby turned her cat's eyes on Eve and stared for a moment, and the effect was unsettling. 'Fortunate in what way?' she said.

'Well,' Eve said uncertainly, 'to live in such a beautiful place, I mean.'

210

Ruby nodded slowly. She didn't reply, yet she looked as if she might have a great deal to say on the matter.

'I suppose it's 'ard work, mind, wi' my brother breathing down your neck.'

'I don't allow him close enough to breathe down my neck,' Ruby said coldly.

'Oh, no, it's just a saying. I mean, Silas can be a bit of a slave-driver.'

Again, Ruby looked stony. Eve reddened.

'I'm sorry. Everything I say seems to be wrong.'

She sounded humble, regretful. Ruby relented, just a little.

'It's better not to speak of slaves in any context,' she said. 'Some people, I suspect, rue the day that emancipation freed our people.' Your brother for one, she thought.

'Your English is quite perfect,' Eve said. 'You put me to shame.'

This was the best possible thing Eve could have said to Ruby: the only compliment on which she placed any real value.

'Thank you, Mrs MacLeod.'

'Will you call me Eve? I really would rather you did.'

Ruby nodded her assent. 'And I am Ruby,' she said, holding out a hand.

In the water, Roscoe tipped his head back and smiled at the sky.

They walked together back up the tunnel of trees and on to the road, Roscoe cantering on ahead with Angus riding piggy-back. The little boy was clearly besotted. He clung on fiercely, as if he might have to fight for the right to stay put.

'This is nice for 'im, to 'ave t'company of another child,' Eve said. The tension had eased, though Ruby still seemed taut and cautious, ready to bolt if she had to. "e misses 'is sisters.'

'Roscoe loves little children,' Ruby said.

'Is 'e your only one?'

'He is.'

Her manner of speaking invited no further comment on the subject. Ahead, Roscoe jogged Angus on his back, so that when the little boy laughed it came out in jumpy little gurgles, which made him laugh more. Eve was glad of the noise.

'I thought I might help you, today, in t'kitchen,' she said.

'I see,' said Ruby.

'I mean, you're overburdened, and I think that's part of t'problem.'

Ruby said nothing. She walked on in her stately fashion, back straight, head erect. She was barefoot, Eve noticed, and yet she didn't flinch or hobble as Eve would have done if she were on this stony lane without shoes. She wore a green and yellow print frock, loose and casual, and her wiry black hair was held back from her face by a scarf of the same fabric. The green was the green of the forest, and the yellow the yellow of the sun.

'Duck *à l'orange*,' Eve said.

Nothing.

'With fondant potatoes and wilted greens. 'ave you cooked this before?'

Ruby stopped walking. 'I have.' Her voice, while not exactly hostile, wasn't exactly friendly either. 'I have cooked everything your brother has asked me to cook. I have wrapped long fillets of beef in that impossible substance you call puff pastry; I have placed chef's hats on the bony limbs of lamb cutlets; I have roasted great lumps of something called venison, which, quite frankly, is not a cut of meat that lends itself to roasting. I have pushed minced pork up the posteriors of English chickens, and plucked and trussed small birds that

212

here in Jamaica we would prize for their song, not for their flesh. I have filleted and cooked fish that do not swim in our seas, but which have travelled across the Atlantic in blocks of ice. Here we cook fish on the day it is caught; we grill our fish whole and pick the flesh off the bones with our fingers. You, however, demand that the bones remain in the kitchen so that the fish may be eaten with a flat, silver knife. This creates work for the cook, and if people have to wait too long for their dinner they may blame their own picky-picky habits and customs. I have learned the language of your cooking with the help of Mrs Isabella Beeton, but I admit I have not yet mastered all of the techniques I need for the delicacies you English seem to demand. It is a lamentable situation, and a trying one.'

'Right,' Eve said. 'So, 'ave you quite finished?'

'I have.'

'You're obviously very upset. It's impossible to cook well when you're agitated, and I'm sure I can 'elp. Help, that is.'

'What is impossible, Mrs Eve, is to cook well for hitey-titey English ladies and gentlemen who, if they ever had any manners, left them on the boat that carried them here.'

Angus, from some distance ahead, shouted, 'Come on, slowcoaches!' His face was flushed with sunshine and excitement. Eve waved at him and smiled, and the women began to walk again, though there was room for two people in the space between them.

'I don't understand,' Eve said. 'It shouldn't matter to you what their manners are like. You're a cook: you should take pride in what you make and send up t'very best dishes you can manage. That venison we ate on my first night was like boot leather just because it was too long in t'oven. And I'm Eve, not Mrs Eve.'

'You are Silas Whittam's sister, that's indisputable,' Ruby said. Her voice was cold again.

'Meaning?'

'Meaning you are rude and peremptory, and you put yourself above me.'

Eve stopped again and all but stamped her foot. 'I most certainly do not,' she said. 'You and I are equals, and if you knew where I'd started you'd think twice before jumping to conclusions. But I'll tell you this for nowt, I wouldn't give t'food you serve to Percy Medlicott's pig.'

Ruby scowled. 'Who is Percy Medlicott?' she said.

Eve flapped her hand in exasperation. 'That's neither 'ere nor there. A pig's a pig, whoever owns it.'

'Indeed,' said Ruby. She fell silent, wondering what Eve MacLeod could mean when she said 'if you knew where I'd started'. It was impossible to imagine anything but affluence for a Whittam. Ships, houses, hotel: could a man acquire these things from a bad beginning? She pondered this, and Eve shot her a sideways glance, thinking Ruby was smarting from the grave insult to her kitchencraft. Best to air these feelings, though, Eve thought. Best to start as she meant to go on: boldly and with authority. She was surprised, then, when Ruby spoke.

'Has your brother known poverty?' she asked. 'Is that what you're telling me?'

Eve laughed. 'Silas and I came from penury, Ruby. We've dined on boiled potato peelings, 'e and I, and drunk t'water we cooked them in for warmth.'

Ruby cast a swift, sceptical look in Eve's direction.

'It's true. I escaped t'slums by marrying a miner, and Silas stowed away on a ship. I didn't see him for sixteen years, and when 'e turned up 'e was a rich man. I'm cutting a long story short, but that's it, in a nutshell.'

They turned off the lane and walked up to the fine iron gates of the Whittam Hotel. It was too early still for Roscoe to go to school, and he was waiting for them with Angus attached, limpet-like, to one of his legs. Thus hampered, he held open the gate for his mother and Eve.

'I've told him I'll teach him to swim,' Roscoe said as they passed through. 'All boys should know how.'

'Thank you, Roscoe,' Eve replied. She ruffled his hair with one hand, and it felt soft and still damp from the pool. 'You're a real little gentleman.'

'You must not promise things you cannot fulfil,' Ruby said.

'But I can teach him how to swim.'

'Like a fish,' Angus said, and made elaborate swimming motions with his arms. Roscoe, freed, surreptitiously rubbed and shook out his leg, as if from a cramp. Eve felt she was becoming fonder of him by the second.

'Only if Mrs Eve is willing to bring Angus to the lagoon. You mustn't assume that she will.'

Oh, thought Eve, Ruby Donaldson could be very vexing.

'Eve. Not Mrs Eve. Of course I will, Roscoe. Angus will love that. And where better to learn to swim than paradise?'

Everyone beamed but Ruby, who walked on up the path.

In the kitchen, Ruby took out the tin of bammy cakes from the larder and dropped eight of them into a bowl of coconut milk. Eve watched her. She fished them out, shook them, then smeared an iron pan with oil and put the cakes in the pan, and the pan on the hob.

'What are they?' Eve said, her curiosity getting the better of her irritation.

'Bammies,' Ruby said, as if it were perfectly obvious. She flipped them with a fish slice and the uncooked sides sizzled fiercely in the pan. The smell, after their early start and big adventure, was heady, intoxicating. Angus clutched his stomach and emitted a small, pitiful moan.

'Here you are, little man,' Ruby said. She flicked two bammy cakes onto a plate, drizzled them with syrup from a jug and slid them along the table. 'Food for that empty belly.'

'Are they drop scones?' Eve said.

'They are not. They are bammy cakes.'

'Yes, but are they made t'same way – flour, sugar, eggs?'

Ruby shook her head, and looked almost as if she pitied Eve her ignorance.

'The grated root of the cassava tree,' she said.

Angus was already reaching for another, his eyes round with longing. Eve sighed and took one from the plate for herself. She would try Ruby's bammies, and perhaps she would enjoy them, but nothing – nothing – would induce her to ask what a cassava was. That, she was determined to find out for herself.

Chapter 25

⌣⌢⌣⌢

Amos had lost the knack of sleeping soundly, and because he blamed the Liberals for everything else, he blamed them for this too. This morning, he was stewing over the budget. It was killing him, very slowly, through sheer envy. In these irrational small hours before night became day he gave free rein to his bitterness at Lloyd George's stroke of radical genius. Increases to land taxes, to duty on coal royalties, to death duties, to income taxes – Keir Hardie could have written it. Keir Hardie *should* have written it. If it wasn't for the work put in by Labour over the past few years, the Liberal chancellor could never have made this sensational assault on the aristocracy. Lloyd George called it his war on poverty, but where had the first salvos been fired? In the Labour Party manifesto, that's where: in the Labour Party's social welfare demands.

Amos heaved himself over, from his back to his side. He had no strategies for countering sleeplessness; count sheep, Anna said, but Amos could never see the good in that – there weren't enough sheep in the Yorkshire and Derbyshire Dales combined to distract him from his thoughts. Moonlight flooded the bedroom, because Anna liked to sleep with the curtains open, and on a clear night like this their bed was lit like a stage. Amos sighed, shifted, shifted again. He felt sorry for himself. These were restless, tormenting times for a socialist seeking justice and a modicum of public glory. Labour might have prepared the ground – ploughed the fields, tilled the soil and even cast the seed – but the Liberals were reaping the corn and claiming the harvest. This farming analogy struck him as not bad: he might use it in a speech, he thought.

Amos turned over again, away from the window, although the silver light actually occupied all the spaces of the room. He didn't mind the dark: liked it, in fact. Thirty years as a miner had seen to that. But Anna preferred to be woken by degrees as the day dawned; she liked the daylight to steal across the bed and stir her from sleep naturally. There was a spare bedroom in this house, all made up and ready to use, and she'd suggested – nicely enough – that Amos might sleep there if he found her habits incompatible with his own. Not on your nelly, Amos had told her. He knew men who'd spent a night in the spare bed, for whatever trivial reason, and had never again regained admittance to the marital one. Anna had laughed at this, and told him he had her word that she would never bar him from their bedroom, but still, Amos preferred to occupy his rightful place in the double bed, curtains or no curtains. His wife was so doggedly independent, he thought, it wasn't beyond her to change her mind and lay claim to the whole mattress.

Next to him, as he tossed and fidgeted and flipped the pillow cool-side up, Anna slept on, her hair spread out in a silken frame for her face, her fingers laced and resting on her chest like a stone angel. In repose she looked even younger than her twenty-eight years – and God knows, he thought, twenty-eight was plenty young enough. Amos had stopped counting at forty: this is what he liked to tell Maya, when she demanded to know his age. That, or, 'Younger than fifty, but older than your mam.' It wasn't that he minded the age gap between him and his wife, just that he didn't want it to grow. Illogical and impossible though it was, he sometimes felt he was heading for old age at a faster rate than she was leaving her youth behind.

Right now, for instance. The very fact that he woke three or four times every night while Anna slept the deep, unbroken sleep of the young was evidence to Amos of a widening gap between them. And her energy, her ideas, her enthusiasms: sometimes they made him feel elderly, grouchy, a stick-in-the-mud. He lay there, watching her sleep, envying her, loving her, and he leaned in and placed a quiet kiss on her right temple, half hoping it might wake her. It didn't, of course. Short of the ceiling caving in, nothing would.

Resigning himself to wakefulness, he lay back with his hands behind his head and began to think about how much he hated the Liberal Party in general and Asquith in particular. This was not a good line of thought for a man who hoped soon to nod off, but there it was. He hated them more, perhaps, than he hated the Conservatives, because at least Balfour had never pickpocketed Labour's social welfare policies and called them his own. Asquith, however, had no such scruples; last year he'd announced the old-age pension as if it had come to him in a flash of inspiration. It was typical of the prime minister, thought Amos, to produce it like a white rabbit from a top hat, and then leave Lloyd George to worry about the finances.

Outside, he could hear the first stirrings of the working day: pitmen leaving their hearth and home for another day at the seam. Terse greetings were exchanged – an ey up, or an 'ow do, gruffly issued, gruffly answered: they were an economical lot when it came to niceties. In his own mining days Amos had enjoyed many a silent walk down the pit lane in the dark, in the company of other men. There was something oddly companionable in being shoulder to shoulder with another miner, with whom you'd exchanged nothing friendlier than a curt nod of the head. You'd fall into step with another man and walk, smoke, say nothing much, but feel a brotherhood that Amos hadn't found since, in the world outside a mine. Never had any trouble sleeping in those days, either. Ten hours hewing coal was a marvellous antidote to insomnia.

He sat up and swung his legs out of bed. Might as well be doing summat as doing nowt, he thought. There was paperwork waiting for him, after all; there was always paperwork. He would brew up downstairs and make a virtue of his sleeplessness. Already he felt more purposeful, less wistful. When he left the bed, Anna murmured something indecipherable and, still sleeping, rolled across into the warm hollow left by his body.

'See?' he whispered. 'You'd 'ave my spot as soon as look at me.'

When Anna came down it was still too early for Norah, which Amos was pleased about because it meant he could pull his wife towards him at the kitchen range and give her a squeeze. She kissed him, too chastely for his liking, then studied his face. She looked concerned.

'Have you been up for hours?'

'Up for one hour, awake for three. Shall we go back to bed?' He lifted her loose hair with his hands and kissed her neck.

'Stop it,' she said. 'Is there any tea?'

'Is there any tea? Is there any tea? When was there ever no tea?' He let her hair fall and ran his hands down over her breasts. 'Ahhh,' he said into her ear, 'you're a torment.'

'You torment yourself,' she said, in her brisk voice. 'Think about hot tea and pour one for me.'

She sat down and pushed back her hair, tucking it behind her ears in a perfectly ordinary gesture that Amos found quite mesmerising. He stared and she rolled her eyes at him.

'So,' she said, 'what kept you awake?'

He poured tea into the coronation mug that Maya had once brought home from a bring-and-buy sale in Ardington parish hall. It amused him, not only that the sale had been in aid of the local Labour Party, but also that he was able to put Edward VII to work whenever he felt like it. High time, he thought, that the useless bugger contributed to the real world.

'Herbert Asquith,' he said. He passed her the tea. The king watched him, reprovingly.

'Hmm, him again. Do you suppose that Mr Asquith loses sleep over you?'

'Not likely. One day, 'appen.'

'Perhaps you should cross the floor.'

She did this sometimes. He had learned not to rise, because by playing devil's advocate, Anna wasn't goading him: rather, she was confirming his beliefs.

'And why would I do that?' he said mildly.

'Because then you could help implement these social policy changes, which you say are Labour's ideas anyway. Don't you want to be in government?'

'Aye, I do,' he said. 'And I shall be, under Labour.'

'Lloyd George seems decent enough. I think you could work with him.'

'Aye, and if 'e wants to join us on t'Labour benches, we'll all shove up for 'im.'

She sipped her tea, then, regarding him over the top of the mug, she smiled fondly, as if at a wilful child. 'What's to be done, though? If Mr Asquith stops you from sleeping, I mean?'

Amos studied the king, who looked back at him through heavy-lidded eyes.

'Nowt, just yet. Except, maybe fresh air an' a bit more exercise.' He wasn't joking, though he sounded to Anna as though he might be. With Amos, it wasn't always easy to tell. 'I might play some cricket this summer.'

'For?'

'New Mill pit team. Sam Bamford sent word: they need a fast bowler.'

'Are you a fast bowler?' She didn't even know he played cricket, and it was admirable, really, how placidly she heard him out, when this scheme was entirely new to her.

'I was, some time back. I reckon I could get my eye in soon enough.'

She nodded. 'Well I never,' she said. But she liked the idea, and in her mind she already had him in cream flannels.

They made a pilgrimage to Netherwood: Amos, Anna and Maya. Anna wanted to see how Daniel was faring and Maya never lacked a reason to see Ellen. Amos, though he'd mooted the outing in the first place, had no particular reason to go except that he wanted to. Sam Bamford was cited as his official business, but he missed his old home town, that was the truth of the matter. Ardington was similar in many ways to Netherwood, but in just as many it was different. Like Netherwood it had three inns, a school and two churches – one high, one Methodist – and like Netherwood its community was close-knit, which wasn't to say people were universally friendly, just that they showed a keen interest in everyone else's private affairs. Being nearer to Barnsley, though, Ardington had less of its own identity and the insidious sprawl of new housing on its outskirts had blurred its edges even further. There was one colliery here and, like Netherwood, coal had originally put Ardington on the map. But it didn't feel like a coal town these days, because plenty of people worked in Barnsley, in its shops and offices. In Netherwood, if a man didn't work at one of the pits, he probably didn't work at all.

They had decided to walk, though it was a distance of four miles. The footpath ran parallel to the railway track, and every so often the little band of pilgrims was taunted by the possibility – now foregone – of covering the journey in an easy ten minutes. However, Anna carried a knapsack of treats and Amos, from time to time, carried Maya, hoisting her up on to his shoulders with exaggerated effort, as if she weighed a ton. It was an old gag, but it always made her squeal in indignation and bat him round the ears with hot little hands.

In Netherwood they parted company. Anna and Maya continued on through the town to Netherwood Hall where, somewhere or other in the grounds, they would find Daniel. Amos took the cinder track to New Mill Colliery, where he hoped to see Sam. He took his time. It was a long time since he'd trodden this particular path and he slowed down to savour it; he liked the hollow crunch of the cinders under his boots. There were ghosts on this path, and two in particular that seemed to fall into step with him now: Arthur Williams, Eve's first husband, and Lew Sylvester, who'd always had the knack of rattling Amos's cage. The times were legion that they had tramped along this path together, blowing Woodbine smoke into the cold morning air, Amos snarling at Lew, Lew buttering up Arthur, Arthur keeping out of it. Lew and Arthur were names on the miners' memorial now, the brass statue in the town centre that had been commissioned by the sixth earl as part of his attempt to atone for a lifetime of indifference: this was Amos's interpretation, at least. Also, it was one he kept largely to himself. The earl's untimely death had resulted in his virtual canonisation among some of the locals.

'Amos Sykes, my comrade in t'struggle!'

Sam Bamford emerged from the deputy's office as Amos

223

entered the pit yard. His greeting sounded ironic, but it wasn't. Sam, whom Amos considered a political protégé, seemed to move ever leftwards in his views, so that by degrees even Amos was beginning to feel like part of the establishment.

'Tha's come to tell me tha'll play?' Sam was as keen on cricket as he was on revolution: the finest judge of off stump Amos had ever seen.

'Aye,' said Amos. 'I'll need some practice, mind.'

'Tha'll get it. Tuesdays and Thursdays, back o' t'miner's welfare.'

Amos looked Sam over. He was a young man, by Amos's standards – thirty, perhaps – with a serious face and, when he applied it, a serious mind. He had a safe job these days, deputy to the deputy, keeping accounts and dealing with the Coal Exchange. He'd developed severe claustrophobia after a rockfall trapped him for a day and a half in a space not much bigger than himself. It had got him out of the pit, this new fear of confined spaces; he never shut his office door, though. Sam liked to know his means of escape.

'Nowt muckier than ink on your fingers these days, eh?' Amos said.

Sam said, 'You can talk, Sykes,' and Amos held up his hands in submission.

'I know, I know. Pen-pushers, both of us.'

'Aye well, tha can still plan a revolution from behind a desk.'

'Trouble is, there's not much appetite for it at New Mill, is there?'

This was true: they were a moderate lot here. Plus, the way the Netherwood collieries were run these days was exemplary: union membership was permitted, the eight-hour day had been introduced before the previous year's legislation and all the latest safety innovations were in place. It must be annoying, thought Amos, to be an agitator at a pit where the men were content. Sam shrugged.

'Cometh the hour, cometh the man. I'm biding my time.'

'And playing cricket in t'meantime.'

'Exactly. We face Thorley Edge next Sat'day. Grudge match. Come on.' Sam set off back towards the office. 'Let's talk tactics.'

Chapter 26

Henrietta's trial had been set for 24 June, which was the day before Isabella's coming-out ball. Terrible timing, with such a lot to accomplish before the event; nevertheless, there was great relief in the family that she would, after all, be freed just in time to attend the party. Henrietta had decided to represent herself, quite against the advice of the family lawyer, who privately thought her a strong-headed madam with an inflated ego and a lamentable lack of satisfactory male influence. He had told her that a more penitent attitude – a simple apology, a letter to Mr Asquith, perhaps – would be the quickest route out of custody. Henrietta, however, was not for turning.

She spent the days before the trial marshalling witnesses and evidence, and for theatrical effect she had subpoenaed the prime minister.

'Really?' her mother said. 'Extraordinary. Can she do that?'

'Well, she has,' said Tobias. They were together in the Fulton House ballroom, where the ceiling was being festooned with swags of jasmine; the waxy white flowers and their dark green leaves had been woven into thick, damp ropes of wire and moss, and they looked marvellous, though the scent was rather high, Tobias thought.

'The hothouse at Denbigh Court must be stripped bare,' he said. 'Don't you find it a bit much, the fragrance?'

'We'll open the windows. By Friday, it'll be almost gone. And has Mr Asquith acquiesced?'

'He has to. That's the thing about a subpoena. She's called him as a witness for the defence. Hilarious.'

'Is it?' Clarissa could see nothing funny at all in a set of circumstances that had resulted in her first-born child being put in the dock. For Henrietta, there would be no living down the scandal, she knew that much, and the issue itself was such a peculiar, unlikely matter on which to skewer one's social standing.

'It is. Very clever stunt, guaranteeing maximum publicity,' Tobias said. 'The pressmen will lap it up.'

Clarissa arched her brows. 'And yet I would have thought that the very least desirable of all possible outcomes,' she said. 'I do hope, when she comes home, she'll behave herself for a while. Don't let her go with you to Cowes if there's any danger of her being rowdy or inappropriate.'

'We'll clap her in leg irons and send her shuffling down the plank, Mama, at the first hint of insubordination.'

'You think me ridiculous.' Clarissa turned away and he kissed her on one petulant, powdered cheek.

'Fret not, darling Mama. I've seen Henry. The wind has been quite taken out of her sails, as we sailors like to say. I should think she'll be good as gold after four weeks in the hell that is Holloway.'

Isabella burst in on the other side of the ballroom. She looked slightly deranged, Tobias thought: hot and bothered, wild-eyed.

'Izzy, what is it?'

'Nothing,' she said, quite calm after all. 'Why?'

'This is how she is, these days,' Clarissa said. 'She looks perpetually on the brink of hysteria.'

'It's not easy, being a debutante,' Isabella said, defensively. 'I have a permanent feeling that I'm late for something. Am I, in fact?'

Clarissa crossed the ballroom, stepping gingerly over garlands that were yet to be hung. They lay in coils on top of sheets, seeping water. Once, when this house had been her own, Clarissa would have fussed about the effect of standing water on the parquet. It was so pleasant, now, to admit the thought and then simply dismiss it.

'Gloves,' she said to Isabella. That was all. Together, they exited the room, followed by a footman.

'Goodbye to you too,' Tobias called out, merrily and then, to himself, 'Don't mind me, I'm sure.'

The courtroom at Bow Street was small and quite friendly, with a pair of bookcases, one on each side of the door, bearing leather-bound tomes, and wooden pews for only a small number of spectators. Henrietta was disgruntled. She wished for a Crown Court and full jury; instead, she had a single, elderly magistrate, who looked at her with irritation, as though she was keeping him from the *Telegraph*. The room was packed, however: the pressmen were squeezed in standing rows behind a small, seated platoon of supporters from the WSPU headed by Christabel Pankhurst, whose presence in court added further to the press interest. Tobias and Thea, front and centre, represented the family and when the earl and countess had walked in, glamorous, glowing with wealth, steeped in confidence, there had been an audible stirring of curiosity, a ripple such as that in a congregation when the bride arrives at the head of the nave. Thea had smiled graciously here and there as if she was, indeed, the reason for the gathering; she had always shone in front of an audience.

Henrietta had been given leave to wear her own clothes rather than the prison uniform, and this she did, choosing also to sport a beautifully embroidered WSPU sash across her chest, bearing the legend 'Law Makers, Not Law Breakers'. It had been a gift from Mary Dixon, and in the gallery her face shone with ardent pride, but Mr Arbuthnot, the magistrate, immediately asked Henrietta to remove it, which she declined to do, thereby causing the first excitement of the morning. She didn't resist as a red-faced police constable divested her of the broad satin band, but neither did she help. Instead she stood with her arms stiffly folded, which forced the constable to rip the sash at its seam to remove it fully. All the while, Henrietta held herself erect and stared at the magistrate with a steely contempt for his petty preoccupations. Thea laughed and gave a small clap; she had come along to the trial in the same spirit with which others go to the music hall, and was determined to be amused. Tobias gave her a nudge.

'Pipe down,' he said, *sotto voce*. 'They chuck you out for enjoying yourself.'

'Oh pish,' Thea said. She sat on the very edge of the bench, leaning slightly forwards so as not to miss a thing. Henrietta had always had a magnificent hauteur, and she employed it now to full effect. She looked thin and taut, though, and smaller: her angular features were more pronounced than before and she was pale. Her blonde hair, in a loose chignon, looked dull and heavy. Thea regarded her with surprised concern. Henrietta – vital, windblown, hale and hearty Henrietta – seemed to have faded and shrunk.

'Is she unwell?' Thea said now to Tobias. 'She looks peaky.'

Tobias studied his wife for a moment. Her understanding of Henrietta's situation was limited, he realised that; if Thea had visited his sister in Holloway she might have been better prepared for the pallor of her skin and the drabness that somehow seemed to cloak her entire person. Even with the advantage of the Ritz dinners, Henrietta had clearly suffered during the past month. She needed to come home, thought Tobias: all would be well when they got her home. To Thea, he merely said, 'She's fine,' then the sharp-tongued magistrate demanded silence, and the morning's proceedings began.

At Netherwood Hall, concern for Lady Henrietta among the household staff was universal, but Mr Parkinson, as ever, set the tone, with sorrowful reflections on shame, disgrace and the tarnishing of the noble name of Hoyland. Anna Sykes, visiting Mrs Powell-Hughes, found the atmosphere sombre indeed.

'There can be no return from scandals such as these,' the butler said with doleful finality. 'Lesser crises have broken nobler families than ours.'

Anna shook her head. 'I'm sure you're wrong, Mr Parkinson. Aren't English aristocrats always in trouble one way or another? It never seems to alter anything for them.'

He regarded her coolly. She was Russian, said his expression; how could she possibly hold an opinion, let alone voice it?

'Also, I've seen her,' Anna went on, impervious. 'In Holloway.'

This was impressive.

'Ah,' said Mr Parkinson a little more humbly. 'And was she in good spirits?' He bitterly blamed Lady Henrietta for the taint of disgrace, but he didn't have a heart of stone. He had, after all, known her for most of her life. His feelings towards her now were those of a kindly patriarch towards an unruly child: disapproving, gravely disappointed, but ultimately very likely to forgive.

'Very good, under the circumstances,' said Anna. 'It must have been hard on her, when the magistrate denied bail, but at least it means they'll set her free after the trial.'

'I see,' said Mr Parkinson. 'Well, that's certainly something.'

There was a brief lull while Mr Parkinson pictured the sixth earl, Henrietta's father, turning in his grave. The wall clock struck four. Anna and Mrs Powell-Hughes exchanged a meaningful glance. At half past the hour Anna would be leaving; she was meeting Daniel and the girls by the wide Dutch canal where she'd left them messing about in a coracle. This was her treat, her indulgence: an exchange of news with Mrs Powell-Hughes. Their friendship had formed four years ago when Anna's commission from the countess had meant daily visits to Netherwood Hall. Now they saw each other only rarely. Each of them wished the butler gone; it was regrettable, but true.

'Lady Henrietta is built of stern stuff,' Mrs Powell-Hughes said. 'I should know, I've nursed her often enough when she's come off her horse.' She spoke briskly, hoping to discourage the Mr Parkinson's tendency to lugubriousness; to discourage, too, his continued presence. However, he had settled into a Carver at the kitchen table; clearly he planned to share his misery in comfort.

'Hardly comparable, Mrs Powell-Hughes,' he said. 'We're talking, here, about the family's name being dragged through the mud by the newspapers. I tell you; they're like hounds after a fox. Merciless.'

'Yes,' said Anna, 'they are. But soon enough, something else will come along to distract them—'

'And then normality will be restored, Mr Parkinson,' said the housekeeper, sensing a way forward in Anna's reasoning. 'We shall all breathe easily again soon enough, Anna's quite right. Was that the bell ringing in the front hall?'

He cocked an ear. He hadn't heard a thing, but he had noticed, since turning sixty last December, that the world was taking on a slightly muffled quality. Either gravel was losing its crunch or his hearing wasn't quite what it had been.

'I think not,' he said, though there was uncertainty in his voice. Anna, quick on the uptake, felt a little sorry to be colluding with Mrs Powell-Hughes's deception but did so anyway.

'No, it rang, most definitely,' Anna said and she smiled regretfully at the butler, as if she were even sorrier than he was that he must now leave them to investigate. He stood, a little stiffly on account of his hip. His face was a study in unresolved anxiety, but the women hardened their hearts and watched him go.

'But there isn't anyone there, is there?' whispered Anna, 'The bell didn't ring. He'll be back in a trice.'

Mrs Powell-Hughes tapped the end of her nose knowingly. 'Mark my words, Mr Parkinson will find another job to do, while he's up there. He can't help it. A mote of dust will have settled on the hall table, or a petal will have drifted from the rose bowl.' She winked at Anna, a surprising gesture from a distinguished housekeeper with a tight grey bun and a starched collar. 'We've done him a favour, dear. Taken his mind off the family's woes. Now . . .' she leaned towards Anna, proffering the teapot '. . . tell me what you've been up to in London.'

Daniel looked strained, thought Anna. There was an unaccustomed tightness to the set of his mouth, as if there were things he wished to say but couldn't. They were crossing the common, having walked the couple of miles from Netherwood Hall to Ravenscliffe. Anna had done most of the talking. Then, quite suddenly, he said, 'The thing is, Anna, I can't be sure he'll keep them safe,' as if she'd asked a question and this was his answer.

'Silas?' she said.

'He's a self-serving individual, always with an eye on his own fortune.'

'Well, yes.' She needed no coaxing to think badly of Silas. She liked him no more than Daniel did, perhaps rather less. Both of them saw him through objective eyes, unclouded by sibling ties. When he'd strutted into Eve's life five years ago – this was how Anna thought of him, strutting like a peacock, flashing his tail feathers – he was the long-lost brother made good, distributing largesse and worldly wisdom, whether or not it was welcome. He had made few friends in Netherwood, but then he hadn't sought friendship from anyone other than Eve. She had been his sole purpose. In a manner of speaking, he had wooed her, thought Anna. There had been an absence of sixteen years: long enough to make a fortune, long enough to lose his humility and plenty long enough to make his surprise appearance seem, to Eve, like a gift from God. All his charm had been lavished on her and, insofar as they could help him win her heart, her children. The rest of them – husband, friends, neighbours – could all hang as far as Silas Whittam was concerned. This was Anna's view, but while her dislike of Silas continued unabated, she at least had no qualms about Eve's place in her brother's affections.

'You can't doubt his fondness for her, Daniel. Whatever you and I feel about him, he's a good brother to her.'

'You're wrong.' Daniel's voice was gritty, twisted with unhappiness. 'He's not to be trusted and they're in his hands, my Eve and Angus.'

Anna tucked her hand through his arm, trying to offer comfort, but Daniel barely seemed to notice.

'He lacks compassion,' he said. 'He lacks a proper regard for others. He thinks he loves Eve but he doesn't know how to love.'

His face, in profile, was dark with worry; too much time in his own company, thought Anna. They'd had letters from Eve, she and he, and there was nothing in them to cause alarm; Port Antonio sounded a fine place, not a forbidding one. Eve sounded exhilarated, if anything: intoxicated by the adventure.

'Well, just supposing Silas doesn't guard them as you would, Eve's quite capable of looking after herself and Angus, you know. Try not to worry.'

'When someone tells you not to worry,' said Daniel, 'it's generally because they don't understand the problem.'

She was stung. For a moment she was quiet, and let her hand fall from the crook of his arm. 'Do you know something I don't?' she said, a little testily.

'It's a feeling, that's all.'

Anna fell silent, leaving him to his bleak reverie. Ahead, by the house, Amos waited, leaning against the gate. He'd had a good day, Anna could see. He was laughing at something with Ellen and Maya, who'd come three-legged all the way from the hall – bound together by a scarf – and still managed to beat Daniel and Anna.

'Daniel,' Amos said as they approached. '"ow do.'

They shook hands. 'Managing all right with no Eve?'

Amos asked the question with merry insouciance, quite disastrously – and innocently – out of tune with the prevailing mood.

'Aye, managing fine,' Daniel growled. 'Though we'll all be better off when she's back where she belongs.' He stomped down the garden path and Amos grimaced at Anna.

'Was it summat I said?'

'Yes,' said Anna. 'And no.'

None the wiser, Amos followed his wife into the house. The little girls careered about, Ellen's left leg tied to Maya's right, and their laughter, which had no regard or respect for adults and their complexities, filled the silence.

Chapter 27

Mr Arbuthnot, the magistrate, was obliged under the strict terms of court conventions to disallow many of Henrietta's questions to Mr Asquith. She kept straying into matters of personal opinion or raising areas of government policy, neither of which avenues could possibly shine any light on the matter in hand. However, even the magistrate, who had little sympathy with violent protest whatever its cause, was finding her hard to resist; for sheer entertainment value, he would willingly admit – later, of course, in the privacy of his club – that he had never encountered the like before, and probably never would again. The journalists bubbled and fizzed with professional glee, and the public gallery listened with enraptured delight as Lady Henrietta Hoyland tied the prime minister in knots.

'What were your emotions when my brick appeared, uninvited, in the entrance hall of Number Ten, Downing Street?' Henrietta asked.

Mr Asquith's handsome face wore the resigned expression of a busy man forced by circumstance to waste his time on nonsense. Disdain and distaste radiated from him like heat from a flame.

'I was angry, just as you would be if someone were to vandalise your property and risk the safety of you and your family.' He was a distinguished man – a barrister as well as prime minister – and debonair; he had clearly dressed with care for this appearance in court. He stood before her, an unwavering symbol of opposition to women's suffrage, the man who had banned females from attending public meetings unless they had a written guarantee from a man to vouch for their character and good intentions. Henrietta smiled, the image of sweet concern.

'Were you afraid, then, for your safety?'

'I was angry, as I said.'

'But, Prime Minister, if you felt the brick threatened your safety and that of your family, would you not feel afraid as well as angry?'

Thea whispered, 'What's she up to? Sounds like the case for the prosecution.' The magistrate pierced her with gimlet eyes and demanded silence.

'I was by no means afraid,' Mr Asquith said.

'Where were you, Prime Minister, when the brick was thrown through the fanlight of Number Ten?'

'I was with members of the Cabinet at the House of Commons.'

'Oh!' said Henrietta, feigning astonishment. 'So the grievous assault on your home posed no physical threat to you whatsoever. Perhaps, though, you were concerned for your wife and your children?'

The prime minister looked at the magistrate. 'Is this relevant, your worship?'

'It is not irrelevant, I believe,' said Mr Arbuthnot, 'if not exactly relevant either. Continue, if you please.' There was a muted ripple of appreciation from the gallery, and Henrietta waited, her head cocked in an attitude of patient interest. Mr Asquith blew out a long breath of irritation. 'My family was at our constituency home at the time,' he said.

Now Henrietta looked at the pressmen and her supporters, and rolled her eyes. There was open laughter, and Mr Arbuthnot smacked the top of his bench and called for order. He glared at Henrietta.

'Lady Henrietta, you will desist from playing to the crowd. This is a court of law, not a variety theatre. Similarly, you are not permitted to either cross-examine or attack the credibility of your own witness.'

'I apologise, your worship,' she said, but there was a light in her eyes now, a flush to her cheeks, a vigour to her movements: she looked altogether stronger than she had when the warders had first brought her in. 'I merely wished to share my surprise that the crime for which I stand here, and for which I have already served four weeks' imprisonment, placed neither Mr Asquith nor any member of his family at any possible risk.'

'You are not required to share anything, least of all your surprise, with members of the public. Do you have any further questions for the prime minister?'

'Just one, if I may?'

The magistrate inclined his head in agreement. Mr Asquith heaved another sigh.

'Prime Minister, does your implacable opposition to women's suffrage indicate an underlying lack of confidence in your own political future?'

Mr Asquith smiled, perfectly aware that his tormentor had just shot her bolt. The magistrate, boggle-eyed at her impertinence, demanded that Henrietta's comment be struck from the record and that her questioning of the prime minister now cease. There was a small uproar as the dogged, devoted Mary Dixon stood and shouted 'Votes for Women!' and 'Shame on you, Asquith!' and, although she was shushed by her WSPU friends, she was herself escorted from the court as the prime minister made his own more dignified exit.

Thea was rapt. 'Isn't Henry marvellous?' she said to Tobias. 'Foolhardy, more like,' he said.

Mr Arbuthnot called for silence, and barked out an order for a short recess. He looked extremely displeased, while Henrietta, standing tall between the two officers who now led her away, looked anything but apologetic.

Amos, Anna and Maya took the train home from Netherwood. To walk there was an outing; to walk home, an ordeal. As it was, Maya laid her head on Amos's arm and slept for the duration of the short journey, worn out by Ellen's inexhaustible fund of games, all involving sticks, mud and warfare of one form or another. Maya's hat was lost somewhere on Netherwood Common and there were grass stains on her white pinafore. Ellen had daubed muddy stripes on their faces for war paint.

Soon Eliza would be back from Paris and Anna felt this could only be a good thing. She worried that, between them, Daniel and Ellen were turning feral; they ate when they liked and not always together, and Ellen had made a bed under a rowan tree: on warm nights she was allowed to sleep there.

'Like a hedgehog,' Anna said now, to Amos. 'On a nest of leaves and feathers. And I don't know that she's had a bath since Eve left.'

Amos couldn't see a problem.

'Nowt wrong wi' a bit o' muck,' he said. 'Anyway, Lily Pickering still comes most days. She'll not let everything go to pot.'

Anna wrinkled her nose. Lily Pickering was taking advantage of Eve's absence too, in her view. By the looks of the linen basket she was at least two weeks behind with the washing and the windows were opaque with that particular mix of dust, midges and dried raindrops that was the speciality of the common in mid-summer. These things went unremarked upon by Anna, of course; the visit was clouded enough, from her point of view, without chiding Daniel about the quality of the housekeeping.

'So,' Amos said significantly. Maya shifted against him and he leaned down and kissed the top of her head, gently so as not to disturb her. There was a leaf threaded through her dark hair but he left it be, in case she wanted it there.

'So, what?' Anna said.

'I expect it was all about t'family's black sheep over at Netherwood 'all? Weeping, wailing, gnashing of teeth?'

Anna gave him a look.

'Not all about that, no,' she said. 'Some of it was about you.'

He grinned. 'I've told you not to brag about your good fortune, Mrs Sykes.'

'I think she pities me. She considers me . . . now what was it? Ah yes, lumbered. Mrs Powell-Hughes considers me lumbered.'

Amos laughed. 'She's not wrong,' he said. 'Whereas I consider myself blessed.'

'You're not wrong, either.'

They smiled at each other, enjoying an unexpected moment of perfect harmony that had come stealthily, from nowhere, and when they alighted at Ardington they kissed on the platform in plain sight of the stationmaster.

After the adjournment Mr Arbuthnot came back a changed man: not a shred of good humour, not an ounce of leniency. Tobias regarded him with alarm. It was clear as day that the magistrate regretted his earlier indulgence and was newly inured to the charms of Henrietta's audacity. He spoke curtly, bringing matters to a close. She was allowed a brief summing up, which she used entirely to promulgate her views on female suffrage, after which the magistrate looked her straight in the eye and declared her guilty of a malicious act of vandalism.

'Your aim, young woman, was to cause the greatest harm to both the property and, I have no doubt, the person of the prime minister. In this latter regard, of course, you did not succeed. However, your disgraceful actions reflect a lamentable and potentially dangerous lack of restraint, added to which you seem determined to ridicule the ancient and serious conventions of our judicial system.'

Henrietta watched his features steadily. His eyebrows were white, as was his hair, and they kicked up and out at their extremities like the ear tufts of an owl. He had thread veins on his cheeks and a florid nose: a port drinker, she surmised, or a lover of claret.

'You are a privileged young woman and your status in society has, I suspect, protected you thus far from facing the consequences of your actions. However, we are none of us above the law and I feel it is my duty to put a stop to your destructive progress with the harshest possible sentence for your crime.'

She heard him and yet she didn't. His words rose up and around the courtroom, perfectly audible but somehow disconnected from her own fate. She looked at Tobias and at Thea, who were staring at the magistrate with horrified faces. Sylvia Pankhurst had her hands clasped at her breast and her eyes cast down, as if she were grieving: for a suffragette, she was surprisingly unsettled by confrontation. Beside her, Christabel kept the magistrate in her sights, her gaze steady and clear-eyed, her expression unreadable.

Mr Arbuthnot paused in his soliloquy to glare at Henrietta, who met his eyes blandly, as if she barely saw him.

'I sentence you to four months' imprisonment,' he said, then paused, and in the courtroom there was a hollow silence, an empty beat of time, before he continued in funereal tones with the formalities. But Henrietta didn't hear because she fell, collapsing down and sideways in a dead faint. Her head struck the corner of the dock with a loud crack and she lay, awkwardly twisted like a broken puppet, on the floor. All about her was pandemonium.

She came to in a narrow hospital bed and for a moment she thought she was paralysed. In fact, her arms and legs were pinned flat by a blanket tucked so tightly under the mattress that it might have been nailed down. She tussled briefly to work herself free but the effort was exhausting so she laid perfectly still again, her eyes closed and her mind empty. Her head throbbed with a hot, pulsing rhythm, insistent and intrusive. She raised a hand, shakily, to the source of the pain and felt a thick wad of bandage, which someone had evidently wrapped round her head. She was puzzled, but in a vague, unquestioning way. There was a smell of carbolic acid and floor polish, and sounds – of voices, doors, trolleys, moans, the clatter of metal on metal – waxed and waned like the sounds in a dream, familiar yet unfathomable.

Slowly, experimentally, she turned her head to the right and opened her eyes. A woman appeared to be sleeping on a chair beside her. She was slumped and slack-mouthed, and her black-clad bosom rose and fell peacefully. The skin of her face was the colour of watery milk and there were soft bristles on the very edge of her jaw. Henrietta stared, and perhaps her scrutiny had a physical quality because the sleeping woman woke abruptly, as if she'd been prodded.

'Back with us, are you?' the woman said. She sounded

resentful, aggressive. Caught napping, Henrietta thought, and this made her smile.

'Funny, is it?'

She was speaking in questions, which Henrietta felt ill-equipped to answer. She looked away, turning her head so that she stared at the ceiling instead of at the cross and whey-faced woman in the chair.

'You've nothing to smile about, I hope you know that. Do you?'

Henrietta decided to try a question of her own. 'Please could you go away?' she said. Her tongue felt too thick for her mouth and she heard her words, slurred and indistinct. The woman gave a sharp bark of incredulity.

'Do you think I'd be sat here if it were my choice? I'm not visiting, you silly bitch, I'm guarding.'

Henrietta turned again, and now her eyes were filled with tears. She had no idea where she was, who this woman was or why she was being so beastly. Her head pounded fearfully; blood rushed against her eardrums and retreated, rushed and retreated, like waves against rock. It was disorientating, this internal thumping; it made all other sounds seem tinny and distant.

'Not so cocky now, are you?'

There she went again, making demands. Henrietta closed her eyes, longing for silence.

'Full of hot air, that's your type. All mouth and no britches. You can dole it out all right, but you can't take it, can you?'

Another figure loomed at the bedside; Henrietta felt, rather than saw, their presence.

'Oh good, she's awake.' Another woman, though her voice wasn't steeped in bile.

'Looks that way, doesn't it?'

'Lady Henrietta? Can you hear me?'

This new person placed a cool hand on Henrietta's arm

242

and spoke kindly. Ah yes, thought Henrietta. I am Lady Henrietta Hoyland. That's who I am. She smiled at the new arrival.

'I can hear you, yes, though my head hurts terribly and my mouth is awfully dry.'

Beside her the cross woman imitated her – 'my mouth is *awfully* dry' – and laughed.

'Do you think you could send her away?' Henrietta said.

'I'm afraid not, dear. She's from Holloway. She has to keep an eye on you. Now, I can't do much about the headache, but I can bring you some water. You just lie still and rest. I'll be right back.'

Henrietta almost grasped her hand so that she might stay, because her kindness was a balm in itself, but her need for a drink was even greater. She sighed unhappily, intensely aware of the baleful presence still at her bedside.

'Lady Henrietta Hoyland? How the mighty are fallen.'

Henrietta turned her head as far away as she could, a childlike gesture that seemed to further infuriate her tormentor.

'Shall I tell you what I can't stick?' she said, and then, without waiting for consent, 'I can't stick the likes of you, shouting the odds at Mr Asquith then collapsing like a half-set jelly when you have to face the consequences. Pathetic, that's what you are. There's women in Holloway doing five, ten, fifteen years and they've nobody sending 'em prime cuts from the bleeding Ritz. They have backbone, you see, unlike you. They have spine and spirit. Give me a pickpocket over a suffragette any day of the week; at least they're only trying to make a living. You lot, though, you make me sick. You think you're something, fighting for the vote, but no. It turns out you miss your four-poster and your silk sheets and your goose-down pillows, and you can't take another few weeks in the clink. Well boo-hoo, I'm sure.'

She sat back, satisfied at having vented her spleen. Her

words prompted a series of fogged images in Henrietta's mind, and she watched them in a detached but interested manner, curious as to the story they told: a courtroom, the prime minister, the faces of her brother and his wife, a white-haired magistrate passing sentence. She saw these things through a mist, however, and their significance to her own fate was unclear.

She would wait for her drink, she thought. There were no plans to be made beyond that. She closed her eyes and let thought be replaced by the smash and roar of the waves in her head.

Chapter 28

~~~~~~~~~~~~~~

Silas expected a great deal from Eve's presence: a transformation, a revolution, a miracle. It wasn't so much his faith in her ability – although he admired her successes back in Yorkshire – as a steely-minded belief that the Whittam Hotel's rightful place was at the top of the pile. His hotel must be the best hotel on the island; he wanted it, therefore it must come to pass. In this regard he was like a child whose belief in fairies made them real: he applied mind over matter, dispensed with the facts in favour of another imagined version of events. This philosophy, perhaps a little odd in a hardheaded businessman, was the product of two decades of easy success. Silas was the stowaway ship's lad who had ended up so entirely the favourite of the boss that the otherwise long, slow, perhaps impossibly steep upward trajectory had been circumvented by the gift of four immaculate steamships to call his own. Granted, he had an excellent eye for business; he had seen the opportunities in shipping from the West Indies, predicted the decline of the sugar cane industry, spotted the potential in bananas – his success was by no means the result of a series of lucky accidents. But his rise had been so fluid and free from obstacle that he had come to regard unmitigated success as a given.

He would not countenance the failure of his hotel venture, for the simple reason that Silas Whittam did not fail. People talked of his Midas touch, but no one believed in its powers so completely as Silas.

It angered him, then, that to his certain knowledge there had since Eve's arrival been no discernible decrease in the number of complaints he was receiving from guests. Time spent in his office was marred by the familiar procession of disgruntled Englishmen whose sensibilities, or those of their wives, had been bruised by daily exposure to a surliness previously unimaginable in the servant class. The food had improved under Eve's authority, but it seemed that this alone was not enough. Golden piecrusts, tender beef, delicately spun sauces: these were all very well, but they didn't compensate for the barefaced insolence of the waiters, porters and house-keeping staff.

'What did you think?' Eve said, facing her brother across a low table. 'That I could erase all your difficulties with my talent for pastry?' She tried to keep her voice light, but there was a perceptible edge to it. His haste for improvement seemed irrational, his demands unreasonable.

They were on the hotel veranda; she drank lemonade, he drank scotch. Eve's face and forearms were flushed with the sun and her frock of pale blue lawn showed her colour off to enchanting advantage, but he scowled at her, less than charmed by her response.

'I thought you might make a better fist of it than you have so far, certainly.'

'You flatter me with your expectations.'

'Then oblige me by fulfilling them.'

'Oh, behave yourself.'

He regarded her while he took another drink, then cupped his cut-glass tumbler in the palm of his hand and, with a steady circular motion, made a small amber whirlpool of the whisky.

She watched him, unperturbed by his mood or his scrutiny. He was her little brother, and if he was troubled by bad manners among his staff, he should consider mending his own first. She'd seen how he spoke to his employees, with his top lip drawn back in a perpetual sneer. It didn't help: really it didn't.

'I think we're making progress,' she said, attempting a conciliatory, if business-like, tone.

'Yes, that would explain why we had four people take themselves off to the Mountain Spring this morning.' His eyes were dark, displeased.

'And I don't blame them. Their beds were unmade two days running and they waited an hour for a pot of tea. I can't put that right with perfect pastry.'

He drained his glass. 'Ironic, isn't it?' he said in a carrying voice. 'To "work like a nigger" doesn't mean hard, but, rather, hardly at all.' He laughed, and his laughter was fuelled by scotch, for this was his third.

A flush of shame coloured Eve's cheeks. 'Don't say that.'

'What?' He was genuinely puzzled.

'If you can't treat your people with respect, they won't respect you.'

'Is that so? News to me. We didn't build the British Empire by kowtowing to the workers, my dear.'

She felt her temper rising in response to the challenge in his voice. 'You've forgotten your own beginnings, Silas. I can see it in Seth an' all. You're teaching 'im to be like you. Seth looks up to you and 'e copies your way of doing things, but I don't want my lad looking down on folk like you do.'

Silas gave a small snort of derision. 'God damn it, woman, take him home with you then. Take him back to Netherwood, send him down a mine like his father before him.'

She stood at once, as furious as she was hurt. Her eyes flashed just as blackly as her brother's, and her voice was loaded with the same suppressed anger. 'There's work to do downstairs,' she said. 'When you're ready to apologise, you know where to find me.'

He began to speak as she walked away, but she wasn't ready to listen. She left the room, letting his protestations hang useless in the air.

Eve was still shaking as she descended the stairs to the kitchen. Her brother's nasty temper stemmed from his own anxieties, she was almost sure of this. And yet, and yet . . . She paused on the bottom step to collect herself, breathing deeply two, three times, leaning on the wall to support herself. Images of childhood, faded beyond sepia, rose in her mind. Their father unbuckling his belt and whipping it with a crack from the loops of his britches, Silas cowering beneath him, covering his head with his arms; their father, seeking oblivion in ale, spreadeagled on the stone floor of their kitchen, growling like an injured beast, cursing the world and everyone in it; their father again, his face an ugly mass of weals and bruising, coming off worse from a brawl in the street; their father, filling the small, cold, filthy house with fear and misery, his wife and children alert to every nuance of behaviour, every possible trap or flashpoint.

As they grew Eve and Silas had cleaved together, comforted one other, escaped the misery with fantastical plans for the future. Their mother's death from typhus was terrifying, shattering, but they would not be dragged down; they were the unfortunate offspring of Dinah and Thomas Whittam but their fates were not bound to their parents, their course was not set. Eve escaped when she married Arthur Williams; Silas escaped on a ship bound for the Indies. They had each flourished and triumphed, shown the world and each other that they were their own selves, not merely doomed copies of their parents' blueprint. So why did Eve now see in Silas's eyes the same glint of unhinged fury, the same unquenched cruelty, that they had seen so many times in their father's? It was unsettling, and in the hot, narrow stairwell she shivered and clung to the wall while the ghosts of her childhood brushed past.

At the top of the stairs the baize door swung open and noisy, living footsteps clattered down towards her. Eve turned as a boy, whose name she hadn't yet managed to remember, barged by and went into the kitchen. He was lowly in the hierarchy, a washer of pots, a clearer of peelings, and yet he gave Eve a look of such bold hostility that it left her winded, as if he'd thumped her as he passed.

This was intolerable. For a moment she stared after him, frozen by the coldness in his eyes. Then she straightened her shoulders and marched in, pushing the door harder than she'd intended so that her arrival in the kitchen was announced by the violent slam of the door handle hitting the wall. She was propelled by indignation, fired up with the injustice of this treatment at the hands of a kitchen lad. Here, then, was the straw that broke the camel's back: this moment would change everything, Eve thought. This would be the precise point at which she might say, in the weeks to come, that she had taken the reins and the reputation of the Whittam Hotel was resurrected and restored, polished back up to a high shine. The boy would look her in the eye and listen to her, and he would do it respectfully. She cast her eyes about the room, looking for his skinny frame, his uptilted nose, his round, disdainful eyes. He was gone.

She stood chewing her lip in frustration, at once entirely deflated. Ruby watched her, keeping one finger in place on *Mrs Beeton's Book of Household Management*, which lay open on the table in front of her.

'That boy,' Eve said.

'Which boy?'

'The thin one. The one who just came through the kitchen.'

'Wendell?'

'That's 'im. Wendell. Where did 'e go?'

'Wendell will be carrying the bins to the garbage carts. Would you rather he did something else?'

'No, no. It can wait.'

Ruby looked down again at her page. Her lips moved as she read. The kitchen smelled delicious, awash with aromas of fish and garlic, although dinner preparations had barely begun. Ruby's three-legged stockpot stood over glowing embers, and in it a fragrant broth bubbled contentedly. Food for the staff, thought Eve. Ruby's suppers were the principal reason that anyone worked here at all. She walked to the pot and peered in. Fish heads winked at her, bobbing merrily alongside onions, herbs and copious rings of the fiery little peppers Ruby held so dear. Eve, irritated at being thwarted in her purpose, said, 'What's this?' in a tone more brusque than was warranted.

'Fish tea.'

Fish tea, thought Eve: what a contradiction in terms. Any hot, light liquid was tea to these Jamaicans. To Eve, only actual tea could be called tea, and here it was not very highly regarded. She folded her arms, tapped a foot on the stone flags, and watched Ruby's head, which was bent low over the text.

'What's so interesting there?' Eve asked, her tone still disagreeable.

'I am reading about Alexis Soyer's recipe for puff paste,' Ruby said with her customary dignity, although she didn't look up.

'Pound of butter to every pound of flour, and not quite 'alf a pint of water,' said Eve.

'Soyer adds egg yolk and lemon juice. But I'm reading it not for the method but for the way Mrs Beeton expresses herself. And this is my break, I might add.'

Eve felt a flash of contrition and her face softened immediately. She sat down opposite Ruby at the table.

'I'm sorry. Wendell upset me, on t'stairs.'

Ruby laughed. 'That scrap of a boy? I advise a clip to his ear.'

Eve, not in the habit of clouting her employees, looked doubtful. In any case, she thought, the way she was feeling now wasn't really Wendell's doing. 'To be truthful . . .' she hesitated on the brink of uncharted waters, then continued '. . . my brother put me out of sorts. I think Silas might be 'is own worst enemy.'

At once, Ruby closed the book. Behind her, Batista peeled red Duke of Yorks and sang soulfully about a balm in Gilead that made the wounded whole. This offered the women at the table not only spiritual succour but also a modicum of privacy to speak as they wished. Somehow, between them, a glass barrier was inching down. Eve said, 'What do you think?'

'What do I think of what?'

'Of my brother.'

Ruby took a sharp intake of breath and shook her head. 'What a question,' she said. 'What a question!'

'Go on, speak your mind. Silas can be nasty, I've seen it for myself.'

Ruby paused, then said, 'Can you picture a monkey's posterior?'

'I beg your pardon?'

'I ask because we have a saying in Jamaica which is very apt for Mr Silas.'

'Right. Go on.'

Ruby adopted the rich, ripe patois she tried never to use. 'De higher de monkey climb, de more he expose,' she said.

Eve laughed, as much at the difference in Ruby's voice as at the image she had conjured.

'Mr Silas has forgotten how to be humble.'

Eve nodded. She'd told him the same thing herself, not ten minutes ago.

'He's so far up the tree that he thinks he's above everyone,' Ruby said, warming to her theme. 'But when we look up, all we see are his . . .'

'Thank you, Ruby. I'm with you.'

Ruby leaned towards Eve across the table. 'He is full of disdain,' she said. She drew back her lips as she spoke, giving each syllable its own and equal weight, investing the words with bitter meaning. 'And the English people who stay here are disdainful too. They have been raised to believe themselves superior.'

'They 'ave, aye. There are plenty of 'em looks down on me for my Yorkshire accent.'

'Then perhaps you understand something of our situation,' Ruby said. She hadn't realised Eve's version of English was considered inferior, although privately she thought it so herself. Did God give us the letter aitch in order for us to carelessly drop it? Ruby thought not.

'You see, in England an extra shilling goes further with a chambermaid or a porter than a please or a thank you,' Eve said.

'While in the West Indies, we have not been free from the slave owners long enough to accept a coin in place of courtesy.'

'I see. So, to wait on white people—'

'Is gall and wormwood to our dignity, yes. Unless, that is, they can be civil-tongued.'

'It doesn't seem a lot to ask.'

'And yet, somehow, it is.'

Batista's song drew to a close and she did what she always did, and began again, from the beginning.

'Sometimes I feel discouraged,' she sang, her magnificent voice invested with devotion to the Holy Spirit, 'and think my work's in vain.'

'Join t'club,' Eve said ruefully. Ruby threw back her head

and laughed, which Eve took as a sort of acceptance, hard won and, more than likely, easily lost.

Wendell appeared through the back door, with the loafing gait he admired so much in Scotty and was keen to imitate.

'Wen-dell Bai-ley,' said Ruby ominously.

The boy looked at her, his eyes big as carriage lamps.

'Over 'ere please, Wendell,' said Eve.

The boy was confused; he was inclined to disobey Eve, yet didn't like to under Ruby's menacing gaze. He tried to honour both instincts and came towards the table with a scowl. Eve confused him further by smiling.

'Next time we meet on t'stairs,' she said. 'You must say, "Excuse me," and I shall say, "Certainly."'

'Do you understand, Wendell?' said Ruby. The boy nodded, although bewilderment and resentment still vied for supremacy in his face.

'Also,' said Eve, 'you can rearrange your features into something more pleasant. I won't put up with you looking daggers at me, as I never look daggers at you.'

'Do you understand?' Ruby said again.

'Do as you would be done by,' said Eve.

The boy looked from one to the other miserably. Something fundamental had shifted and altered in the short space of time between putting out the garbage pails and returning to the kitchen. He felt caught, like a coney with its head in a trap: pulling away would only tighten the wire.

'Off you go, Wendell,' Ruby said now.

'And thank you,' Eve added.

'Fo' wha'?' he said, his face clouded by incomprehension.

'For being the last straw,' Ruby said. 'Now, go about your business before we lose Batista underneath a mountain of potato peelings.'

Wendell smiled at last. 'That gonna be one big moun'n,' he said.

Chapter 29

It was later on the same afternoon that Eve had her eureka moment, and it was so brilliant, and so simple, that she laughed as the thought formed, and clapped her hands together gleefully.

When this happened, Ruby was busy with fondant potatoes – a terrible, shameful waste, those identical squat cylinders of potato that could only be created by carving half of them straight into the compost bin. She had resisted them when Eve first arrived, arguing that they would do just as well baked whole. No, Eve had said, not for fine dining. Flat on their bottoms, flat on their tops, like little barrels. She had stood over Ruby until she turned out a tray of perfect fondants, and now she turned them out in dozens, buttery, rich, drunk on chicken stock. Roscoe was also in the kitchen, which meant that Angus was too, and the two boys had been put to work washing spinach leaves at the sink. Angus's contribution to the task was questionable – he stood on a chair and played with the water – but Roscoe was compensating for him as he always did. Batista was seated as she could only stand for short periods before her ankles ballooned, and happily employed stringing runner beans while talking to the Lord, while Scotty was setting Wendell a bad example, standing at the open door of the larder and juggling with five onions. He was deft and sure, and deaf to Ruby's reprimands.

Roscoe looked at Eve and started laughing too, because there is something infectious about another person's amusement, whatever its source. Angus, with a small boy's self-importance, assumed that he must be the joke and began to toss wet leaves higher up into the air, in an exaggerated version of what he had already been doing. One of them landed on Roscoe's head like a dark green cap, and Angus bent double in the throes of unbearable mirthful bliss.

'What on earth?' said Ruby, looking between the spinach at the sink and the onions at the larder, and then at Eve, who grinned at her idiotically, full of the joy of her scheme. 'What variety of madhouse is this?'

Eve said nothing, only smiled; Ruby, impatient with her, tutted and rolled her eyes, and returned to the potatoes. Eve went to the dresser where she kept a wooden box containing the menus from the past few weeks. She had instigated a simple filing system of the dishes they served, in order to keep an eye on their balance, variety and originality, and now she pulled them in a bundle from the box, a month's worth of meals, all of them based on the elegant traditions of an English luncheon or dinner party: sole *à la crème*, vermicelli soup, pot-roasted pheasant, rolled breast of veal, apple charlotte, greengage jelly. The menus were printed on cream paper vellum of the best quality, because Silas Whittam could be accused of many things, but not miserliness. Their quality, though, worked against Eve now, making them difficult to rip in half, which was her intention. At first she tried to tackle the whole bundle in one go. Then, when they resisted, she took batches of four or five and tore up the menus with a sort of grim pleasure, as if the task were long overdue.

'There,' she said when the job was done. 'Very good

riddance.' She dropped the remains into the bin and dusted off her hands.

Ruby, all eyes again and the potatoes temporarily forgotten, said, 'Too long in the sun?' Scotty chuckled and said, 'Little man An-goose, your mamma gone cray-zee.' Angus, interested only in spinach and water, was oblivious, but Roscoe stared, shocked by the episode; it seemed to him too close to vandalism, too much like the sort of offence that at school would result in a caning.

'Now, Ruby,' Eve said – quite rationally, for she was still perfectly sane – 'This is t'plan. We continue as we 'ave been doing for this coming week. Then you and I will compile an entirely new menu, of Jamaican dishes. Food you make for yourself, food you eat at 'ome. Nowt – I mean, nothing – will be cooked in this kitchen that 'asn't been raised or grown on this island. You won't be needing Mrs Beeton, except for what she can teach you about English.'

There was a short, stunned hiatus, broken by Batista, who took up her strange half-wheeze, half-chuckle and said, 'E-e-e-e-e, bakra 'im no like curry goat in 'im hotel, 'im no like rice 'n' peas an' mackerel rundown.'

Eve felt her announcement, her great scheme, had been somehow undermined. Needled, she said, 'Why do you call Mr Silas "bakra"? What does it mean?'

Scotty and Wendell looked at their feet and Ruby coughed. Only Batista, to whom the question was addressed, seemed unabashed.

'Bakra, 'im plantation slave masta, laang time ago,' she said, giving her words a singsong lilt. 'Bakra 'im crack 'is whip on flesh, mek de slaves work all de laang day.'

Scotty, emboldened by Batista, chipped in with a plainer definition. 'Bakra: back raw,' he said. 'Raw from de sting of de whip.'

'I see.' Eve looked at the faces in the room, at Batista,

Scotty, Wendell, and at Ruby and Roscoe. They were all watching her, wondering what her reaction might be to this small but significant insight. At the sink Angus made *plap-plap* noises in the water with his hands.

'Well, do you think you might stop it? Only, if we're to make this 'otel a better place to stay it first must be a better place to work. If you can all show willing, I'll make sure my brother does too. I've seen what 'e can be like; I'm not blind. Everything in this hotel must change, even Silas Whittam. Leave 'im to me. But please' – she paused, and looked at them all, looking back at her – 'don't keep calling 'im bakra.'

There was a long silence, which she decided to take for agreement, and smiled. 'So. Next job, tonight's dinner. Roscoe, is that spinach still fit to eat?'

He nodded.

'Good, then drain it and dry it off. I need to pop upstairs.'

She left, and Batista drew a long, noisy breath through her teeth.

'Call 'im whatever, 'im bakra by nature.'

Ruby, who couldn't in all conscience disagree, said, 'But his sister has a good heart.'

Batista pursed her lips and shook her head, and settled back to the beans.

Silas had left the hotel for the day, Seth told her: gone to Sugar Hill, on business pertaining to bananas.

'Why do you want him?' he asked.

He was sitting in Silas's office, behind his uncle's desk, and – to his mother, at least – he looked for all the world as if he were playing at being in charge. Eve almost said, Mind your own business, but then she remembered he was not only

257

her son but also assistant manager. Even so, she wasn't quite willing to disclose her plan.

'Just an idea, that's all, a possible way forward. When will 'e be back?'

'Tomorrow, perhaps. Or the next day. He has to show his face at the plantation from time to time, otherwise they'll start taking liberties.'

'Who will?'

'The pickers,' said Seth unthinkingly. 'Constitutionally idle.'

She looked at him through narrowed eyes. 'Really? And I assume you've witnessed this for yourself?'

He flushed a little, and said, 'All right, Mam, I know what you're saying.'

'Right. Well, think on before you start voicing your uncle's opinions. Now, I need you to keep an eye on Angus for me, and I need a lift to Sugar 'ill. I shan't be there long.'

'What's your idea, then? Must be good if it can't wait.' His voice was truculent, his expression sulky. The little boy was very near the surface of this young man, Eve thought.

'It is good,' she said. 'You'll 'ear it soon enough.'

Now he looked disconsolate, and she relented, but only fractionally.

'The thing is, love,' she said, 'I'd prefer to speak with Uncle Silas first. Now, who can take me?'

'It'll have to be the trap,' Seth said and, pleased to be able to exercise some authority in front of her, he fetched Maxwell and issued him with instructions: Hitch the mule to the cart and convey Mrs MacLeod to Sugar Hill without delay.

'Please,' said Eve to Maxwell, though it was rather transparently for the benefit of Seth, who was beginning to find this chastising habit of hers very wearing, not to say undermining. The assistant manager of the Whittam Hotel should not, he felt, be subjected to daily lessons in good manners from his mother. Maxwell sloped off to lead Edna to the cart, and Seth called after him to take the coast road, restoring to himself a modicum of self-regard with this display of local knowledge.

'It takes longer,' he said, turning to Eve, 'but it's less rutted.' At least he had this, he thought; at least he knew where the potholes were.

Eve, bumping along on the seat of the trap, wondered what the rutted track might be like if this were the better one. Beside her, Maxwell chewed tobacco and, from time to time, squirted a jet of brown saliva from the corner of his mouth. There was no conversation, and the silence was the uncomfortable type, quite as intrusive in its own way as unwanted chatter. She kept her eyes on the road and was glad when Edna slowed and turned, at a sharp tug on the reins from Maxwell, into the gates of Silas's estate. This was only the second time that Eve had been here; Silas seemed to see no reason to entertain his sister in his home when the hotel served perfectly well. Her previous visit, in her first days on the island, had been at Eve's suggestion, not his. Silas had driven her and Angus down tracks lined with banana plants, explaining, in terms too technical to follow, the process of cultivation from rhizome to mature, fruiting crop. Afterwards his housekeeper had served them tea in a drawing room so pristine that it felt like an assault to leave a dent in the cushions. Eve thought about this now, as Maxwell drove her up to the great house; thought, too, about Silas's solitary life up here at Sugar Hill. He had welcomed Eve and Angus on that day, but his smile had seemed warmer when they left than when they arrived. She was fond of her brother, but she didn't claim to understand him.

'I shan't be very long,' Eve said to Maxwell, hopping down from the seat as the mule slowed to a halt at the sweeping curve of the steps outside the house. 'No more than an hour, anyway. I need to get back.' But Maxwell shook his head and was already moving on. He turned his head and spoke over his shoulder.

'Me kyaan wait here,' he said – the first words he'd uttered since they left the Whittam. 'Edna take fright at de duppies.'

'What?' she said, in some alarm. 'What's Edna afraid of? Maxwell? I'm going to need a lift back soon.'

'Me kyaan wait here,' he said again, and he chivvied the mule into a trot with a rattle of the reins. 'Me take de trap to de lane, an wait dere.'

Helplessly, she watched him retreat. There was dust on her skirts and sweat ran in warm rivulets through her hair, down her neck, down her back. She'd been bitten on the journey: mosquito hour, Ruby called it, this point in the afternoon when day began to meet dusk. Two hot red lumps had risen on Eve's wrist and another on the back of her right hand. She stood, feeling overheated and uncomfortable and – and this was irrational, since she'd asked to be brought here – abandoned. Maxwell had unsettled her with his silence and, now, his flight.

'*Madame? Bonjou', madame.*'

Behind her, on the steps, Silas's housekeeper had appeared, and her voice, low and husky, startled Eve, although it was welcome. They had met on that first visit, though they had not been introduced. Eve wished, now, that she knew her name.

'Come,' said the woman. She smiled a little hesitantly and beckoned for Eve to follow her, which she did.

'My brother isn't expecting me,' she said, but the housekeeper merely turned and smiled again. She wore not a housecoat, nor a frock, but a long swathe of fabric in brilliant blue, wrapped and twisted around her to form a garment, which fell in folds from one shoulder to mid-calf. Her arms were thin, her ankles too, but her belly seemed softly rounded, as if she might be expecting. Her skin was glossy black and her eyes, though modestly dipped, shone with a mysterious inner light, as if she had a cherished secret. Beside her, in her pale grey frock, Eve felt leached of colour: drab and ordinary. The birds of the island – the hummingbirds, the yellowbills, the orioles – were none of them more colourful or exotic than this woman who led her up the steps and through the tall French windows into Silas's expansive drawing room.

He was there, artfully arranged, a study in white: white couch, white linen suit, feet up on a white ottoman. For a fraction longer than was necessary, he continued to look at the newspaper in his hands before raising his dark brown eyes to his visitor.

'Evie!' he said, though his surprise seemed feigned, Eve thought, as if he had heard her arrival, watched her approach, then placed himself in this casually elegant attitude. 'Justine, take my sister's hat and bring her some lemonade, *tout de suite.*'

'*Oui*, masser,' Justine said, and flowed like a blue stream from the room.

'Justine,' Eve said to Silas. 'Bonny name.'

He shrugged and patted the couch. 'Sit,' he said. She did, but she chose not to share, taking a chair opposite instead. He raised his eyebrows.

'You're still angry? Come, come, Evie, don't nurse a grudge.' He pouted at her and made unhappy eyes, as if nothing could make him sadder than this grievance she clung to. She folded her arms, sat back in her chair and watched him for a moment. He was king here at Sugar Hill, she realised; there was no one, not a soul, to puncture his self-regard. Here, in the supreme comfort of his plantation house, no one ever challenged his supremacy. Well then, she thought: she would.

'I've 'ad an idea for your 'otel,' she said, and it threw him, because he was all set to coax her back to good humour but here she was, apparently perfectly unruffled.

'First, you need to change t'name.' She hadn't meant to say this – hadn't had the thought until this very moment – but now, struck by his enduring and complacent belief in the legend of Silas Whittam, it seemed to be the key to everything.

He gave a short bark of incredulous laughter. 'I see. And that's the root of the problem?'

'Yes,' she said, undeterred. 'Yes, I think so, in a way.'

'Ri-ight. So, what's wrong with the present name, pray?'

'You,' she said, simply and brutally. 'You've named it after yourself.'

'I named it after my company, which happens to bear my name.'

'Aye, and I reckon that was your first mistake.'

He laughed again, without amusement. 'So, who or what should my hotel be named after?'

'Jamaica.' She leaned forwards and her face was alive with her plan. 'Make your hotel the first on the island to celebrate Jamaica: its food, its customs, its colours, its plants. That's where success lies, Silas.'

He gave a short, explosive laugh. 'You've seen our guests. Do you suppose they'll thank us for feeding them fried green bananas and boiled okra?'

'They might. They've travelled all this way, so why would they expect t'food to taste like 'ome? You 'ave Jamaican cooks in your kitchen; let 'em cook Jamaican food. Be different, Silas. Be bold.'

'And the name of this brave new venture?' he asked, his voice heavy with scepticism and something else too: resentment, perhaps. She waited for a moment, reluctant, suddenly, to reward his churlishness.

'Eden Falls,' she said finally. 'I don't know why it never occurred to you before. The Eden Falls Hotel.'

Chapter 30

Henrietta's sentence had been reduced to three months on account of the time she'd already spent in prison, and, until she had fully recovered from her fall, she would be allowed to remain in hospital. Meanwhile, if she was quiet and submissive the three months might well be reconsidered: six weeks, perhaps, or eight. This was what the solicitor told Tobias, and what Tobias duly relayed to his mother, who merely closed her eyes, as if shutting out the distasteful facts of her daughter's current existence.

'Quiet and submissive might be too much to ask,' Isabella said. 'She's had a lifetime of being exactly the opposite.'

'You should visit her,' Tobias said. 'You both should. You'll see how changed she is.' They had recovered indecently quickly from the shock of Henry's continued imprisonment, he thought. An awkward silence ensued. Tobias sighed.

'After the ball, that is.'

'I'll go, but it'll have to be Monday now,' Isabella said. 'Not that she'll want to see me. She thinks me silly and irrelevant.'

Tobias, who yesterday evening had sat at Henrietta's bedside trying to steer her through a coherent conversation, didn't contradict Isabella, but said, 'She's not yet quite herself,' which was putting it mildly. 'She's . . .' He paused, at a loss for the words to describe his sister's present state. Humiliated? Demoralised? These things, certainly, and also timid and querulous, quite altered.

'Thoroughly ashamed of herself, I hope,' cut in Clarissa. 'The only blessing is that her father isn't witness to all this. Now, Toby, you'll have to excuse us: we have two hundred young people descending in a few hours' time. Henrietta's difficulties will have to be set aside, and since they're entirely of her own making, my conscience is clear.'

'Good for you, Mama,' said Tobias, and Clarissa, who heard only what she wished to hear, smiled at him. He wandered from the drawing room, leaving them to their ecstasy of minute detail; they had no need of his input where Isabella's dance was concerned. His own contribution had begun and ended in drumming up a few extra young men – there never did seem to be quite enough of them – from his own fund of friends: brothers of friends, generally, or friends of brothers of friends. It hardly mattered how distant the connection with Isabella; if they were bachelors under the age of twenty-five, and if their social credentials were impeccable, they could be added to the list.

A hundred debutantes required, ideally, a hundred chaps, especially if there was to be dinner. It happened, here and there, that two girls would have to be placed side by side at the table when a list was one or two men short, but such contingencies smacked of failure in Clarissa's eyes. The whole point of every gathering was to dangle tender, debutante flesh under the noses of eligible young men. She considered any ball where there was a shortfall of white tie and tails a flop. Tobias grinned to himself at the memory of those seasons – not so very long ago – when his own name was on the list of every titled girl in London. The mantelpiece in the drawing room of Fulton House had been stacked with invitations for dances, dinners, garden parties. He went to everything, and didn't behave particularly well either: that is, he didn't propose marriage to anyone. He had never been able to see the appeal of these alabaster-skinned virgins whose mothers sat on the periphery of every occasion, scrutinising potential suitors like farmers at a cattle auction. His younger brother Dickie – foolish, gallant, eager Dickie – had dutifully played the game: attended the balls, fallen for girls, even proposed to one of them. But Mimi Anderson had been after a bigger fish; the second son of an earl wasn't enough of a catch for her. That was why Dickie was now drifting around the Italian Riviera, and why Mimi Anderson was unhappily married to a buck-toothed viscount, whose father looked good for another couple of decades at least. Poor Dickie. Poor Mimi. Poor viscount.

Tobias laughed, although he was alone with his thoughts. He had wandered into the library, where he poured himself an early scotch from the decanter and rang the bell for ice. He thought about Thea, who had gone to the hospital against all her instincts and inclination. She ought to be home by now, he thought: at least, she ought to be home very soon. He closed his mind to suspicion and made himself think instead how kind it was of his wife to visit Henry; it was a mark of how affected she had been by the sight of her in a dead faint in the courtroom. Tobias hoped the friendship between the sisters-in-law might be rekindled as a result of this drama: a silver lining, as it were, to the cloud.

Once, when he and Thea were first married, the two women had been very close, and this had been the source of considerable happiness to Tobias. Their intimacy had somehow underpinned his own relationship with his wife, giving it ballast, tying it down. True, he had at times felt excluded by their mutual affection – had felt, indeed, like an occasionally unwelcome third party – but this had, at least, left him free to come and go as he pleased. Certainly it had been preferable to the enigmatic coolness that had characterised their relationship for the past couple of years. For a fellow with vast experience of women, Tobias was prepared to admit to bewilderment in this matter. He wished for harmony between his wife and sister: his own life had run smoother when this happy state had last existed.

Ballatyne, the butler, slid into the room. He was holding an ice bucket and silver tongs, which he immediately put to good use, dropping two cubes into Tobias's glass. Tobias gave him a perfunctory nod of thanks. Ballatyne was one of Thea's finds and the absolute antithesis of his predecessor, a most unaesthetic fellow named Munster with an expression and bearing more suited to the funeral cortège than the drawing room. This chap, on the other hand, wore his butler's worsted tight and with panache, and his eyes were a dark liquid brown.

'Will there be anything else, Your Lordship?' Ballatyne had a musical Edinburgh lilt. His tidy black eyebrows lifted in gentle enquiry and a small smile played about the corners of his mouth. Tobias gave him a hard look. There was good looking and too damned good looking, and this fellow bordered on the latter.

'No,' Tobias said rudely, and he stared at his whisky while Ballatyne left the room, then, when the door closed he stood and walked to the window, sitting down on the cushioned sill to watch for Thea's return. He saw rivals everywhere; that was his problem. He saw rivals even among the servants. This was the price he paid for the privilege of calling Thea his wife.

The ballroom glittered with diamonds; afterwards, when those who had been there relived the occasion moment by moment, the flash and blaze of precious stones remained in the memory, along with the music, the conversation, the food, the gowns. In the dancing flames of the candelabra and the steady glow of the chandeliers, arrows of diamond light darted constantly across the room like glorious, abundant fireflies. The debutantes were relatively modestly adorned with discreetly precious family jewels, but their mothers were quite weighed down, all of them rising to the challenge set by Clarissa, whom everyone knew would be wearing the Plymouth tiara. It was famous – had been famous, in fact, for decades – and was always rather resented. Garrard had made it in the 1840s for Ursula, the third duchess, and Archie, keen to avoid the disastrous consequences of a wife with a tiara-induced headache, had spent a small fortune having it adjusted to sit perfectly atop Clarissa's head. She wore it well: regally, in fact. And all around, the very finest ancestral stones vied for similar glory, and fell fractionally, crucially, short.

At dinner Isabella sparkled with conversation. She had sought a tutorial from Tobias a few days earlier. Sometimes, she had said, there were awkward silences. At another girl's dance one could blame the seating arrangements: tomorrow, though, she would only be able to blame herself.

'When in doubt, talk about ghosts,' he had said. 'Don't mention the weather or the food; never yet met the fellow who gives a damn. But hauntings, everyone likes.'

'Right,' Isabella had said, tempted to make notes. 'What about world affairs? Should I be mugging up on Home Rule or unrest in the Balkans?'

'Good God, no. The skill lies in being clever enough not to sound too clever,' Tobias said. 'Steer clear of politics, since you know nothing about it anyway, and it comes over as bluestocking. Motoring goes down well. Mug up on motors – six cylinder over four cylinder, Rolls-Royce over Daimler, you know the sort of thing. That should do it. Well, and sailing,' he added, remembering his yacht. 'It's not every debutante who has a boat named for her.'

'I wish I could have you on one side of me,' Isabella had said.

He had smiled, thinking how very glad he was to be out of it. 'Who do you have?'

'Matthew Peverill and a German chap, I think. No one knows much about him, but Continentals can bring a splash of colour, Mama says, and I think he's connected to the Hohenzollerns so . . .' she trailed off, and shrugged.

'That middle aitch is silent, darling,' Tobias said.

'Oh! Well, thank you. One less trap to fall into,' she said and then grimaced at a sudden new thought. 'Gosh, I do hope he doesn't resemble the kaiser.'

'The kaiser's not bad looking, apart from the moustache and the withered arm, and they're not hereditary.'

'Well anyway, the connection's rather tenuous, to be honest. He's a cousin of a cousin of Wilhelm, or some such. Mama's making the most of it, naturally. You'd think he was next in line, to listen to her.'

'And does he speak English?'

Isabella's face fell. 'Gosh,' she said. 'I should jolly well hope so. They all do, don't they? It's not as if anyone else speaks German.'

He did, of course, speak English. Very well, with just enough of an accent to single him out as interesting, but not so much that listening to him was a strain. His name was Ulrich von Hechingen, and he had an endearing habit of looking directly into Isabella's eyes when she spoke, as if there was nothing or no one quite so fascinating as she at this immense gathering. They didn't talk about ghosts, motorcars, or yachting, and yet their conversation was easy and lively. He was the oldest son of a Bavarian count – he didn't mention the kaiser and Isabella thought it vulgar to ask – but he described a Romanesque family castle on a rock, with turrets and towers, such as Rapunzel might have recognised. She told him about Netherwood Hall and made him laugh with stories about her childhood that she hadn't known were funny until she saw them again through his eyes. His dark blonde hair was Brilliantined into submission, but Isabella could see that it curled, or would curl, if allowed to. His eyes were navy blue, and between his two front teeth was a narrow gap, which, as imperfections went, was of no account; if anything, it rather added to his appeal. Isabella turned reluctantly to Matthew Peverill after the consommé and for the duration of the *filet de truite*, and worried all the while that Ulrich would forget her before the *mignon d'agneau*; each peal of laughter from Helena Lalham, next-door-but-one, prodded at her confidence like the sharp tip of a small knife. But then there he was, turning back to Isabella as she turned to him, and his smile radiated interested warmth.

'Your mother is watching us,' was what he said, without preamble. 'Do you suppose she approves?'

Isabella glanced across the room at Clarissa, who instantly looked away.

'Of you, or of me?' Isabella said.

'Of you *and* me.'

Isabella's pulse quickened and she felt suddenly short of breath. Now, when she must be coolly sophisticated, she found she had nothing to say and a juvenile blush was spreading upwards from her throat. Thea, she thought; in this situation, what would Thea say?

'Well, *I* approve of you, certainly,' Isabella said and smiled archly. She felt her heart fluttering like a trapped butterfly against the blue satin of her gown.

'And I of you.' Ulrich let his gaze stray from her eyes to her lips and held it there. Isabella, lightheaded, was grateful to be sitting down.

Later, the tables were whisked away and Ulrich claimed Isabella for the first dance and every alternate one afterwards. He slipped the card off her wrist and, leaning against the dove-grey panelling of the ballroom, wrote Herr von Hechingen again and again with the tiny silver pencil. She watched him, and found herself thinking that Isabella von Hechingen sounded very fine.

'Look at those two.'

This was Thea, who appeared at Tobias's shoulder as he stood at the open door of the ballroom, staring in with an expression of gloomy preoccupation. He turned at his wife's voice, but he didn't smile, because he was still feeling cross at her late appearance earlier this evening. Visiting was strictly limited, this much he knew; so why had she been gone for almost four hours, kissing him blithely on her return, the smell of cigarettes on her breath and a look in her eye of secrets withheld? She had gone to change, letting him stew, and now she was back in a loose black evening gown, beaded all over with jet. The beads shook and shimmered as she moved.

'Isabella, I mean. And the boy.' Thea pointed at them with a pale finger and smiled up at Tobias.

'Yes.'

'We could dance.'

He was silent, then said, 'Where were you?'

'When?' She knew what he meant, but felt disinclined to respond helpfully to his truculence: it disappointed her.

'After seeing Henry and before coming home.'

'Why Tobes, you're cross-examining me,' she said mildly. 'Poor Henry's still very vague, by the way. She'd forgotten all about Isabella's coming-out ball. Mind you, I think Isabella's forgotten all about Henrietta.' She nodded towards Isabella and Ulrich, who were dancing now, their faces flushed, their expressions intent. 'Isn't that a little close, for a minuet?'

Where Tobias would usually have laughed there was

another silence. She regarded him with a level gaze. The band in the ballroom moved on to a Viennese waltz and that, along with the rise and fall of chatter on and around the ballroom, gave Thea the feeling that she was standing in the wings of a stage.

'OK,' she said, finally, decisively. 'I went to see Henry and we talked in a desultory way about hospital food and the disagreeable warder who's detailed to watch her, even when she sleeps. Then I took a cab to Harley Street, to see my doctor. He subjected me to an examination, with extremely cold hands, and he told me that I was pregnant. Then I walked around and around Regent's Park, smoking quite publicly and unapologetically. Then I came home to you.'

He stared.

'You look such a dope, with your mouth hanging open,' she said.

'Did you just tell me I'm going to be a father? Is that what you said?'

'That would be the likely outcome of my pregnancy, yes.'

He leaned towards her, stooping so that his cool forehead rested on hers, and he closed his eyes, overwhelmed by the sweet completeness and simplicity of his relief and his joy.

Chapter 31

Alderman Simpson had appeared to accept with good grace Anna's refusal to stand for election to the council, yet he wore his quiet disappointment as openly and obviously as his chain of office. He managed to be everywhere. She had no recollection of ever bumping into him on previous visits to Ardington, but now his genial face, clouded by regret, seemed to loom at her wherever she went: the bank, the grocer's, the post office. He was following her, she told Amos; but Amos, who wanted her to stand too, had refused to smile and said the alderman was too busy with town matters to waste his time in such a way.

Still, whether or not the alderman was guilty of engineering these apparently chance encounters, again and again she saw him, and it was as if her own ubiquity about town was proof that, if she had an ounce of public spirit, she would put her name forward. It became embarrassing, and now and again Anna found herself wishing she were elsewhere. Still, she had absolutely intended to spend the whole summer in Ardington, so she could hardly be blamed when Clara, one of her two student artists, had telegraphed to say a family crisis was taking her home to Brighton for the foreseeable future and she must leave at once, even though the de Lisle job in Kent wasn't quite finished. William, Anna's second assistant, distracted by the demands made upon him by the Slade, would be hard-pressed to finish the job alone and on schedule, so Anna was needed to complete the final panel of the summer-house, and to recruit someone to fill Clara's shoes.

She would be alone in the London house for a whole week, and the shudder of pleasure she experienced at this prospect felt almost illicit. Amos had hidden his disappointment at her temporary departure, but she knew he wanted her with him. Maya and Miss Cargill were off on one of their educational jaunts, and that left Norah as Amos's sole companion; she would talk too much and burn the toast, and belt out Irish folksongs in her oddly flat voice which was somehow more melodic when she spoke than when she sang.

On the day she left, Anna had walked to the railway station, swinging her small leather bag and hoping the cheerful woman who had a cart on the corner of Gower Street would be there this evening with her pea soup and jellied eels. Then she had chided herself for looking forward to a London supper when Amos had been so evidently sad at her departure. He would be fine, of course; she had no worries on that score. In Ardington, he was famous: the people's champion returned from battle. They didn't know, in this corner of the kingdom, how little was achieved on the Labour benches, or how radical were the plans for the Liberal budget. It was always beneficial to Amos – to his morale – to revisit the scene of his triumph and live for a while among the men who'd voted him into Parliament. Always, when he returned to London from Ardington he felt a renewed vigour for the cause and a renewed faith in his party. Also, he was the New Mill Colliery cricket team's secret weapon these days. Tuesday and Thursday evenings, and sometimes all day Saturday, were spent in pursuit of the precise mastery of the line and length of a speeding cricket ball. He had volunteered Anna for the tea rota, which privileged position required that she make egg-and-cress sandwiches and iced buns for home matches. To date, she had been required to do this only once, and, with the tea prepared and laid out on a trestle table, she had sat on the pavilion steps and watched the match with a growing sense of despair as she failed utterly to make sense of the progress of play. It had seemed at once static and frantic, which she found unsettling. Amos's job was to try to hit the stumps, she realised, but that had been her only insight into the tactics of the game, which had taken hours to conclude and had ended, bewilderingly, in a draw, even though according to the board one team had scored more runs than the other. On the way home, on the train from Netherwood, she had said she thought it odd that two teams could tie when their scores weren't the same.

'We didn't tie, it was a draw,' Amos had said.

'Is there a difference?'

'I'll say,' he had replied, and while he explained the variety of possible outcomes of a cricket match, Anna had designed murals in her mind's eye, then dozed off.

She would miss her next turn on the tea rota, she had realised, as her train headed south towards Barnsley and beyond. She had smiled wickedly and wondered whose wife would step into the breach. None of them would find it the imposition that she had, she was sure. Outside, a gust of steam belched from the chimney and wrapped itself around the train, and for a moment the view was lost. Anna thought about the boilerman, wielding his shovel back and forth, feeding the hungry firebox with coal while she sat here in perfect comfort, in a carriage that was empty but for her, and warmed through by the sun. Its plush seats were the colour of port wine, and there were pleated curtains of the same, rich colour at the window, held back with brass clasps. Anna had cast an approving gaze around her, and wondered how she might occupy the carriage in such a way as to discourage anyone else from coming in. She spread her coat out on the opposite seat and brought her bag down from the luggage rack to put next to her, then she settled down again, stretched out her legs and allowed herself a few moments' admiration of her new boots – cream leather, soft as butter, better suited to London than Ardington – before delving into her bag for a notebook, in which she started a list of everything she must accomplish before returning to Yorkshire.

The following day, she met William at Charing Cross Station, and together they travelled to Kent. Lady Marcia de Lisle lived in a Jacobean manor house in the soft green countryside near Tunbridge Wells. By the recent standards of Anna's commissions this was a modest property, with only five acres of grounds surrounding a house with no pediments or porticoes, no colonnades or cupolas. It was unimposing in the best possible way, which is to say it was a house one could imagine oneself living in and growing to love. It was a pinkish colour, which gave it the permanent appearance of standing in the light of the setting sun. The windows were of mullioned stone and there were red tiles on the roof. Its most remarkable feature was a grave old door, carved four hundred years ago from Kentish oak and so heavy and wide that another, smaller door had been cut into it for the practical purpose of coming and going.

Anna only accepted commissions at places, and for people, she liked. This could be extremely awkward when, as sometimes happened, she walked away from a spluttering, titled lady of the house whose drawing room, or ballroom, or personality, fell short in some indefinable yet critical way. Marcia de Lisle had written to Anna in praise of her work at Houghton

Hall in Derbyshire, where she and Clara had painted a Mediterranean citrus grove on the long dining-room wall. The illusion was startling; lemons and oranges bright against the green gloss of abundant leaves, the fruit heavy and ripe on their bowing branches. So Anna had journeyed down to Tunbridge Wells to meet Marcia, who was dark-haired and olive-skinned, and who told Anna that she had seen the painted citrus grove and wept because it reminded her of Spain, and her childhood. Her husband was away all week, working for the Colonial Office, and she had too many evenings on her own thinking about the bustle of family life in Seville. She had shown Anna into the dining room, but Anna shook her head sadly; too dark, and anyway, she made it a rule not to duplicate work in the homes of other clients.

'Each piece is unique,' she had said. 'Houghton Hall, I'm afraid, get the lemons.'

They had walked together around the ground floor of Ashdown Manor, and then had toured the upstairs rooms, looking for a place to paint. Marcia had felt panic rising in her Andalusian breast, plus a certain confusion at the artist's scruples. Anna herself had been concerned that, lovely and personable though Lady de Lisle undoubtedly was, none of the rooms in her charming house quite lent themselves to the purpose. Then, from the window of an upper-floor dressing room, Anna had seen the summerhouse, a beautiful six-sided wooden building with a shingled roof and the mellow patina of great age. It seemed to be marooned in the centre of a pond, but in fact, when Marcia took her out there, Anna saw that there were two paths across the water, one on each side, made from duckboards hammered on to sturdy posts hidden in the weedy depths. The slatted wood appeared to float on the surface of the pond.

'Here we are,' Anna had said, as if it was hers, and Marcia was the guest. 'Isn't it perfect?'

And Marcia, who had realised almost as soon as they met that this idiosyncratic woman was beyond her influence, had said, 'I suppose it is, yes.'

Now, inside the summerhouse, Anna stood and turned, very slowly, to absorb the impact of their work. It began with a dawn mist and would end with a wash of silver moonlight, the phases of the day shown through a panoramic painting of the de Lisles' pretty garden, each of the six panels a continuation of the last, but each quite different in light and feeling. She was pleased. The panels, though entirely non-religious, gave the little building a holy air, like a tiny Renaissance chapel. Anna had designed it, drawn out the plans, sketched them on to the wooden walls and, with Clara, had got the project under way. But then she'd let Clara and William take over, so it was a while since she'd seen it. She looked at William, who stood beside her, waiting for her verdict.

'It's very fine,' Anna said. 'Really very fine.'

William, relieved, smiled at her. 'It is, isn't it? Classic English pastoral.'

'But it looks Italianate, too, doesn't it? Like the Sistine Chapel. This blue distemper, it's remarkable.'

She touched the panel, completed weeks ago, showing the garden under the hot, clear blue sky of a summer noon.

'Clara's,' William said loyally.

Anna looked at him sadly. 'We need a new Clara,' she said.

'I may have found one for you. She's better at life drawing than landscape, but that's what we need, I think.'

'Good boy. Come. We'll stop for tea.' She put her arm through his and led him out of the summerhouse and on to the duckboards. He was only five years younger than she was but

277

she treated him with a maternal air, to which he responded like a dutiful son. She patted his arm with her free hand and asked him who he had in mind, and he told her – Jennifer Hathersage, a third-year fine art student at the Slade, poor as a church mouse, rich in talent, easily the best of the women and possibly the best of the men – as they took a circuitous path back to the house where a small wing off the kitchen had been made available for their use.

They stayed one night and two days at Ashdown Manor, then Anna left William with the cleaning and finishing and returned to Bedford Square. Marcia de Lisle had clasped Anna's hands and breathed effusive thanks, promising to sing her praises far and wide. 'Not too far, not too wide,' Anna had said, alarmed. At this rate, she said to William, she would have to hire everyone at the Slade.

She let herself into the house, took off her coat and hat in the quiet front hall and hung them on the empty stand. It was odd, being here alone: the small noises – the tock of the grandfather clock, the clip of her heels on the tiles – were hollow-sounding and amplified. All the post that she hadn't had time to look at when she first got to London was heaped on the hall table, and there was a new batch on the floor. She picked it up and added it to the pile, which she carried through to the sitting room. There she sat in Amos's armchair, to see if she could discover why he was so attached to it. Herself, she would have everyone sit anywhere, just as she would as happily sleep on the right-hand side of the bed as the left. Amos, though, was a man of dogged habits, and he was encouraged in them by Maya, who liked to plump up his cushions and declare his chair ready whenever he walked in from work. It was a decent-enough wing chair, but nothing out of the ordinary, Anna decided. However, she stayed where she was and began to shuffle through the envelopes, looking for somewhere to begin. All the letters for Amos she collected in a separate pile to take with her back to Ardington. All those for Anna Sykes Interiors she placed on her lap, not yet in the mood to contemplate more work. And then she saw Eve's left-sloping handwriting, in blue ink, on an envelope scuffed and scarred by its long voyage from Jamaica, and she let everything else fall to the floor.

She tore at the seal with a pounding heart. For no very good reason she felt certain that the letter contained bad news, and she wondered if Daniel's concerns, irrational though they had seemed, had perhaps stolen into her own consciousness, so that where she had previously imagined Eve in an adventure lit with permanent sunshine, now some indefinable darkness played at the fringes of the picture.

'My dearest Anna, she read, 'Well, the Whittam is now the Eden Falls Hotel, I've learned how to make curry goat with rice and peas (though the peas are not peas, but kidney beans) and Angus is learning how to swim . . .'

Anna smiled, and breathed a long sigh of relief. She read on:

I wish you were here with us, in this remarkable place. Jamaica is so beautiful, Anna! The colours are so vivid, and the weather extreme. The midday heat hits you like the slam of air when you open the door of the top oven on the range. The rain, when it comes, soaks you as thoroughly as if you stood in a water butt under a downspout. The winds – I'm told – can lift a building off a hill, and carry it away through the skies. All being well, we'll be home before the hurricane season, because if a house can be swept off I'm fairly certain an Angus can be too! It's hard enough to keep an eye on him, without fretting about the wind whisking him away too.

Now Anna shifted in the chair, and curled her legs beneath her like a contented cat. She could hear Eve's voice, as clearly as if she were in the room.

At the hotel, it's all go. Silas isn't happy, because I've made him change the name to the Eden Falls Hotel, and he likes to see Whittam written on the things he owns. But with the help of the Jamaican staff I'm turning this place into a Jamaican hotel, rather than an English hotel in Jamaica. Heaven knows what our guests are going to make of it when the transformation is complete. Ruby – you'd like her; she's the cook here, and finally I can call her a friend – says we should ply them with rum from the moment they arrive, and I believe she may have a point. Or perhaps Ruby and I should have the rum, and then we shan't care what the guests think!

Ruby, thought Anna: who are you? She looked up from the letter, and tamped down a small flash of childish envy that Eve's adventure was being shared with a friend other than herself. She looked down at the letter again. There were three more pages of writing paper, and both sides of each were filled. She shivered with anticipated pleasure and gratitude, and then she dived back in.

Chapter 32

⧼⧽

The first guests to arrive at the Eden Falls Hotel had of course booked to stay at the Whittam, so they all had to be briefed by Eve in the charabanc on the way from the port. She had explained to them, brightly and with no suggestion of apology, that they were privileged to be on the brink of a new adventure at this English-owned hotel, which aimed to celebrate all things Jamaican. Their comfort would remain paramount, but many things would be unfamiliar. The staff, the food, the decor – all would reflect the vibrancy and colour of this tropical island.

'If the staff seem a little informal,' Eve had told them, 'it's only because it's their way. If you're looking for a starchy doorman, you'll be disappointed. If you snap your fingers at a waitress, she'll probably ignore you. But a smile and a "please" will get you everything you wish for. There's no formal English service at dinner because it's not t'Jamaican way. But I think – in fact, I know – that what you'll find at t'Eden Falls Hotel is something far more memorable, and entirely unique.'

Still, when they arrived and the guests stepped down from the running board of the bus, they looked about with trepidation, as if they'd been told there were savages with poison-tipped spears. There was something inherently and comfortably English about the name Whittam; something familiar and dependable and, after all, it was also the name on the liner that had carried them over the sea. Eden Falls, on the other hand . . . perhaps it alluded to man's expulsion from paradise, said one gentleman, quietly, to his wife, who blushed at the suggestion of sin.

But their qualms evaporated in the Jamaican sun and their inhibitions, met with exuberance, were quickly vanquished. Rather than an indifferent version of their own gracious homes, the Eden Falls Hotel presented them with something quite different. There was Scotty on the top terrace, in a clean shirt and shorts, playing the guests into the hotel with jangling riffs on his old banjo, accompanied by Wendell shaking a dried calabash filled with seeds. Jamaican punch came out on rattan trays, in glasses half filled with crushed ice. The cold of it, chased by the heady warmth of the rum, made people gasp and smile. Little plates of sweetmeats, unimaginably exotic to the English palate, were passed around the gathering: guava doasie, tamarind balls, coconut drops. They were roughly made, in the country style, and heaped in bowls in bountiful quantities, so that they begged to be tasted and sighed over, and tried again, then washed down with more head-cooling, belly-warming punch.

Laughter bubbled and brewed and floated out through the jalousies and into the hot, damp air. The staff, some of them new, drawn by the promise of a different ethos, still moved languidly about their business, but they smiled as they went and nodded at the guests; the atmosphere was of harmony, not mutiny. The Constables and the Gainsboroughs were still on the walls, and poppies and peonies still bowed their heads sullenly in the borders, but it was early days: one step at a time.

Eve watched from a distance. There were two new girls, Precious and Patience, circulating with icy pitchers of punch. They were summer leavers from Port Antonio School, the memory of scripture lessons still ringing in their ears, and they carried the rum punch reverently and poured it with infinite care. They wore name badges to discourage anyone from calling them 'girl'. Everyone had badges now, first names only, and it had become a game among some of the new wide-eyed guests, to lean tipsily forwards and read aloud what they saw.

'Rrrrrrruby,' said a tall, foppish man with a blond fringe, who peered at her badge through a monocle. 'Jolly good name for a gem of a woman, ha!' Pleased with his flattery, he rocked on his heels and looked around, hoping vaguely for praise.

'Yes, sir,' Ruby said. 'It is. Tamarind ball?'

It sounded a little like a threat, and he hastily declined. Ruby crossed the room to Eve and said, 'These badges encourage the gentlemen to take liberties.'

'Do they?'

'They encourage them to be too familiar.' Ruby puffed out her chest and gave a creditable imitation of her admirer: 'Jolly good name for a gem of a woman.'

'Oh, well,' Eve said, smiling. 'That sounds 'armless enough. Quite nice, even.'

'One thing can lead to another.'

'Ruby,' said Eve, 'I think you're looking for things to complain about.'

Ruby considered this, and thought it might be true. She had fallen into the habit of finding fault, and perhaps, in the absence of real grievances, she was inventing false ones. Already Eve had managed a miracle; there were callaloo fritters and jerk chicken on the menu of Silas Whittam's hotel. Callaloo fritters, jerk chicken, turtle stew, boiled crabs, curry goat, fried plantain . . . all the food of Ruby's childhood, cooked as her own mother had cooked it, in the duchy pot and over a flame, and even – this truly was remarkable – over a smouldering pit of pimento wood in the garden. The dining-room tables were decorated with small vases of poinciana and jacaranda flowers, and where there had once been starched white linen on the tables there were now humble tablecloths of printed cotton, bought for a song from Musgrave Market.

Ruby said, 'Perhaps so.' She studied Eve's face for a moment and said, 'You look weary.'

'I am,' Eve replied. 'I could lie down right now and sleep.'

'You should rest. I can manage tonight's dinner.'

Eve laughed. 'I should say you can. You could do it all blindfolded. You don't need me any more.'

Ruby regarded her, as if weighing things up. 'Need, perhaps not. But I do prefer it when you're in the kitchen.'

'Why, thank you.'

'You're most welcome.'

They both laughed, but Eve had blue shadows under her eyes and Ruby felt a twist of concern. Life at the hotel had taken a sharp turn for the better, but they'd been run ragged to achieve it. When the new name went up, each letter picked out in green on a board painted as blue as the Caribbean Sea, Ruby had felt a rush of fierce gratitude to Eve that she hadn't expressed, except in her smile. But she knew what they owed her, for showing Silas Whittam how to honour the island he seemed to think he owned. It struck Ruby that Eve would be going, perhaps sooner than planned. You don't need me any more, she'd said, and Ruby found it pained her to think of Eve and Angus gone from Jamaica.

'But still plenty to do,' she said now, thinking only of herself and feeling immediately guilty.

'Oh aye, more than enough,' Eve said gamely, but she pressed her left temple and closed her eyes on what she knew were the beginnings of a pounding headache.

'I have feverfew in the larder,' Ruby said, 'and lemongrass

tea. Come.' She put an arm around Eve's shoulder and steered her towards the kitchen stairs. Eve allowed herself to be led. Really, she was done in, she thought; half past two in the afternoon and all she longed for was to sink into sleep.

Silas made himself scarce, on the pretext that this was Eve's show and so she should be allowed to bask in the glory. Really, though, he was feeling sour and a little mutinous, like a pirate captain who found his crew making a better fist of the ship's business than he had. He felt detached, surplus to requirements, usurped by his sister in status and acumen, and bested, entirely, in the battle to win the cooperation of the Jamaican staff. To avoid having to examine these uncomfortable feelings he drove to Port Antonio, and, alone at a bar in a dusty street off the market place, steadily drank himself into a simpler state of mind.

The problem was, he explained to himself with rum-induced insight, Evie had overstepped the brief. What he had wanted, what he had brought her here for, was to make the hotel work on his terms. The Whittam Hotel – a fine name, if ever there was one – was meant to be a gracious home from home in the tropics for visitors from England. Embraced by the familiar, they were supposed to sink gratefully into the ease and comfort of an English country house. They were not intended to be picking the bones out of red snappers with their fingers and trying to make themselves heard above Scotty's island music.

He banged his tumbler twice, sharply, on the bar, and held it out to the barman, who looked at him with distaste but took the glass and refilled it with rum. He knew Silas well: a dogheart who didn't need the help of liquor to turn nasty. But Silas took the glass without looking up and kept his mouth shut, except to pour more rum down his throat. When he slid down from the bar stool it was almost six o'clock; he'd been drinking since two. He steadied himself before setting off towards the door, which, when he reached it, seemed to shift each time he went for the handle, sliding from left to right, eluding him. The barman watched, coolly amused. Silas, with a grunt of concentrated exertion, lunged again and this time hit the mark, thrusting open the door and exiting the shadowy interior sideways and in a rush, as if he'd just been thrown out.

The light, after four hours in comforting gloom, was brutal. He screwed up his eyes against it and cast about for his car, the whereabouts of which he had forgotten. But it was close, just a short way up the street, and he weaved towards it gratefully and clambered in with a sigh of profound relief. For a few moments he sat there, holding the steering wheel and puzzling over his lack of progress, until a passing man said, ''im can't move till 'im cranked, mon.' Silas turned his head, which was unaccountably heavy, and slowly focused on the man, who spoke again, but this time it was to another passer-by, a woman, who laughed, and stood by the car, preparing to be entertained.

'You wan' me crank de 'andle?' the man said, and his voice, to Silas, seemed to be coming through a conch. It swelled and echoed, like a voice in a dream.

'You wan' me crank de 'andle?' he said again, only louder. The woman laughed once more and looked about her, encouraging others to stop and watch the show.

'It Mr Mention, from de Whittam,' someone said. A chicken, one of a small flock free ranging in the dirt, flapped up and sat experimentally on the bonnet of the car. It eyed Silas beadily, without fear, and a goat, tethered to a post, watched him with mean yellow eyes. This, thought Silas through the fug of rum, was the real Jamaica: primitive and bestial, and too damned hot. He took off his hat and flapped it at the chicken, which merely settled into a more comfortable squat on the sun-warmed metal.

The man, the first one, gave up conversation and instead mimed an elaborate winding motion, which triggered a memory in Silas, so that his face opened up with understanding and he nodded with precision. Someone said, 'Leave 'im to sweat,' and the woman chuckled and said, ''im fool-fool Englishman, too full a rum to drive,' but the man only rolled his eyes and, walking to the front of the motorcar, grasped the handle. With two easy turns he sparked the engine into life. The roosting chicken threw itself off, an indignant ball of feathers, and everyone took a step back for safety then watched, pityingly, as the Ford Model K lurched into motion, weaving out of the market place, scattering dust and chickens and leaving in its wake a feeling of general disdain at the folly of the bubu who couldn't hold his drink.

In his sozzled wisdom, Silas decided to call in at the hotel and so drove there pell-mell in first gear, the six-cylinder engine screaming in protest. At the gate he brought the vehicle to a halt by stalling, and swung out his legs with the theatrical flamboyance of the drunkard trying to demonstrate his sobriety. He plunged through the gate, stopping first at the new sign to shake his head sadly at the incontrovertible evidence of the name change, then threaded his way up the terraced path to the colonnaded entrance, where the doors were flung open to admit the breeze that blew in warm, comfortable gusts from the sea.

In the foyer he stood and observed from a safe distance what appeared to be a party in the bar. The place was hopping with people and music. Was someone drumming? He peered cautiously round the corner and saw Maxwell rapping out a beat with his hands on the wooden bar in time to the music of a small ensemble, while Scotty performed a loose-limbed dance and crooned, *'I got de blues, I beg to be excuse, dat why I refuse, I feelin' all confuse.'* There was general tipsy laughter, and some of the English guests were dancing too, copying Scotty's rangy shimmy, picking up the words to his song, which didn't, after all, deviate from those same four lines.

Silas shrank back, unseen. He felt out of place here, and this was disconcerting as it was his hotel, built on his land, with his money. The injustice of this made his mind turn to Eve, the architect of this new incarnation. There was no sign of her in the jamboree next door. Or Seth, for that matter. This aggravated him; he cupped his hands at his mouth and twice bellowed 'Seth!' in a manner that, had he been sober, would have appalled him in any other man. The music was loud, but not so loud that Silas couldn't be heard. An uncertainty crept into the merry-making, as people looked around for the source of the uncouth interruption.

'I say,' someone said. 'Isn't that the owner, three sheets to the wind?'

There was a small outbreak of hilarity and Silas, with only the scantest idea of the impression he was making, stood his ground, his feet planted apart on the parquet floor of the foyer; he seemed to be swaying gently in the evening breeze.

'Uncle Silas!'

Here was Seth, bounding down the staircase, two steps at a time, in the natty linen suit paid for from the profits of Whittam & Co. He looked brisk and capable, and Silas regarded him through narrowed eyes. Seth, bright and friendly, said, 'I wondered where you'd got to. Are you all right?'

But he patently was not. His eyes were glassy and his mouth moved silently, as if he were practising speech before properly attempting it. In the bar the music had stopped, and while some of the guests were milling about with drinks, taking the air on the terrace, others were looking at Silas with knowing smiles, as if to say, there's a fellow about to make an ass of himself. Silas turned away from Seth, moving his head in that steady, over-cautious manner of the pie-eyed, until he faced the onlookers.

'Yond Cassius has a lean and hungry look,' he slurred, pointing an accusatory finger at Seth. 'He thinks too much; such men are dangerous.' Then he executed a sweeping bow, which caused a rush of blood to his head, and proved too much. He fell to the floor in stages: first, all fours; next, hands and knees; finally, flat out, face down.

'God damn it!' he said, speaking into the parquet with a spirit that belied his helplessness. 'God damn it all to hell!'

There was a ripple of applause and someone called, 'Encore!' Seth, who would have liked the floor to open up and swallow him whole, took his uncle in an underarm grip and dragged him into the office and out of sight.

Chapter 33

Silas woke up with a fierce, hard pressure behind his eyes and a mouth as rough as stone. He was full length on the leather couch in his office, his shoes on the floor beside him. He had no idea how he had got here, although he did remember the car ride, and a chicken. He eased himself up on one shoulder and the room ebbed and flowed before him, so he put himself back again, gingerly. The carriage clock on his desk began to chime, and he counted the strokes: ten o'clock. He wondered, was it morning, or night?

An hour passed, and another. Finally, a searing thirst proved stronger than the desire to quietly die, and he found the courage to move in small, careful increments towards the door and across the foyer. It was past midnight now, but there was still the murmur of conversation coming from the bar, so Silas headed instead for the dining room and the door at its far end, which led down the casement stairs to the kitchen. He had expected darkness, but a yellow glow seeped through the sides of the closed door, lighting his way, and when he pushed open the door Ruby Donaldson was sitting at the table. There was a deep, warm smell of baking bread; on the dresser behind her eight loaves had been left in tins to rise and prove. On a folded rug, on the floor by the stove, Roscoe lay like a comfortable puppy, sound asleep. Silas stared at the scene; there was something unutterably reassuring about it. The mother, the child, the halo of light from a lamp on the table, the warmth; like a stranger to comfort, Silas stared, drinking it in.

Ruby had expected to see Seth, not Silas, but she hid her dismay behind a neutral expression and waited for him to speak.

'Ruby,' he said, and his voice was almost humble.

'Yes?'

'Why are you here? It's night time.' His tongue felt fat and dry in his mouth, and he went to the sink and drew a glass of water. He was behind her now, and she felt the habitual fear that he might reach for her when she wasn't looking. Still, though, she didn't turn around, so he couldn't see her face when she said, 'Your sister has a fever.'

This startled him.

'What sort of fever?' he said stupidly.

'The usual kind.' Her voice was cold, but then she seemed to relent and added, 'Her temperature's up and she says her limbs are heavy. She's sleeping now. I said I'd stay.'

He came around the table and sat down, opposite her. He noticed, now, that she wasn't only sitting at the table, but also doing some mending. She had a grey sock stretched over a darning mushroom, and the long needle with its thread was poised in her hand. Roscoe's school sock, Silas thought. When had he last given her money for the boy's clothing? He didn't ask her this, but said, 'What do you think it is, then?'

'She might be over-tired,' Ruby said, half-heartedly.

'I doubt that. She's a Yorkshirewoman.'

Ruby had her eyes down, avoiding his gaze. She wanted him gone. The room was no longer safe with him in it, because the version of Silas who sat before her now was not to be trusted. She knew this better than anyone.

'God, my head hurts,' Silas said. He let it drop, with his forehead resting on the table. On the floor, Roscoe stirred and whimpered, but he didn't wake, only turned so that his back was pressed against the lower part of the stove. Ruby stood and went to him, moving him gently away from the heat, and when she turned again Silas had turned his head on the table, and from this curious position was looking at her with a crooked half-smile, as if he knew everything about her, and one of the things he knew was this: she was his, if he wished it.

'She may have yellow fever,' Ruby said, partly to shock him but also because she feared it could be true. She had helped Eve into bed, when it was still just four o'clock in the afternoon, and her skin was hot over her whole body, burning up, bringing an unnatural flush to her face and neck. Eve had complained of aches deep in her bones and Ruby had given her fever-grass tea to bring out the perspiration, then covered her with a cool sheet. Eve, who had forgotten what it was to be sick, had looked at her with wild eyes. Ruby had thought she was afraid of the sickness, but really Eve had been afraid because she had realised, at last, how far away from home she was, and how very badly she wanted to be back there.

Silas sat up and said, 'She can't have yellow fever.'

'Oh, really. Why is that?' Ruby said.

He stared, having no good answer.

'I've seen yellow fever,' Ruby went on. 'Have you?'

His mouth hardened into a cruel line. 'I expect you've seen all manner of ailments, yes, raised as you were in the gutter.'

There, thought Ruby: there he is, the real Silas Whittam. She swallowed and moved towards him, to show him she wasn't afraid.

'I was raised in a poor home, but a loving one,' she said. 'I didn't live in squalor though, as you did in Grangely.'

Her words cut like a blade; he could have howled with rage. She saw this and took pleasure from it. That Eve had discussed their childhood with Ruby Donaldson was a kind of treachery, in his view. Silas saw their impoverished childhood as a shameful stain on their reputation; Grangely was their secret, to be acknowleged only privately and to be buried so far beneath their success that even they might begin to believe it no longer existed. There was no honour in triumphing through adversity; to the world, he wished to appear invulnerable, invincible, a man of substance but a man without a past.

Without compassion, Ruby said, 'Your mother died from typhus – Eve told me. And your father, who was a drunk, hanged himself rather than share your burden.'

Through clenched teeth Silas said, 'Shut your filthy mouth.'

'Filthy mouth? You considered it fit to kiss, once upon a time. You considered my mouth beautiful, as I recall. I tasted of vanilla, didn't I?'

Rarely had Ruby felt so powerful; she hadn't realised that Eve had given her such a weapon. She rose above him like the wrathful Nemesis, calling him to account for his excessive pride, his undeserved good fortune, his absence of humanity. But he met her hot, red anger with his own, and he stood and stalked round the table so that she no longer looked down on him, but up.

'You were nothing, nothing at all, when I met you,' he said, and his mouth was twisted with spite. 'I raised you to this, and I can return you to the gutter whenever I wish.'

'You cannot. Once, perhaps. Not now.'

'I can take him,' Silas said, indicating Roscoe with a contemptuous toss of his head. 'I can take him with me, back to England. Perhaps I shall.'

Ruby was unbowed. 'You took my innocence. You will not, now, take my son.'

'Our son. *My* son.'

'The law would not allow it.'

293

He laughed, scorning her. 'Really? I wonder where an English court might judge his best interests to lie? With you, barefoot in the Jamaican dirt, or with me, in a fine house in Bristol?'

Now Ruby began to feel afraid. The madness had gone from Silas's voice and he spoke calmly, as if he were merely presenting a hypothesis, not threatening to rend her small world. In his cool stillness she sensed true danger.

'You have no love for him,' she said, her voice low with emotion. 'Whereas I love him more than life.'

'Actually, I find I'm almost fond of the little fellow. As he grows I begin to see myself in him.'

She struck him, fast and furious like a cobra, and her hand left its imprint on his cheek. He touched it tenderly with his fingertips, and smiled at her.

'There is nothing of you in my beautiful boy,' Ruby said, and her voice shook with contained anguish because she knew this wasn't true.

'Ruby?'

Eve stood at the open door to the kitchen, supporting herself on the frame. Her face was ghastly pale, and her hair was wet, plastered to her face and neck. In her nightdress, in this condition, she looked as if she'd risen from the grave. Ruby and Silas stared at her, she in horror, and he with a sort of savage amusement. Briefly, Ruby clutched at the hope that Eve hadn't overheard their exchange, but it was a fleeting and insubstantial thought, because her expression dispelled all possible doubt.

Silas left the kitchen, with a sideways glance at his sister.

'I'll be in the office,' he said, but she didn't reply. He saw her glittering eyes, but thought that Ruby had almost certainly exaggerated the seriousness of Eve's fever. It would pass by daybreak, more than likely. Now, Ruby would doubtless spill the beans, which was perhaps just as well and saved him the trouble. Before the door closed he turned to Ruby and winked. 'Don't keep her up too long,' he said, and she returned his words with a silent stare.

'Go on,' Eve said.

'It can wait,' Ruby said, taking in her friend's pallor and the way she sat heavily in the chair, as if dragged down by weights.

'It can't. It's waited too long already.'

So Ruby told her, in a strange, detached style, as if she was recounting a tale of someone other than herself, and Eve didn't interrupt, only listened.

'The old plantation at Sugar Hill – the great house, the fields, the sugar mill and boiling house – had been bought outright by a young Englishman whose steamships had become a regular sight at the Port Antonio dock. He had no interest in sugar, and the instant the estate was his, he employed local men to hack down and tear up the old crop, and to till and feed the soil that, over the decades, had been thinned and depleted. The cane had grown high and wild, and it didn't give up its ground without a fight; it stabbed at the men's hands and arms, cutting into their flesh, and its deep roots clung tenaciously to their place in the baked earth.

'Silas Whittam, the new master of the estate, was an impatient man, and he ordered the men to torch the crop. They hesitated, knowing – as he did not – how fire in Jamaica could rush like floodwater across the island's fields and forests, ceasing its destruction only when it reached the sea. Their foreman, a thoughtful man named Roscoe Donaldson, stepped forwards to speak, and advised the hot-headed young master to wait for the rains, which would soon arrive, and would help contain and control the power of the blaze. Silas Whittam roared with contempt at their lily-livered concerns, and he pulled, from the crowd of women looking on, a young girl in a white slip, with bare feet and her hair falling to her shoulders in a mass of narrow braids. Roscoe Donaldson flinched and protested, for this was his only daughter, Ruby, but Silas only laughed because he intended her no harm. He smiled at the girl, who regarded him solemnly with her almond eyes, and he handed her a roughly made torch of wood and cloth. She held it at arm's length, and he struck a match and lit it, then pushed her gently forwards to the edge of the cane fields.

'She crouched, and held the burning ball of cloth against a long, dry stem, and at once the fire caught hold and a lizard's tongue of orange flame licked upwards, dancing madly along and across, until another, then another was alight. In seconds, the blaze was too hot to bear and everyone stepped back, mesmerised by its power. Silas Whittam and Ruby Donaldson, architects of this immense destruction, looked at each other with shining faces, and they laughed. He placed a hand on her shoulder and together they watched the crops burn. Occasionally she sneaked a look up at him, because to her he seemed as thrilling and exhilarating as the fire itself, and it felt like a privilege to be by his side.

'Time passed. The banana plants grew and thrived, and Ruby and her mother, with a hundred other women, carried the fruit every day in loaded cottas to the Rio Grande. She rarely saw Silas Whittam, although when she did he would smile at her and show her that he remembered what they'd done together. He had silky brown hair that she longed to touch, and pale, refined skin. His nose was narrower than hers, and his lips thinner. She was fourteen, and her mother called her beautiful, but Ruby thought him more beautiful than anyone she had ever seen, and she would fall into a silent fury when the other pickers called him "bakra" and blamed him for their aching backs and limbs. Sometimes, he gave her books to read, or a peeled orange, and once, in the heavy, red light of the evening, he had sat her by him on the steps of his porch and given her rum punch – just a sip, he had said, for now – and talked to her about England. It was companionable, cosy, and it seemed, to Ruby, to hint at a shared future. This was why, when he kissed her and slid his hand inside her blouse, she allowed it, and shivered with pleasure at his touch.'

Ruby stopped talking. She looked at Eve's ashen face, watching her across the table. Her eyes were wild and damp with fever.

'You must go back to bed,' Ruby said. 'I'll prepare you a herbal tea and help you upstairs.'

She stood, but Eve said, 'And now you 'ate him,' and her sickness, or the shock, made her voice shake. 'Did 'e force you, in t'end?'

Ruby shook her head.

'I was willing. I loved him. I thought he loved me.'

'You were just a child.'

'I was fourteen.'

'A child.'

'There were younger girls than I with a child on their hip, but yes, I was a great deal younger than him.'

'And was it just once?'

Ruby shook her head.

''ow many times?'

Ruby shrugged. 'A few,' she said, feeling a natural defensiveness rise in her breast, although it was all such a long time ago. 'I went to him after dark and we would lie together in his bed. I loved him,' she said again. 'And then, one evening, I had to tell him that I was expecting his child.'

'And?'

'And he changed. Everything changed. He suddenly

couldn't bear the sight of me. He denied that he was the father. He said it could be any man from the Port Antonio docks to the Blue Mountains.' There were tears in her eyes, and she wiped them away angrily.

'What did you do?'

'I was hardly faced with a multitude of choices. There was an obeah woman on the plantation and my mammy wanted her to . . .' Ruby hesitated, searching for an acceptable word '. . . intervene. But I had felt the baby move, and I knew I could love this child because it would be mine alone.' She glanced at her son. 'And it was Roscoe,' she said.

Now they both looked at the sleeping boy, as if to confirm the reality of him. Eve shivered, though her face was damp and her nightdress clung to her skin.

'Please,' Ruby said. 'Let me take you back upstairs.'

'I can go alone,' Eve said. She stood, but she didn't leave. Instead, she said, 'Yet 'ere you are, working for 'im when I should think you can hardly bear to look at 'im.'

'It was an agreement,' Ruby said. 'I had no choice but to accept the terms.'

'What sort of agreement?'

'That I preserve the secret, if your brother supported us financially. My daddy thought him the very devil, but he was not wicked through and through. He gives me money sometimes, for Roscoe, and he employs me here. But no one knows the truth, except, now, you.'

'And Roscoe? Does 'e ask?'

'Not yet. One day he will, and I shall tell him his father was a good man who loved us both.'

'Ruby, I—'

Ruby held up a hand. 'It can all wait. Go to bed. I'll bring you feverfew, when the water's boiled.'

Eve, finally, did as she was bid, moving like a wraith through the shadows of the hotel. A light was on in Silas's office and his door was open, but she walked past without even a glance. He saw her slip soundlessly by, and he was shocked; he had thought – in fact, he had been sure – that she would hear the tale and then come to him in sympathy.

Chapter 34

They took Henrietta from hospital to Holloway in a Black Maria drawn by a pair of old dray horses. There was a narrow slit in the side of her locked compartment, and through this Henrietta watched the outside world where dreary people in drab clothes went about their desultory business: freedom was wasted on them, she thought. If she were free she would wear a scarlet hat and a magenta coat, and she would run everywhere and always be happy. Then she thought, Imprisonment is making me foolish.

She closed her eyes, to shut out the spectacle of unworthy, liberated people, and she didn't open them again until the horses lumbered to a halt in the prison yard. Her door was unlocked and she came unsteadily down the metal steps of the carriage on to the cobbles. Her hands were cuffed, tighter than was necessary, and it was raining: fine, sharp, soaking rain that suited her mood. A silent wardress led her through the yard and Henrietta let her mind drift north to Netherwood Hall and to the comforting image of Parkinson. She pictured the butler, erect and immaculate, descending the steps of the house in order to receive her from the Daimler, his dear, familiar face a study in restrained joy at her arrival, and she was consumed by a sudden longing to see him.

She hung her head and followed where she was led, only dimly aware of the sounds around her, and the other prisoners in front and behind. She knew the drill, and was at least spared the intimate physical examination she had previously endured. A roll of bedding was pushed into her arms, along with a brick of yellow soap wrapped in a fold of paper. The smells of Holloway Prison, she imagined, would stay with her for ever, and one of them would be carbolic acid. She thought about the late summer fragrances of lavender and pot pourris, and the stillroom in Yorkshire where rose petals were turned into eastern-scented jellies, and she allowed fat tears of self-pity to roll down her cheeks.

The wardress, behind her now, shoved Henrietta in the small of the back and moved her along through a series of barred doors – unlocking them, locking them again, each time with a different key – toward the iron staircase and the tiered landings. Her face wore an expression of grim contempt and Henrietta, passive and obedient, thought this only right. For a while, when all this began, she had felt like a warrior, a Boadicea for the modern age. But essentially, she thought now, she was a spoilt child who had wandered too far from home.

Henrietta lay on the thin mattress of her bunk and counted the squares in the grille at her window. There would be seventy, she knew this already. It was a different cell from her previous one, on a different landing in a vast prison, but there was a symmetry to the place that could almost be comforting.

She was alone, although there was a second bunk below hers and she knew it might be filled at any time. Outside the iron door of her cell prison life seethed and swelled and she knew that solitude, in this relentless cavern of noise, was to be cherished while it lasted. She thought about the strangeness of the past days and how, when she had opened her eyes in the hospital bed, she had remembered nothing of how or why she got there. Her noble cause, her great reforming zeal had dimmed and dissipated, like the lights from a firework that explode into the sky and seconds later are gone, forgotten. Later, of course, she had pieced together the sequence of events, remembering – with Toby's help – the brick, the remand, the court case, the sentence, the fall. She remembered, too, the fury she had felt when she ran down Whitehall to Downing Street, and the white heat of moral outrage that sent the brick flying through the fanlight of Number Ten. But she didn't quite feel it now, she found. Votes for women seemed less imperative than the immediate problem of her extended incarceration, which had filled Henrietta with a kind of hollow, debilitating despair.

The blanket she lay on was grey and coarse; it prickled her skin even through her clothing. She shifted position to relieve the irritation, though it barely helped, and the springs beneath the thin mattress creaked and complained, which only served to remind her how difficult it would be to sleep. She thought she could not endure another night here, and the certain knowledge that she must gave her, at last, a small spark of resistance, enough to lift her just far enough out of her passive state to consider her options, which she decided were four: escape, suicide, endurance or protest. The first two she ruled out immediately, having no wish either to live life as a fugitive or to cease living life at all. The third she rejected too, because although it was, strictly speaking, possible, it was also unthinkable. That decided, she concentrated her mind on the fourth and final option, and found it a simple matter, after all, to settle on a plan.

That evening, when dinner arrived from the Ritz,

Henrietta refused to eat it. There was a duck breast with crisp, salty skin and a puree of parsnip, but she let it congeal on the plate in front of her, then sat silently while the women next to her and opposite took turns with their forks, devouring Henrietta's superior food along with their own stewed beef shin. They were welcome to it. She took no water either, and the emptiness she felt by lights out had an ascetic, religious quality that gave her renewed purpose and inner strength. The following day she returned untouched her porridge and her tin mug of tea, and at lunchtime she watched her potato soup grow cold without once picking up the spoon. At this point a canteen warder realised what was going on and alerted the prison governor to the fact that they had a refuser on their hands. By mid-afternoon the entire prison population seemed to know that Lady Henrietta Hoyland had decided to neither eat nor drink until she was released.

Ulrich had been invited for supper with his aunt. It was supper, not dinner, because they were to eat late, following *Tristan und Isolde* at the Royal Opera House. Liese von Hechingen, the aunt, had once met Richard Wagner on a holiday in Sicily, and this had made her an authority on the man and his music.

'He was writing *Parsifal*, you know,' she said imperiously. 'As I recall, he worked better in the mornings than the afternoon, and he told me Palermo was just far enough away not to be a distraction to him.'

A footman slid up to the table, offering a large dish of softly scrambled eggs. Aunt Liese took half of the contents without ceasing her flow.

'It must have been the fifties, I suppose,' she said. 'Late fifties. But he completed it much, much later. Such a brilliant man. He called it not an opera but *ein Buhnenweihfestspiel.* Uli, *was ist das in Englisch?*'

Ulrich said, 'It really doesn't matter, Aunt Liese,' but he smiled at her, so that his rebuff wasn't too unkind and Isabella saw yet another reason to love him.

Peregrine, Isabella's stepbrother, took what was left of the scrambled eggs and said, 'Is that what we heard tonight, then? Parsi-what-not?'

Isabella would have liked to say, loudly, that she was unrelated to the very stupid son of the duke, but instead she said, 'No, Perry. We saw *Tristan und Isolde.*'

'Almost five hours of it,' Clarissa said meaningfully.

'It was a long time to sit,' Ulrich said, although he had held Isabella's hand in the dark and she had stroked his skin with her thumb, so the duration of the opera had not seemed excessive to either of them. Everyone waited, quietly, for the footman to return with a replenished dish, and when he did, Ulrich took a modest portion for himself. There was a small silver pot of beluga caviar beside his plate, with the tiniest silver spoon imaginable. He dotted his plate, admiring the startling contrast of the black glistening against the creamy yellow, then furtively licked the spoon and found, when he looked up, that Isabella's mother was watching him closely. The duchess was an exacting woman, he had discovered: keen to identify one's shortcomings. He tried to disarm her with a smile but she only inclined her head gravely, as if to say the jury was still out, the verdict as yet unknown.

'So, our renegade relation is back in the news.'

This was Peregrine, who often spoke with his mouth full and did so now. Of all his dreadful characteristics, thought Isabella, this was surely the worst. She glared at him and he blinked back. Amandine, Peregrine's wife, said, 'Renegade relation,' and tittered.

'What's that you say, Perry?' barked the duke. Clarissa

had banned his ear trumpet from the table, so Archie always missed a good deal of what was said.

'Henrietta, Papa,' Peregrine said, cupping his hands to make a megaphone. 'Back in the newspaper. Starving herself to death in the clink.'

Isabella and Clarissa exchanged a look of perfect sympathy and united distaste. They knew about this latest development; Tobias had been to see them, bearing the news with remarkable sangfroid. The authorities wouldn't be prepared to watch her waste away, so she'd soon be back home, he had said. In that case, Clarissa had murmured, why didn't all prisoners refuse their food all the time? Tobias hadn't known how to answer so he had said nothing, only drummed his fingers on the arm of the couch and looked thoughtful. That was this morning, when Henrietta was already a day and a half into her fast. Clarissa, who herself subsisted on less food than a sparrow, was concerned not so much for her daughter's health as for her increasingly degraded reputation. Peregrine's crowing pronouncement was, she believed, one more nail in the coffin of Henrietta's future prospects.

'Good Lord!' Archie shouted. 'Why would the gel do that?'

Peregrine, full of eggs and toasted brioche, sat back in his chair and laced his fingers across the swollen expanse of his stomach. 'It's what these suffragettes do, Papa,' he shouted. 'Ups the ante, y'see. Martyrs to the cause.'

'I believe Henry just wants to come home,' said Isabella. 'Toby says she's not angry any more, just desperately unhappy.'

'Well, put it how you will, she's a damned embarrassment to the family and I'm jolly glad she's not a Partington,' Perry said. Amandine swelled with wifely pride and Isabella, who had always found it easy to cry, fought the onset of tears because Peregrine was not worthy. 'I'm jolly glad she's not a Partington too,' she said passionately, driven not so much by loyalty to Henrietta as loathing for Peregrine. 'Because then you'd be my actual brother, and that would be more embarrassing than anything Henrietta has done.'

Ulrich laughed. Peregrine stood up.

'Outrageous,' he said. 'I will not be insulted at my father's table.'

Clarissa could not abide bad manners, whatever provocation may have preceded them. 'Please sit down, Peregrine,' she said evenly. 'Isabella, you must apologise at once.'

Isabella held her tongue. She looked at Ulrich, who offered a smile of warm encouragement and then spoke calmly into the hostile silence.

'From what I understand, those campaigners for women's suffrage who have broken the law are political prisoners and deserve to be treated differently – more respectfully, one might say – from common criminals. Lady Henrietta has been treated abysmally by the judicial system, and I think she is quite justified in taking this latest course of action. If she were my sister, I should be proud.'

Ulrich had never met Henrietta, and had only a scant understanding of the details – it was not something Isabella wished to discuss – but he spoke with the authority of a barrister, although he was no such thing. Somehow, he had bridged the chasm that had opened between Clarissa's demand for an apology and Isabella's unspoken yet evident refusal to oblige; he had fogged the issue, and with great éclat. Isabella pressed a hand against her heart, for she thought it might burst. That she deeply resented her older sister's attention-hogging conduct was, for now, neither here nor there. Ulrich had managed to confer nobility upon Henrietta's actions, and by so doing had got Isabella off the hook. She wondered if anyone had ever loved another human being so entirely as she loved Ulrich von Hechingen.

Peregrine, purple faced, had nevertheless reclaimed his seat. The wrong done to him had not been righted; his indignant fury had not been assuaged. However, a platter of crêpes Suzette had been carried into the dining room, and their buttery fragrance immediately distracted him from his ire.

Aunt Liese clapped her hands gleefully and turned to Clarissa with eyes lit by a childlike excitement. 'Well!' she said. 'I'm sure even your naughty daughter would be tempted by these.'

It was such a spectacularly silly thing to say. Clarissa, from ingrained politeness, gave the older lady a gracious smile, but she was much displeased. She remained to be convinced that this family was entirely suitable. In the pages of the *Almanach de Gotha* she had followed the labyrinthine roots and branches of the German imperial family to its further-flung scions, and while the connection with the von Hechingens could certainly be verified, it was tenuous indeed. No, she thought now; Isabella's future is far from settled. She enjoyed a frisson of satisfaction that this might very well be the last time the Prussians dined with the Plymouths.

'Now then young man,' Archie bellowed in the direction of Ulrich. 'Tell me, do you ride? We have a couple of absolute top-notch hacks in our stables, right here in London. Take one or other of 'em out for a canter any time you like, eh?'

He smiled broadly at his own largesse. His deafness inured him to every nuance at the dining table, and in particular chilly disapproval. This was his misfortune. Unbeknownst to Archie, his wife's grievances against him were stacking up into teetering piles, like the unpaid bills of a bankrupt tradesman.

On her third day of hunger strike, Henrietta was moved once again from prison to a locked single room in the Highgate Hill Infirmary. There, her arms were tied to the bedposts and a nurse pinched her nose closed while another pushed the sloppy constituents of cottage pie into her gasping, open mouth. Henrietta closed her eyes and her mind, and swallowed nothing. After fifteen minutes of pitched battle the nurses left her to stew in her own juice, her face and chest covered in mince and mash, her wrists still tied painfully tightly to the iron bars of the bedstead.

She felt lightheaded with victory.

Chapter 35

J ennifer Hathersage might be poor, thought Anna, but she shared no other characteristics with a church mouse. She was confident and garrulous, and their meeting in the Antique Room at the Slade was constantly interrupted by cheerful greetings from, or merry conversations with, a stream of other students, both male and female. She was tall and altogether bony, with wrists that jutted out from the sleeves of her smock and a long, rather sharp nose. She wasn't remotely attractive in any conventional sense – or any sense at all, in fact – but by sheer force of personality she seemed to have overcome her obvious physical disadvantages. Anna, there to offer her paid, and rather prestigious, employment, felt a little superfluous and when Jennifer accepted the job, she did it with a certain amount of condescension, as if the favour was hers, not Anna's, to bestow.

Her portfolio was excellent, though, and later, as Anna walked out on to Gower Street, she considered the irrefutable fact that each of the young artists she employed were, technically speaking, more talented than she. Both of them were being expertly tutored in the craft that she, without really thinking much about it, had turned into a profession when she painted a beach house on Thea Hoyland's bedroom wall. And then, just as this thought passed through Anna's mind, there was a tap on her shoulder and she turned to find Thea herself in the flesh, standing right before her, smiling broadly. 'Thought it was you,' she said and Anna jumped: actually jumped. Thea laughed.

'Sorry, did I spook you?' she said. 'I must look a fright today.'

'I just conjured you out of thin air,' Anna said. 'I thought of you, and there you were, *pouf*!'

'Sorry to disappoint, but I arrived here the usual way, by car. Gee, it's good to see you!'

She said this so warmly, so convincingly, that Anna felt a wash of fondness for this woman who, after all, was more former client than friend.

'What are you up to?' Thea asked. 'I saw you coming out of the Slade and I yelled at Charlson to stop so I could catch you.'

'Oh well, yes, I had things to do: a new artist to hire, you know.' Anna gesticulated vaguely backwards, to the entrance to the art school.

'And are you through?'

'Pardon?'

'Through. Finished. Free.'

'Oh, I see, yes. I'm heading for Regent's Park,' Anna said, which was true; she had thought of a stroll in the sun.

'No, come with me,' Thea said, which seemed to be an order, not an invitation.

'To?'

'Luncheon at Fulton House. We're very glum, with Henry locked away still. We need variety.'

Anna frowned. 'Is Lady Henrietta still in prison?' she said. 'I thought she—'

'Oh boy, are you out of date.' Thea looped an arm through

Anna's and turned her round so that Anna noticed, then, the Rolls-Royce waiting a little way down the street. It looked incongruous in the plain uniformity of Gower Street: sleek and pale against the sooty brick of the terraced buildings. Thea, still talking, propelled her towards the motorcar and Anna, who had neither agreed nor disagreed to the scheme, found herself climbing in and settling on the leather seat. Inside, the car smelled of beeswax and Thea's cologne. The driver, immaculate in his Hoyland livery, sat straight-backed and awaited instructions.

'Thank you Charlson, home we go,' Thea said merrily, and then turned to Anna. 'So, poor Henry gets another three months in that vile institution, which everyone agrees is far too harsh a punishment for throwing a silly brick, and now she's taken matters into her own hands and stopped eating.'

'Stopped eating?'

'Hunger strike,' Thea said in a comically gothic voice laced with doom.

'Oh, how dreadful.'

'You see, they let out Marion Wallace Dunlop after four days when she stopped eating, so unless Mr Asquith wants Henry to actually die, he must release her too. That's the plan.'

The motorcar, moving smoothly through the streets of Bloomsbury, drew attention from passers-by and Anna was glad that Amos couldn't see her, perched on the soft leather upholstery with the Countess of Netherwood; he would have demanded explanations, justification. The air between them would have been thick with reproof. Anna said, 'And how long has she been refusing food?'

Thea counted on her fingers. 'Saturday, Sunday, Monday – three,' she said. 'Which is nothing, really. I swear I've gone without food for longer, without even meaning to.' She laughed, though Anna looked concerned.

'Have you visited?'

'Oh, sure, but I prefer to send Toby. He's better than I am at that sort of thing.' She looked away, out of the window. 'Gosh, London is so drab,' she said, alighting, butterfly-like, on a new topic. 'I'm longing, now, for the regatta.' She looked at Anna again. 'It's so important, isn't it, to ring the changes? I can't bear to be stuck in one place for too long.'

This sounded shallow, self-absorbed. Anna didn't answer.

'Do you sail?' Thea asked.

'No.'

'Me either: well, not for years. But we should all try these things. I did a bit of boating as a girl and of course I sailed here from New York, but frankly those liners are so huge that I might have been in a hotel for three weeks for all I saw of the water.'

Anna said, 'Well I sailed here too, for that matter, on a steam ship. My first husband and I were escaping persecution.' It was a kind of reprimand, but it was too hidden, too oblique, to hit its mark. Thea widened her eyes. 'Golly,' she said. 'That sounds thrilling. Do tell.'

'Not now,' Anna said, regretting her impulse; regretting, too, the earlier passivity that had put her here in the first place. Thea's insouciance was suddenly unappealing. 'And look,' Anna said, shunting forwards on the seat of the car as if she might jump out there and then, 'I think I should go home, to Bedford Square. I have rather a lot to do.'

Thea's face fell. 'Really?' she said. 'Lucky old you. I have absolutely nothing at all to do.'

As problems went, this hardly merited sympathy. Still, there was something so wistful about the way she looked and spoke that Anna softened, but only fractionally.

'Then let's go and visit Lady Henrietta,' she said. 'I'd like to see her, see how she is.'

Thea sighed and pulled a face. 'Really?'

'Yes, really.'

'But you can't just waltz in, you know.'

'Certainly we can't, if we don't go.'

'I mean, there's a visiting hour, and it isn't now.'

'Never mind, we can deal with that.'

'But . . .' Thea, used to pleasing herself, cast about for another objection, more out of habit than conviction. 'I'm expected back,' she said, but half-heartedly, because the truth was no one ever expected Thea until they saw her walk through the door. She looked at Anna, whose expression – determined, disapproving, implacable – gave her no cause for optimism.

'Charlson,' Thea said resignedly. 'About turn.'

The cricket pitch at the back of the miners' welfare was as hard as stone after a few weeks of sun, and the wicket was brown, not green. Amos spent hours here; it was less lonely than home and, anyway, he loved the weight of the leather ball in his hand and the supreme satisfaction of letting it fly at its target. They had practice nets and Amos found that there was usually someone around who was willing to face a few overs. Before Sam had brought him into the fold, Amos hadn't played cricket for years. Now, this summer, he'd begun to feel that this was one of the principal reasons he had been placed on earth. His body was made for it: his body, and the effect upon it of the years he'd spent hacking coal out of its seam. His shoulders and arms were strong, his legs powerful. He had balance and timing, accuracy and speed, and he had a fierce ambition to hone this natural ability into perfectly consistent genius. He was a formidable foe with a ball cupped in his hand, and he took no prisoners. When Amos bowled, the batsman either went for the shot or ducked; Lofty Vickers, in the practice crease, chose the latter option now.

'Bloody Nora, Amos, I'm on t'same team as thee!' He bent

to pick up the ball, which lolled in the folds of the net, devoid of its killer power.

'There'll be nowt Wharncliffe can show you that you 'aven't already seen,' Amos said. 'They can do their worst come Sat'day – you'll be ready for 'em, Lofty.'

'Aye, or dead,' Lofty said. 'I should bat in a bloody pit 'elmet.' He tossed the ball back to Amos, who spat on it and rubbed it hard on the cloth of his trousers. He walked backwards, slowly, watching the batsman through narrowed eyes.

'Easy,' Lofty said. 'You don't want my death on yer conscience.'

Amos stopped, drew up his shoulders, rocked back on one heel, then took off at full tilt towards the wicket, bringing back his right arm at the precise moment, which was more about instinct than technique. He sent a yorker, just because he could, and because he knew that if he judged it right, Lofty would dance out of the way of the ball and the bails would fly.

'Out!'

This was Sam Bamford, ambling past the back of the nets, heading for the welfare hall, which on match days they called the pavilion. He raised a hand in salute to his pace man, his demon bowler. Amos, waiting for Lofty to replace the bails and regain his nerve, considered the possibilities for his next delivery. He considered, too, the fact that, if it was practical and within his power, this was how he would live his days: time and again, outfoxing a batsman with a well-aimed cricket ball.

Lofty tossed him the ball and it landed in his palm with a soft, satisfying slap, but when he turned to walk away from the wicket he saw Eliza Williams streaming across the field towards him, her face full of anguish. He dropped the ball and went to her; she barrelled into his arms, sobbing and fighting for breath.

'Eliza, sweet'eart, what is it?'

He was truly alarmed. Eliza was sunshine and laughter: always had been.

'I need Anna,' she said, through juddering breaths. 'Will you take me to Anna?'

'Now then,' he said, holding her tight, kissing the top of her head. 'Calm yourself, then tell me what's up.' He smiled at her. She looked up at him, helpless, hopeless, and he knew that whatever it was, it couldn't be as bad as she thought.

'It's Mam,' Eliza said. 'I think she's dead.'

He could get no sense out of her, so he took her back to Ravenscliffe, where a telegram had arrived earlier that day. Daniel was in the kitchen, and when he looked up at Amos and Eliza his expression was twisted with grief and fury. The telegram lay on the table, and he pushed it towards Amos. He picked it up and read: EVIE ILL STOP YELLOW FEVER STOP GRAVELY CONCERNED STOP SILAS

Amos looked at Eliza and said, 'She's not dead then, Eliza. She's badly, but she's still with us.'

'I want Anna,' Eliza said. She sounded younger than her fourteen years, and the tears still poured silently down her face.

'She could be dead though, couldn't she?' Daniel's voice was cold and hard in the warm kitchen. 'Since that was sent she could have died. And if she has, I shall wring that bastard's neck.'

Eliza wailed.

'Where's Ellen?' Amos asked. He felt entirely out of his depth.

'Outside, up a tree,' Eliza said. 'Will you take me to Anna?' She turned pleading eyes on him, and he could understand this at least: Daniel had turned inwards in his rage and anxiety, and the child needed a woman's comfort. He placed a hand on her head. 'Anna's in London, pet. As soon as she's back I'll bring 'er to you.'

Daniel brought his fist down hard on the table. 'I should have stopped her going,' he said in a strangulated growl. 'I should have forbidden it. He's a self-serving bastard, and my wife and son are at his mercy. Oh God!' He laid his head on the table. 'My boy,' he moaned. 'My wee boy.'

Eliza patted his shoulder ineffectually, then let her hand rest there. She looked like a small, inept guardian angel, and was the very image of suffering. Just lately she had come home from Paris, bubbling with excitement, brim-full of joy. Now she was a terrified child trying to be brave. Amos's heart went out to her. He smiled and she attempted a watery smile in return.

'Look,' he said, 'your mam's sick, but she's a strong woman and I'd put good money on 'er pulling through. There's nowt to be gained from weepin' and wailin' for summat that 'asn't 'appened.'

'I should've kept her here,' Daniel said.

'You couldn't,' said Amos. 'Eve's like my Anna: she knows 'er own mind. She went to Jamaica for Seth as much as for Silas, and we've all read 'er letters. She called it paradise. She likes it out there. Mark my words, she'll pull through this.'

Eliza's expression brightened as she drank in the words of reassurance. This was what the child needed, thought Amos, not drama and unwarranted grief.

'Nip outside and fetch Ellen down,' Amos said. 'We'll all share a pot o' tea and some o' Lilly's baking. Does Lilly bake?'

Eliza nodded. 'Buns,' she said. 'They're not nice though. They're not like my mam's.' Her lip began to wobble again, but she left the room through the back door to coax Ellen out of her tree. Swiftly, Amos sat down opposite Daniel.

'Frame thi'sen, Daniel MacLeod,' he said, and not gently. 'Can't you see what you're doing to that bairn?'

Daniel looked at him, stunned.

'Eliza needs you to be strong. She's terrified, and it's your doing.'

'If Eve dies—'

'Aye, we know: you'll throttle 'im, and if I get to 'im first you'll find you don't 'ave to. But Eve's not dead, so you mun stop acting like she is and start showin' these bairns 'ow to go on.'

Daniel looked bleak. 'I feel so damned helpless,' he said. 'And I feel certain I'm going to lose her.'

Amos reached across the table and placed a steadying hand on Daniel's arm. He understood what it was to love Eve Williams because he had once done so himself, fervently. Water under the bridge, he thought, and Anna had all of his heart now. But still, he understood.

Outside, on the lower slope of the common, Eliza climbed Ellen's tree and sat beside her on a long, wide bough. She put an arm round her sister's shoulders and said, 'Amos's come. It's better in there now. Kettle's on.'

They stayed put in the elm, though, each taking some comfort from the closeness of the other. Ellen sucked her thumb. Eliza thought about happiness and how, now it had slipped away, it was impossible to remember the feeling or to imagine it ever coming to her again.

Chapter 36

The speed of Eve's decline shocked everyone. She couldn't stay at the hotel, so she was moved to Silas's house. Shaken into tenderness by the severity of her illness, and riven with guilt for assuming she would conquer it, Silas wrapped her in the sheet she lay under and carried her to his car, placing her on the back seat as if she were made of spun sugar. Angus howled, but was held back by Seth. The little boy hammered at Seth's hands and screamed infant curses at his uncle, demanding that he bring back his mam, but Silas paid him no attention and Seth was firm. Eve knew nothing of any of it. She was drifting between unconsciousness and semi-consciousness and her yellow-tinged skin burned with fever. If her eyes flickered open she seemed to know no one, even her sons. She was lost to a different world and Silas, more than anyone, was terrified; he believed she would never come back.

There was a doctor in Spanish Town, rumoured to be experienced in cases such as these, and though he had been sent for he had yet to appear. Ruby said, What did everyone expect? He lived way over on the wrong side of the Blue Mountains, and unless he had the power of flight it would be days before he came, if he came at all. Anyway, she said, Eve didn't need leeches and dubious science. While they waited for the doctor, Ruby had been nursing Eve with the herbal infusions she swore by, cloudy and bitter smelling, dispensed in five daily doses. When Eve was moved Ruby moved too, ministering to her still, bringing feverfew, cowfoot and bitter bush leaves, and calabash syrup in a stoneware jar. She still had her work in the hotel kitchen, so during her absences Justine was briefed to keep vigil, a task she seemed preternaturally suited to as she sat placid and silent at the bedside.

Ruby would have preferred that Eve be moved to her own little house, but Batista told her not to invite sickness into her home, and anyway, Silas would have none of it. Swamped by a desperate devotion, his heart heavy with grief, he tried to assuage his own suffering by lavishing every comfort on Eve. He had her settled into a large room on the first floor, where the double jalousie windows were swagged on the inside with white linen to diffuse the light. The sheets on her bed were of cool, smooth Egyptian cotton, and an additional ceiling fan was fitted to stir the thick, Caribbean air into something approaching a refreshing breeze. She was to have everything she needed: that was his instruction.

The day after Eve went to Sugar Hill, Ruby came at first light, driven there by Scotty in the trap. The big house was silent, but Henri slid from the shadows and directed her upstairs, and when she pushed open the door of Eve's room Silas and Justine were both in there. They stood several feet apart, but something about they way they stared – Silas at Ruby, Justine at her feet – suggested collusion, a shared secret, and when Silas left the room Ruby said bluntly, 'Is that his baby you're carrying?'

Justine nodded. Ruby shook her head, as if she pitied the other woman her plight, but Justine placed a protective hand on her swollen belly.

'Masser is good,' she said. 'Is kind.'

Ruby looked away. She felt a jolt of absurd hurt that when her own pregnancy had been discovered by Silas the goodness and kindness had ended, not begun. On the bed, Eve moaned and Ruby, grateful for the diversion, went to her side. Eve's eyes were open, and Ruby murmured hello, though there was no response. She sat down on the mattress and said to Justine, 'Come, help me lift her.' Justine did as she was asked, propping Eve up with one strong arm so that Ruby could offer her sips of vervine tea. Later, she held a strange-smelling poultice to Eve's brow, brushing Justine's hand away when she offered to take over. At length she stood, turned Eve's pillow, shook out and smoothed her sheet, and made to leave. Justine, watchful, silent, ventured a smile, but Ruby found she couldn't return it, though she didn't entirely understand why. Instead she said, curtly, 'I shall come back as soon as I'm able,' and left the room. Justine lowered her eyes but her face was serene. She was still seated at the bedside, and she lifted up Eve's hand and let it rest in the coolness of her own palm.

Silas was waiting for Ruby at the bottom of the stairs. He watched her descend, but not with his usual sneer: rather, he looked vulnerable, ragged with anxiety, and his voice was laced with uncertainty.

'Do you think she'll live?' he said. 'I can't rid myself of the certainty that she won't.'

'We don't know the answer to that, do we?' Ruby said.

'Then you do think she'll die.' His voice was bleak.

'That is not what I said. Many people survive yellow fever.'

'She should've shaken it off by now, though. Why hasn't she shaken it off?'

'She has a bad dose. We have to watch her closely.' She

felt no sympathy for Silas in his evident distress. For Eve, however, she was gravely concerned.

'I've telegraphed her family, in Yorkshire.'

Ruby tutted, much displeased. 'Have you? Spreading the misery seems an unhelpful course of action. What can they possibly do, besides worry desperately?'

'Better that than wire them out of the blue with the worst possible news.'

'Cho! Enough,' she said, and walked towards the open door. She could see Scotty waiting on the trap, with his back to the house.

'Ruby!'

Silas lunged and grabbed at her arm, and she spun round. 'Do not touch me,' she said with quiet force.

'I don't think you understand,' Silas said. 'I can't bear the thought that I might lose her.' Tears welled in his eyes and he left them there, to fall onto his cheeks. Ruby saw that he was in real distress, and wondered if this was the first time Silas Whittam had shed tears.

'I will do all I can,' Ruby said. 'But I'll do it for her, and for her little boy. Not for you.'

'Stay,' he said. 'Stay with her. I'll put another woman in the kitchen.'

Ruby shook her head. 'The very last thing your sister would want is for the hotel kitchen to go to rack and ruin once again. I've given her something to calm her and to cool the fever. She'll sleep for a few hours. In any case, she has Justine – as, I gather, do you.' Ruby turned again and he didn't try to stop her, but followed her to the steps of the house and watched her spring up beside Scotty, who snapped the reins and made the mule move off at a lick along the drive to the lane.

321

Edna trotted peaceably down the sharp incline of Sugar Hill, past cotton trees whose fluffed branches lined and filled the lane, so that for this short leg of the journey the trap was in complete shade. Ruby sighed and rubbed her eyes with balled fists, like a child, and Scotty sucked his teeth.

'What?' said Ruby, putting down her hands and looking at him sideways.

'You dog tired, nuh?'

'A little weary. Not for the first time, however, and not for the last.'

Scotty nodded, and held his tongue. Privately, he thought Ruby Donaldson put herself out too much for people who weren't worth the trouble.

'How are the boys?'

'Pickneys fine.'

'I was worried Angus would cry when he woke and found himself in a new place, but I thought it best that he should rest so I had to leave him sleeping, to get up here and back again in time for—'

Scotty held up a hand, a flat palm against her rush of words.'Ever'ting cook an curry,' he said. 'An-goose happy as a snapper, him splashin' at Eden Falls.'

'Oh lordy, that's where I must go then,' Ruby said. She yawned widely, forgetting to cover her mouth. 'I'd thought to go home first and make a little breakfast.'

'Roscoe done thought a that,' Scotty said, and he laughed and would tell her no more, only whistled through his teeth and let Edna lead them to the narrow path to the falls, where Ruby climbed down.

'No need to wait Scotty, I'm sure you have a good deal to do,' she said, with the haughtiness that never quite left her. In reply he winked at her, then lingered to watch Ruby's sweet backside as she swished through the grass, unconsciously alluring. It was a kind of sport for Scotty and for Maxwell, catching a glimpse of Ruby from behind, without her know-ledge. Now he fell solemn at the beauty of it.

When she reached the water Angus and Roscoe were squatting on the bank like little bush piccaninnies, cooking crayfish on a small fire. They had on baggy shorts, but their torsos were bare. Angus poked experimentally at the orange embers, watching the sparks, while Roscoe used two sticks to pick up the crayfish and turn them. They were utterly absorbed, but in the way that children had of rarely being startled, they didn't jump when she spoke, but merely turned to her and smiled.

'Look Ruby, Roscoe catched janga,' Angus said.

'Caught,' Ruby said. 'Crayfish.' She gave Roscoe a look.

He shrugged. 'Janga, crayfish, same thing and one as tasty as the other,' he said, risking cheekiness, full of confidence in his role of guru and guide.

She let it pass but said, 'Crayfish, nevertheless,' then she pointed to the soft heap of cakes, damp and warm on a tin plate, and added, 'and bammies?'

'And this.' Angus said, pointing to a jug of lemon syrup. He'd been charged with the task of carrying it himself, all the way from Roscoe's house to Eden Falls. The top of the jug was covered with another tin plate, to keep out the ants.

Ruby sat down between the boys. 'How clever of you,' she said. The crayfish popped and fizzed over the fire, and their fanned tails began to blacken at the fringes, so Roscoe took the plate from the jug and flipped the shellfish onto it, then he bopped Angus lightly on the head with the singed end of one of the sticks. 'One more turnabout before breakfast?' he said. 'Let the crayfish cool?'

And Ruby watched them swim, Roscoe leading, Angus following, like a duckling after its mother. Roscoe kept to the shallows and swam smoothly, with barely a break to the surface of the water, while behind him Angus's limbs went like the clappers and his face was all motion, laughing and gasping. He was a different child, thought Ruby, to the one yesterday who'd screamed for his mother as she was lifted away from him in a sheet wrapped about her like a shroud: a different child, yet the same. He had forgotten, for the time being, that all was not well. He'd remember soon enough. For now, though, she would leave the magic of Eden Falls to do its work, and she allowed herself to savour the moment: their laughter, the sublime beauty of the lagoon, the salt smell of cooked crayfish and the benediction of the morning sun.

By the time they left the falls a bank of cloud as wide as the horizon had begun to move with stealth and speed across the sky, and the dust and leaves on the lane were whipping against their ankles. Angus walked most of the way, skipping and dancing as if the wind had him in its clutches too, but when Roscoe carried on towards school Ruby picked the little boy up and he curled and clung to her with his hands laced tightly behind her neck and his skinny legs wrapped around her waist. His skin against her own was translucent; on his wrists and at his temples blue veins showed through and this made him seem fragile, though Ruby supposed he was no more so than any other little boy of three. They were almost nose to nose and she studied his face at these close quarters: heart-shaped, like Eve's, but darker-eyed, and his hair was darker too. Perhaps he took after his daddy in this regard.

'Where's my mam?' Angus said, although he knew.

'At Sugar Hill, where your uncle lives,' Ruby said.

'But I want 'er.'

'I know you do.'

'Can I see 'er?'

'Soon, but not yet.'

He pouted, his young face clouded by thwarted wants; he was about to cry. But then Seth appeared on the terrace above them and called down – pompously, irrelevantly – that there was a severe storm forecast, high winds and heavy rain, and at the same moment the darkening clouds burst and in a matter of seconds Ruby and Angus were drenched by a torrent of warm rain, implausibly heavy, as if a sluice gate had opened high above them.

Angus, thrilled and entirely distracted from his imminent lament, pushed at Ruby until she released him, and then he zigzagged up the garden towards Seth, who hurried inside. Ruby followed, keeping her usual, languid pace, and instead of heading off to the kitchen, she walked into the hotel via the main entrance, expecting that Seth would want news of his mother. But when he saw her at the open door of the office he affected puzzlement and said, 'What is it, Ruby?'

'I just came from Sugar Hill, where I'm nursing your mother.'

'Indeed. Mr Silas will be here soon, thank you.'

She raised her eyebrows. He strived so desperately for dignified authority, but he always looked like a boy in a gentleman's suit. Angus sat cross-legged in the leather chair and sucked the end of a pen thoughtfully, as if he was writing a letter and found himself stuck for a word. His wet shorts would mark that soft hide seat, thought Ruby; well, let them.

'I wonder if you quite understand the gravity of the situation,' she said to Seth.

For a few moments they stared at each other, but Seth was resolute. He was conscious of a dangerous blurring of boundaries caused by his mother's sudden illness and the speed with which they had all had to act. Ruby's bush medicine was doubtless soothing as far as it went, but hardly the thing on which they all should now depend; she should not be given the status of a medical practitioner. It was Seth's duty to restore order, to reassert his position – and hers – in the simple hierarchy, whatever heroics Ruby Donaldson might feel she had performed. This, he was sure, was what his uncle would expect of him. Often enough, Seth had heard him say, 'Iron fist, my boy; anything less and they'll run rings round you.'

'Thank you, Ruby,' Seth said again. 'Mr Silas will inform me of developments. For now, your place is in the kitchen.'

She laughed at him, flatly. 'Have a care,' she said, turning to leave. 'Your heart is turning to stone.'

Justine watched Silas until he spun out of sight in his red motorcar. The taste of him was still in her mouth; he had come to her for comfort before he left, unbuttoning his trousers and pushing her gently down onto her knees. She was glad that he wanted her, glad that he needed her; certainly, she wanted and needed him. Her breath came fast and shallow at the thought of him, and she longed already for his return. She pressed her forehead against the pane to cool her thoughts and she saw Henri – poor old Henri, was how she thought of him lately – gallop round the side of the house with a rake and a barrow, running from the sudden downpour. In Jamaica, as in Martinique, rain came not gradually but in a deluge, overwhelming and complete, a veritable flood flung from the heavens; then, as suddenly as it had come, it would stop and the sun would bear down once again on the newly washed world.

From the bedroom window, Justine watched Henri; he had crouched under a cabbage palm, and appeared to be contemplating the rivulets that carved small furrows in the dusty drive. Henri had told her he would leave Sugar Hill when he could. He was lonely without her companionship. Justine understood this, and although she didn't want him to go, neither could she offer him a reason to stay. Sometimes she imagined a life as Mrs Silas Whittam, in which Henri lived with them in the great house, passing off as her brother – which he was, in spirit and in her heart – and dressed fine and fancy. At other times this happy vision eluded her, refusing to form or slipping out of reach of her mind's eye, while other, starker futures rose up, uncomfortable and unwelcome.

Behind her, Eve shifted in a sudden spasm of pain and called out sharply, a name that Justine didn't know. She had turned on to her side, and when Justine went to her, Eve seemed to know her and tried to speak, but instead began to retch violently, her eyes wild with panic and pain. She vomited before Justine was able to fetch a bowl; Justine held back Eve's hair and wiped her face, and spoke to her in a soft patois that sounded like music. When the convulsions left her and Eve dropped back exhausted on to the pillow a livid trail of blood snaked from the corner of her mouth and down into the hot, wet crevice of her neck.

Justine knelt at the bedside and uttered a few words, an ancient incantation for the spirit of this suffering woman. Then she cleaned Eve's sleeping face and, without disturbing her unduly, remade the bed with fresh linen, so that when the spirit departed, as Justine now believed it would, the mortal remains would be respectable and Silas would know that she, Justine, had carried out her duties, precisely as instructed.

Chapter 37

~~~~~❦~~~~~

Ulrich, who was nineteen, and therefore too young, had proposed marriage to Isabella, who was seventeen, and therefore far too young. He might as well have thrown a hand grenade into the Park Lane drawing room: it could have caused no more alarm to the duchess, and perhaps, even, a little less.

The boy had asked the duke for his permission. Archie, pleased and flattered to be – for once – involved in the matters of the day, had granted it. This fact, among all the others that stacked up to represent the case against, was the one that caused Clarissa so much pain that she took to her room and refused to let Flytton so much as open the curtains, let alone dress her. She wouldn't come out until the scheme was declared null and void. She would speak to Isabella only when the engagement was broken. She would never speak to Archie again.

Archie knew she was upset, but he hadn't realised that he had been sent to Coventry because his wife barely spoke to him anyway, and when she did he rarely heard her. Therefore he was not, perhaps, as helpful as he might have been. Ulrich was part of the family now, as far as the duke was concerned. Permission, once granted, could not be withdrawn: a gentleman's

328

word was his bond. He took Ulrich with him to White's and put the boy's name on his account at Davies and Son, so that Uli's tailoring would be as impeccable as his command of English. After four days of lonely languish in the crepuscular conditions of her rooms, the duchess emerged – dressed, bejewelled, magnificently chilly – to find that Uli had his own Arabian mare in the stables and his own Buick under cover in the courtyard, and that Isabella wore a Hohenzollern diamond, which was, at least, a material confirmation of the connection with the royal line.

'Extremely distant cousins,' Clarissa said when Tobias made this very point.

'Which is more than we are,' he said. 'I should imagine Aunt Liese has telegraphed Frau von Hechingen at the schloss to warn her that Uli is marrying down.'

'Baroness von Hechingen,' Clarissa corrected, a stickler for correct form.

'Oh well, there we go, splendid. German nobility, with a line to the kaiser, albeit a circuitous one.'

Clarissa sighed, feelingly. 'I do miss your father,' she said.

'Don't blame Archie for this, Mama. Izzy would have won Papa's permission in a heartbeat. She had him in the palm of her hand.' Still though, he privately thought it a bit rum that Ulrich had gone to the duke. He felt it an unfortunate omission that his own assent hadn't been sought. But Tobias, unlike his mother, didn't bruise easily, and in any case it was difficult to imagine a more likeable cove than Ulrich, who certainly seemed to adore Isabella.

'I just feel . . .' said Clarissa, then stopped to press a limp hand to her pale brow. Tobias waited.

'I just feel,' she continued, 'that this is folly. She is so young!'

'Headstrong,' Tobias said. 'Make her wait, perhaps?'

Clarissa brightened. 'Yes. At least a year, perhaps two.'

'Well, certainly one, at any rate. We would all suffer fright-fully if Izzy was thwarted for longer than that.'

The duchess straightened her shoulders and tilted her delicate chin. 'She shall wait a year, or there will be no wedding,' she said, as if it were her idea entirely. 'Excellent.' Tobias could see the improvement in his mother's spirits at this proposed assertion of her authority. For himself, he thought Isabella might just as well get on with it. Tobias was not the sort of fellow to put obstacles in the way of anyone's desire.

'Still, though,' said Clarissa, a little wanly, 'I should have been more involved from the outset. It's a mother's job to steer her daughter towards the right match.'

'Well, who wrote the table plan, on the night of Izzy's ball?'

She nodded, taking his point. She had been thinking, when she drew up the seating arrangements, of the Peverill boy on Isabella's left. He was heir to a dukedom, although the seat was in Cornwall, which was a bore.

'I believe you were very clever, Mama,' Tobias said. 'Extremely prescient.'

She narrowed her eyes at him, searching for mockery, but found none. He merely smiled and raised his teacup as if it were a champagne flute.

'*Prost!*' he said.

Clarissa frowned, not sure what he meant by this, but she felt a little more cheerful anyway. Archie's presumption had been beyond the pale and he was far from forgiven, but Isabella's conquest, she was prepared to accept, could certainly be seen in an agreeable light. At the very least, she thought, it detracted attention from Henrietta, whose name was in the newspapers yet again.

Her elder daughter's hunger strike in Holloway Prison had prompted not mercy, but the opposite; after twelve days of starvation, Lady Henrietta Hoyland was to be forcibly fed. The pressmen had fallen on the story like crows upon carrion, and Christabel Pankhurst, wishing with all her heart that she and Henrietta could swap places, did the next best thing and publicised the outrage for all she was worth. It was a call to arms, she said; the government had declared war on women.

None of the family was quite sure what force-feeding involved – a question, perhaps, of insisting very firmly that she eat, ventured Thea – but they were told that Henrietta's health, which had been severely jeopardised by starvation, would now improve, so they tried, on the whole, to consider it a good thing. Certainly, when Thea saw her Henrietta had looked horribly peaky. She had gone to the infirmary with Anna Sykes and found Henrietta unable to summon the energy to move. Thea and Anna had sat in near silence on either side of the hospital bed while Henrietta lay between them, flat as a runner bean and staring at the ceiling.

When she got home Thea had told Toby that she wouldn't visit again if Henry couldn't make an effort. She had placed an artful hand on her belly, to remind him – as if she needed to – that in her new condition she mustn't be made to do anything she didn't wish to do. Clarissa hadn't visited since Henrietta was incarcerated, and Isabella, who at least had intended to visit her sister, was now engaged to be married, which apparently precluded any unpleasant duties of any kind. Then, yesterday, a matron, acting on instructions from the governor of Holloway, had politely and respectfully turned Tobias away from the hospital with the gentle advice that family members should wait until Lady Henrietta's condition was 'stable' before visiting her again. Tobias had accepted this, though he had thought it sounded a little fishy; and then today he had opened the *Telegraph* to see an item on page three detailing the horrors of the 'daily ordeal' that Henry was now facing, as described to them by Miss Pankhurst, who apparently had inside information. It sounded simply ghastly, and Tobias was sure she must be mistaken, or simply whipping up alarm for the sake of publicity. She had gone on to denounce the prison authorities as barbarians before denouncing in a similar vein the king, the prime minister, the home secretary and any other fellow who had ever disagreed with her.

Tobias, sitting in the drawing room with his mother, spoke of none of these things, concentrating only on guiding her back into a reasonable humour. However, he was deeply troubled, and, worse than that, he had no idea what to do.

Amos Sykes was back in London and he was looking for his wife. Her place was in Ardington. She was needed there, by Eliza, by Ellen, by Daniel and – God knew – by himself. He felt the present situation amounted to an emergency, but he disliked the limitations of telegrams and their impersonal nature; he had never sent one in his life. Instead he had journeyed to London, a man on a mission, to explain to her fully that nothing was right and that the longer her absence continued, the worse everything would become.

She was out, though. He had let himself in and stood in the entrance hall, and had known at once that the house was empty. It had that essential stillness of a home without its family. He had made himself a cup of tea, rifled through the post, which had clearly been sorted by Anna earlier in the day, then put on his coat again and walked to Tottenham Court Road to buy a newspaper. He bought the *Daily Mirror*, rolled it up like a baton, tucked it under his arm and set off back again, and this is when he saw her, outside their house in earnest conversation with the Earl of Netherwood. There was a motorcar idling in the road, a cream Rolls-Royce with tan leather upholstery, and a chauffeur so motionless he might have been stuffed. Tobias Hoyland wore a mid-tan lounge suit, a cream silk scarf and two-tone shoes; Amos thought him ridiculous. Anna, however, was taking him extremely seriously; she listened, nodded vigorously, responded, listened again, and Amos's heart filled with resentment. She had no idea that her husband was approaching until he was almost upon them. Then, when she saw him, she gave a little bark of surprise and flung her arms around him in evident delight, and he instantly felt like an undeserving curmudgeon.

'Well I never!' said Anna.

'Speak of the devil, as they say,' said Tobias. He held out a hand, which Amos was obliged to shake.

''ow do,' he said, just as he would have done if it had been Sam Bamford in the pit yard. 'Talking about me, were you?'

'Indirectly,' Tobias said. He barely knew Amos Sykes, except by reputation. In his father's day, Sykes had been an agitator, a glowering malcontent whose name sometimes came up over the kippers when the late earl and Henrietta were talking shop at the breakfast table. Now that he'd taken his rabble-rousing tendencies to Ardington their paths no longer crossed. He still looked a crotchety devil though, thought Tobias. A shame for the wife, who was pretty as the day and all smiles.

'We were talking about Lady Henrietta, in fact,' Anna said, with a brightness that she hoped would detract from Amos's scowl. Silently she willed him not to fly off the handle, here in the street.

'Poor girl's got herself in a pickle,' Tobias chipped in. 'Being force-fed eggs and milk, by all accounts.'

'She's starving herself, in Holloway Prison,' Anna said. 'So now they've decided to forcibly feed her. It's quite brutal.'

Amos, silent thus far, said, 'Right,' very flatly, acknowledging the information without betraying the least interest in it. Tobias, acutely aware of the new awkwardness that had arrived with Amos, smiled tightly at him and warmly at Anna and said, to her, 'Righto, I'll leave it with you. Any influence you can bring to bear would be simply marvellous.' He was holding a Homburg – again tan, lighter than the suit but exactly the same shade as the shoes – and now he placed it on his head and climbed into rear seat of the motorcar. Through the window he said, 'Cheerio then,' and the vehicle moved smoothly away.

Amos looked at Anna. 'Does 'e always dress to match 'is car?' he said.

She smiled thinly. 'Let's go inside.'

In a windowless room of the infirmary, Henrietta was half-pushed, half-lifted onto a hard, narrow bed, which stood at about waist height and was not, she immediately realised, meant for sleeping on. There were eight warders, waiting in a grim line, and they stepped forwards to surround Henrietta. One of them began to pound at an unseen pedal, which tilted the head end of the bed upwards, so that Henrietta, who was now being held in place by the warders, was lying not flat, but at a slight angle. Two doctors entered the room, one of them carrying a glass flask of thick, milky fluid and the other bearing a length of rubber tube, which was coiled over his arm like a snake on a branch. They were laughing as they entered, at something one of them had said, but then they fell silent and neither of them uttered another sound. Henrietta, quite helpless, closed her eyes in despair, though she didn't speak and she didn't cry. Exactly this had happened to her yesterday, and the very worst part was about to come. Her head was gripped and held rigid in the iron vice of a warder's hands, and her limbs were pinned by the others, then the pipe-bearing doctor – greying, bewhiskered, severe – began the tortuous process of pushing the tube not into her mouth but up her nose and along the nasal passages then down into the gullet. Her eyes opened wide at the assault; the pain was indescribable, a suffocating invasion, an attack on those tender, delicate, secret places of the human body that should never feel the harsh edges of man-made implements brutally deployed. She bucked and gagged, and the warder who held her head slid her hands further down so that, with her fingers, she could clamp Henrietta's mouth shut. She was expert at this; it was her speciality. Henrietta looked into her face and saw gritted teeth, clenched jaws, eyes of steel. Her own body was limp now, unresisting, but the eight warders still pinned her down with fierce dedication as the doctors went silently about their business.

The milk came next, roughly a pint and fortified with beaten eggs, pumped from the flask, along the tube and down into Henrietta's gut. This part, the feeding, was accomplished quickly, and when the flask was almost empty the doctor called a halt and whipped out the tubing, swiftly, without care or compassion. Immediately, Henrietta vomited, a great upsurge of fluid that caught one warder in the face and splattered on the doctor's polished black boots. Someone – she didn't know who – slapped her hard, across the cheek. Then everyone exited the room and she was left alone on the bed, where she lay as still as death, imagining herself elsewhere, imagining herself free. She knew, because Mary Dixon had written to tell her, that in the world outside, she was a cause célèbre. Her heroic martyrdom, Mary said, was the movement's single most effective weapon against the government. Every woman fighting for the vote owed Henrietta a debt of gratitude. She was marvellous, inspirational, a symbol of valour in the face of contemptible cruelty.

Henrietta closed her eyes. She didn't want the vote. She only wanted to go home.

Tobias had gone to Anna at his wife's suggestion. 'She can do anything,' Thea had said. 'Try her.' It was true, Tobias had thought, that Anna Sykes seemed capable and caring, and the fact that she was married to an MP couldn't hurt, even though he was from the wrong benches. It was all about access and influence, after all. So Charlson had driven him to Bedford Square and he had knocked on her door and persuaded her to have tea with him at the Lyons Corner House on Coventry Street – Thea's suggestion again; he had no idea why she knew the place, but it fitted the purpose. Anna had listened to the tale of woe, and had been horrified at what he told her.

'Bad enough,' he had said, 'that darling Henry is kept away from us. But to be tormented in this manner, and for us to discover it through an article in the newspaper . . .'

He was very upset: shaken, almost tearful. Anna's heart filled with pity, and she promised – perhaps unwisely, she later thought – to do all she could to help Lady Henrietta. Then Charlson had driven her home and that's when Amos had arrived, out of the blue and with a face like thunder. He looked no happier now, sitting in his wing chair in the drawing room, listening to her account of the story.

'Well, anyway,' Anna said, tailing off, discouraged. They looked at each other and Amos said, 'Aye, "well, anyway" sounds about right.'

'Meaning?'

'Meaning, well, anyway, that's their problem. You 'aven't asked me why I've come.'

This was true. She had been over-anxious to tell her tale, madly hoping to deflect his anger, and so now she said, 'Oh, yes, I suppose I just assumed that it was Labour business.'

'It isn't,' he said brusquely. 'I came after you. You're needed back 'ome.' The north – Yorkshire – would always be home for Amos; here in London he felt like a visitor.

'Eve's badly,' he added. 'Daniel's out o' kilter and them girls need you.'

'But I had a letter from Eve, full of high spirits,' Anna said.

'There's a lot can change before a letter sent from Jamaica arrives in London. They got a telegram from 'er brother. Seems to think she's at death's door. Daniel 'as 'er dead and buried.'

She blanched, and stood up. Amos thought she was going at once for her hat and coat, but she held her ground and her eyes were filled with hot anger. 'You pig!' she said.

'Ey? Don't shoot t'messenger,' he said indignantly, but he knew he'd been unkind. There were ways and ways of delivering bad news.

'You just want to make me feel as bad as possible, don't you – about being away, about sometimes living life separate to you? You want me to be someone else! This is truth of it.' Her voice rose to a full-blown shout and he shrank from it, appalled. 'Well,' she raged, 'I am who I am, and you should not have married me, perhaps.' Her heart thumped in her chest, and she felt lightheaded with fury and distress. Amos seemed stupid with shock; lost for words, staring and staring but saying nothing at all. He was thinking hard, however, because he knew that in many ways she was right; he had come to London in a spirit of self-righteous indignation at her absence; he expected her unstinting support at home and in his work; he resented her chosen profession. But, emphatically and categorically, he didn't think he should have married anyone other than Anna Rabinovich.

He didn't say any of this, though; he was stumped, and he was stubborn. Unhappiness was plainly written across his face, but Anna, just at this moment, didn't much care. She sat down again and took a moment, collecting herself before she spoke again.

'Tell me about Eve,' she said, calmly enough, and he told

her in a surly, mechanical voice what little he knew. Anna closed her eyes and breathed in deeply, absorbing the information. It was a body blow, but she was sustained by the certain knowledge that she would know in her heart if Eve were gone. This she believed fervently.

'Poor Daniel,' she said. 'Poor girls. How they must be suffering.' Amos's spirits lifted with love for his extraordinary, compassionate, generous wife, who could seethe with anger one moment and forgive the next; but then she said that her plan was to remain in London for the time being, because she had given Lord Netherwood her word that she would petition the government on Lady Henrietta's behalf. In an instant Amos's world turned dark again.

'You put that lot before Eve?' he said, incredulous.

For a moment she looked down at her hands, which were clasped in her lap. Then she looked up and fixed him with a look of such disdain that he felt a jolt of actual physical pain. 'No,' she said, 'of course not. That's not what I'm doing. I am, however, putting them before you and your demands, in this instance.'

She paused now, and drew breath, and Amos could see that she was shaking. If he could have moved he would have stood and wrapped her in his arms and apologised again and again, but he seemed compelled by an inner destructive force to merely sit and stare. So Anna went on, in a measured, rational way that felt worse, to Amos, than the shouting. 'If Eve were in England you know that I would be by her side. But she's thousands of miles away, while Henrietta Hoyland is imprisoned here in London. I shall see if I can help, and then I shall come back to Yorkshire and do what I can there.'

Her expression was unreadable, but he knew she was angrier with him than she had ever been. He had used the crisis of Eve's illness for his own ends. He wanted her by his side; whatever the needs and wants of Daniel, Eliza and Ellen, his own came first; his own were paramount. She had understood this at once, and now it had dawned on him too.

He said, 'Anna,' in a faltering, questioning voice, as if he couldn't see her, but she didn't answer. She only stood once more and left the room.

PART THREE

Chapter 38

It did Isabella Beeton no credit that there was not a single mention of goat in her book of household management. Ruby had looked in the index months ago, not because she needed to know how to cook goat but because she wondered what the English did with it. There had been plenty of recipes for lamb, even more for mutton, but for goat nothing at all. It was as if the creature's four tasty feet had never walked the earth. Ruby pitied Mrs Beeton in particular, and the English in general. Speaking for herself, there was no animal flesh that she held in higher esteem.

This morning, Scotty had carried in two whole carcasses, intact from their heads to their hooves, one over each shoulder. On a butcher's block in the kitchen annexe, which was reserved for the grislier aspects of meat preparation, Batista – a maestro with a cleaver – had set about them with swift expertise. Heads, feet, shins, necks and all variety of offal went in a tin bucket for safe keeping, while the prime cuts came through to the kitchen for currying. Ruby cut the meat into chunks and seasoned it with a mix of chopped scallion, garlic and curry spices. It needed, now, to be massaged into the flesh, but this, she thought, could be accomplished by someone else, and she looked across the kitchen to where Angus sat on the floor with Scotty, playing four-five-six with a trio of dice.

'Angus,' Ruby said. 'Come and rub the goat meat.'

This sounded interesting so the little boy stood up immediately, and Scotty said, 'An-goose, you kyaan just walk away from de game,' although that's exactly what he did and Scotty held out his hands in mock despair.

'Sorry Scotty,' Angus said importantly. 'Ruby wants me.'

'Good boy,' she said, and lifted him on to a stool at the sink. 'Now, wash your hands, then drag the stool over there, where the goat's waiting for you.'

He did as he was bid, and she said, 'Good boy,' again. 'Now, get your hands right in there, and rummage about so that the spices colour the meat.' She showed him what she meant and he copied, revelling in the squelch of the fresh, cool meat in his palms. 'That's the way,' she said. 'That's the way to curry goat.'

She was pleased and so he smiled with equal pleasure; he loved Ruby almost as much as he loved Roscoe. He was sleeping at Ruby's house for the time being, sharing Roscoe's narrow bed. He slept in the warm lee of the older boy's body, curled up like a cashew nut in the space Roscoe made for him, listening to stories about a clever, tricky spider called Anansi; they were mesmerising tales, but always, always, Angus fell asleep before the end. He didn't mind, though: it meant that Roscoe would have to tell him again. Angus couldn't imagine a nicer way to go to sleep, or a nicer bed to sleep in, or a better friend than Roscoe.

Ruby watched him for a while. She marvelled at his capacity for happiness, which she supposed was common to all children, not just to this child. He grabbed the simple joys from each new day, and if he asked about Eve it was because Ruby had mentioned her first. For now, Angus had a new normality and he was satisfied with his stand-in family of

Ruby and Roscoe, and a cast of interesting extras – Scotty, Maxwell, Wendell – who provided additional entertainment. Just as well, thought Ruby, because his actual family members were a dead loss. Silas paid him little heed, so Angus paid little back, and Seth was kind but oddly formal; he always seemed to be stuck for something to say.

Batista, busy with the cleaver at the butcher's block, raised her voice in song, and the sound of the blade splitting bone provided a sort of grisly percussion. Angus glanced at Ruby, alarmed. Batista, alone among the kitchen regulars, scared him without ever meaning to. She had a way of rolling her eyes back in her head when she spoke to the Lord. Also, she puffed and wheezed and sometimes tried to grab him as he passed, then said, 'Why you torture me li'l man?' when Angus dodged her fat arms and refused to let her squeeze him. Angus thought it impossible to like Batista, although Roscoe did and Ruby too. Perhaps, Ruby told him, he would grow to like her, given time. This he doubted very much. She staggered into the kitchen now, heaving with both hands the tin pail of unspeakable goat parts, and Angus cut her a wary glance. Ruby, catching it, laughed and rubbed his hair, then said, 'Here comes Batista with the fifth quarter of the goat, all washed and ready for the pot,' and Angus looked down sternly at the basin of meat and spices, cross with Ruby for trying to meddle. He would not look up, he thought, until Batista was busy, or gone. Seeing this, Ruby laughed again and left him to it. She had work to do before she left for Sugar Hill.

Ruby had been about the same age as Angus when her mammy taught her what to do with the fifth quarter of the beast – the bits, her mammy told her, that the slaves used to get because no one else had any use for them, and more fool them. Now she followed the method in precisely the way she was taught as a girl, tipping the contents of the bucket into a five-gallon pan of boiling water. Never, ever – she could hear her mammy's grave voice even now, in her head – put meat and its bones into water that was cold.

'It sit there like something evil and gather scum,' she had said. 'Skimming the scum off of soup is about as low as a girl can go, and you'll never, ever, catch it all.'

What Mammy said Ruby did; she did it now, standing at arm's length so the rolling boil didn't splash and scald her. With the new addition the tempest was temporarily becalmed, so she waited a minute before adding green bananas, hot peppers, carrots, turnips, chochos, yam, thyme, more scallions and four flamboyant, generous pinches of sea salt. The head of the goat rose magisterially to the surface of the water so she pushed it down out of sight with a wooden spoon. Three hours from now this would be mannish water, a hot broth that was reputed to grow hairs on a young man's chest and put snap in an old man's celery. Ruby, who needed neither of these benefits, simply liked the taste; it recalled innocence, childhood, a mother's love. It also made enough to feed a village, and the hotel's guests would sup but a fraction of it, served to them – sieved and sieved again to a dark, clear broth – in earthenware beakers, the like of which none of them had ever used before. There was plenty of porcelain in the cupboards, of course: the soup could have been served in Royal Doulton so fine you could see the shadow of your hand through it. But this was the Eden Falls Hotel, where fine china, like beef en croute and sole *Veronique*, was a thing of the past. This formula – perverse, perhaps; brave, certainly – had proved to be a winning one. By offering the guests nothing at all that was familiar Eve had succeeded in pleasing them. Each meal had become an adventure. The handful of guests who baulked at goat and yam and ackee were offered a plain griddled steak, or spit-roast baby chicken, but these dishes carried with them the taint of woefully limited horizons. There was a new and infectious spirit in the dining room, and a new informality too. Napkins were tucked into collars; occasionally, cutlery was abandoned for the sensuous pleasure of picking up a pork rib and sucking it clean.

Ruby gave the brew one final poke and the scallions bobbed like corks. 'There,' she said, as if this had made all the difference, and then she started to take of her apron. Angus, who wasn't looking but had a sixth sense about these things, said, 'Where are you going?' although he instantly regretted it, because Batista gave one of her low, wheezy chuckles and said, 'Pickney eyes in back of im 'ead.'

'Roscoe is expecting to find you here, at the end of school,' Ruby said, pre-empting the second question, which would certainly have been whether he could come too. 'You mustn't disappoint him, must you?'

Angus shook his head gravely. 'Is Scotty staying?' he asked.

Scotty said, 'An-goose, leave de goat an play tree-four-five, mon.' He was squatting against the wall, rattling the dice in his big hands and grinning, showing all his long teeth. Angus looked at Ruby.

'When you're finished,' she said. 'And only then.'

She was just as strict with him as she had ever been with Roscoe. Yes, his mammy was sick and his daddy was far away, but no child was ever improved by over-indulgence or shirking. He nodded, and his expression was so endearingly conscientious as he returned his attention to the basin of meat that she wanted to reward him, so she said: 'And yes, of course Scotty will stay.'

Ruby looked at the porter, who winked at her. Batista, with a glassy expression of beatific calm, rocked back and forth in her chair and said, 'Jesus, lawd Jesus, me comin' soon to de pearly gates, me hear de bugle blow,' and Ruby could see that Angus had a point. The old woman, with her patois and prayers, wasn't – to use an expression she'd learned from Eve – everybody's cup of tea.

When Ruby arrived at Sugar Hill Justine shrank away from the bedside with her eyes dipped, afraid of the other woman's displeasure, but Ruby only nodded and smiled tautly. She had corralled her complicated feelings towards the housekeeper and claimed only to pity her.

'Thank you Justine,' was all she said, keeping her eyes firmly away from the swell of her belly. 'How is she?'

Justine said, 'Same-same,' without looking up.

'No more blood?'

'*Non*.'

'And has the doctor seen her today?'

'*Oui madame*, but now he gone.' She looked up, and added, 'to Spanish Town.'

Ruby rolled her eyes at his uselessness. Justine, who had been backing towards the door, now slipped from the room. There was something so cowed and craven about her, thought Ruby; she should stand tall and proud, not creep about like an apology.

Ruby turned to Eve, who lay on her side on the bed. She looked unbearably fragile: insubstantial and weightless. Her eyes were closed, her breathing shallow, and the skin of her face was still tinted parchment yellow, although when Ruby laid a hand on her forehead the heat of the fever seemed to have abated. Ruby sat beside her and tenderly stroked her head, and Eve seemed to stir, as if somehow, from the depths of her sickness, she might be trying to make the journey back. Ruby watched her closely and said her name. Eve's lips, pale and painfully dry, moved fractionally, although there was no sound. There was a pot of balm on the bedside table so Ruby dipped a finger into it and drew it across Eve's mouth, rubbing the salve gently into the cracked skin. Again she stirred, but her eyes stayed closed.

Ruby sighed, and in the quiet room her sigh sounded doom-laden, although in fact she felt some hope. There had been no bleeding since that first, terrible time, when Justine had practically had Eve laid out for the coffin, and the doctor, who had finally arrived, cross and dusty, from Spanish Town after three days' travel in a pony and trap, had declared her to be 'in God's hands'. This had hardly seemed, Ruby told him, an appropriate verdict for a supposedly reputable man of science. There had followed an icy silence, which had intimidated Ruby not one jot.

'We are all, when it comes to it, in God's hands, Dr Hennessy,' she had said. 'What we would like to know from you is what can you give this poor lady to hasten her recovery?'

Silas had been there, clutching his mouth in horror and defeat at the doctor's verdict, as good as useless. He was an insubstantial man for all his swagger, Ruby thought. When she had stood up to the doctor, challenged his complacency, Silas had stared at her as if he hadn't realised she was in the room.

Dr Hennessy had ignored Ruby. 'When yellow fever continues on to its second phase,' he had said, addressing his words to Silas, one white man to another, 'the chances of recovery are remote. Your sister has begun to haemorrhage due to the damage caused to her internal organs. Her vital signs are weak. By all means let your girl' – here he indicated Ruby, without looking at her – 'tend to her comfort and keep her hydrated. The rest, I'm sorry to say, is out of our hands. Now, I trust you have a room prepared for me? I have had an arduous journey.'

Ruby had stepped between Silas and the doctor, and skewered him with a defiant glare. 'My name,' she said, 'is Ruby Donaldson, and I am no one's "girl", Dr Hennessy. If you have no b tter advice than this, I wish for all our sakes you had been spared the trouble of coming at all,' and Silas had opened and shut his mouth like a guppy on dry land.

So now, Ruby thought, Dr Hennessy was gone. She

wondered what he had charged for his expert opinion: a hundred times what it was worth, in any case. On the floor, at her feet, she had a loose hemp bag containing a collection of leaves picked from the trees and plants of her garden, and one or two gleaned from the roadside. She picked it up now and, holding it open, dipped her head into it and inhaled the complex, familiar, bitter aroma: ackee, soursop, liquorice bush, joint-wood, pimento, cowfoot, sage, guava, jack-in-the-bush, cerassee, thistle and elder.

'Justine!' she said then, because she knew the other woman would be only on the landing, awaiting instruction. The door opened a crack, and Justine whispered, '*Oui, madame?*'

Ruby held out the bag. 'I want you to take these and boil them in four pints of water, until the water has taken on the same colour and smell of the leaves. Do you understand?'

'*Oui madame.*' She took the bag from Ruby's outstretched hand.

'When I come back later this evening I believe Mrs Eve will be awake,' Ruby said. Justine listened, placidly, for her part in the plan. She had utter faith in Ruby, and utter respect for her authority; she was only sad that she seemed to have lost her as a possible friend. 'Together,' Ruby said, 'you and I will give her a bush bath.'

'*Très bien,*' Justine said. '*Merci, madame.*'

Ruby nodded. 'The child,' she said abruptly. 'When will it be born?'

Justine furrowed her brow, as if she had never asked herself this question and was only now working out the answer. The baby signalled dangerous territory, Justine felt, and she was wary as she replied, '*Novembre, madame.*'

'Will he allow you to stay?' Ruby asked and it was evident from her tone that she herself thought this unlikely. Again Justine seemed to be considering the question, but she met

Ruby's eyes quite steadily when she answered, '*Mais oui*. This is my home.'

'No,' said Ruby. 'This is Silas Whittam's home. You, Justine, are merely passing through.'

She felt vicious towards her. And she felt ashamed.

Chapter 39

‿୨⌒᷿⌒୧‿

The demolition of the glasshouses, when it had first begun, had seemed like an act of desecration, as if a temple was being razed to the ground, not a hothouse. They were surprisingly flimsy, these structures. One dismantled joist had led swiftly to another, and glass had rained down in lethal shards. The area had had to be roped off to prevent an accident. As for the plants, they had to go too. Some of them had been able to be saved; the best of the ferns and the tropical palms were carefully dug up and temporarily potted, and were now huddled together in a suntrap by the coach houses, out of place and inconvenient, like refugees from a war. But everything else had been ripped out, the roots, stalks and foliage burned on a vast smoking pyre, the blooms sent to the still room for stripping and drying, or placed in barrels of water at the end of Oak Avenue so that anyone from the town could walk up and help themselves. For a fortnight in late May carnations, freesias, lilies and orchids had flaunted their gaudy colours in front-parlour windows up and down the miners' terraces.

Now it was July, and the building of the new plant houses was under way, and already, from the footings and the length and depth of the beds, it was plain to see that they would be

352

magnificent. But what was also plain was that Daniel MacLeod had lost all interest in the scheme. Indeed, the head gardener seemed to have lost all interest in everything. There were thirty-four gardeners beneath him, and it was just as well they knew their business, because there was no guidance from him. He had turned inward; everyone saw it, and it was because his wife, who had taken off to Jamaica, was ill: dead, some folk said, but this was surely only morbid speculation. Mr MacLeod brought himself into work each day, but his demeanour and bearing were that of a man bowed down by life's burdens.

'If he would only talk about it,' said Mrs Powell-Hughes. The housekeeper was watching Sarah Pickersgill bottle chutney in the kitchens of Netherwood Hall. The air was pungent with the sweet-sour smell of Demerara sugar boiled with vinegar and Sarah's fingertips were yellow with turmeric. 'You should put that in with a spoon,' Mrs Powell-Hughes said. 'Terrible stuff to remove, turmeric.'

The cook sniffed dismissively. 'I can't gauge t'quantity unless I do it in pinches,' she said. 'Mrs Adams were t'same.'

They both were briefly silent, remembering Mrs Adams, the old cook who died of a seizure in the cold store.

'I'm minded to seek him out,' said Mrs Powell-Hughes. She was back to Daniel again, but she'd lost Sarah, who looked up blankly.

'Mr MacLeod,' said the housekeeper. 'He won't come in for meals, or for a brew, so I shall have to find him myself.'

Sarah looked sceptical. 'I'd leave well alone if I were you,' she said. 'He's grown a beard.'

'Well, and is that a reason to keep my distance? Plenty of men grow beards.'

'Aye, because they mean to. Mr MacLeod's grown a beard because 'e's forgotten to shave, I reckon. That's quite another matter.'

Mrs Powell-Hughes saw Sarah's point. The Daniel MacLeod she knew had always been a clean-shaven man, and now he had a wild look about him: unkempt and, she suspected, unwashed. She wondered if she might call in at that house on the common. She could find out a little more of the facts because, try as she might to disregard gossip and rumour, it was impossible not to overhear and then to worry. It would be irregular, calling in; she realised that. Then again, she'd been once before, when Anna Rabinovich married Amos Sykes and they'd held a little reception on the grass outside. She could call in one evening, perhaps. She could take a pie. That would surely be better than ambushing him in the garden. She'd seen him yesterday, with his hands thrust down into his trouser pockets, walking up through the kitchen garden without once glancing at the beans or stopping to pull out a dandelion, and he hadn't looked approachable in the least. She hadn't said hello: had slipped out of range to spare them both awkwardness. Could she summon the courage to knock on his door, then? It would be the Christian thing to do, but would it be pleasant or comfortable? These questions passed silently like clouds through her mind, and her brow furrowed as she contemplated them.

'Not that long to go now,' Sarah said, and the housekeeper knew at once what she was referring to: the regatta and their trip to Cowes.

'Mmm,' said Mrs Powell-Hughes.

'I've drawn up menus and sent 'em on for approval.'

'Yes, you said.'

'As soon as Lady Netherwood gives me t'say-so, I shall start packing some non-perishables. Pity this chutney won't be ready.'

'I hope you've something better than chutney in mind. It's not a parish picnic, you know.' The housekeeper's tone was quite altered; mention of the regatta made her sharp-tongued.

Sarah glanced at her, amused.

'Don't whittle so much about it,' she said. 'It's just a week on a boat.'

Mrs Powell-Hughes didn't deign to reply. It needled her that Sarah Pickersgill, born and raised in landlocked Yorkshire and with no idea what she was talking about, nevertheless presumed a worldly air whenever she spoke about Cowes, which was often. In the silence, Sarah bottled on contentedly, and because the conversation seemed to have dried up, she hummed a cheerful tune as she worked. It sounded, to the housekeeper, suspiciously like a sea shanty.

The family had been absent all summer, but Netherwood Hall had buzzed with activity. From the attic rooms to the basement cellars there were myriad tasks to accomplish. This was a period of recovery for the house, a respite from the rigours of lavish living. During these weeks the household staff moved more freely through the corridors and entered rooms without knocking, but it was by no means a holiday. Rather, this was the time when the chipped gilt of picture frames was retouched; when the rugs were rolled and carried out for beating; when the wooden panelling was fed with linseed oil and the wooden floors waxed; when the lightly tarnished brass of the tapestry rails, high up on the drawing-room walls, could be buffed back to a high shine; when the individual crystal droplets on the ballroom chandeliers could be washed, dried and polished until each one glittered in the electric light with diamond brightness.

Parkinson, conducting a tour of duty through the house, gazed at it now in appreciation; it was as if they'd harnessed the sunshine, he thought, and this was so uncharacteristically whimsical that he reddened, even though he was alone. He busied himself at once, patrolling the perimeter of the gracious room, pleased with the gleam of the parquet floor and the glow of the lighting. Not so very long ago it had been all candles and oil lamps, in here and throughout the house. Then, they'd kept a boy whose only job was to trim the wicks and fill the lamps, and he'd never had an idle moment. Jimmy, Parkinson thought, that was his name. The lad walked miles in the course of a working week. Now one flick of a brass switch and lo, there was light. In this room, and the dining room, the old sconces were still on the walls, although the scorch marks left by the flames were long gone, painted over. The butler stood, lost in the past, remembering the hunt balls, the Christmas balls, the birthday balls. He thought of Lady Henrietta at eighteen, her coming-out ball held not at Fulton House but here at Netherwood Hall, which was perfectly right and proper. Two hundred and fifty young guests, the blur of silk and satin, the windows flung wide to cool the dancers, the dear, departed sixth earl and the then Lady Netherwood watching the proceedings with quiet satisfaction and thanking him, Parkinson, very especially for his tireless quest for perfection. Those were the days; the family complete, the house in its pomp. The past was a happier place than the present, he felt, and the future, in the hands of a young earl and a flighty countess, was worryingly unpredictable. Parkinson enjoyed predictability; it was a very undervalued quality. Outside, the bell in the cupola struck midday, reminding him that time waited for no man, and especially not for butlers. 'Ah well,' he said out loud, 'better get on.' But he stood still, fixed to the spot by nostalgia and something akin to sadness, or regret.

There were four doors to the ballroom, and one of them opened now to admit Mrs Powell-Hughes, who looked extremely perky, and a little bit smug. 'There you are,' she said. 'I'm glad I've found you. Lady Henrietta looks likely to join us in Cowes.'

The very best type of good news – just like the very worst bad – comes quite out of the blue, and these tidings were so entirely unexpected that the butler clapped his hands to his mouth and the housekeeper laughed.

'I know,' she said. 'Isn't it marvellous?'

'Are you quite sure?'

'Sure as I can be.'

It struck Mr Parkinson now that as head of the household staff he would usually have been the first to hear any developments regarding the family. He said, 'And how do we know this, Mrs Powell-Hughes?' as if he doubted the truth of it, or the reliability of the source. The housekeeper pursed her lips in irritation and said, 'I can assure you, Mr Parkinson, that I'm not peddling idle rumour,' and then she paused for a worrying moment, as if she might tell him no more, so he swiftly reassured her that he had meant to imply no such thing.

'Very well,' she said, mollified. 'I saw Mrs Sykes in Netherwood and she's visited Lady Henrietta in prison and then again in the infirmary.'

The butler winced at these details; the specifics of Lady Henrietta's whereabouts caused him pain.

'She's thin as a lath, apparently,' Mrs Powell-Hughes went on. 'Not herself at all.'

'But she's home?'

'Not as such. There's a bit of paperwork, legalities I expect. But' – she hesitated, trying to remember what Anna had said – 'the prime minister has chosen to be merciful.'

'We might do well to wait until the earl confirms the news, however,' said Mr Parkinson, asserting, albeit in a small way, his seniority. 'That is, without wishing to question the authority of Mrs Sykes in this matter, we perhaps should keep it to ourselves?' He did wonder, privately, what Anna Sykes could possibly have to do with the sorry situation, or why she might

357

be in a position to predict an outcome. Mrs Powell-Hughes seemed to know better, though.

'Oh, if Anna says so, it'll be so,' she said rather breezily, and bobbed across the room to the door with a distinct spring in her step. 'Anyway,' she said, pausing on the threshold, 'she spoke to Mr Asquith, so she should know.'

Mrs Powell-Hughes had been in Pickering's, ordering blue and white ticking, when she bumped into Anna, who used a draper's shop like other people used a library; she came for the peace, and to think. This morning she had been contemplating the vagaries of life over a rack of jewel-coloured slubbed silks: a boldly optimistic order by the young Mr Pickering – whose father, old Mr Pickering, had always thought mostly of worsteds and wool flannel – in this town of working-class housewives.

Mrs Powell-Hughes, seeing Anna, had voiced her concerns, *sotto voce*, about Daniel MacLeod, and Anna had reassured her that she was here, now, for a few days and would be looking after him. Lighter of heart, relieved of her imagined obligation, the housekeeper had asked if Anna was thinking of making herself an evening gown out of garnet silk. Anna, surprised, had said, 'No, why do you ask?' which had thrown Mrs Powell-Hughes, since the younger woman had the fabric between finger and thumb and was rubbing it speculatively.

'Oh! I see,' Anna had said. 'No, no, I'm not buying.' She let the cloth drop. 'I just like it in here. It's soothing.' And she smiled and shrugged, as if to say, There's your explanation, do with it what you will.

Mr Pickering, at the counter, looked crestfallen. If the likes of Mrs Sykes weren't tempted by the silks, he wondered if anyone would be.

'Beautiful colour on you,' he said. 'It's not everybody could wear it, but you could.' He was known to have an eye, the young Mr Pickering; his opinion was valued. Also, he was the only shopkeeper in Netherwood to wear a three-piece suit to work, and a necktie with matching handkerchief. This, while conferring status upon him and earning respect, also – in truth – made him feel out of his element here. Sometimes he dreamed of moving lock, stock and barrel to Sheffield.

'No time for dressmaking, Mr Pickering,' Anna said, crushing his hopes, and then, because she saw his disappointment, she said she might make some cushion covers and bought two yards. She left the shop with Mrs Powell-Hughes, and together they strolled along King Street, which was how the housekeeper came to learn the news about Lady Henrietta and the part Anna had played in her deliverance. It had just been a letter, she said; but in the end, it had been delivered in person to Mr Asquith.

'Never! At Parliament? Did your husband take it?'

'No,' said Anna levelly. 'At Downing Street, and I took it.' This had seemed even more remarkable to the housekeeper, whose eyes widened in wonder. Anna, however, remained perfectly casual. 'I hadn't expected to see him,' she said, 'which is why I put it all in a letter. I was going to leave it with the constable on the doorstep, without much hope of it ever being seen, but then the door opened and someone I knew stepped out, and he showed me in. Mr Asquith was extremely pleasant, although he's very angry with the suffragettes. Still, he listened to me most obligingly.'

'Hang on, who came out?' said Mrs Powell-Hughes, struggling to keep up. 'Who showed you in?'

'Oh, a man I know: Sir William de Lisle. We painted his summerhouse. Wasn't that a stroke of luck? He's something in the Colonial Office.'

'Well well,' said the housekeeper. 'Fancy that.' She was

beginning to feel rather parochial. Her own world was so very small compared to Anna's.

'Yes, very fortuitous.' She seemed to be stopping at that, so Mrs Powell-Hughes pressed her further; what had she said to the prime minister?

'Oh, well, just that the best way to keep the WSPU out of the newspapers was to let Lady Henrietta go. She was becoming a martyr to the cause, you see.'

'Yes,' said Mrs Powell-Hughes. 'I think so.'

'Mr Asquith finds them maniacal,' Anna said. 'He's sick of being pelted with missiles, he said.'

The housekeeper tutted. 'He would be, yes.'

'But he agreed with me that the present publicity is bad for the government and good for the suffragettes.'

'Did he?' There was a respectful pause while Mrs Powell-Hughes digested the information. It seemed astounding to her that Anna could tell the tale in such a nonchalant manner, as if recounting a conversation with the postman or the butcher. Thinking this made her ask, 'So, were you nervous?'

'Mmm?' Anna's mind had drifted again, to Eve, and to Daniel.

'Talking to the prime minister, I mean? Were you quaking in your boots? I should've been.' She laughed; she felt nervous at the mere thought of it.

Anna looked at her askance. 'No, not at all,' she said. 'Why?'

'Oh, no reason,' said Mrs Powell-Hughes. Then Anna turned the conversation to other matters, which occupied their walk to Turnpike Lane, where their paths diverged. It didn't escape Mrs Powell-Hughes's attention, however, that instead of walking briskly towards Netherwood Common and Ravenscliffe, Anna dawdled and checked her silver fob, and this was all done with purpose, as if she expected someone to join her. And then – this was just visible, through a break in the terrace on Watson Street – the housekeeper saw a young man, black-haired and coffee-skinned, striding towards Anna with the type of broad, open, charming smile that must surely bathe the recipient in warmth. Mrs Powell-Hughes thought she had seen him before – he was conspicuous enough, heaven knew – but she couldn't place him or name him. It vexed her that she wouldn't be able to quiz Anna directly, without betraying her own somewhat covert behaviour, and all the way back to Netherwood Hall she racked her brains, but his identity eluded her.

'Penny for 'em,' said Sarah Pickersgill, who had shoved the kitchen tabby off the kitchen step and was taking two minutes from the tyranny of pickling and bottling.

'If I described to you a handsome young man with an exotic complexion . . .'

'I'd tell you it was Mr Oliver of Whittams,' Sarah said obligingly. 'Why?'

'He's in Netherwood,' said Mrs Powell-Hughes.

'I could 'ave told you that, an' all,' said Sarah. 'They've a colliery at Dreaton Bridge, where my brother lives. They come up from time to time, Mr Oliver or Mr Whittam. Keep an eye on things, like.'

Mrs Powell-Hughes lowered herself on to the step because it looked so pleasant in the sunshine, and Sarah knew so many interesting things.

'He seemed very pleased to see Mrs Sykes,' she said meaningfully.

Sarah raised a worldly eyebrow. ''e's gorgeous,' she said.

'Sarah!'

'Just saying.'

'Does he know Mrs Sykes well, do you suppose?'

Sarah shrugged. 'Silas Whittam, Eve MacLeod, Anna Sykes, Hugh Oliver – there's your connections. I expect they know each other well enough, yes. This step's a right suntrap, int it?'

'It is. I can see why the cats like it.'

They sat on, wilfully and uncharacteristically idle, in plain view of the estate offices across the courtyard where the bailiff, a diligent oddball named Absalom Blandford, twitched and fumed at their audacious time-wasting, and jotted down their conduct in his special ledger, under the day's date and with the precise time recorded alongside.

Chapter 40

Like a pair of bookends, Enoch and Amos sat side by side in the sunshine, watching boaters on the Serpentine from underneath the brims of their hats. They both wore pewter-grey Homburgs – neither would be seen dead in anything made of straw – so each perspired gently around the hatband and felt the occasional bead of sweat breaking for freedom towards the collar. They didn't have a lot to say. They were both brooding, pondering the consequences of recent events: in Enoch's case, entirely political, in Amos's, wholly personal. Their expressions repelled those passers-by who might have thought of sitting too. They looked stern, in their contemplative state: as if they might judge a fellow and find him lacking.

For his part, Amos was considering the irony of being back in London now that Anna was in Ardington. He'd been called down on party business and he felt a small stab of shame – not for the first time – at the drama he'd made of trying to fetch her home, and then the drama, again, when she'd gone to Asquith – Asquith, of all people! – on an errand for the earl. He had raged, as if her sole intention had been to betray his principles: as if he was the centre of the universe and all actions were significant only so far as they related to him. Anna had heard him out in white-faced, dignified silence, then had with-drawn to pack a suitcase. They had travelled north together, in a train carriage so full of their mutual discontent that there was barely room for themselves. Later, in the sanctuary of his old office at the miners' union building in Barnsley, he'd had a talking-to from Enoch. It was high time that Amos conquered the black dog of his temper, his friend had said: Send it packing otherwise you'll drive her away. His words had sounded over-blown and theatrical at the time, but now, in the clear light of a summer's afternoon and with a hundred and seventy miles between him and Anna, it seemed like sound advice.

On the water, young men and women larked about in wooden boats and their laughter bounced across the lake like skimmed stones. To Amos there seemed no point to their activity; what was the purpose of a boat on a body of water that went nowhere? He thought this first, then he asked it out loud.

'Merriment,' Enoch said.

'I'd want a river, me.'

Enoch didn't reply.

'On a river,' Amos said, 'you get somewhere. T'landscape changes, t'river widens, there are mills, bridges, villages, towns, all that sort o' thing. This,' he said, gesturing towards the hilarity on the lake, 'is just going round in circles.'

'Very apt,' Enoch said.

'What is?'

'That. Going round in circles.'

'Well, they are.'

'And so are we, except we're 'avin' a lot less fun than that lot.'

Amos fell silent. He was supposed to be the pessimist, Enoch the optimist; he hated it when Enoch lost his pep. How could he, Amos, fight the good fight without Enoch's wilful, stubborn buoyancy?

364

'It's an 'iatus, that's all,' Amos said. 'A short interruption to our upward progress.' He tried to put a spring in his words, a jokey lilt, but it sounded stilted and unconvincing; certainly, it was uncharacteristic.

Enoch snorted. 'More like a bloody big brick wall.'

'Claptrap,' said Amos, reverting to type. 'There's no brick wall, and don't you be building one.'

'I'm not,' Enoch said flatly. 'It's not of my making.'

'They will deliver less than they promise,' Amos said. He was quoting directly from one of Enoch's Fabian Society pamphlets. 'The Liberals, ultimately, will fail the working classes, because at heart it is the party of compromise – Enoch Wadsworth, *The Impoverished Liberal Legacy*, 11th April 1909.'

If Amos expected a smile he was disappointed. 'All well and good,' Enoch said, 'but if this budget of Lloyd George's delivers even 'alf of what it promises, we'll be pushed so far to t'margins of politics that we might as well join t'ighland Land League and start campaigning for crofters' rights.'

'Good cause that,' Amos said. 'Except we don't want an independent Scotland. We need Scotland.'

Enoch tilted up the brim of his hat and let the sun fall on his face, which was pallid and softly lined: the face of a scholar, Amos always thought. It was hard to imagine that Enoch had ever worked underground, except that he had a way of heaving his shoulders when he breathed, and when he coughed he sounded as if he was trying to bring up half a lifetime of coal dust. Amos could tell, now, that his friend was cogitating; his political uncertainties never lasted very long.

'The problem, as I see it, is one of faith and respect,' Enoch said.

This was better. Amos waited as Enoch formed his thoughts.

'Faith in our own future as a viable political party, and respect for ourselves as a radical force entirely independent of t'Liberals.'

There was a pause, a thinking silence.

'We've fallen into a trap set years ago by Gladstone,' Enoch said. 'We've been patronised by t'Liberals, we've been grateful for t'crumbs they've thrown, stepping back for us 'ere and there so we can fight seats they don't need. We've been used, in effect, as a gauge of working-class opinion, nowt more.'

Enoch turned and looked at Amos. 'They don't feel threatened by us. They don't feel us nipping at their 'eels.'

'Their folly, then,' Amos said, taking his cue. 'And our triumph will be all t'sweeter when it comes, for being completely unexpected.'

'Soldier on,' Enoch said. 'We mun soldier on and stay true to our founding principles. From now on, we fight every by-election, irrespective o' MacDonald and 'is Liberal appeasement. We educate t'unions so they follow t'miners and affiliate wi' Labour. We push for a sea change in our way o' thinking, so that every Labour MP sees 'imself in government, not forever agitating for change from t'fringes.'

'Hallelujah,' Amos said. 'And amen.'

'One day, we'll run this country . . .'

'. . . fair and square . . .'

'. . . without Ramsay MacDonald and 'is Lib-Lab deals.'

They turned to each other and grinned, because they'd enjoyed this conversational journey before, and it always led them towards a better frame of mind. Then they shook hands, as if sealing a deal, and individually, privately, tamped down the fear that it was all pie in the sky.

There were a few catcalls from the landings when Henrietta left Holloway, but otherwise she was ignored. What a difference to her arrival, she thought. Back then there had been a series of degrading encounters, in which first her possessions, then her clothes and finally every last scrap of dignity had been taken from her. She had been dressed in a prison-issue frock, harangued with a long list of rules and lectured on what she may and may not expect in terms of contact with family and friends. When the time came to leave, however, she was simply shown the door. Her own clothes, the ones she had arrived in, had been brought to her, wrapped in brown paper, the night before. Her silk camisole, drawers and waist-petticoat had all been laundered, but her skirt and blouse had been neither washed nor hung, so they were marked here and there with smuts and were horribly crumpled. The WSPU sash, on the other hand, was pristine, carefully folded and placed almost respectfully on top of the pile of garments like a gift. The sight of it had given Henrietta a jolt, in the same way that an old photograph can startle a person: showing them, perhaps, who they once were.

On the morning of her departure Henrietta dressed herself – this took time; the buttons and laces resisted her fingers – and then sat on the edge of her bed with the sash on her lap. She held it at one end and let it unfold in a noiseless stream to the floor. Purple, green and white: dignity, hope and purity. Mary Dixon was a skilled seamstress; Henrietta traced a thumbnail along the tiny, near-invisible dots of silk thread and wondered at the patience required for such a task, and the perfectionism. She wondered, too, at the pride and passion for the cause that seemed to her to be miraculously embodied here, in this lovingly worked length of cloth. A small part of her wished to keep it as a memento, but when a warder rapped on her door and she stood to leave she carefully hung the sash over the end of the metal bedstead. It looked festive in the plain, grey cell.

Unaccompanied, she crossed the cobbled yard and passed through the great fortified entrance to the world outside the prison. When the door swung shut behind her she felt the vibration in her bones. Tobias was there in a voluminous linen car coat that flapped open on either side like two vast wings as he strode towards her. He enveloped her, pulling his coat around them both. She breathed in his cologne, a sharp, delicious mix of lemon, lime and lavender, and surrendered herself to the utter relief of freedom, the certain promise of comfort and the safe, firm embrace of her brother. All their lives she had regarded herself as stronger than him. Now she could see that she had been wrong; or rather, if he was weak, she was weaker still.

Tobias had brought a two-seater Daimler, pillar-box red with a hood lined in tartan. This was folded back, and Henrietta's motoring hat and cape were on the passenger seat. He placed the hat on her head and tied the chiffon scarf into a soft, floppy bow under her chin, then took the cape and arranged it on her shoulders, fastening the row of mother-of-pearl buttons as if she were a child and indeed, like a child she submitted to his attentions. He held her face, and with his thumbs he stroked the blue-grey shadows under her eyes and looked at her with such loving sorrow that tears of self-pity welled in her eyes.

'Come on then,' he said. 'Let's get you home.'

He held open the door of the car and she climbed in. She was glad to be sitting down. Her head spun with the effort of so much movement after so many days of torpor. She leaned back in the seat and closed her eyes to ease the giddiness. Tobias glanced at her with concern.

'You look all in,' he said.

She nodded. It hurt to speak.

'I haven't told Ma that you're out today,' he said. 'I thought the very last thing you'd want is any kind of reception committee, or fuss of that kind.' He was driving now, but he kept darting anxious looks at her to gauge her reaction. She smiled wanly to show her approval.

'I'll tell her you're coming out tomorrow. She's delighted, you know' – again, a sideways glance – 'that you're being released, that is. I know she hasn't been to see you, but that's not to say she doesn't think about you.'

Henrietta held up a hand. 'Tobes,' she said in a strange, rasping whisper. She coughed, and held a hand against her throat. It felt damaged, but the pain was deep inside and if there was scarring, it was hidden. 'It's quite all right,' she said, trying again. 'Don't make excuses for Mama.'

He laughed ruefully. 'Righto,' he said. 'Fair do's.'

The little coupé was performing well, and even in the present rather strained circumstances he could take pleasure from that. Tobias generally drove as if each new journey were a rather speedy game of chess. There was nothing more disappointing to him than an entirely empty road, free of other traffic. What he enjoyed was the check, cross-check and checkmate of motoring strategy: the triumph of getting ahead in the nick of time and against the other fellow's will. Now he nipped through a narrow channel, between a Buick and an old-fashioned brougham, and was rewarded with shouts of protest from either side as he sped on

'Tight squeeze,' he said without the slightest concern.

'The horses,' whispered Henrietta, 'didn't like that.'

He couldn't hear and whizzed on, jinking through the traffic as they negotiated the teeming urban swathes of Holloway. Henrietta reached over and tugged at his sleeve, and when he turned she half spoke, half whispered, 'Please can we go via Bedford Square?'

He pulled a face. 'Must we?'

She nodded, and he opened his mouth to argue then closed it again, as it seemed, after all, a small thing to ask. She didn't speak again until they got there, and then she only said, 'Wait here, Tobes,' when he started to get out. He watched her make her way to the front door of the Sykes house and felt like a bounder because she looked so vulnerable, and so unsteady on her pins. She had doubtless hoped to find Anna, but it was Amos Sykes who opened the door and Tobias's heart sank for his sister: she'd get nowhere fast with him. He adjusted his position in the car seat so that he had a clearer view of Sykes's expression which, for a tub-thumping left-wing zealot, was relatively benign. Henrietta was obviously doing most of the talking; Tobias could see Sykes leaning towards her, straining to hear. Tobias did the same, but he couldn't hear a thing over the engine and from this distance. Sykes nodded, answered, grimaced – unless that was a smile – and then closed the door as Henrietta turned and made her way back to the motor.

'All well?' said Tobias. 'Message delivered?'

She nodded. She'd used up her voice for the time being. Tobias longed to know the details of the exchange, but when Henrietta was settled once again in the passenger seat she patted him on the leg as if he were a loyal hound, then closed her eyes for what remained of the journey to Belgravia, and Fulton House.

Chapter 41

◦⌒◦⌒◦

Seth still hadn't visited Eve. He wasn't sure how to, since his uncle had carried her off to Sugar Hill. There was an unspoken veto on casual visitors, and Seth lacked the confidence to turn up uninvited, even if his mam was there on her sick bed. He lacked the confidence, too, to ask permission, and this made him angry with himself for being such a sap. But also – and this third reason was, in truth, the principal one – Seth was hamstrung by guilt: burdened and held back by the dull weight of it. He hadn't visited because he couldn't bear to face the truth, which was that she might not be on the island if it weren't for him, and if she wasn't on the island she wouldn't now be dangerously ill. This was the term Uncle Silas always used: not critically or chronically, but dangerously ill. She was in peril, and he, her son, was not only powerless but culpable. This fact, and it had, by now, hardened into solid fact in his mind, made Seth's heart pound and the bile rise in his throat. On the brink of manhood, he felt like a helpless child and he hated himself for it.

When his thoughts alighted uncomfortably on the letter dictated by his uncle but written by him he blushed with shame and berated himself for the weasel words that had lured her here. In his heart he had known that Uncle Silas should have sent a businesslike letter: open, transparent, frank. There had been a good chance that his mam would have come anyway, without the need to draw her by her heartstrings. No, the right way to go about things would have been for Uncle Silas to write to his mother, stating their present difficulty and the proposed solution in clear, objective terms. Seth knew that not only would this have been the correct way to go on; it would also have been *normal*. It was not normal, not at all, to manipulate, cajole, or deceive in the pursuit of one's own selfish, professional interests.

So.

This was where Seth always stopped. He shifted in the desk chair, stood up, paced the perimeter of the room, adjusted very minutely the position on the wall of a framed map of Jamaica. The incontrovertible truth, and the nub of the problem, was this: if he knew that his uncle's behaviour was unacceptable in this regard, he supposed that it was unacceptable in others. This was a thornier subject for Seth. He loved his Uncle Silas and he admired him, and he resisted with all his might the diminishment of those important feelings. From the day he had left Netherwood to work alongside him, Seth had felt it an honour, and a remarkable opportunity, to listen and learn. From nothing – literally nothing – his uncle had built an empire and stamped his name all over it, so that Whittam was known across the world to be synonymous with quality. At the docks, in Bristol and here at Port Antonio, there were wooden crates of bananas stacked high, with Whittam & Co. printed on the sides in dark blue ink. A warehouse towered over the wharves with the same words emblazoned above the main entrances and again, in smaller letters, above the gantries. In Yorkshire, at Dreaton Main Colliery, a glossy blue board bore the same company name and – best of all, in Seth's opinion – there it was again, painted on the prows of the finest fleet of liners to sail the Atlantic Ocean.

How, then, when he had made his mark on the world in such a bold, emphatic, indelible way, was his uncle capable of the sort of wily selfishness that even Seth, who was not yet seventeen, could see was almost childlike? How could his brilliance, skill and business acumen exist alongside this stubborn determination to please himself at any cost? It troubled Seth deeply that the uncle to whom he had paid such avid attention, the man he had copied in all matters of style and substance, was perhaps not everything that he should be. Something had changed, thought Seth; something had altered his outlook so that his drive and ambition, and his ruthless eye for a deal, seemed to be mutating into wild unpredictability and morose self-absorption. In Seth's mind the letter to Eve had been the catalyst and there, again, he was able to lay the blame at his own feet. Since they had colluded over the letter everything good had been twisted out of shape. Uncle Silas had begun to drink too much; he reached for the Scotch whisky at any time of day and drank it greedily, as if he were parched. He shouted, not just at the staff but at Seth, and it happened too often and in public. He shut himself away at Sugar Hill and made a mystery of his life there. He stayed away much of the time, then, when he did appear, he scattered ill will and cynicism about him, as if his aim was to sow misery and watch it grow.

Seth, out of his depth in so many different ways, considered his situation. His uncle's frequent absence meant he was, he supposed, in charge, and yet he felt just about the least capable person on the premises. None of them – Ruby, Maxwell, Batista, Scotty – ever sought his opinion about anything. The menu, the decor, the drinks they served in the bar: all were organised and overseen by the Jamaican staff. Even the new waitresses, Precious and Patience, who were younger than Seth, didn't seek his direction. Rather, they stared at him boldly and made him feel hot to his roots. They wore knee-length sleeveless frocks in vibrant colours and their slender brown arms and legs were alluring but also innocent, and this provoked some turbulence in Seth's soul. He was unequal to their silent poise; without ever uttering an insolent word, he felt they mocked him.

All of these anxieties drifted through Seth's mind now. They were familiar thoughts, and he was weary of them. He stared out of the window and comforted himself with the fact that Hugh Oliver would soon be here. When Hugh came everything would be better. He was urbane, competent and calm, and he was due any day now. By rights, Uncle Silas would then sail back to Bristol for a few weeks, although Seth wondered if his mam's illness might keep his uncle here. Miserably, he acknowledged that, at the moment, he hoped it wouldn't. He wanted Uncle Silas to go away, and that seemed terribly wrong: a sort of betrayal. He had to cling to his respect for his uncle. All of Seth's pride, all of his standing in the world, was invested in that.

Outside, he could see his little half-brother Angus talking to the gardener. The child was squatting on his haunches, chirruping away to Bernard who, Seth could see, now and again nodded or smiled or said, 'Uh-huh,' which was all Angus needed for encouragement. Seth felt guilty about Angus too, although not as guilty as he did about Eve. He couldn't summon any genuine interest in the child, who resembled Daniel too much to feel like flesh and blood. Seth didn't mind Daniel, but he was part of a chapter of his mam's life that Seth felt didn't include him, just as Jamaica was a chapter of his own life that probably shouldn't have included his mam. Watching Angus, he felt a swell of resentment at the child's ease in Bernard's company. He might be a native, hunkered down like that, barefoot and tousle-haired, and then Ruby Donaldson appeared and the three of them – the cook, the gardener, the child – all laughed at something she said.

'God damn it!'

His uncle's favourite curse in Seth's voice sounded unconvincing, so he tried again: 'God damn it all to hell!'

This time it was louder than Seth had intended. Bernard and Ruby turned impassive gazes towards the sound, and Angus, confused and alarmed, stood up and stepped sideways, closer to the cook. Ashamed, Seth ducked down, and moved quickly away from the window.

Ruby had seen him. White-faced, jug-eared, peering out at them from the safety of his office, which none of them were meant to enter without first being summoned. She kept her mouth shut, because here was little Angus and that strange individual at the window was, after all, his brother. Whatever Ruby might think of Seth, she didn't wish to alter the little boy's view of the world, whatever that might be. But, over the top of Angus's head, Ruby and Bernard exchanged a look that said plenty.

Bernard was Batista's cousin – 'From de laang, lean branch o' de family,' he said when he first came to work here. Ruby had looked up at him, and then down again to short, fat Batista with a sceptical smile. He was devout, like his cousin, but less mournfully so; he regarded life not as a long, deep river of human suffering but more a pleasant sojourn in God's earthly garden. They shared a similarity around the eyes, though, and a certain quiet belligerence. Bernard was digging up peonies, which he'd planted six years ago, under sufferance, knowing full well they wouldn't thrive; it was too hot for them here, and when it rained the few blooms they'd mustered soaked up the water like sponges and bent in a sorry, sodden arc to the soil. Bernard planned to make a bed of Jamaican orchids, which is what he'd recommended to Mr Silas at the time. Well, now, Bernard thought, a bucket with a hole is no use at the riverside. Mr Silas should learn to mind those parts of his business that he knew about, and leave the rest to others. He carried on thinking and digging, as if Ruby and Angus weren't there. The orchids would be pink, like the peonies, but they would hold their heads high in the sun and the rain. There were two hundred species of orchid on the island, Bernard knew: only a white man would want peonies instead.

'His daddy's a gardener,' Ruby said now, placing a proprietorial palm on Angus's head. The novelty of his hair – soft, like silk thread – never failed to charm her, and she twirled a strand around her finger and watched it slip away.

'My *pa's* a gardener,' Angus corrected her. 'Not my daddy.'

'I do beg your pardon. Your pa, of course.'

'Gardeners fine fellows,' Bernard said, tuning in, though only briefly. 'Fine fellows.' He had a slow drawl, difficult for Angus to understand.

'My pa has a big garden,' Angus said. 'As big as this island, I think.'

Bernard chuckled. 'Dat some plot.' He stooped to worry with his fingers at the earth, where old roots clung with desperate tendrils to the loamy soil. Angus helped him, burrowing with two hands into the bed, wheedling out the parts of the peonies that the spade had missed. Ruby left them to it and walked down the path to the road where Maxwell and Edna were waiting – for the second time that day – to take her to Sugar Hill.

'Can I come?' Angus called, but he stayed by Bernard's side and there was no real urgency to his question, or any expectation of success.

'Soon,' Ruby said over her shoulder. 'Maybe next time.'

376

Eve was propped up in bed, pale and slight against the bolster. Beside her was the small pile of letters, sent from England and, until today, unopened. The curtains were drawn closed, but behind them a window was open and the cream fabric billowed and swelled in the warm breeze, like the sails on a boat. Eve's eyes were bright with recent tears. Ruby understood, and said nothing about it. Instead she cocked her head jauntily and said, 'Well aren't you a sight to gladden the heart?'

Eve smiled. The yellow taint had almost entirely gone and her complexion was now merely wan. She said, 'Justine's gone to fetch tea. I feel like Lady Muck.'

Ruby put down her basket. 'Who's she?'

'Figure of speech,' Eve said. 'I just mean, I'm being waited on. I'm not used to it.'

Ruby perched on the edge of the bed. 'You've been waited on for some weeks,' she said. 'Waited on, and watched.' When she'd left Eve this morning she was awake, but barely so, and Ruby had had to support her while she took small sips of bitter bush tea. There was more of it in a flask in the basket; it was a dark brew, foul tasting, but it was helping mend Eve's poor, ravaged insides. The herb-filled bath that she and Justine had given her a few days ago had worked differently, from the outside in. It had enveloped her in a pungent steam that every Jamaican mother knew could work miracles when other medicines failed. Look at her now, thought Ruby: a living soul, brought back from the very edge of death.

'Do you remember the bath?' Ruby asked now; she was wondering what Eve knew and what she didn't. They had carried her from the bedroom, lowered her into the bath, supported her while the aromatics rose up from the hot water in a healing cloud, lifted her out, dried her and placed her back into bed, all without any sign from Eve that she knew what was happening.

'Oh,' Eve said. 'Yes, vaguely, I think I do. It smelled of sage, I think. Made me sweat.'

She had no idea, thought Ruby, of how close she had come to death, or how miraculous were the plants that had saved her. She had no idea, either, that Roscoe was Silas's son; the conversation in the kitchen was forgotten, the memory of it trammelled by the fever's progress. Ruby looked at her and wondered how and when she could tell her again; she felt she must, now that it had been told.

'What is it?' Eve said, but Ruby only smiled and said she was glad to see her so much improved.

'Will you bring Angus next time?'

Ruby nodded. 'He's very well, your boy. I left him gardening with Bernard.' She saw Eve's eyes fill again. She took her hand and Eve laid her head back on the bolster, letting the tears run unchecked down her face.

'Cho! Come come, now's not the time for tears.'

'I want my family,' Eve said. 'I want to go 'ome.'

Justine crept in on bare and silent feet, carrying a tray with a china teapot, cup and saucer. Ruby hadn't been there when she had left the room but she showed no surprise, only smiled cautiously and nodded, then placed the tray on the bed beside Eve. Then, with infinite humility, she retreated. Eve turned her head wearily and watched her leave, then said, 'She never stays if there's anyone else 'ere, and she never speaks unless someone speaks to 'er.'

'She's a very humble person,' Ruby said. 'Too humble, perhaps.'

'She's 'aving a baby, by t'looks of things.'

'She is.' To discourage further speculation – it was too soon for this conversation, just as it was too soon for the other – Ruby reached for the teapot and said, 'What have we here?'

'Real tea,' Eve said, smiling damply. 'Not fish tea, or fever-grass tea, or bitter bush tea.'

Ruby pulled a face as she poured. 'English breakfast, I suppose. All very well, but it never brought anyone back from yellow fever.'

'Ruby,' Eve said, and the other woman looked up from the task.

'Yes?'

'Bless you. Bless your goodness and your kindness. And thank you.'

Ruby waved away the words, but she was deeply gratified, and moved. She passed the cup, just half full so it wouldn't spill, to Eve, whose expression, when she took a drink, was full of bliss, like Batista's when she imagined the comfort that waited for her in heaven. This brew that the English loved so much, thought Ruby, it might not be beneficial to their health, but she was willing to accept it could be beneficial to their souls.

Chapter 42

⧖

Anna and Eliza were wedged together on the garden swing, the one that Daniel made for the children when he and Eve were first married and he moved in to Ravenscliffe. Anna had an arm around Eliza, who leaned in to her, drawing comfort from the closeness. As well as Anna's particular smell – not cologne but something toasty, definitely something edible – Eliza breathed in the sharp, fresh scent of grass that rose up from beneath their feet and, on the breeze, the smell of the pits, a rich, acrid, coal-and-smoke smell that, when you lived here, you almost stopped noticing. Over the picket fence, where the garden ended and the common began, Ellen and Maya were stalking ladybirds and holding them captive in a matchbox. Watching them, seeing their absorption, Eliza felt older, somehow, than she wanted to be. She had lost the knack of forgetting, of living in the moment.

'If she's dead . . .' Eliza said.

'She isn't dead,' Anna said quite calmly, because they'd been over this ground before and Anna realised that the girl only said it for the simple solace of her answers. 'If she was, we would know.'

''ow would we know?'

380

'Well, we would be told by telegram. That's the ordinary way. But also, I know in my heart that Eve is still with us. If she had died, my heart would've told me.'

Eliza sighed. 'I wrote again. Daniel posted it yesterday.'

'That's what she needs, letters from home.'

'She 'asn't written to me for a long time.'

'That's the illness. When she can, she will. Hugh said he'd send news, too, the moment he got there.'

'I like Mr Oliver,' Eliza said. 'I like t'way 'e talks to me in t'same way 'e talks to you and Daniel. I like being included. Some grown-ups just talk over you, as if you're invisible.'

Hugh Oliver, on a brief visit to Netherwood, had come to Ravenscliffe and shared a meal, a Russian dish made with beef short ribs and rice, and all the exotic seasonings that Anna had brought to Ravenscliffe when she lived there. 'This cayenne,' she had said, waggling the jar at a bemused audience of children, 'has not been used since I left for Ardington. Shame on you all!'

'No call for it in meat 'n' tatie pie,' Lilly Pickering had said. She was disgruntled by Anna's recent return to the fold: in Eve's absence, Lilly herself had been at the domestic tiller. But her standards were not ambitiously high and when Anna had arrived, wielding a wet mop across the front-hall tiles and filling the kitchen with foreign smells, Lilly had taken her coat from the peg and said she was off. 'You mun call me,' she said to Daniel, 'when she's gone.' Her offspring had trailed after her, reluctantly because they preferred this house on the common to their own in Beaumont Lane. But Anna had been unapologetic.

'Place is pigsty,' she had said hotly. 'That woman is disgrace.'

They knew not to argue, even though they all felt an injustice had been done. Any port in a storm, after all, and they had been able to depend on Lilly, bad-tempered and hatchet-faced though she often was. Plus, the Pickerings were poor; what would they all eat if they didn't eat here, Eliza had wondered. She resolved to bake scones and take them to Lilly; they would be a peace offering with a practical application. In her mind, the Pickering children would fall on the home baking with cries of ecstatic delight.

The truth of it was that Lilly had done what she could. Daniel had been the problem, dragging the house and everyone in it into the pit of his crippling despondency. Part of Anna's anger when she first arrived had been founded in shock: the house seemed to sag with the weight of Daniel's misery. She had always regarded Ravenscliffe as invulnerable, a province set apart from the outside world, a place of comfort and renewal; when she first saw it – and it had been empty and neglected, standing firm on its flattened and windblown portion of the common – her spirits had soared. It wasn't that the house was beautiful or elegant. It was heftily built from local stone and it hunkered down against the wind, with its back to the town. But it had a visceral quality, and a mind of its own; when Anna persuaded Eve to move her family into it, it was as much that Ravenscliffe had chosen her as she had chosen Ravenscliffe. But under the slack stewardship of Lilly, and with Daniel grieving for a wife he thought he had lost, the house had filled with shadows. It took every ounce of Anna's will, every last scrap of her optimism, to chase them away. She and Maya had come to stay and would remain, she told Amos, until Ravenscliffe felt right again. When he protested, she reminded him that this was, after all, what he had wanted.

'You can stay too, Dad,' Maya had said. 'Can't he, Mam?'

But Anna didn't appear to have heard, and Amos had only kissed Maya and left them there.

'Can I talk to you about Paris?' Eliza said now.

Anna looked at her in surprise. She'd talked to Eliza a good deal about Paris already: the glamour of the Rue du Faubourg Saint-Honoré where they had stayed; the glory of the Ballet de l'Opéra; the whirling, breathless excitement of the Ballets Russes and a dancer named Nijinsky who so thrilled the audience at the Théâtre du Châtelet that they leapt to their feet as if the seats were on fire and roared their appreciation. All of this had poured forth from Eliza, who, until Anna's arrival, had felt she had no one to tell. But now, she was saying, there was more.

'Go on,' Anna said, patiently.

Eliza looked at her hands, which were knotted together in her lap. 'Well,' she said, then stopped again.

'Eliza?'

'There was a man there . . . two men, actually . . .' again Eliza hesitated, and panic filled Anna's chest at what the child was about to say. Terrible images flashed through her mind of the potential dangers on the streets of Paris for a beautiful young girl, inadequately chaperoned. 'They were in charge of the Ballets Russes,' Eliza said, and looked up into Anna's face, as if she'd finished.

'Oh!' Anna said, trying quickly to mask her relief. 'Do you mean Sergei Diaghilev?'

'Yes, I do. 'e was one of 'em.'

'And?' Anna's heart still raced, but now for a different reason.

'They 'eld a sort of audition. We didn't know anything about it, Mademoiselle and me; we didn't have my things, even. But Mademoiselle knew one of t'company from her own days as a dancer, and she mentioned it when Mademoiselle told 'er. About me, I mean.'

The words tumbled out in a hectic rush, and Anna's face bore a small scowl of concentration.

'So we went, and I wore borrowed pointes, which you never should do, but I had to because—'

'You didn't have your things, Eliza, you said that already.'

'Exactly, so anyway, I danced for them. There were millions of girls, and they were all French, and they were all in pink tulle, and I had somebody's satin skirt that kept trying to slip down, so Mademoiselle tied a ribbon round the waistband. The pointes fitted, though, but after I'd started dancing they told me to take them off and dance barefoot, so I did.'

'Eliza!'

'What?'

'What are you telling me? Are you telling me you danced for Diaghilev?'

'I am, yes.'

'Then stop talking about your clothing!'

'Sorry. Mr Diaghilev and t'other man – I think he was a choreographer – they asked my name and told me to dance. I could do whatever I liked. There was a lady at a piano, and she played something I've never 'eard.'

'That must've been difficult for you. What did you do?'

'I just danced. It was nice,' Eliza said simply.

'Eliza, what an extraordinary thing! My darling girl, did you tell any of this to Daniel?'

She shook her head. 'Nobody knows, just me and Mademoiselle, and now you.'

Anna gave her a squeeze. 'Well,' she said. 'I'm very, very proud of you. So will Daniel be when you tell him, and your mam too. You know, Sergei Diaghilev is from Russia, just like me.'

'He is, yes,' Eliza said, nodding fervently. 'St Petersburg, Mademoiselle said.'

'Your Mademoiselle sounds interesting.'

'She is,' Eliza said, proud as punch of her teacher.

'Well I never, what a time you had! Shall we go in now? Have some tea and toast?'

'The thing is . . .'

'Mmm?' Anna was already off the swing, looking around for Maya and Ellen. She turned back to Eliza and smiled at her fondly, wondering what could possibly be left to say.

'Mr Diaghilev asked me to come back t'next day, and then there were only about eight of us.'

Anna stared. 'Go on.'

'I danced again, in bare feet, to some music that Mr Diaghilev said was so new nobody had ever danced to it before. He told me to forget everything I'd ever been taught. That sounded a bit rude, I thought, because Mademoiselle was there, and she likes us to do exactly what she says, but she nodded at me so I listened to t'music and started to dance.'

'Was the music nice?'

'Beautiful. Lively and cheerful.'

'Just like you.'

Eliza beamed.

'And did Mr Diaghilev enjoy your performance?' Anna was rapt; she could barely believe what she was hearing. Eliza sat, swinging gently and making what was quite extraordinary sound exactly the opposite.

'At the end we all stepped forwards onto t'stage and stood in a line, and Mr Diaghilev stood up. He said' – here Eliza adopted a fruity baritone, with an accent borrowed from Anna – 'I'll take the girl with the smile on her face; she dances with her soul.' We all looked at each other, to see who was smiling.'

'And was it you?'

'It was,' Eliza said. 'Yes.'

The next day, Anna and the three girls went to Barnsley, to see Evangeline Durand at her school of ballet. Daniel had been only semi-engaged the evening before, when Anna told him what Eliza had now told her. She had been able to see how entirely impossible it must have been for the girl to share her excitement with him. When he came in from work, hopeless misery trailed in behind him through the door. She had waited until the children were in bed and then she had spoken to him, dealing in blunt home truths. He was grieving for a loss he hadn't suffered, she said. He was doing a disservice to Eve, and to her children, who needed his loving support and a semblance of normality in their home. He was not honouring his love for Eve by wallowing in this way. All of this he listened to with a brooding countenance and then, when she'd finished, he merely said, 'You cannot know how I feel, so don't presume to judge me,' and walked out of the room. The silence he left behind was profound and unsettling. Anna, though, was unrepentant. She was gravely disappointed in him: he was being tested, as they all were. This was not his crisis alone. In the morning, when Anna rose, he had already gone to work, and she was grateful for it.

She had instigated a new regime at Ravenscliffe since her arrival, so before they could leave for Barnsley each girl had a task to accomplish. Eliza tidied away the breakfast things, Ellen swept and mopped the floor, and Maya beat the mats and collected wild flowers from the common, and put them in a crisp Cornishware jug on the sill. Anna cleaned the kitchen window with vinegar and water until the panes were as clear as a mountain spring. Show the house you love it, she told them, and it will always give you a warm welcome. The girls swapped sidelong, eye-rolling glances, but even their mutual scepticism was cheering, somehow, and by the time they left for the station the mood among the four of them was almost jolly. When the train passed through Ardington Maya waved at the stationmaster, who lifted his cap at her and bowed.

In Barnsley, Eliza led the way to the dance school, although they all knew perfectly well where it was. Even Ellen indulged her, falling in line as they processed along Mill Street to the towering building that housed Mademoiselle Evangeline's little domain. Inside, they climbed a dark staircase, then passed through the loom room and into the wide, bright studio where twenty little girls at the barre turned their heads to stare with solemn faces at the intruders. Ellen and Maya stared back.

'Eliza, *chérie*!' This was Mademoiselle Evangeline, pit-patting across the wooden floor with her arms outstretched. She resembled a matryoshka doll, thought Anna: neat and rosy, with shining black eyes and glossy black hair so tightly bunned it could indeed have been painted on her head. She kissed Eliza once on each cheek and then said, 'Who do we have here?'

Eliza made the introductions, and Mademoiselle Evangeline cast an assessing gaze over Ellen and Maya, looking instinctively for a dancer's bearing. Maya, she thought, looked promising. Anna said, 'Eliza's told me all about Paris.'

Mademoiselle Evangeline said, 'Ah,' and nodded vigorously. '*Très bien, chérie*,' she said to Eliza and then, in a whisper to Anna, 'I began to wonder if Monsieur Diaghilev had scared her away.' She gave a quick smile, a fleeting acknowledgement that she was not wholly serious, then clapped twice and the little girls at the barre changed position, although she had her back to them.

'Not at all,' Anna said. 'But life at home is a little—'

'Difficult, *oui*, I understand. Prepare, one, and two, second position, arms down, *demi plié*.' Behind their teacher, the little ballerinas responded as one. Eliza watched them with a critical eye; she watched them as someone who had danced for Diaghilev and been chosen. They were only young – seven and eight, she thought – but she could see they were unpromising. A favourite word of her dad's popped into her head:

387

clodhoppers. This made her smile, and some of the girls at the barre smiled back.

'And, of course,' Anna was saying, 'until her mother returns there can be no decisions made on Eliza's behalf.'

'Reverse your arms, *grand plié*, stretch side, two, three, four. Perhaps,' said Mademoiselle Evangeline, 'you might prefer to return when my class finishes?'

But there was no need to come back, Anna said. She merely wished to reassure the teacher that Eliza was quite as honoured and excited as she should be, but had simply not wanted to burden her stepfather with any of the details. This was why nothing had been said or done in the past few days.

'He is . . . distracted,' Anna said judiciously, 'by his wife's illness.'

Mademoiselle Evangeline made a sympathetic moue and shook her head sadly. '*Je comprends*. But what wonderful news for Madame MacLeod to return to! Fourth position girls, *demi*, and two, three, prepare, *demi*, two, three, four.' She turned as she spoke and studied her little dancers. 'Tummies in!' she said. 'Shoulders back! You look like *petits cochons*: a line of little pink pigs.' Ellen gave a small bark of laughter and Eliza shushed her, which always, with Ellen, had the reverse effect so that as they left the room she said, quite loudly, 'It looks stupid, ballet.' Her pugnacious little face dared Eliza to challenge her, but her sister only pirouetted past with a gracious smile, as if she pitied Ellen her resentfulness and was prepared to forgive.

'Each to their own,' Anna said. 'If we all liked t'same things, life should be very dull.'

'Why are there all these looms?' Maya asked as they retraced their steps through the mill.

'For t'weavers,' Eliza said. 'They made cloth 'ere once. There's a ghost, we call 'er Dolly Treddle; she comes and works t'loom where she used to sit.'

'Why?' Maya was not scared in the least, only puzzled. 'Does she miss the work?'

Eliza had never been asked this before. 'She's just 'aunting,' she said and then, for authenticity, added, 'They say that she died when t'bobbin shot off and hit 'er on t'temple.'

Ellen snorted. 'That's stupid too.'

'Stupid is as stupid does,' Maya said, quoting a line of Miss Cargill's, without at all understanding what it meant. Ellen didn't like the tone and stuck out her tongue. She felt cross and bored, and secondary in importance to Eliza, who – in Ellen's view – was now all puffed up with pride. Maya stared at her with hostile eyes.

'Let's have a treat,' Anna said. 'I know just place.'

She took them to the Barnsley branch of Eve's Puddings & Pies, where Ginger Timpson, the manageress, gave them such a warm welcome even Ellen began to thaw. Ginger had a mesmerising, louche glamour, a rarity in these parts. Her hair, which she always wore in a tousled bun, was a lavish shade of orange and she put rouge on her cheeks, and although she wore the same style of navy twill apron that all Eve's employees were given, Ginger always belted it twice, tight, around her wasp's waist and tied a bow at the front. Her bosom was arresting too: generous and well supported. Altogether she drew the eye, and although one might say all these attributes were wasted in a café on Market Hill, she was marvellous at her job. She had a word, a wink or a smile for every customer, and it was plain to see they were there for Ginger as much as for the produce. Anna and the girls sat at a sturdy scrubbed-pine table and Ginger brought them tea, dandelion and burdock, toasted teacakes and lemon-curd tarts. She sat with them while they ate, and told funny stories about the things people said. It was lovely, Eliza thought, but it was sad too, eating Mam's food when Mam was so far away. She hid her sadness, though; it would spoil the treat for them all if she drifted into melancholy. She licked the lemon curd out of its pastry shell, and managed not to cry.

Chapter 43

Three days after her release, Henrietta announced that she wished to recuperate at Netherwood Hall, not at Fulton House. For weeks now she had been longing for the specific comforts of her Yorkshire home, where the servants knew her best and where she had always been happiest. Word was sent north and Maudie, Henrietta's maid, attended to the packing, which would take at least two days. Such a fuss, said Clarissa, with Cowes round the corner and everything to pack, once again, for that. She was genuinely puzzled; wasn't one feather bed much the same as another? Wasn't the company more stimulating in London? Plus, if Henry was in Belgravia, it was but a hop and a skip from Park Lane.

'How will we visit you, if you're all the way up there in Netherwood?' the duchess asked in a plaintive voice; she included Isabella in her enquiry, as they had arrived together, each of them still sufficiently interested in the prodigal's return to pay her a call.

'I don't suppose you *shall* visit,' said Henrietta and then added brutally, 'but as you didn't visit me in prison either, I can't imagine you'll suffer too greatly as a result.'

She was lying on a daybed in the smaller of Fulton House's

two drawing rooms, wearing a mint-green tea gown that Isabella eyed covetously. She'd never seen it before, and she had thought she knew every item in her sister's wardrobe. It made Henry look uncharacteristically wanton, Isabella thought, and resolved to add something similar to her trousseau when the time came. She imagined Uli's face when he saw the hills and valleys of her body through the layers of chiffon; he would never look at another woman because she would be constantly alluring. This was her plan.

'Well, if you're going to be unpleasant,' said Clarissa, rising, 'Isabella and I will leave. Isabella?'

Her younger daughter looked at her with vague, glassy eyes, and then turned to Henrietta. 'I do like your gown,' she said. 'Is it new?'

Henrietta laughed. 'Izzy, please pay attention. You're meant to be leaving in a huff after being insulted. Mama, I'm sorry I was so sharp with you, please do sit down; and no, it isn't new at all, Izzy. In fact, I think it was probably once yours, Mama.'

Intrigued, and distracted from her pique, Clarissa gave the garment closer inspection and was able to confirm that yes, the tea gown had once been one of her own. Now she looked at Henrietta with new interest. 'You must be very slender,' she said, 'to fit into anything of mine.'

'The Holloway Prison reduction plan, Mama – it's all the rage in fashionable circles,' and Clarissa took a moment to consider whether her caustic daughter was being unkind or amusing. She had always found Henrietta impossible to read: even as a little girl she had been mercurial and contrary; occasionally quite unmanageable. Her father's daughter, in many ways; she had his cleverness and his temperament. But dear Teddy had been softer-edged, and had known how to coax Clarissa from the tyranny of her own petulance, while Henrietta knew only how to provoke it.

'I expect you're teasing me,' the duchess said now, 'but I think you look all the better for your time away.' This was such a patently facile point of view that there would certainly have ensued a spat, except that Henrietta found she hadn't the will. She closed her eyes and swallowed experimentally. Each day that passed, the pain was less. Isabella, uncomfortable on a scroll-backed slipper chair, watched her uneasily and wondered how soon they might leave. She felt squeamish about the precise, medical details of what had been done to Henrietta; this fastidiousness, however, didn't extend to the prison itself. This she found thrillingly, darkly fascinating.

'Did you see the place where they have the hangings?' she said with what Clarissa thought a lamentable lack of good taste. 'Did you see the scaffold?'

Her mother shot Isabella a look of reproof, but Henrietta just said, 'No, it's all rather hidden away. Anyway, there aren't very many hangings, you know. On the whole it's a very dull, repetitive, drab life in there. Everyone looks the same: wrung out and grey-faced. I was immensely unhappy.'

Isabella's large blue eyes filled with compassionate tears. She knew she hadn't been at all kind; she knew she had been selfish.

'I'm sorry I didn't come, Henry,' she said, and just at that moment she was.

Henrietta, rather ungraciously Isabella thought, only nodded.

'Are you still a suffragette?' she asked, feeling rash. Henrietta glanced away, as if her feelings were hurt, but when she answered her voice was mild.

'In spirit. From the sidelines, for the time being.'

Clarissa huffed.

'I sincerely hope you've learned your lesson,' she said. She was standing now, pulling on her kid gloves, stirring the still air of the drawing room with her sudden determination to be off.

'I learned all sorts of lessons,' Henrietta said significantly, 'about all of us.' She would not give her mother the satisfaction of drawing from her any promises about the future. Her feelings, in any case, were extremely confused. Yesterday Mary Dixon had left her card on the hall table, and a note containing passionate good wishes. She had signed it 'Ever yours, in the sisterhood of the struggle', and Henrietta had felt a flash of shame at having had her sent away. It was easy enough to convince any unwanted visitor that, following her ordeal, Henrietta needed peace and quiet. In fact, she felt she was gathering strength by the hour. But she simply couldn't face her fellow combatants from the WPSU because, when she did, she would have to reveal herself as not so much a figurehead as a flop. In Yorkshire she would be safe, however, and free to be herself again; she would ride and review the estate with Jem Arkwright, and connect, once again, with the steady certainties of Netherwood Hall. The cause could manage without her for a while.

Isabella stooped over the daybed to kiss her sister, a perfunctory peck on the cheek. Henrietta thought she looked very pretty, in a dress of rose-pink shantung. 'This is nice,' she said, taking a pinch of the silk between finger and thumb. 'In Holloway we all wore ugly frocks of grey ticking.'

Isabella's eyes widened in sympathy. 'Golly. How perfectly ghastly.'

'There were worse things,' Henrietta said drily, 'but yes, it was pretty horrid. Mine was stained under the arms when it was given to me.'

Clarissa stamped her foot. 'Enough!' she said hotly, so that both her daughters flinched. 'That is the very last detail I wish to hear on this odious subject. It is insufferably vulgar to discuss it in this casually prurient manner. The entire episode is one of which I am thoroughly ashamed, and I hope you know, Henrietta, that your darling papa would have felt exactly as I do. I only hope I live long enough to see your reputation restored and the incident consigned to obscurity.'

She seemed drained by her tirade, and sat down, again, on the Chesterfield. Her face was ashen except for two bright spots of red, high on her cheeks. She brought one hand to her heart and another to her forehead; she looked stricken.

'Mama—' Henrietta began, but her mother shook her head vehemently. 'Not another word,' Clarissa said. She looked at her elder daughter and her eyes were cold. 'Not another word, even in apology. The subject is closed. Now, Isabella, we shall take our leave.'

Isabella, marooned on the Turkey carpet between her sister and her mother, looked glumly from one to the other. Now Mama was in a bate and would be difficult all day long, and the mention of Papa had upset all of them. Instinctively she reached for her lucky charm, the Hohenzollern diamond, and thought of Uli. She felt immediately cheered, and as she followed her mother from the drawing room she turned and blew Henrietta a kiss. Poor old Henry, she thought: what was the point of diaphanous chiffon when she had no one to love her?

Lady Henrietta's arrival in Netherwood had been managed quietly and without fanfare. She was there to convalesce, Mrs Powell-Hughes told the assembled household on the morning she came. She needed peace, quiet and building up. To this end, the housekeeper had bought in three bottles of Parrish's Chemical Food, and she watched Henrietta every morning at breakfast to be sure she took the requisite spoonful. Henrietta complained that it tasted of rusty nails, to which the housekeeper replied, 'That'll be the iron,' in a manner that told Henrietta that she might be mistress of

Netherwood Hall at the moment, but she must do as she was told in this regard.

As well as the Parrish's, there was spinach with every meal and, three times a week, softly cooked liver in one form or another. Mrs Powell-Hughes had been shocked, she told Sarah Pickersgill, at the state Her Ladyship had come home in.

'Shocked to the core,' she said. 'I never thought much of the London lot, but I'm afraid they've plumbed new depths. You only have to look at her to see she needs iron, and there was that Mrs Carmichael sending up milky puddings.'

Sarah had never met the Fulton House cook, but she saw no particular advantage in trying to be neutral. 'Typical,' she said. She was rubbing chicken livers through a sieve, for a parfait. It was strange, she thought, preparing fine food for only one person. Stranger still, the house hadn't felt empty when none of the family was here, but with Lady Henrietta living alone on the upper floors suddenly they all seemed to be rattling around like peas in a drum. When dinner went up on a single silver tray Sarah felt a shiver of apprehension, as if Miss Havisham was waiting to receive it in her tattered wedding gown. There was no one below stairs with whom she could share this fanciful notion, however. Even Mrs Powell-Hughes, the closest Sarah had to a confidante, and something of a reader, wasn't familiar with Dickens.

'She's doing well now, of course,' Mrs Powell-Hughes said. 'Filling out a bit. Lady Henrietta always liked her food, even as a tot.'

'Mmm,' said Sarah, trying to communicate a lack of interest. She hadn't worked here long enough to know Her Ladyship's childhood eating habits: they'd all been grown by the time she came, apart from Lady Isabella, of course, who was so much younger than the rest. Sarah was a meticulous diarist, so she knew it was eight years, two months and four days since she'd started here, and she remembered Lady Henrietta, in those early days of her employment, as a haughty figure with a bony profile, like a Roman centurion. Nice enough, but very grand. Personally, Sarah slightly resented her unscheduled arrival this week. Mr Parkinson and Mrs Powell-Hughes had been in raptures the day word arrived that Lady Henrietta was coming: you'd have thought it was their own long-lost child returning to them. When Atkins had fetched her from the train and swung the Daimler around the carriageway to the south front, the butler had broken into a little trot in his haste to get to the car door before the chauffeur. Sarah, standing dutifully on the steps, playing her part in the servants' guard of honour, had half expected him to sweep Lady Henrietta into his arms and carry her. Instead he offered his arm and she took it, and they walked like Darby and Joan into the house, with Mrs Powell-Hughes flapping and fluttering behind them. 'An honour,' Mr Parkinson kept telling them all. 'An honour, and the greatest of compliments.'

Well, thought Sarah now, her fingers sore from the sieve, and stained the same reddish-brown as the disintegrating livers, it was an imposition and the greatest of nuisances as far as she was concerned, and it would put them in a proper pickle when the time came to leave for the Isle of Wight. There was enough to be done without firing up the kitchen range and bringing down the bright, clean copper pans to dirty them all over again.

'You can swear by Parrish's tonic, though,' Mrs Powell-Hughes said.

'Sets my teeth on edge,' Sarah replied nastily. 'Mind you, so does spinach.' She banged a pot on to the hob and sloshed in a measure of Madeira, and something in her manner inspired the housekeeper to find something urgent to get on with, somewhere other than the kitchen.

Jem Arkwright, the land agent for the Netherwood estate, was a bluff, dependable, supremely loyal man, and also the closest Henrietta now had to spending time with her late father. This was how she saw him: Teddy Hoyland's representative here on earth. For this she treasured him. Certainly he was the only person whose knowledge and understanding of estate matters surpassed her own. He was the only man in the world from whom her father would ever take advice, and together the two men would walk the paths and perimeters of the land twice a week, sometimes three, so that they each knew this acreage – its boundaries, its drainage, its yield – as well as they knew the secrets of their own hearts.

Not that Jem gave much away. His silence was one of his defining characteristics, like his broad barrel chest and mutton-chop whiskers. Spending time with Jem could be much like spending time alone, unless he brought his Jack Russell terrier along; then you might feel you had some company. But Jem's was a reassuring silence and he would always answer a question, although not often very fully. In any case, Henrietta didn't mind any of this. She valued his quiet good sense and his total acceptance of her as, if not his superior, then at least as his equal. She had found him as she entered the yard on the big black hunter that Dickie used to ride, and Jem had done the job of the groom, holding Marley's halter in his gnarled grip and seeing Henrietta safely to the cobbled ground. He agreed, when she asked him, that he was just setting off towards Harley End, and when she suggested she might accompany him he nodded his assent. Could he wait just a moment, until she'd swapped her riding habit for her tweeds? He could. She wanted to visit Mrs Sykes at Ravenscliffe she said, so she would continue on there without him from Harley End. He made no reply to this – for what was there to say? – but simply stood and waited in the centre of the courtyard, peaceful and solid, puffing on his old pipe. Behind him the bailiff's door opened, and although Jem heard it he didn't turn around.

'Arkwright,' said Absalom Blandford in his peremptory, scolding voice: the one that Jem had never responded to, and didn't now.

'Mr Arkwright,' said Absalom more peaceably, or, at least, as peaceably as his nature allowed. Jem tossed him a glance over his shoulder. 'Aye,' he said, as if merely confirming his own identity. A plume of smoke emerged from the corner of his mouth, and although they stood in the open air the bailiff held a handkerchief over his nose. He was afflicted with too powerful a sense of smell, which was unfortunate for a man whose office was adjacent on one side to the stables and on the other to the garaging for the earl's growing collection of motorcars. He was assailed by fumes, of either a mechanical or organic nature, whenever he set a fastidious foot forth. Jem smiled, very much to himself.

'Your receipts and invoices for the third quarter,' said Absalom, 'appear to be incomplete.' He trotted closer, taking care where he trod.

Jem took the pipe from his mouth. 'That's because they are,' he said.

'Are what?'

'Incomplete.'

Absalom gave a small, incredulous laugh. 'Then how am I expected to balance the books, without the full cooperation of the land agent?' he said.

Jem had in his head, and under his feet, all the evidence he needed that the estate – those parts that fell to him to manage – were in fine fettle. The acreage he walked, the fences he mended and the stakes he planted, the coppices he managed, the leases, grazing rights, building rights and trading rights he granted: this was where Jem's checks and balances existed, not between the black leather covers of an accounts ledger.

Sometimes, he was the first to admit, the numbers didn't quite add up. But Jem said none of this now; he merely blew smoke into the clear sky.

'Mr Arkwright, may I remind you that, in the business of accounts, the principal object is perspicuity.' said Absalom. 'Perhaps you might find it convenient to do as I do and carry a pocket memorandum book at all times.'

Jem said nothing. Across the yard, Lady Henrietta emerged from the kitchen door with two arthritic Labradors in tow. Jem's terrier zigzagged through their legs and barked, and Henrietta bent down to tickle him behind his ear. 'Now then little fellow,' she said to the dog, and then, addressing Jem, 'I thought I'd bring Min and Jess, unless you think they'll slow you down.' They were the late earl's dogs, trained to the gun, although the soft weight of a pheasant in their mouths was but a distant memory. Now their most useful service was as foot warmers on a winter's evening, or footstools in the summer. In either case, they would lie still for as long as anyone required them to.

'Master's dogs're allus welcome,' Jem said. He set off towards the arch, which led to the open countryside and Harley End, and the bailiff clucked with indignation. Henrietta gave him a questioning look.

'I was querying Mr Arkwright's inadequate record-keeping,' he said treacherously.

'But it's your job, Mr Blandford, to keep the accounts,' said Henrietta. She didn't like the bailiff, or even trust him especially; she believed he had delusions of superiority, and they had had run-ins in the past, when she had had to check his arrogance and put him in his place. But her father had rated him highly, and for this reason he had kept his position; this, and the fact that it would be more trouble than it was worth to dismiss him. The estate properties were numerous indeed, and Absalom Blandford knew the details of every last one: the rents, the tenants, the leases. He looked at her now with his hard, conker-brown eyes, and said, 'My accounts ledgers bear the closest possible scrutiny, Your Ladyship, but the land agent persistently refuses to oblige me by keeping even a rudimentary tally of expenditure.'

The bailiff was probably right, thought Henrietta; she imagined Jem was as sparing with his figures as he was with his conversation. But she said, 'Please don't trouble Mr Arkwright again with such matters,' which forced him to bow his head and say, 'Very well, Your Ladyship.'

She set off after Jem, and the dogs plodded single file behind her. Absalom watched the small procession. In his world a goodly number of people fell short of his own high standards, and among them was Lady Henrietta Hoyland. She allowed her heart to rule her head, and she smelled strongly of horse. He again held his handkerchief over his nose and mouth and took a dose of its lavender scent. Thus restored, he hurried back to his office where, from time to time, he was free to imagine Lady Henrietta on her knees in front of him, begging forgiveness for her foolishness and pleading with him not to leave her for the Devonshires at Chatsworth, where his unequalled talents and hawk-eyed acumen would be properly appreciated. In his way, he mourned the passing of the sixth earl more than anyone. The unswerving loyalty that he had always tried to show to Teddy Hoyland now had nowhere to reside.

Chapter 44

Silas gave Eve his arm and walked her from the car to the hotel with a smile of benign triumph, as if he alone had nursed her back to health. It was lunchtime, and there were chicken wings and pork ribs griddling over the jerk pit; the air smelled of green pimento wood and peppers. Hotel guests mingled on the terrace with tall glasses of rum punch. There was a sense of lively camaraderie and a smattering of music, and in the thick of it all was Hugh Oliver, straight off the boat. He emerged from the throng with his arms wide.

'I wish your husband could see you now,' he said, and to his great surprise, this stopped Eve in her tracks. Silas, however, strode on up to Hugh and shook his hand boisterously. 'As I live and breathe,' he said. 'The "and Co." in Whittam & Co. How the devil are you?'

But Hugh was looking at Eve's face, which was full of alarm. 'Why?' she said.

'Because he has you knocking at death's door, my dear woman, and here you are, as palely, beautifully alive as an English rose.' He had a silken tongue, Hugh Oliver, but it made little impact on Eve, who only stared.

'Marvellous, isn't it?' Silas said, loudly and more robustly than seemed strictly appropriate. 'Full recovery from the nastiest bout of yellow fever I've ever seen. We have a fighting spirit, we Whittams: never say die. We should put it in Latin, above our doors.' He laughed, but no one joined in.

'But Daniel doesn't know, does 'e?' Eve said to Hugh. 'None of them know, thank goodness.' She was halfway up the path, and appeared rooted to the spot, so Hugh began to walk down to her. Behind him the music and laughter seemed suddenly at odds with the mood here, on the herringbone path in the fragrant garden. Eve had worked a miracle in his absence; he had shouted for joy when he first arrived and found the staff – the same staff as before, with a few new faces too – greeting guests with wide, Jamaican smiles and a calypso beat. But now some strange, unexpected current ran between himself and Eve: a fundamental failure of understanding or communication. She was rigid with the new anxiety that his words had caused her, and Hugh couldn't comprehend the reason. Behind him, Silas said, 'I thought it best to let them know.' He sounded defiant and defensive. 'If the worst had happened, it seemed better to prepare them for it.'

'But it didn't,' Eve said. 'The worst didn't 'appen.'

'And aren't we all deeply grateful for that!'

Eve fixed him with an unsmiling gaze. 'So did you send another telegram, to let them know I was on t'mend?'

On the terrace above her Seth appeared, looking shy and uncertain of his reception. Eve, seeing him, smiled and said, 'Seth, sweetheart.'

'Hello,' Seth said. 'You look well.' He would have liked to hug her, but everyone was looking now, including the guests.

'Seth did, didn't you Seth?'

This was Silas, addressing his nephew with a confident smile. 'That is, I asked you to.'

403

'What?' said Seth. 'Sir,' he added, not wishing to sound insolent. He had no idea what his uncle was talking about.

'The telegram, telling the Netherwood clan that all was well; did you deal with it?'

There was a silence, long and uncomfortable, which was broken by Eve. 'Not to worry,' she said quickly. 'Fact is, I'm fine, and we can let 'em all know now, can't we?' Seth's ears were puce-coloured; always, the physical manifestation of his emotions began here. He looked as if he might cry. 'It's all right, love,' she said, and Silas laughed. Seth, confused by his uncle, was angry now at his mother, for treating him like a child. He glowered silently.

'A mother's love for her child knows no bounds, isn't that right?' Silas said. 'I was about to be torn off a strip for being at fault, yet now you discover the failing is Seth's the offence is forgivable.'

Seth, struck mute, tried to remember being asked to dispatch a telegram, but couldn't. If he had, he would have been forced to ask how to go about it, never having sent a telegram in his life. But it was inappropriate, he felt, to challenge his uncle in front of everyone, on this happy occasion, and in any case Silas was already ushering everyone inside, introducing Eve to some of the new English guests, spreading bonhomie, so the moment for any form of self-defence was lost. His mam didn't blame him, he could see that, but neither did she realise the truth. She had merely excused his supposed forgetfulness, in a very public and shaming way.

Later that day Hugh showed him how to word a telegram and how to send it via a telephone call to the Western Union in New York City. This made Seth feel a little better, a little less like a hapless dunce. He didn't know what to say about the injustice done to him by his uncle, so he said nothing at all.

Eve had an afternoon nap with Angus, who had given up the habit in her absence but made an exception in honour of her return. They slept for two hours, holding hands, and then, when they woke, he led her downstairs to the kitchen where, he told her with great authority, Ruby would have jobs for them both. She didn't, in fact, but to oblige him she sent him down to the entrance gate to wait for Roscoe to return from school, as if, without Angus, her son would never find his way into the hotel. Eve sat down and for a while she watched Ruby moving purposefully around the kitchen, and then she said, 'I owe you a great deal, Ruby.' Ruby put down the spoon she had been using and said, 'You owe me nothing at all.'

'I don't know 'ow you make that out. You nursed me and you cared for Angus. I don't know what would've 'appened without you.'

'I did what any mother would do for another,' Ruby said, although she knew there had been more to it than that. It had been a sort of devotion. She busied herself at the range, where scallions and tomatoes simmered. She was making codfish fritters, which would be served as canapés before dinner, and now she added two fat cloves of garlic, chopped small, to the skillet on the hob. They popped and hissed in the hot oil and juices, and their particular smell rose up at once, filling the kitchen.

'Well, anyway,' Eve said, 'I'm grateful. I shan't forget what you did, and I shan't forget you.'

'Forget me?' Ruby said, turning from the pan with an expression of mock astonishment. 'What an idea! No one can forget the person who first fed them curry goat.'

'Not to mention callaloo, and ackee with saltfish,' Eve said, smiling. 'Can't get any of that at t'Co-op in Netherwood.'

Ruby turned away again, and with her back to Eve said, 'When will you go?' She hardly wished to know the answer.

'I don't know. Quite soon, I expect, but it all depends.'

This seemed vague enough not to cause Ruby any immediate consternation. She didn't like to think of Eve gone at all; somehow Eve stood between herself and Silas Whittam and made her feel stronger. And Angus; the thought of him made her catch her breath. He was the sort of lovable, trusting child whose friendship was a gift. No: she knew they didn't belong here, but she didn't want them to go.

A clatter at the back door heralded the arrival of Roscoe, accompanied by his little shadow.

'Roscoe said we can swim,' Angus said. 'Can we, Ruby?'

'Please,' Roscoe said, in a reprimanding voice that made Angus scowl, although he repeated the word dutifully enough. Ruby felt a jab of concern that the child was seeking her permission rather than his mother's, and she looked across at Eve, who was, in turn, looking at the boys, from one to the other.

'Mam?' said Angus, redressing the balance. 'Please can we?' His childish lisp was endearing, and it wasn't too much to ask, but Eve didn't answer. She only turned and looked back at Ruby with an expression that the other woman understood at once.

'Certainly,' Ruby said to Angus, and then to Roscoe she added, 'but be back before five.' He grinned at her by way of assurance, slung his satchel into the scullery and took a banana from the hook by the larder, then said, 'Race you,' and ran out of the door. Angus flew out after him with a howl of indignation, leaving Ruby and Eve alone again. They were held still for a moment by a heavy, significant silence, and then Ruby said, 'You remembered.'

Eve nodded slowly. 'Strangest thing. I saw Roscoe, and thought there was something of Silas in 'is face, and then I recalled that night when you talked about it all. It's like remembering a dream.'

'It was quite a night,' Ruby said, a little tightly.

'I think, if I didn't already know, I wouldn't see any resemblance at all. I see you in Roscoe, usually.'

'Well, he's my life's work,' Ruby said and tried to smile, although she felt tense, and sad, as if everything now would be different, and none the better for that. All Roscoe's life she had hidden the identity of his daddy. She believed it to be right that Eve should know the truth but even so, she couldn't see a happy outcome.

Behind her, the sweet smell of caramelised scallions began to spoil, so she turned at once to shove them around in the skillet and stop them from blackening. There was some small comfort in this everyday activity. She took the pan off the heat and flaked the salted cod into it, breaking up the firm white flesh between her fingers and thumbs. Her heart raced, although she didn't precisely know why, and beneath her feet the ground seemed unfirm, like the deck of a boat in a heavy swell. Eve said nothing, but Ruby could feel her eyes upon her – at least, she thought she could, but when she turned Eve seemed to be looking inward, at her own private thoughts.

'That woman,' she said now. 'Justine.'

Ruby waited.

'Is she carrying Silas's child?'

She hadn't been sworn to secrecy, so Ruby said, 'Yes.'

'Does 'e 'ave others?'

This was a question so obvious that Ruby was astonished she had never asked it herself. 'I suppose he might do, yes.' She thought of all the long-limbed young women who harvested his fruit and carried it on their heads down the track to the Rio Grande. She thought of their strong, slender arms and the softness of their breasts and bellies beneath the gaudy cloth of their dresses. It was inevitable, she thought now, that one or other of them would have been plucked from the ranks like ripe fruit, to be enjoyed by their employer. He was greedy. He had no restraint. Who knew how many offspring he had sired?

'Ruby, I'm so sorry. I feel ashamed.'

'Not on my account, I hope.'

'No, no, of Silas, of t'way 'e carries on.'

Ruby shrugged, and Eve thought how much the gesture reminded her of Anna, which in turn made her long for her friend.

'Mr Mention,' Ruby said, 'that's all he is, checking off his conquests with notches in a stick. He likes Jamaican girls.'

'And Justine – do you think 'e likes 'er?'

'For now, I think he probably does. In his way, that is.'

'Ruby, when we talked, the night I fell ill, did you tell me you loved Silas?'

Ruby said, 'Once, a long, long time ago, I thought I loved him, yes.'

'And now?'

'I hate him. Many people do. I don't want people to know he's Roscoe's daddy. Especially, I don't want Roscoe to know, although I think that's a vain hope, because he'll probably tell the boy himself one of these days.'

Eve sighed, a long, despairing sigh that touched Ruby's heart because she could see how different these siblings were, and how difficult it must be for Eve to hear these truths. Ruby thought for a moment, searching for something good to say, and then, 'He's morally lax, Eve, and he's selfish and arrogant. But he isn't absolutely wicked.' Eve looked at her with gratitude, for trying to be kind.

Chapter 45

⌘

When Seth had first come to Jamaica he had found its beauty oppressive. The abundance of colour and the crushing, endless march of foliage had seemed too much, and certainly most unlike Bristol. But then, Bristol had seemed exotic compared to Netherwood. The Avon Gorge had made him gasp the first time he saw it: the towering limestone cliffs and the depth and breadth of the Avon were as dramatic a natural landscape as he had ever seen. Also the lively, filthy, crowded docks where the seagulls – massive birds, Seth thought: cruel beaks and talons, and mocking, wheeling cries – filled the skies when the cargo steamers came in, dropping like feathered rocks to steal what they could from the decks. It was all as foreign to Seth as another country, and indeed he had felt as if he spoke a different language from the clerks he worked with, whose Somerset burr was as odd to his ear as his Barnsley tyke was to them.

But Jamaica had stunned him. Something like claustro-phobia came upon him the first time he walked from the hotel to the waterfalls, which were only accessible through a tunnel of vivid, dripping green. He remembered looking closely at the construction and feeling repelled by the vines and the creepers that had knotted themselves into and among the leaves to make a woven roof and walls that would surely, ultimately, strangle anything tender, anything soft. It had reminded Seth of the tangle of briars around Sleeping Beauty's castle: sinister and defensive. He would have liked to take a machete to it, or a sword, just as the prince did.

He had only been once to Eden Falls, and that was because of the tunnel. It annoyed him that his mam loved the falls so much that she'd named the hotel after them, and that Roscoe Donaldson took Angus there most days and had taught him to swim. Seth couldn't swim. There was a large pond on Netherwood Common where he pretended to swim, so no one knew he couldn't. He knew where the shallower parts were and stuck to those. That, or he sat on the edge saying no, he didn't fancy a swim today – and that was always a plausible stance, because it was a mucky hole where sometimes people drowned unwanted puppies and kittens in tied sacks. He should probably have learned here, in the warm waters of the Caribbean Sea: how to begin such a thing, though, at the great age of almost seventeen? He could hardly ask Roscoe for help.

These thoughts streamed through his mind and darkened his expression as he sat on the terrace of the hotel, listening to the sounds of the jungle. The solitaire bird, hidden some-where in the tree canopy, had set up its plaintive whistle, which was supposed to be hauntingly melodic but Seth thought sounded more like a metal gate with a chronic squeak.

'Spot of oil, lad, that's what you need,' he said to the bird, and jumped when Hugh Oliver said, 'Beg pardon?'

Seth blushed and said, 'I was talking to myself.' Hugh smiled, then sat down next to him in a seat that swung, very gently, as it took his weight. Seth's admiration for Hugh was unbounded. He had a way of dealing with life that Seth longed to emulate: an equable approach to disruption or disorder. Seth had never seen him lose his temper – that is, never in the way that Uncle Silas did, making cruel verbal parries, shouting down even the most timorous of counter-arguments. When Silas tried this approach with Hugh, he would employ a quiet, steely smile to throw him off kilter and then walk away until tempers had cooled. Seth had seen it many a time – had tried the smile in front of a mirror – but he couldn't pull it off. He looked merely simple, not steely. If Seth found the courage to confide, Hugh would probably help him achieve the same sangfroid, or something approaching it, because he was a kind man, and generous too. For all these reasons, Seth admired him, but especially he admired his good looks. Hugh was a Bristolian of very unexceptional parentage, but somewhere along the line of his ancestry, an English seafarer had bred with an African slave. This was the legend, at any rate, and certainly Hugh had never attempted any other explanation for his glossy dark curls, his wide-set dark brown eyes and his skin colour, which seemed unremarkable – pale, even – here in Port Antonio, but so markedly exotic in Bristol and Netherwood.

'I saw Eliza and Ellen,' Hugh said now. 'They said to say hello.'

Seth looked surprised, as if this were unlikely. 'Did they? Are they all right?'

'In fine fettle, both of them. Eliza's been to Paris, you know, to see the ballet.'

Seth raised an eyebrow to show his manly disdain for such pastimes. 'How's business at Dreaton Main?' he said, as if, to him, coal production was the thing.

Hugh didn't mock, as Silas might have done. 'Very good. They mine a quality grade of coal from those seams. What we don't use ourselves fetches an excellent price at the Exchange.'

Seth nodded, pleased to be taken seriously. 'How long will you stay this time?' he asked.

'Not sure, now. Theoretically, your uncle should be heading back to Bristol, leaving me here, but he seems adamant that he should stay, at least until your mother books her passage home.'

'I suppose she'll be keen to go sooner rather than later?'

'She is, yes. Certainly her family – your family – are keen to clap eyes on her after the scare they've had.'

Seth said, 'Uncle Silas blamed me for that, but it was his fault.'

'It's water under the bridge,' Hugh said. 'The telegram should be with them by now.'

Seth eyed him covertly, wondering if he should press for some small acknowledgement of the injustice, but Hugh was gazing at the middle distance with a rapt expression. 'Look at that,' he said, pointing ahead. 'Fireflies.' There were scores of them, their tiny phosphorescent lights blazing in the dark crevices of the lawn.

'You can see why they were thought to be fairies, in the olden days,' Seth said, more beguiled than he wanted to let on.

'You can,' Hugh replied. 'They're magical.'

'It's the females, attracting a mate. Once she's mated she turns her light out, lays an egg and dies.'

'Sad story,' Hugh said. 'Still, at least they shine while they're alive. That's more than most of us can say.'

He smiled at Seth, who smiled uneasily back and wondered if he meant something by that, and if so, what.

The atmosphere in Silas's office was thick with resentment and recrimination. His handsome face was surly, and he looked at his sister with an entirely new, but entirely heartfelt, dislike.

'You're a sanctimonious bitch,' he said. 'Holier than thou, the worst kind of critic.'

Eve, reeling from his anger, tried her best not to show it.

'All I said was you should do right by Justine. What does she 'ave, if you forsake 'er?'

'Forsake her? Forsake her? Listen to yourself! She's a slave girl from Martinique – she hasn't set her sights on the white master, I can assure you of that.'

'*You* listen to *yourself*! In case you 'adn't realised, slavery was abolished last century, Silas, and while you might be Justine's employer, you are most definitely *not* a white master. She's a beautiful woman who's carrying your bairn.'

'So what? She's not the first.'

Appalled at his shamelessness, she was momentarily silenced. He slid his eyes away from hers and spun his chair so that he faced the window, then he stood up and, plunging his hands into the pockets of his trousers, stared moodily out into the garden at nothing. His mind, apart from the obvious annoyance caused by his sister's moralising, was largely untroubled. Nothing had changed, except that she knew the truth about Ruby Donaldson and had guessed the truth about Justine. Well, he said to himself again, so what? So bloody what? He was the same man he had ever been and would ever be. His life was his own and would never – God willing – resemble Evie's. She had done well, granted, but she had settled for relatively little in the end. He was disappointed in her.

'You want to know your problem?' Eve said. He turned round, and shook his head.

'Not especially,' he said. 'Not from you.'

She told him anyway: 'You 'aven't grown up. You're still a child, grabbing what you can, running from responsibility. Look at you, nothing but t'best from your collar to your boots, but you're still that stowaway boy in rags underneath it all.'

'Oh, very profound.' He looked at her with derision. 'Do you charge for your wise counsel?'

'Silas,' she said, and it was an appeal to the brother she

had once thought she knew. For a moment she thought, too, that he might respond, but instead he walked slowly, casually, towards the door of the office and held it open for her with a gracious flourish of his free arm.

'Time you were on your way,' he said. 'You bore me with your small-minded concerns.'

She stood and folded her arms so that she might stop the trembling that threatened to betray her. 'What 'appened to you, Silas? When did you become so cold?'

'To you? Just this evening, when you presumed to meddle in my private affairs. Prior to that you were one of my favourites, but I will not be judged by you or by anyone. Now, what is it they say where you come from? Ah yes' – here, he mimicked Eve's accent – 'sling your 'ook.'

'We come from t'same place, you and I. And everyone judges you, except, perhaps, Justine. Is that why you keep 'er close? Because she's too spineless to make demands? Is that why you shunned Ruby, eight years ago – because she *did* make demands?'

'Get out.'

'I will. I shall leave Port Antonio on t'next available sailing.'

'Excellent.'

'And I shall take Seth with me.'

He threw back his head and laughed at this, then said in a mocking falsetto, 'Please, no, anything but that!' Eve was filled, suddenly, with a new sort of anger, because she could weather any amount of vitriol thrown at her, but she couldn't bear to have her son held in contempt too. She stormed from the room before he saw her cry, and he threw the door closed after her with such force that the bang it made resounded through the ground floor of the hotel and made the guests in the bar look at each other and wonder what they'd heard.

Seth and Hugh were still on the terrace when Silas emerged, and when he saw them he seemed delighted.

'Join us?' said Hugh.

'I came out for a smoke. But your company will be a bonus.'

He sat down, next to Seth and opposite Hugh, and he offered them both a cigarette, which both declined. He lit his own, and the tip of it glowed like one of the fireflies.

'What was the bang?' Hugh asked.

'My office door,' said Silas. 'Through draught, I suppose. Made me jump out of my skin.'

Seth, wary of this calm and pleasant Uncle Silas, but encouraged nonetheless, said, 'Sometimes, if the kitchen door's open, you get a hot gust of air come right through the building, almost solid.'

'You do,' Silas said, and he nodded, as if pleased with this observation. Seth relaxed further still. Hugh laced his hands behind his head and gave a contented sigh. 'I must say, this place is transformed.' He looked at Silas. 'Isn't it? Eve's done a marvellous job. What a stroke of genius.'

Silas took a deep pull on his cigarette and blew the smoke out in a series of perfect rings before he answered. 'Genius. Not least because the expense has been minimal. We can serve our guests the scrag ends and plantain that the locals revere and they go home feeling spoiled. Hilarious.'

Hugh regarded him levelly. 'There's more to it than that.'

'Just being facetious,' Silas said. 'Evie has spun a miracle. I shall be for ever in her debt.'

Seth glanced across at his uncle, looking for clues, but his face was unclouded; he caught his nephew's eye and smiled. 'Do you want to go back with her when she sails?'

'Do you want me to?'

'Up to you, my boy. Take a bit of leave if you like. Or stay here with Hugh, showing him how to go on.'

This sounded nice, thought Seth: a few weeks in the steady, benign company of Hugh Oliver.

'Think about it,' Silas said. 'You've worked hard, you deserve a break. On the other hand, you're always needed by the business. Entirely your choice.' He took another long draw of the cigarette, then pinched out its glowing end between finger and thumb and flicked it up into the night sky. They knew it had landed when the crickets fell silent, and, like a conductor, Silas raised his arm and brought it down at the precise moment the chirruping struck up again. The three of them laughed at his perfect timing. 'God,' said Silas, 'it's a wonderful life, isn't it?'

Ruby found Eve in the bedroom, moving quietly so as not to wake Angus. She had piles of clothes stacked on surfaces, and the doors of the wardrobe hung wide, revealing a stripped interior. Ruby was shocked.

'Are you going now?' she whispered. 'What's the hurry?' When she looked properly at Eve she could see her eyes were swollen from crying, and this shocked her further still. She said, 'Eve, stop,' because the other woman was going about her task with a desperate, unsettling intensity. Ruby placed a restraining hand on Eve's arm and Eve dissolved into heaving sobs, regardless now of her sleeping son, although he barely stirred. Ruby held her but said nothing, only waited for Eve to collect herself.

Later they sat in sombre silence, side by side on Eve's bed. Nothing Eve had told her had surprised Ruby, but still she felt a great wave of compassion for her suffering. Eve's hand lay on hers and Ruby studied it, then enclosed it with her other hand.

'The preacher at my chapel tells us all shall be well and all shall be well and all manner of things shall be well,' Ruby said.

Eve shook her head. 'Not this time.'

'It shall, Eve. Time passes, wounds heal, life goes on. So there's a rift between you and your brother. Time and experience may change him, or it may not: all of it just adds to the sum of human existence.'

Eve almost smiled. 'You're full of philosophy all of a sudden,' she said.

'Jamaicans are very philosophical. We've had to be. One island, countless injustices, but we can still find joy in jerk chicken and rum and a tuneless banjo.'

Now Eve did smile, but half-heartedly. She was doused in homesickness, sodden with it. She yearned for Daniel's kisses, Eliza's smile, Ellen's stiff-armed embrace. She wanted to bake a Victoria sponge in her own kitchen. She wanted to spend an afternoon with Anna, spilling her soul. Even if she boarded a steamship right now, she was still three weeks away from any of these things. And yet here was Ruby Donaldson, whose heart had been trodden into the dirt by Eve's own brother, offering comfort and sympathy with such gentle humour and generosity that Eve felt humbled.

'What will you do?' she asked now. Ruby looked at her askance.

'Do?'

'When I'm gone.'

'Nothing's changed for me, Eve – except that Roscoe and I have made two new friends.'

'But will you stay 'ere, working for Silas?'

'I prefer to think of it as working for Roscoe. His future is still full of promise. That's why I work here – to help him fulfil his potential. One day he'll leave Jamaica and spread his wings properly.'

'You're only twenty-two yourself, Ruby. That's nowt. Nothing.'

Ruby shrugged. 'Well, even so, I'm not exactly spoiled for

choice, am I?' She didn't look sad, exactly: resigned and very serious, but not sad. They exchanged weary smiles, but then Eve's face brightened and she said, 'Come with us.'

'Where?'

'To England. We're family, aren't we? Come back with me. I've a big house, room for you and Roscoe, and there are good schools and a college in Sheffield, and open spaces, and my girls'd—'

Ruby held up a hand to stop her. 'No. Thank you, but no.' She sounded very decided.

'Why?' Eve asked, and when Ruby considered her answer she found she had nothing to say.

Chapter 46

Anna and Maya left Ravenscliffe the day after the telegram arrived to say that Eve was well on the road to recovery. It was a Thursday in late July, and they stayed to share dinner, then packed their small cases and took their leave. Daniel gave Anna such a hug that she was lifted off the floor, her feet dangling uselessly while he squeezed her.

'Thank you, and I'm sorry,' he said. 'I've been like a bear with a sore ear.'

A bear with a sore ear would have been infinitely better company, she thought, although she smiled and said, 'You're very welcome.' She had decided to forgive his lapse into gloomy introspection because, really, there was no alternative.

The telegram had said: TO ALL STOP MAM MUCH BETTER STOP MUSTN'T WORRY STOP HOME AUGUST STOP PROBABLY ANYWAY STOP SETH. It had made them laugh, partly out of sheer relief and partly at Seth's expense.

'"Probably anyway",' said Eliza. 'That sounds just like 'im.'

'That's why it's sweet,' said Anna. 'He can't help but be himself.'

'Probably anyway sounds good enough to me,' Daniel said. 'As long as she gets here.'

He'd been deadheading sweet peas in the garden, and singing, when Anna and Maya left. Maya, thinking of her English lessons with Miss Cargill, had said, 'It's as if the sun has come out from behind a lowering cloud,' and then she'd been cross when her mother laughed. Anna's fervent apologies were still being snubbed when Lady Henrietta Hoyland rode up to them on a towering black horse, and Maya's annoyance was eclipsed by round-eyed awe. She gazed up at Henrietta, who smiled down at her from what seemed a very great height.

'Looks like I'm lucky to have caught you,' Henrietta said, and for an awful moment Maya thought she might be required to speak, but her mother said, 'You are, we're heading off home. Did you ride over to see me?'

Henrietta dismounted in a fluid, athletic bound. She wore a chic top hat, a long velvet-collared riding jacket and a pair of chocolate-brown trousers, which looked very comfortable, Maya thought, although she'd never seen a lady in anything other than skirts. She hadn't noticed she was staring, but realised she must have been because the lady laughed and said, 'Hello, I'm Lady Henrietta Hoyland, a friend of your mama's, and I'm afraid I borrowed a pair of my brother's breeches because they're so much more practical for riding – promise you won't tell?'

Maya, quite speechless, looked at Anna, who helped her out. 'You can trust us,' she said. 'We won't utter a word.'

'Good, good. Now look,' she said to Anna, 'I've had the most exciting brainwave. I wondered if you might come to Cowes, as my guest. It's the first week of August, and we have an enormous yacht with empty cabins because it's only me, Tobias and Thea. What do you think? The regatta will be such fun, and something quite different, don't you think? A proper thank you from me to you. Do say you'll come.' She directed a radiant beam at Anna, pleased with her own bright idea, and then said to Maya, 'You too, if your mama will allow it.'

Maya stared and then, because she didn't want to seem rude, she said, 'Thank you. I do like cows,' and for a short, puzzling time Lady Henrietta asked her when she'd last been and had she sailed while she was there, until Anna realised the mistake and untangled the crossed wires. She wasn't able to give an answer to the invitation, though. She knew she must say no but couldn't, quite. Her first thought had been of the thrillingly different world conjured by the word 'regatta'. Her second thought, of course, was of Amos.

'Well, look,' Henrietta said, 'have a think, and let me know. I shall take our train to London and travel on by motor to Portsmouth, and we'll sail to Cowes from there. I'd love to have you two for company, and if the little one has a nanny you might send her on ahead with our household staff – not all of them, of course, just a handful.'

Privately Anna winced at what her husband would have to say at Miss Cargill being dispatched with the Hoylands' servants. She wondered, too, what Miss Cargill would have to say. Maya said, 'I have a governess, and I don't need a nanny because we have Norah.'

'Splendid, bring the governess: she can teach you all about Cowes with an e and a capital C.' She threw herself back up into the saddle, and the black horse nickered and took a few delicate, prancing steps backwards.

'Steady, Marley,' she said, and immediately, he steadied. Henrietta said, 'Send me a note, or call in at the hall if you'd like to come. And *do* come,' she added, then she raised her crop in salute and spoke crisply to Marley, who set off at enough of a gallop that for a while Maya could feel the vibration of his hooves on the hard turf all the way up her legs.

'May we go?' the child said. 'I think Miss Cargill would believe it worthwhile.'

Anna looked down at her, marvelling at the child's sober precocity; she was becoming more like her governess, and less like either of her parents, every day. 'We'll have to see,' she said: an unsatisfactory grown-up answer, thought Maya, that usually meant no.

Because it was Thursday, Amos was at the nets, so Anna and Maya went there and watched him for a while, unobserved. He was lost in his purpose; even as he walked towards them to take another run-up he looked only at the ball in his hand. His lips moved, as if he were talking to it. When he bowled Maya flinched. 'He seems quite mean,' she said to her mother. The batsman had to spring out of the way to avoid being hit, and he shouted, 'Fuck's sake, Sykes!' at which point Anna thought it best to herald their arrival, so she applauded and Maya joined in. Seeing them. Amos tossed another ball in a lazy curve at the nearest cricketer and jogged across the pitch. He smiled at Anna a little uncertainly, then to cover his awkwardness he grinned widely at Maya.

'Now then, sunbeam,' he said, and he lifted her boater to kiss the top of her head, which was warm and smelled of straw.

'You look very cross when you throw the ball,' she said.

He pulled a snarling face at her. 'All part of t'game. If t'batsman's worried, I'm 'alfway there.'

'Halfway where?'

''alfway to bowling 'im out.' He tapped the side of his head. 'Psychology,' he said, 'is a very important part of a cricketer's arsenal. You ask Miss Cargill when she's back. I expect she'll 'ave an opinion.'

'She says it's important to be fair, and never to cheat,' Maya said. 'Even at Happy Families.'

'I should say so,' said Anna.

'All's fair in love, war and cricket,' Amos said. 'Famous

saying, that.' He nodded at their bags, which were set to one side. 'I like t'look of them. Them say to me that you're coming 'ome.'

'We are,' Maya said. 'Daniel got a telegram and Eve's nearly better.'

Amos looked at Anna for confirmation and she nodded. 'That's grand,' he said. ''ow about we celebrate with a shandy?'

'At the Hare and Hounds?' Maya said. 'In the beer garden?'

'You read my mind!' said Amos. 'Ten more minutes work 'ere, and I'll be with you.' He glanced at Anna and said, 'Is that all right, love?' He looked anxious, so in reply she stepped forwards and kissed him, and behind them the cricketers gave a ripple of applause and somebody whistled. 'Off you go,' she said. 'Play nicely.'

The lemonade at the Hare and Hounds came in marble-stoppered Codd bottles, which was the main appeal of the drink as far as Maya was concerned. At home in Ardington she had twenty-three glass marbles in a velvet drawstring bag, and now she would have twenty-four. This one was cobalt coloured and looked, to her connoisseur's eye, to be one of the polished ones: a prize indeed. In a separate glass Amos had mixed a splash of his bitter with lemonade from the bottle. Maya sipped it and listened to the adults talk, about politics mostly. It was dull but very pleasant too, to be sitting with them in the garden at the back of the pub. Amos had bought a paper bag of pork scratchings, and the saltiness stayed on Maya's lips even after a drink. She could see the winding gear and headstocks of New Mill Colliery from where they were sitting, and Maya wished the wheel would turn to bring the men up from under ground. It wasn't the right time of day, Amos had said. He'd told her, too, that the pit ponies were coming up in a few weeks for some sunshine and fresh air, and he'd promised to take her to see them when they did. There was nothing like it, he'd told her: the ponies would be mad with joy. *Mad with joy.* The phrase had stayed with her. Maya thought about it again now, and shivered slightly at the idea of being so full of happiness that you lost your mind. That, she considered, would be being *too* happy. And she was worried, already, at how the ponies felt when the time came to go back to work in the dark tunnels of the pit.

Next to her, her mother was talking about her new girl, Jennifer, who painted for her with William. 'Such a talent,' Anna said. 'Her family are potters, from Burslem,' and Amos said, 'Ah, one of t'five towns. Very interesting union 'istory in Staffordshire.' Maya glanced at her mother, who winked at her, and seeing this Amos said, 'I'm only saying. Carry on,' but Anna said she'd finished, really, and if Amos wanted to tell them about unionisation of the potteries they were all ears. Amos said, in a voice that showed he was sorry, 'Tell me some more about this Jennifer girl,' so Anna did, and Amos listened without interrupting.

Under the table the grass was worn by peoples' feet, and there were cigarette ends, some of them quite long: certainly long enough to re-light and smoke. Not that Maya would do such a thing; she simply wondered why, if people liked the taste of smoke and tobacco, they wasted such a lot of it. Then, suddenly and quite out of the blue, she remembered the invitation.

'Dad,' she said. Amos was speaking again now, recounting a tale about a market stall near Cheapside that sold chamber pots with an image of Mr Asquith's face on the inside, and Anna, who was laughing, said, 'Don't interrupt, sweetheart,' but Amos stopped and smiled. 'No,' he said to Maya, 'You're all right, go on.'

'We've been asked if we'd like to sail to Cowes on Lady

424

Henrietta Hoyland's boat,' Maya said in a voice that gave away just how much of an honour she felt this to be. But instead of answering her Amos just looked at Anna, and no one said anything at all.

Norah was in the parlour with her feet – still shod – up on the ottoman when they walked in. She leapt up like a scalded cat and, for once, was stumped for something to say. Maya, a great one for propriety, raised her eyebrows but Anna didn't seem to notice.

Not even a hello, thought Norah, switching instantly from the fear that she might have given offence to being mightily offended herself. She began to bustle pointlessly round the room, lifting and replacing objects, trying to look occupied.

'Are you back now, then?' she said. She sounded peevish, as if she never knew where she was with all this coming and going.

'For the time being, yes,' Anna said. She put down her suitcase and said, 'Will you unpack please, Norah? The garments that need to be washed are at the bottom,' and then left the room. Norah looked at Maya, who was standing like a lost soul, still hanging on to her bag, and said, 'Is your daddy not with you'se?'

Maya shook her head, and her brown eyes filled with tears.

'I think he's angry with me,' she said with a tragic expression. 'He said he had some business at New Mill, but I don't think he does. I just think he doesn't want to be here.' Tears rolled freely now down her face and Norah, overwhelmed with sympathy and love, wrapped her arms about the girl so that she knew she wasn't alone.

'Now, child, your daddy loves you more than the king

loves mustard, and you know how much the king loves mustard, don't you?'

It was a book they'd read together lots of times, about a king whose kingdom ran out of condiments. Maya nodded into Norah's soft bosom and sniffed.

'Wipe your nose on my pinny,' Norah said. 'No one's looking, and the Good Lord knows I've done it myself plenty.'

She stood there holding Maya for a long while, and let the child be. It was all well and good, thought Norah, having grand, important, busy lives, but sometimes all a wain needed was to stand still and be loved.

'Will I make a brew for you missus?'

It was much later, and the gas lamp that stood on the street, directly outside the house, filled the parlour with a diffuse and greenish glow.

'No, thank you Norah,' Anna said. She was sitting on the couch with a pile of letters on her lap, though how she could read anything in the gloaming was a mystery to Norah.

'Will I light the lamps for you then, missus?'

'I suppose so,' Anna said, as if it was of no interest whatsoever.

Norah moved around the parlour, putting on the gas and lighting the wall lamps, cheering up the room. 'Do you know the poem about the street lamp, missus?' she said to fill the wretched silence. 'For we are very lucky with a lamp before the door?'

'And Leerie stops to light it as he lights so many more.'

'There, that's an improvement,' Norah said as the last lamp glowed into life. 'Well, I always thought it a stroke of luck myself, to be lit from the outside as well as in. But you can't be managing with only a street lamp if you've letters to read.'

She nodded down at the stack on Anna's lap, desperate to know who they were from, and – uncharacteristically – not quite bold enough to ask.

'Oh these,' Anna said. 'They're old ones, from my friend in Jamaica.'

'Old ones is it?'

Anna nodded; quiet as a clam, thought Norah.

'Can I get anything at all for you, missus?' She was reluctant to leave her, looking so small and sad and lonely. Anna shook her head. 'Nothing, thank you.'

'Is the mister coming home, missus?'

Anna looked at her. 'That'll do, thank you Norah.'

So the maid retreated, but as she climbed the stairs she heard his boots on the steps outside and heard his key turn in the lock, so instead of continuing on up to her attic room she stood in the shadows of the first-floor landing and listened to their voices. Norah had never seen the harm in eavesdropping; she did it at every opportunity. Now, though, it seemed almost a question of duty. If no one would tell her what the bejesus was going on, she had no option but to find out for herself. She quietened her breathing and held herself still, and tuned in her ears to snatches of a conversation that sounded bitter and resentful, and altogether bleak.

Chapter 47

The king's yacht had dropped anchor off the south railway jetty at Portsmouth Harbour, and out at sea the entire Northern Fleet of the British Navy was assembling for the Spithead Review. Aboard the *Lady Isabella* there was a general, pleasing sense of being in the right place at the right time. Tobias was on deck with *The Times* spread out before him, pinned down against the breeze with four brass weights he had pinched from the galley.

'This is simply fascinating,' he said. 'Thea, look.'

She had been recumbent on a jauntily striped deck chair, but she obliged him by clambering out – there was no elegant way to exit a low-slung canvas chair – and wandering over to look down at the newspaper. She cocked her head and squinted at the complex chart he was poring over. 'What on earth?' she said.

'It's a plan of the ships' positions,' he said. 'See? Twenty-four battleships, sixteen armoured cruisers, forty-eight destroyers and so on and so forth. Here, you see, are the flagships – *Dreadnought*, *Indomitable*, *Inflexible* and *Invincible*.'

'Indomitable and inflexible: that reminds me, what time does your mother expect us?'

She waited for him to laugh, but he was intent on reading the tiny names attributed to the ships and hadn't heard. For a confirmed landlubber, Tobias seemed extremely committed to the details of ocean life, thought Thea. But then, her husband was a man of readily adopted enthusiasms. She admired this about him; it helped bring out the enthusiast in her. Too many people of their acquaintance believed it the height of sophistication to display ineffable ennui, as if they were so boundlessly privileged, so limitlessly wealthy, that everything in life that should be seen or done *had* been seen or done, and now they were simply having to do it all again. Thea recognised in herself the tendency to fall in with this fashionable affectation, when, in fact, one could always find something interesting to do if one would only drop the pretence of world-weariness.

Granted, what Thea found interesting was not always within the parameters of acceptability and usually involved sex. Out of sheer curiosity she had made passionate love repeatedly to Henrietta in the weeks up to and after her marriage to Tobias, until Henrietta discovered an enthusiasm of her own and cooled off the affair. Then, during the Eugene Weeks – which is how she thought of that period: capitalised, like Cowes Week or the Boer War – she had filled her days with either sex or the pursuit of sex, which had been interesting but fundamentally unrewarding: a sort of gluttony, a greed for something that was in any case too readily available. Eugene Stiller might have been an almost-renowned artist, but still, his remarkable capacity for gaining and maintaining an erection was far and away his most fascinating characteristic. Dropping Eugene had been terribly easy for Thea, because London was full of erections, if that was all one wanted. She had turned back to Tobias in the end because he was more fun than most. He came up with schemes and followed them through. He didn't trail doe-eyed behind her, waiting for crumbs from her plate. He was always up for a romp in the

429

sack – or anywhere else, for that matter – but it wasn't his only form of diversion. He looked up now from his chart, and the sunlight on his reddish hair made him appear gilded. He smiled. She hoped, not for the first time, that the baby was his. Certainly, she would make sure the next one was.

'It'll be a sort of naval ballet spectacular,' he said. 'A hundred and fifty vessels across eighteen nautical miles. Let the kaiser stick that in his pipe and smoke it.'

'Is that what it's all about? Sabre rattling?'

'More or less, yes. We're very good at showing off, here in the British Isles. All these naval vessels on display and not a single one has had to be recalled from our foreign outposts; we're magnificent. Wilhelm will be spitting with fury.'

'Poor little kaiser,' Thea said. 'He seems a very striving sort of man.'

'He is. It's the withered arm and the Hohenzollern personality defect,' Tobias said. 'Quite bonkers.'

Thea raised her eyebrows. 'We don't see it in Uli, do we?'

'Not yet,' he said, and crossed his eyes. She laughed.

'It's all such a game,' she said, looking again at the parallel lines of the fleet depicted in the illustration. 'Keeping Ahead of the Kaiser.'

'He's a sneaky cove, though. Never quite know what he's up to. He's put the wind up the Admiralty, who've heard he's building more warships than he says he is. That's why we have to build more ourselves, y'see. Up the ante.'

'How silly,' Thea said. 'Who's counting anyway?'

'Oh, well, best to stay on top if we possibly can. He built the fastest yacht in the world, did Wilhelm. Spent four and a half million marks on it, just so he could beat his uncle at Cowes, which he did the very next year. Put Bertie right off racing. He packed it in after that, if I recall.'

'How like the king,' Thea said. 'So petulant. He shouldn't expect to win all the time.'

Tobias, no ardent fan of Edward's, nevertheless felt the need to defend him since Thea was, after all, American. 'It isn't that he's a bad loser,' he said. 'Rather, that the kaiser is such a frightful bore about his victories. Takes all the fun out of the race.'

There was a breeze across the harbour, and Thea pulled her shawl tighter around her narrow shoulders. Tobias, all concern, moved over to her at once and, positioning himself behind her at the rails, wrapped his arms around her and laced his hands across the subtle bump of her belly. He lowered his head and she felt his breath in her hair.

'I'll keep you both warm,' he said into her neck, and she experienced the familiar, liquid rush of desire that the onset of pregnancy had done nothing to diminish. She arched her back and pressed herself into his groin, and felt, immediately, his response to the pressure.

A discreet cough alerted them to the arrival on deck of a third party. Parkinson allowed them precisely long enough to appear respectable before approaching with a silver salver balanced on the flat of his white-gloved hand.

'Mrs Pickersgill has sent hot beef tea,' he said, feeling at once the superfluity of the gesture. The countess smiled a little archly for his tastes and said, 'How kind of her, and how timely. Darling,' she said, turning to the earl, 'I can manage without you now I have beef tea.'

The butler blushed and placed the tray on the nearest flat surface. At Netherwood Hall he would never dream of seeking out the earl and countess to offer them unasked-for hot drinks, but here on board what he now had to accept was the family yacht, the usual rules seemed not to apply. As Sarah Pickersgill delighted in telling him, he was all at sea. The beef tea had been entirely her idea; he should never have listened to her. Still, he thought, the countess was sipping at her drink now, and looking contentedly across the choppy greyish-green waters towards the open sea, and the earl had given him a friendly nod by way of dismissal, so perhaps it hadn't been too great a blunder. His personal pride was all but restored, when the boatswain shouted at him for leaving the salver and the silver pot on a case that contained life jackets and must never on any account be obstructed. With pink cheeks Parkinson retrieved the tray and beat a retreat below deck. If he was sharper than usual with Sarah that afternoon, she had – he felt – only herself to blame.

Anna had arranged to spend two days and three nights in Cowes. This did not, she believed, seem excessively indulgent, or suggest that she went with any intention of damaging her husband's political career. She and Maya would travel alone – on the public rail network, and without Miss Cargill – and rather than stay on the Hoyland yacht she had rented rooms in a small house in old Cowes. This demonstrated an appropriately modest spirit, as well as an independent one. Together she and Maya would explore the town, watch a few races and experience something utterly new and exciting. Anna would collect ideas for future commissions; Maya would collect memories. No harm was meant, and none would be done. If Amos wished to come too he would be very welcome. She expressed all of this in a letter, which she sent to him at Bedford Square, where he was currently staying. If she declined Lady Henrietta's invitation, she wrote, it would be entirely because his will had subjugated her own. If she didn't go, she didn't think she would ever be able to forgive him for this.

'And if she does go – and she will – what if I can't forgive 'er either?' Amos said. 'She doesn't see both sides o' t'coin.'

Enoch listened, and had nothing to say. He always took Anna's part in the tussles of will that from time to time afflicted their marriage, but now he was silenced. There was no getting away from the fact that, at this remarkably volatile and critical point in the nation's political history, it was provocative of the wife of a Labour MP to accept the hospitality of one of the richest families in Britain. One thing to charge them a small fortune to paint their walls; quite another to raise a glass with them at the glittering pinnacle of their social season.

'Of all t'years for 'er to go,' Amos said, 'it 'ad to be this one. Naval bombast, and that Romanov despot to boot.'

''appen that's why she wants to go,' Enoch said. 'Being Russian, like.'

Amos had his head in his hands, and if Enoch intended to be funny, his humour missed its mark. Amos's name was on a list of seventy MPs making a formal complaint to the government about the tsar's visit to Cowes. In the Foreign Office, Sir Charles Hardinge was peddling a story about improvements in Russian civil liberties to excuse the king, but everyone knew Nicholas presided over a murderous regime, and his close family ties to the British royals were an embarrassment and a disgrace. He was the spitting image of the Prince of Wales; Amos could just imagine the pair of them in Cowes, playing sailors. It made him feel sick with rage. And to know that Anna would be somewhere there, among them . . . he moaned out loud, a low, soft bellow of pure misery. Across the table, Enoch stared into his pint and wondered if it was time they left.

Talk about rubbing salt into the wound, thought Enoch when they left the comfortable little pub half an hour later. At Amos's behest they were off to hear Lloyd George address a public meeting in East London; a battle cry, doubtless, to one of the most impoverished parts of the city. Speaking for himself,

Enoch would have given it a miss. The message would be all over the papers the following day, and the pair of them were already as glum as a wet Monday morning without the additional pain of witnessing first hand the splendid oratory of the chancellor. But Amos had always believed that forewarned was forearmed; listen to the opposition, he said, before drumming them out of office. He attended more Liberal meetings than most Liberals, and always he watched in dour silence with his mouth set in a grim line. He was like an opium addict, thought Enoch: he knew it was bad for him, but he couldn't give it up.

They walked in silence down Rhodeswell Road towards the incongruous crenellations of the Edinburgh Castle. It had been the biggest gin palace in Limehouse until Thomas Barnardo got his reforming hands on it and converted it into a mission church, where the strongest drink a man could buy was coffee. Spiritual succour on tap but no spirits, thought Enoch, with his pamphleteer's habit of finding bons mots for every occasion. Another time he would have shared this with Amos, but he glanced at his friend's stern profile and decided to keep it to himself.

From the windows of the houses around the hall, WSPU banners had been strung and women leaned out shouting abuse at any man they suspected of being a Liberal. The pavement, too, was crowded with jeering, jostling suffragettes. Amos and Enoch pushed their way into the building and found a place to stand by the back wall. The hall was packed – there must be thousands, Enoch said, and Amos nodded – and even with every window in the hall pushed wide it was stiflingly hot. The taunts of the women outside threatened to drown out the speaker, but from the moment he began Lloyd George had his audience in thrall and somehow, something of the charged atmosphere filtered through the open windows so that even the militancy out on the street began to ebb.

The chancellor started on the Navy's new warships, insisted upon by landed noblemen who were not, he said, remotely interested in how the government paid for them. 'Somebody has got to pay; and then these gentlemen say: Perfectly true; somebody has got to pay but we would rather that somebody were somebody else.'

There was laughter, and Amos and Enoch exchanged a look. There was something of the class warrior about Lloyd George tonight, and the massed bodies in the hall sensed it too. On he went. The building of the eight new dreadnoughts had begun, he said, so the government had passed round the hat. 'We sent it round amongst the workmen and winders of Derbyshire and Yorkshire, the weavers of High Peak and the Scotsmen of Dumfries, who, like all their countrymen, know the value of money. They all dropped in their coppers.' He paused here, and waited for a few beats. 'We went round Belgravia,' he said, 'and there has been such a howl ever since that it has completely deafened us.'

A great roar of contempt went up, a rousing endorsement of the chancellor's unequivocal ridicule of the country's toffs. Here was a man with his feet planted firmly on their side of the divide: an ordinary man, speaking from the heart for ordinary men. When Enoch looked at Amos he had his eyes closed and a strange look on his face: despair, envy, admiration.

'I went down a coal mine the other day,' Lloyd George said now, and Amos's eyes sprang open again.

'We sank into a pit half a mile deep. We then walked underneath the mountain and we did about three-quarters of a mile with rock and shale above us. The earth seemed to be straining – around us and above us – to crush us in. You could see the pit props bent and twisted and sundered until you saw their fibres split in resisting the pressure. Sometimes they give way, and then there is mutilation and death.'

Enoch leaned in to his friend and whispered, 'We could

leave. We've got 'is gist,' but Amos didn't reply, only stared ahead at the man who was taking the very words from his mouth.

'And yet when the prime minister and I knock at the door of these great landlords and say to them; "Here, you know these poor fellows who have been digging up royalties at the risk of their lives? Some of them are old. They have survived the perils of their trade, they are broken, they can earn no more. Won't you give them something towards keeping them out of the workhouse?" They scowl at us, and we say: "Only a ha'penny, just a copper." They say, "You thieves!" and they turn their dogs on to us and you can hear their bark every morning. If this is an indication of the view taken by these great landlords of their responsibility to the people who at the risk of life create their wealth, then I say their day of reckoning is at hand.'

The stamping and whistling was tremendous; he had the crowd in the palm of his hand: silent when he wished to speak, baying for blue blood when he paused. Amos wondered how soon the king would learn of his chancellor's treachery. He pictured the fat monarch, just about to settle down to a slap-up dinner on the royal yacht down there in Portsmouth, on the eve of the Spithead Review. But never mind the kaiser and his quota of battleships, Amos thought: the king's most dangerous adversary was right here in the mission hall. Amos clapped and whistled with the rest of the crowd, and there was nothing grudging about it; credit where credit was due, he thought.

Chapter 48

Hugh took Eve for lunch at the Mountain Spring Hotel. Soon she would be sailing back to England, and Hugh said he wanted to treat her before she did. They talked, as he drove, about her girls and how they'd been when he saw them. She wanted precise details – what they said, how they looked, what they wore – which Hugh struggled to supply. 'I'm a man,' he said. 'I don't notice the finer points.' But he did tell her that Eliza looked prettier than ever and danced for him on the slate floor of the big kitchen, and Ellen deigned to eat lunch at the table in his honour.

'Where else would she eat it?' Eve said.

'Up a tree, by all accounts. She's turned wild in your absence.' He started to laugh, but stopped when he saw her expression. 'No, it's fine. She was fine.'

'Was she filthy?' Eve had an image now of Ellen, caked in muck and feathers, foraging in hedgerows.

'Clean hands, but the rest of her was a little grubby,' Hugh said honestly. 'Anna was there, remember – she has standards, even if they're not quite as high as yours.'

She looked at him when he mentioned Anna, for signs of the old attachment, but he just smiled blandly, although he was perfectly aware of her curiosity. He had proposed to Anna once, trying to step in front of Amos, pip him at the post: she had turned him down and married the man who – in Hugh's considered opinion – was far less likely to make her happy. At Ravenscliffe, over lunch, he had noted her reluctance to talk about her husband, and an absence of radiance when she did; noted, too, his absence from the gathering, which went unexplained. All of this had been very interesting to Hugh: never say never, he had thought. Picturing Anna now, he allowed himself to think it again. Sometimes life was a long game, and the patient man the victor.

Eve gazed at the sea, which glittered turquoise, and read aloud the quaint and captivating road signs: Alligator Church, Fellowship, Nonsuch and, ahead, a left turn to Frenchman's Cove. She felt a sudden sharp regret at how little of the island she had seen. The hotel, Musgrave Market and Eden Falls – these three points, marked on a map, would accurately plot the tiny triangle of her existence here in Jamaica.

'I've 'ardly seen anything,' she said now, in a sort of plaintive wail. 'I should've done more while I had t'chance.'

Hugh smiled across at her. 'Yellow fever tends to put the kibosh on touring.'

'I suppose so. But before I fell ill, I didn't stray far either.'

'Well you strayed from Netherwood to Jamaica. It's further than a lot of people go in a lifetime.'

'True.' She smiled, and he allowed himself an appreciation of her beauty. The illness had left her thinner than before, and more fragile in appearance, but this enhanced her allure, Hugh thought. 'What?' she said, and he looked away at once.

'I was just thinking,' he replied, his eyes back on the road, 'how very much you've done for us, and what an absolute brick you've been.'

'Why thank you, kind sir.'

He inclined his head graciously and then swung the

motorcar into an almost-concealed right turn, which took them on to the long, straight, spectacular driveway of the Mountain Spring. It was lined on each side with jacaranda trees, whose spreading branches formed a canopy through which the sunshine filtered in leopard spots of light. Eve stretched out an arm and trailed her hand through the lower, softer shoots, and Hugh told her that they'd missed the glory of full bloom, when the flowers gave the entire driveway a purple-blue glow.

'You see, there's something I should've seen,' Eve said, although until he mentioned it she had thought it uncommonly charming already.

'Another time.'

She looked across at him. 'You know as well as I do that I shan't be back.'

'We-ell,' he said, slowly. 'As I just said, never say never.'

'Did you say that? I didn't 'ear you.'

'Didn't I?' He laughed at his own mistake, but kept it to himself. 'Well, anyway, it's a firmly held belief of mine that one should never rule anything out.'

'You can rule out me coming back, believe you me. Boats and bridges are all burned.'

The hotel suddenly revealed itself as they emerged from the tunnel of jacaranda. It was a long, three-storey building with a pitched roof, tiled red: functional rather than picturesque. It possessed no immediate charm, said Eve; it lacked personality. Hugh said that so did its owner, the president of United Exotics.

'But what Vernon Dowe lacks in personality he makes up for in personal wealth, a fair amount of which he's ploughed into this place. They wanted the Whittam, y'know. Silas wouldn't sell. I thought he was mad, but now I think perhaps I was.'

An immaculately liveried doorman stepped forwards and Hugh slowed to a halt.

'Good afternoon madam, and welcome to the Mountain Spring Hotel. Good afternoon sir, and welcome back.'

Very slick, thought Eve, very clever to know she was new and Hugh wasn't. The young man flashed a toothy American grin and held open the door for Eve, who hadn't realised it was quite time to get out of the car. She shot Hugh a quizzical look. 'They park the motor for us,' he said, then adopted a New York twang – softly, so as not to offend – and added, 'All part of the Mountain Spring experience.'

The interior of the hotel was wonderfully cool, thanks, Hugh said, to Vernon Dowe's investment in some new-fangled electromechanical apparatus that could draw in warm air and blow it out chilled. 'Never,' Eve said, but the evidence was all around her; at the bar, some of the women wore furs. She and Hugh were ushered to a table with two clubby leather chairs, given plump, promising menus and each offered a flute of perfectly cold champagne, on the house. 'A token of our appreciation to loyal customers,' the waiter said.

'So, Mr Oliver, do you come here often?' Eve said, affecting a passable drawl when the waiter had gone and they had toasted one another's good health and happiness.

'Between you and me, absolutely as often as possible,' Hugh said, and they laughed. She could see the draw. Aside from the blissful effects of the cool-air machine, the place was a sanctuary of competent calm. A string quartet played Brahms among the potted palms and the waiters moved about the room as if they were on oiled castors; their obliging smiles accompanied every word and deed. They were all white-skinned, though: not a local among them. This seemed odd, to Eve: a startling contrast to their own enterprise on the other side of town.

'New Yorkers and Bostonians,' Hugh said, 'to a man. Silas grinds his teeth in frustration whenever I persuade him to come here with me.'

'Even now?' She was thinking of the merry atmosphere at the Eden Falls Hotel: the busy terrace, the barbecue nights.

Hugh nodded. 'Even now. He'd swap places in a heartbeat.'

''e's ungrateful. 'e wouldn't know a good thing if it slapped him in t'face.'

'He's conventional, that's all. He'd like to be not merely a successful hotelier, but a *conventionally* successful hotelier, like Dowe.'

'The Whittam was a disaster before we changed it.'

'No, you're right, and I'd tried often enough to talk him into selling up. But he's dogged, your brother.'

'That's one word. I could think of others.'

Hugh raised his eyebrows and smiled. 'You're still angry.' This was an observation, not a question, but she nodded in any case.

'Certainly am.'

'Let it be, Eve. You've done him a favour and he knows it.'

'Actually, it isn't really about the hotel.' She halted, unsure what Hugh knew and what he didn't.

'Ah. More personal, is it?'

She took another sip of champagne and eyed him across the rim of the glass. There were too many secrets already, she thought; she wouldn't add to the morass.

'Roscoe's 'is son,' she said, feeling bold and rash. 'And now t'ousemaid's expecting too. Justine.'

'Ah, right,' he said, quite unruffled.

'You knew?'

'Eve, he might be your brother but I've known him a lot longer than you have.'

She replaced her glass on the table. 'So it's quite acceptable, is it?' She felt the anti-climax of revealing a great, shocking truth, only to discover it was already known.

'It's not how I would live my life,' he said. 'But men have

done worse things down the centuries than father illegitimate babies.'

Put like that, it sounded almost reasonable. But it wasn't so much the fact of his cavalier philandering as the manner in which he went about it, she thought. She had seen at close quarters the cold, careless streak, the easy way he had with hard words and cruel barbs. He now seemed, to her, a different man from the one she thought she knew. He seemed wicked.

'Are you ready to order sir, madam?'

The waiter had appeared soundlessly at their table, but their menus were still unopened. 'Give us a couple more minutes, will you?' said Hugh smoothly, and the waiter slid gracefully away. Eve opened her menu and tried to concentrate, but almost at once gave up. She looked up again at Hugh.

'It's just, 'e's not who I thought 'e was,' she said.

'Who did you think he was?'

She didn't answer.

'Look,' Hugh said, with the patient air of a man who had said all this before. 'Silas can be a charmer, a heartless bounder, a sparkling conversationalist, a ruthless bastard, a true friend, an ill-tempered curmudgeon. Yes, he likes to goad, he can be a bit of a gadfly and he drinks more than he should. But Eve, you can't reform him, so don't try. He's not the easiest of men, but he's not dull. You could never call him that.'

She seemed so sad and silent, he felt sorry for her disillusionment. 'You just have to take the mixed bag, with Silas, or take nothing at all.' He picked up his menu and said, 'Shall we decide?' but she ignored him.

'When 'e came to Netherwood, after all those years away, I was swept away by 'im. My bairns were too. Now I feel we were fooled.'

'You might have fooled yourselves,' Hugh said. 'But I'd bet a pound to a penny that he didn't aim to fool you.'

'Well I don't see much difference, in t'end.'

'World of difference.' He drained his glass. 'Anna didn't like him. Amos couldn't stand him. Daniel didn't trust him. You, however, loved him at once. I'm not here to apologise for Silas, or to justify his behaviour. But Eve, he is who he is. Yes please.' This last was to the waiter, who replenished Hugh's glass and then hovered hopefully.

'Bring us today's special,' Hugh said to him. 'Whatever it is. We're all of a dither here,' and Eve, who at the moment couldn't care less what or whether she ate, said, 'I've asked Ruby to come back to England with me.' It was meant purely to shock him; it did.

Over lunch – a divine filet mignon with chive butter: exactly the sort of dish Ruby would once have cremated – he tried to talk her out of the scheme. It was patent madness, Hugh said, to pluck a Jamaican woman and her child from the only home they'd ever known and expect them to thrive in industrial Yorkshire. Ruby and Roscoe Donaldson in Netherwood? Lambs to the slaughter. Eve put up a stout defence. Ruby was a strong woman, emotionally and physically, and Roscoe was a delightful boy whom anyone would love. In any case, the pair would be under the protection of her and Daniel at Ravenscliffe. Ruby would have employment, Roscoe would have excellent schooling and, later, the chance of further education. He was her nephew; she wanted him close.

'Will I send Justine to you in due course? With her offspring? Keep them all in the bosom of the family?' He sounded like Silas, she thought, and wondered for a moment whether the two men were more alike than she'd realised. Her powers of judgement were flawed, she now believed; her discernment was questionable. But then he said, 'Sorry, that

443

was uncalled for,' and he seemed to mean it. He sawed at his beef, and popped a slice into his mouth, and across the table, they watched each other. It was quite true, thought Eve, that she was as closely related to Justine's unborn child as she was to Roscoe. But he'd misunderstood her purpose if he thought for one moment that all of Silas's cast-off women were welcome in her home. For all she knew, they could be legion.

'All I'm saying,' said Eve, 'is Ruby and I are friends now, and Angus and Roscoe are friends too, as well as cousins, and in England, there'll be a world of opportunity that doesn't exist in Jamaica.'

'No sunshine, or not much,' he said, trying to lighten the mood. 'No sea or sand. No ackee and saltfish. No humming-birds, no jacaranda.'

'All right, all right, that's all true,' she said, not ready to be amused, 'but none of those things are reasons to stay.'

'She's a negro, Eve.'

'I've noticed.'

'Well, how do you think it'll feel for her and Roscoe, being the only black-skinned residents in Netherwood? In the entire county, for all I know.'

'Anna was – is – the only Russian. She's managed well enough.'

'Absurd comparison,' he said. 'Anna is blonde and blue-eyed and five foot two, not statuesque with ebony skin. Anna doesn't stand out like a sore thumb in the Netherwood Co-op, does she?'

Eve conceded the point with a curt shake of the head, which swam a little when she moved it, after two glasses of champagne. Now a deep red claret had arrived, to drink with the beef. 'Try it,' he said, nodding at her glass. She did, and its mellow liquid weight slipped warmly down her throat.

'Eve,' he said. 'This is something I understand, believe me.

I'm a shade or two darker than most of the people I live and work among, and it can be difficult, being different.'

She looked at him, the gloss and polish of him, the cut of his jacket and the crisp white of his shirt against his light brown throat: hard to imagine him suffering a failure of confidence in the company of anyone. Though it was also hard to imagine anyone getting the better of Ruby, and the fact was she didn't even know yet if Ruby would come. What she did know, however, was that she profoundly regretted mentioning it today.

'Please don't mention this to Silas,' she said, and he held up his hands in a non-committal way.

'I think that if you're planning to abscond with the cook the boss should probably be told.'

'She's not an indentured slave, you know.'

'I do know that, thank you.'

'Then she's free to leave your employment if she wishes.'

'She is indeed.'

They moved on, then, to speak of other things, but the air between them had cooled and it proved difficult to completely regain the friendly footing on which they'd begun earlier in the day. Even the first-rate hospitality of the Mountain Spring began to grate, and by the time they left Eve was ready for the authentic, if slightly unpredictable, charms of the Eden Falls Hotel.

What Eve hadn't told Hugh was that she wanted to take Seth back with her too; she wanted to take him but he wouldn't go. She had asked him the very same evening of her row with Silas, the evening she'd begun packing – far too hastily, of course: it had all had to come out of the trunk again – in her frenzy to be away. She had found Seth sitting alone on the terrace late at night, long after the hotel had fallen quiet and still. He had seemed very content, and she remembered thinking this was odd, given the drama of the day, the ripples of which had surely not escaped him. Even Wendell, the kitchen lad, had looked at her with saucer eyes when she passed him on the stairs. She had told Seth her story, recounted her conversation, left nothing out; this all must be in strict confidence, she had said, but if he didn't know the truth he would never understand how much it mattered that he left with her and Angus, that he remove himself from his uncle's influence. Seth had heard her out in placid silence, and then had simply said no.

His uncle valued him, Seth said. He had told him so, just this evening; he saw his potential – more so, perhaps, than she did. His uncle had told him, more than once, that the company would be his in the end. And the paternity of Roscoe Donaldson, while admittedly a surprise, was neither here nor there. 'Not my concern,' he had said. 'Not yours either.'

Eve had looked at her son, her firstborn child, and although she was close enough to have taken his hand, she had never felt further away from him. He held her gaze, with the defiant challenge that, over the years, he had always reserved for her, and she felt, amid her sadness, a slender but quite distinct thread of relief at his decision.

'Mam,' he had said, 'you look after yourself and Angus. I'll look after myself.'

So she had left him in the dark, with just the crickets for company. After she'd gone he tried to smoke a cigarette, a habit he longed to acquire, but the taste was too bitter and he stubbed it out. He thought about Ruby Donaldson, whom he disliked, and felt glad that his uncle had spurned her. If he hadn't, then her little bastard – he felt a thrill at

446

the ugly word – might be a threat. As it was, so long as he, Seth, could make himself indispensable to Uncle Silas, he was on a straight, clear road to success. He lit another cigarette, determined, this time, to see it through to the end.

Chapter 49

The *Victoria and Albert* was only ten years old and very fine, but even so she was eclipsed in grandeur and elegance by the Russian imperial yacht, which had sailed with immense grace into Cowes harbour, masts gleaming like golden spars in the soft morning light. The day before, Tsar Nicholas, gaunt but elegant in the white uniform of a British admiral, had stood at salute, shoulder to shoulder with the rotund and somewhat florid Edward, to review the mighty armada of British battleships at Spithead; but now the sailing races were about to begin and, with them, the fun.

Tobias invited the household staff up on deck when the *Lady Isabella* took her place in the busy harbour, so that they could properly observe the *Standart*, the tsar's yacht. She was a magisterial craft. Four hundred feet long, with a gleaming black hull and a bowsprit adorned with gold leaf. There were three towering, varnished wooden masts and two vast white funnels, and her deck seemed to be crowded with people, so that it was difficult to pick out Nicholas and Alexandra, although everyone claimed they could. Parkinson stood at the rails, mesmerised: that the tsar and tsarina were practically within hailing distance was a remarkable and memorable thing.

Poor Mrs Powell-Hughes, he thought; she had had to send up her sincerest apologies from the darkened sanctuary of her cabin.

'She's feeling decidedly seedy, Your Lordship,' Parkinson said with a knowing smile, one sailor to another. That neither he nor the earl had ever sailed before seemed to escape him, although Lord Netherwood said, 'Poor soul, me too, and it was only eight miles.'

Sarah Pickersgill was a natural, however. She didn't even hang on to the rails but stood twitching her nostrils in the breeze like a foxhound, and shading her eyes with her hand so that she appeared to be saluting the other vessels. All the while, she kept half an eye on the boatswain, who wore his best blue coat with brass buttons and, if she wasn't mistaken, had winked at her when she emerged from the galley, slightly flustered from cooking for the first time on the move and tucking rogue strands of unruly blonde hair into her cap.

There were hundreds of yachts at anchor, and all of them were required to keep a respectful distance from the king and the tsar, who were moored side by side in the centre of the harbour and closely guarded by a circle of small gunboats. Nicholas was famously anxious, Ulrich told them – not about his own safety but that of Alexis, the sickly little tsarevich; in Russia, he said, assassination was a constant threat, and subversives came in the most unlikely guises. Ulrich was a fount of information. He knew the yachts of all the European royals, and pointed them out as they passed: the Prince of Battenburg's *Sheila*; the King of Spain's *Hispania*; the old, exiled French Empress Eugenie on her beloved *Thistle*; and the kaiser's racing cutter *Meteor*.

'All of Cowes is *en fête*,' Isabella said gaily. She had been giddy since their arrival at Cowes, as if the salt air itself were intoxicating. Here, in this remarkable melting pot of continental nobility, her own status – as bride-to-be of Ulrich von

Hechingen – had hit new and dizzying heights. Uli appeared to know absolutely everyone who wasn't English, and at a regatta overrun with crown princes, archdukes and romantically exiled French royals, this was a distinct and exciting advantage. He wasn't on terms with the kaiser, being too distant and obscure a relation, but nobody minded that, as Wilhelm was such an angry-looking, off-putting little fellow. It was enough, for Isabella, that the kaiser's cruising yacht was named *Hohenzollern* and there was she, sporting a fat diamond with the very same pedigree. Small wonder that she currently existed in a state of exultation. Even her mother was finally impressed; her daughter's fiancé had secured invitations for dinner with the Crown Prince of Bavaria, whom Uli called Rupert. 'He's not much fun,' Uli warned the duchess. 'He's very much the military man.' But Clarissa didn't care a jot; in her view, fun was overrated anyway. Certainly, it played second – even third – fiddle to connections, especially those of a royal nature. She had half hoped that Edward VII would remember her kind hospitality at Netherwood Hall five years earlier and bring her and Archie aboard the *Victoria and Albert*, but it quickly became evident that the king's attention was all taken up by the tsar, who didn't seem to want to meet anyone. He had yet to set foot on dry land. Crown Prince Rupert, while rather a minor royal, was nevertheless better than nothing, and Clarissa was very glad that the Plymouth tiara would get another outing so soon after the last.

Anna and Maya's rooms were in a quaint, blue-painted cottage in a street just behind the Parade. They had a bedroom and a sitting room, and a key for the front door in case they came in after dark. 'I hope we do,' Anna whispered to Maya as their landlady led them down the front hall to demonstrate the idiosyncrasies of the lock. 'Otherwise we shall be having a very dull time.'

She was pleased, though, that she hadn't accepted Henrietta's invitation to occupy a cabin on the *Lady Isabella*. The modesty of their rented dwelling was perfectly in keeping with Labour ideals, she felt. Was it her fault if, whenever she and her daughter stepped out of the house, they were cheek by jowl with all of England's aristocracy?

They met Henrietta on the lovely, lawned sweep of land behind Cowes Castle. She was arm-in-arm with Thea, and they made a small spectacle with their hugs and hearty hellos. Maya looked beguiling in a sailor frock and red patent-leather shoes, and Thea, who was in white embroidered linen and lace with a navy satin ribbon trim, at once took her by the hand and said, 'Look! We're the best-dressed pair on the Parade.' They walked ahead, and Henrietta and Anna followed.

'To be perfectly frank,' Henrietta said, when they were far enough behind the others not to be overheard, 'I thought you wouldn't come. I gather the chancellor has rather put the spotlight on the idle rich with his Limehouse speech.'

Anna said, 'Well yes, and I did waver. I think if my husband hadn't been so against the plan I might have stayed at home.'

Henrietta laughed. 'I never could bear to be told no myself,' she said. 'When I was young, my dear father was always forbidding things. I think that's why I became such a rebellious soul.'

'I don't wish to make Amos unhappy. But he does try to bend me to his will.' She glanced at Henrietta. 'And he disapproves of some of my friends.'

'Well he was extremely kind to me, the last time I saw him,' Henrietta said, and Anna frowned, trying to think when that might have been. Certainly, outside the Caxton Hall back in May, his manner had been far from kindly.

'I called on you in Bedford Square,' Henrietta said. 'Toby

took me, after he had fetched me from Holloway. I wanted to show you I was free, and to say thank you, but you'd gone to Netherwood. Amos answered the door.'

'Oh?'

'He said he was happy that you'd been able to help, and told me to look after myself.'

'Did he? That doesn't sound very much like Amos.'

'And yet it was, unless you have a very gruff housemaid. He didn't tell you, I suppose.'

'Not a word.' She wondered why. Perhaps the silence that so often existed between them lately had proved too intractable. Ahead, Thea and Maya had settled in a sunny spot on the grass at Prince's Green, and were looking at the boats on the water. They were chatting animatedly, each of them speaking and listening in equal measure. Anna allowed herself a rush of pride at her daughter: her grave, sweet face, her sociability, her curiosity about the world. Maya saw her and patted the grass.

'Come and sit down, Mama. This is the best view of the races.'

'Is that so?' Anna said. She smiled at her daughter and sat down, and Henrietta joined them. The grass was warm and dry, and although there were deck chairs for hire, it suited their unceremonious mood to sit on the ground. The four of them made a picturesque group, and a photographer, roving the Parade with his Box Brownie, insisted on taking their picture exactly as they were. Afterwards he gave them a small card bearing the address of his studio. Before she left Cowes, Anna bought a copy of the photograph from him: there she was with Maya, sitting on the ground between the Countess of Netherwood and Lady Henrietta Hoyland. Three attractive young women and a child. Thea and Maya were squashed up close; a more decorous gap separated Anna and Henrietta. All four wore happy smiles. No one would be able to say, from looking at their images, which of them were titled and which were not. This fact seemed to Anna immensely significant; it lay, she felt, at the very heart of everything she believed.

In the galley kitchen of the *Lady Isabella*, Sarah was managing terrifically well. It was an acknowledged fact that for a head cook of a large private household she was very young. When Mrs Adams – her predecessor, mentor and bully – had keeled over in the cold store and died, she had been two days shy of her fiftieth birthday. Sarah wasn't yet thirty. But perhaps it was precisely because of her inexperience that she was so undaunted by a challenge. This was Mrs Powell-Hughes's theory, which had come to her as she watched Sarah assemble nine platters of lobster Thermidor, and a plain boiled lobster with mayonnaise for the child. This, after mixed hors d'oeuvres and stuffed artichoke hearts, and before roast saddle of lamb and a frozen chocolate *Bombe Nabob*.

'I take my hat off to you, Sarah Pickersgill,' said the housekeeper. 'I can't imagine Mrs Adams would've taken this in her stride in the way you have.'

Sarah snorted. 'I'd like to have seen 'er in this kitchen. We should 'ave 'ad to get 'er out with a shoe 'orn.'

It couldn't be denied. Mrs Adams had had arms like hams and the girth of a beer barrel. 'Anyway,' Sarah went on, 'it might be small, but it's very well thought out. Everything in its place, and a place for everything. I walk miles in t'course of a week in my kitchen at Netherwood 'all. At least on a yacht your legs are spared.'

Mrs Powell-Hughes smiled at her. 'Well, I think you've done a marvellous job in very difficult circumstances.'

Sarah stopped what she was doing. 'Thank you,' she said. She was touched. 'And I'm glad you're back on your feet.'

The housekeeper pulled a wretched face. 'Only because we're steady now. As soon as that anchor's pulled I shall be queasy again. I tell you, I'm not like you; I can't adapt.'

'You should ask leave to travel up on deck when we sail for Portsmouth. You'll do better in t'fresh air.' The boatswain had told her this, but she delivered it as her own advice. The less Mrs Powell-Hughes knew about her conversations with Mr Clough – for that was he – the better. Even Sarah blushed to think of the confidences they'd swapped in the close confines of his cabin. Not to mention the rest of it. He was a very ardent man when his coat was off. As soon as she'd told him she was only Mrs Pickersgill because she was the cook, not because she was married, he had been after her with all the unbridled eagerness of a ferret down a rabbit hole. She smiled at the half-hearted way she'd tried to halt his advances. In the end, she'd thought why the dickens not? Soon enough, she'd be back below stairs at Netherwood Hall and his salty lips and firm flesh would be a distant memory.

The cautious clip of Mr Parkinson's shoes on the narrow galley stairs heralded his imminent arrival, and sure enough he appeared in due course with a loaded tray. He held it out to the housekeeper and said, 'If you wouldn't mind, Mrs Powell-Hughes.'

She took it, and put it down carefully. Glassware, mostly; lovely plain crystal, with gold-plated stems, all bought new for the boat. 'Are you managing?' she said. 'Up there, I mean.'

'Oh, I'm managing perfectly well,' the butler said with a sort of snippy stoicism that, in spite of his words, suggested some displeasure. He was unhappy with the guest list, Mrs Powell-Hughes suspected. He didn't think the Earl of Netherwood's butler should have to wait on Anna Sykes and her little girl. She didn't want to hear about it, so she just said, 'Excellent,' in a bracing voice that left him no opportunity to expand his views. She handed him an empty tray and he turned on the stairs and disappeared, little by little, from view.

The seating plan for the upper-deck dining table on the *Lady Isabella* was thus: Tobias at the head of the table, Thea at the bottom. Anna was on the earl's right, and to her right was Henrietta, then Peregrine Partington, Isabella, and Ulrich. Thea had insisted on having Maya at her right-hand side, and next to the child was Archie. Amandine, Perry's wife, came next, and then Clarissa, who was displeased to find herself opposite Anna Sykes, whom she found inappropriately opinionated for one so lowly. Neither, in her sadly unsought opinion, should there be a child at dinner, but somehow the fact that they were afloat had changed all the rules. She shared an occasional, comforting glance with dear Parkinson, whom she knew would perfectly understand, and share, her discomfiture.

Tobias was in full flow. Earlier in the day he'd bumped into Sir Francis Knollys, who as the king's private secretary was meant to be a tower of discretion, but instead was rather a gossip. He had told Tobias that the king was wild with fury at Lloyd George over the Limehouse speech.

'Knollys says he's already fired off a letter to Lord Crewe, demanding that he kick up a stink about it, and he's asked Asquith to tell Lloyd George he's gone too far this time.'

'It was a little inflammatory,' Henrietta said.

'Goodness,' said Clarissa. 'Politics at the dinner table. How very *outré*.'

'Sorry Mama,' Tobias said.

'I believe Lloyd George knows exactly what he's doing,' said Anna, who had no compunction about discussing politics at the dinner table: quite the contrary, in fact; at her own dinner table it was what they did much of the time. 'He's determined to push his budget through. I admire him enormously.'

'Aren't you meant to be for Labour?' said Peregrine, with an expression of milk-curdling sourness.

'Oh, well of course,' Anna replied sunnily. 'But still, I admire the chancellor for the strength of his conviction, and his courage. I don't speak for my husband, or the Labour Party, naturally. This is just my opinion.'

Peregrine looked across the table at his wife, whose mind was blessedly free of opinion, and said, 'Dear one, if you can't manage all your lamb?'

'But Anna,' Henrietta said, 'Surely the chancellor knows there's nothing to be gained by antagonising the very people with the power to veto his plans? The peers will never allow this budget to pass through Parliament.'

'Heavens, Henry,' said Clarissa. 'Please desist.'

'Exactly. It's a clever trap, I believe,' said Anna. 'Traditionally, peers don't interfere with finance bills. The last time they did there was a civil war and the king was beheaded.'

Amandine gasped. 'The king, beheaded?' she said. Ulrich laughed, and Isabella said, 'Charles the First, Amandine, not Edward the Seventh.'

Perry said 'Damned disgrace,' through a mouthful of his wife's lamb. 'If Lloyd George thinks he can topple Bertie he'd better think again.'

'No, no,' Anna said. 'I'm sure the chancellor means no disrespect to the king. But if the upper house rejects the finance bill and throws out Lloyd George's budget, the king will have to dissolve Parliament and the Liberals will take their case to the country.'

'Goodness, what a lesson we're enduring. Parkinson, I think we have finished,' the duchess said meaningfully. The butler shot her a small, colluding smile and began to clear the dinner plates.

'And so?' said Tobias to Anna, lured back into the debate in defiance of his mother, who looked at him coldly, her mouth pinched into a tight, straight line. 'What of it? We have nothing to fear in the House of Lords from another general election.'

'You might have, if the Liberals go to the country on the peers' excessive powers of veto as well as on the budget.' Anna smiled pleasantly at the peer whose hospitality she was currently enjoying. 'Your days as a member of the ruling class could be numbered.' There was a short, rather stunned silence, and then Peregrine said, 'I say! That's quite enough politics. There are ladies present, you know.'

Anna laughed, and said she hoped she could count herself among their number; Clarissa looked at her doubtfully. At the other end of the table Thea clapped her hands for silence and said that clever little Maya knew a Russian folk song and had agreed to sing it for them, loudly enough that the tsar might hear.

'On your chair, sweetie,' she said to Maya, who looked at Anna for a nod of permission and, having received it, clambered nimbly into a standing position on her seat. 'Now, the tsar's yacht is just over there,' Thea said, pointing to the middle of the harbour. 'So face that direction and give it everything you've got.'

Well, thought Clarissa, this really is the limit. The two people in the party who had least cause to draw attention to themselves were now dominating the evening. She glanced down the table at Archie to convey her displeasure, and saw that he was fast asleep.

Chapter 50

When Anna was thirteen years old, Tsar Alexander died and the news was a shock to all of Russia. Anna's parents, in the cataclysmic spirit of the moment, undertook the long and arduous train journey from Kiev to St Petersburg, in order that they and their children might pay their respects. It was November. Anna and her brother Alexei were wrapped in wool and fur but, even so, their hands and feet lost all feeling, standing amid thousands of mourners in the dirty snow of Nevsky Prospect. Anna was so cold that she forgot to mourn, and while all around her people hung their heads, she instead stared boldly at the red and gold carriages, trying to pick out their occupants. The cortège moved at a snail's pace, advancing slowly towards the Cathedral of Peter and Paul, where all the Romanov tsars were buried. Behind the imperial family, alone in a coach of her own, the young and beautiful Princess Alix of Hesse was hidden behind heavy veils, but little Anna saw what she believed was a sad half-smile, directed only at her. She started, as if she was about to run to the carriage, and she believed she might have done if her mother hadn't grabbed her arm roughly and hissed, 'Be still! Bow your head and pray.'

'It's the new tsar's bride, Mama,' Anna had whispered, and her mother had crossed herself and said darkly, 'She has come to us behind a coffin.' The next day they had shuffled in a line of thousands past Alexander's bier while priests chanted litanies and a hidden choir sang sorrowful hymns. Anna's father had lifted her so that she could say a respectful farewell to the dead emperor. He had a holy picture in his hands, which seemed a simple thing to be carrying after all the luxury of his life. His face wore an expression of mild contentment, although his skin was waxy and pallid like a doll's. He looked, to Anna, as if he had never actually been alive. 'What a shame I only ever saw him dead,' she had said, too loudly; her father put her down at once, and her mother slapped the back of her head.

These were the memories that ran through her mind now as she stood at the harbourside, looking out at the *Standart* with the same frank curiosity as she had shown for the cortège fifteen years earlier. The hull of the imperial yacht looked freshly blacked in the bright morning light, like a new kitchen range. Her decks were swagged with awnings of white canvas and there were wicker chairs and steamers set out, some of which were in use, though it was hard from this distance to know by whom. The people on board were indistinct; she could tell women from men, but not empresses from servants. There was a relaxed informality on deck, though – she could tell that – and there were children too, who must surely be the daughters and son of Nicholas and Alexandra. There had been three girls before Anna fled Russia: Olga, Tatiana and Maria, three little grand duchesses. Then, after she arrived in England, she read that Anastasia had been born, and finally Alexis, the tsarevich. They must worry for their frail son, Anna thought: a terrible burden to be heir apparent to the monstrous powder keg that was Russia. She wondered what he understood of his responsibilities at not quite five years old. If she were tsarina, she would bring him ashore to play on the beach.

Anna considered the size of the vessel. Really, she was meant to drop anchor in the Finnish fjords or a remote Baltic cove, or beneath the towering cliffs of the Crimea, where her mighty bulk would be in proportion with the surroundings. Here, in the confines of Cowes harbour, she dominated the scene, a colossus of the seas. The yacht was still surrounded by its security cordon of destroyers, and there was doubtless a whole platoon of guards on board to ward off assailants. This meeting of the emperor and the king had been arranged here precisely because the harbour was easy to seal off and guard, but the scheme had placed the socially reticent tsar into the very centre of a whirlpool of glamorous posturing and pageantry. Anna felt sorry for him; he appeared careworn in photographs, and she thought she could detect kindness in his eyes.

This was not an acceptable view for the wife of a Labour MP, or indeed for a Russian émigrée who had fled the pogroms. She knew she was meant to hate him and, certainly, his empire was corrupt and unjust and cruel, and when she'd escaped with her first husband, she hadn't felt safe until their ship set sail from Bremen. But in all fairness, could one man be held responsible for the evil prejudices of a million others? The vast empire was ungovernable, the potential for wickedness immense. She knew by heart all of Amos's strident opinions on the evils of imperial Russia; from the sidelines, he cheered the revolutionaries on. But she wondered how he would have managed, if by an accident of birth he'd become Emperor of all the Russias on his father's death. This made her smile; the thought of Amos in his pit boots and cap acknowledging the crowds outside the Winter Palace. He would make rather an effective autocrat in another life. His belligerent bearing and stubborn self-belief would serve him well.

She scanned the decks of the *Standart* one last time, looking for the empress, but stopped when she realised that she was being watched by a heavily bearded officer who was out to bag an assassin before lunch. The poor Romanovs, thought Anna; they see a throng of gaily dressed people and wonder who among them would like them dead.

Thea had made quite a pet of Maya, and today the two of them had been sea bathing together, taking a dip from the back of a quaint bathing machine that had been towed for them to the water's edge by a horse. Maya had a lavender-coloured costume, with straight, knee-length knickers and a skirt with a white-trimmed frill. She was proud of it – rightly so, Thea told her – and she bemoaned the fact that it hardly ever got an outing. She wanted to keep it on while they ate ices on the grass by the bandstand, but even Thea, who didn't exhibit nearly so many dull, adult preoccupations as most grown-ups, would not allow it, so they both changed into their normal clothes in the privacy of their rented mobile hut.

Anna was already waiting for them on Prince's Green when they arrived, pink and exhilarated from the sun and the cold salt water. Maya told her about the horse, and said she should have come too; Anna said it would have taken more than one horse to get her into the chilly waters of the Solent. They talked about plans for later: Thea said they were dining with the Duchess of Manchester in the house she'd taken for the week, but Anna and Maya were welcome to dine on the *Lady Isabella* if they wished. Anna said she wouldn't hear of putting their staff to such trouble on what would otherwise be an evening off. They would eat fish and chips, and then see what they could see. That sounded nice, said Thea a little wistfully, and Maya said, 'You're more than welcome to join us,' which made her mother and

Thea laugh, even though Maya knew it had been exactly the right thing to say. Then, suddenly, the child shot up, dropping her ice and startling a seagull, which cawed and flapped and caused a small outbreak of chaos on their part of the green.

'Dad!' she shouted. 'We're here! Amos!'

She turned her shining face to Anna and Thea and said, 'It's Amos. My dad,' and then she pelted across the grass and Anna saw him, dressed in his summer suit and his winter Homburg, and her heart leapt at the incongruity of him, and the shock.

They made an unlikely party, Amos, Anna, Maya and Thea, but if Amos was feeling uncomfortable, it didn't show in his face, which was arranged into an expression of benign interest. Thea was talking about her plans for opening the gardens of Netherwood Hall to the public, because she thought it a waste and a shame that so few people were able to appreciate their magnificence.

'I thought, perhaps, every Sunday, but Toby thinks that might be too much, so he suggested bank holidays, but that seems too little.'

Amos nodded very nicely. 'Also,' he said mildly, 'you don't close your pits on bank 'olidays.'

'Don't we?'

'Not when I worked in one, anyroad.'

'Ah, back in the bad old days,' Thea said merrily. 'I think Henrietta's reformed us now. Anyway, it's neither here nor there, because I've plumped for the last Sunday of the month, from May to August. We'll have one at the end of this month, because I can't wait until next May.'

She paused, as if waiting for applause. Anna said, 'It sounds an excellent plan. Does Mr MacLeod know of it?'

'No-o,' Thea said, 'I haven't seen him in weeks and weeks. But it's for him, really, so I don't see how he could object. He works so hard, and sometimes entire borders bloom and die without anyone other than Henry and me showing an interest.'

They were standing on a jetty, waiting for the boat that would carry the countess back to her yacht. When it came, Tobias was in it. Amos's face was unreadable, but he shook the earl's proffered hand. Tobias turned to Anna.

'I didn't know your husband was in Cowes, Mrs Sykes.'

'Neither did I,' Anna said.

'Ha! Very good! Well, in you hop, darling, steady as you go.' Tobias reached for Thea and handed her carefully into the craft: she was precious cargo. 'I say, Mr Sykes?' he said, when Thea was seated.

Amos didn't exactly answer, only looked at the earl and raised an enquiring eyebrow. This could have been construed as rude, but not, apparently, by the earl. 'I was thinking about a cricket match. My wife here has decided she wants to fling open our gates to all and sundry, and I thought an inaugural cricket match would be entertaining.'

'Oh?' Amos said neutrally. Toffs *v.* Nobs, he thought: no thank you very much.

'So, I wondered if you might know anyone in Netherwood who could field an opposition? I'll provide the house team – call in some favours, get any available chaps over from Chatsworth, Wentworth Castle and whatnot. Do you know any cricketers?'

Now here was something. Amos rocked on his heels and smiled. 'One or two,' he said.

'Splendid. Could you field a team, do you suppose?'

'Leave it with me. Last Sunday in August, did you say?'

'That's it. Not much notice, but it'll just be a bit of fun. I'll bet some of your mining pals could probably wield a bat if we gave them one.'

'They do say,' said Amos, 'that if you need a decent cricketer you should whistle down a mine shaft.'

The earl chortled at the thought of recruiting a team from anywhere other than the playing fields of Eton and Harrow. 'Jolly good,' he said. 'Tell them it's a six if the ball hits the house, and there's a prize of twenty-five pounds to any man who can break a window.' He barked with laughter. 'That should kindle some interest, what?'

'Oh aye,' Amos said. 'I should think so.'

'Right we are, anchors aweigh.' The little motorboat chugged off from the jetty, and Thea made Maya squeal with laughter by waving her silk handkerchief and pretending to cry. Anna gave Amos a shrewd look and said, 'One or two?'

'One or two bad 'uns, I meant,' he said. 'Eleven or twelve belters.' He grinned at her, but she resisted him and said, 'Anyway, why are you here?'

'Oh that's nice, I must say.'

'I mean, have you come to stir up trouble?'

He held out his arms in mute appeal. 'Do I look like a troublemaker?'

'You do, actually, Dad,' said Maya. 'Your hat's at a funny angle.'

He roared with laughter, picked her up, and rubbed his stubbly chin on her soft cheek until she begged forgiveness. Anna watched them and felt lighter and happier than she had for weeks.

'It's good to see you,' she said.

He put Maya down. 'It's *very* good to see you.'

'Why did you come, though? You were dead against it.'

He shrugged, shoved his hands in his pockets, jangling his change. 'Fancied some sea air,' he said. He looked about him, left and right; everywhere there were lords and ladies in bespoke versions of casual yachting costumes, and the harbour bristled with masts and sails. 'It's busy though,' he said. 'Is there summat going on?'

'Seriously,' Anna said.

'Seriously, I wanted to see you. Correction, I *needed* to see you. I needed to see you to tell you I'm sorry. I've been a brute and a clot, and I'm sorry.'

'I don't remember you ever apologising to me before.' She felt a little churlish, reminding him of this now, but nevertheless it mattered. It had always been her, never him, who broke a silence.

'Then you'll know what it means that I'm saying it now.'

'And now, you should kiss,' Maya said, so they did.

When Henrietta came to find them the next day she was taken aback to see Amos, although she managed very well to hide her surprise and he managed very well to be polite. They were hiring bicycles, Anna said: could she join them? Henrietta demurred, reluctant to impose, and in the end it was Amos who insisted. 'More t'merrier,' he said. 'You can ride a bike, can't you?' It was this indirect challenge that Henrietta couldn't resist. She could ride a bicycle perfectly well, and in fact led the way from Cowes to a sandy cove, where they ate cheese and pickle rolls.

Maya collected shells and those stones which, to her, and sometimes inexplicably, were interesting. The adults watched her, and talked, and Henrietta showed such an informed interest in the ructions created by the chancellor that, before he realised what was happening, Amos found he had complimented her on her grasp of the matter.

'Thank you,' Henrietta said, 'but I can't take all the credit.' She smiled at Anna. 'We had a lesson in radical Liberal tactics from your wife. My mother is still lying in a darkened room with an ice pack on her forehead.'

Anna said, 'Did she think I was dreadful?'

'Shocking.' Henrietta looked at Amos and said, 'Anna was quite magnificent. We were all quaking, by the end, at the thought of the House of Lords razed to the ground and all the Tory peers castrated. You would have been proud of her.'

Amos looked at Anna, who was laughing with Henrietta, and his heart was full. 'Oh, I am' he said.

His wife smiled warmly at him, pleased at the effort he was making, and Amos, who didn't want to give the impression that he was warming to Lady Henrietta Hoyland, had to look away. He was here in Cowes for Anna, and for his marriage, and for Maya. He wasn't here to make friends with the foe.

Chapter 51

❧❧❧❧❧

Silas's great rival on his home shores was the Fyfield Steamship Company, which ran a small fleet of banana boats between Jamaica and Bristol. He had hoped to have drummed them off the seas by now, but it seemed there was room for two international banana shippers, because Fyfield's were no less of a presence at Port Antonio docks than Whittam & Co. It gave Eve some considerable satisfaction to tell Silas that, rather than wait for *Pegasus* to dock in a few days' time she and Angus would sail home on the SS *Avonmouth*, a Fyfield vessel. It was in now, she said, and would leave tomorrow for Bristol.

'You'd do that?' he said. 'You'd sail home on a cargo ship?'

'I would and I will.'

'Out of spite?'

'No,' she said, 'out of expediency. I want to get back, and this is t'quickest way.' It was perfectly true, though, that it gave her an occasional pulse of satisfaction to be sailing home without his help. The Fyfield captain had promised her a comfortable berth, though nothing like the standards of the *Pegasus*.

'All said and done, it's a banana boat, madam, not a passenger liner,' he had said. Eve had told him that if all he could offer her was a seat on an upturned crate she would still prefer to sail with him tomorrow than wait. Also, she added privately, Silas would be on the *Pegasus*.

After she told him, he rallied swiftly, as was his style, and dismissed her from his office with a shrug of indifference. Then she and Angus walked to Eden Falls so that he could swim with Roscoe, and from there the three of them went to Ruby's little blue and yellow painted house for lunch. For the first time in a long time, Ruby had given herself a day off; Batista, Precious and Patience were running the lunchtime service, which in any case was much simpler these days, since Mrs Beeton and her recipes had been jettisoned.

Ruby had stuffed and baked a yellow-tail snapper, and she served it whole on a long fish-shaped platter with rice and peas and pickled peppers. They ate outside, at a rough wooden table. It had recently rained, but now the sun blazed and behind them, steam rose up from the vegetation, and a loamy, fertile smell mingled with that of the garlicky fish. I need to remember moments like these, Eve thought. Angus licked his fingers and asked to get down, and Ruby said, 'In a moment, because there's something we have to say.' Eve looked at her in surprise, but it was Roscoe who spoke.

'We have decided, Ruby and me—'

'Ruby and *I*,' Ruby said.

'Ruby and I, I mean, have decided that we would like to come with you,' he said.

'That is, if we are still welcome,' Ruby added. Her heart was pounding at the enormity of what Roscoe had said with that handful of simple words.

'Oh Ruby,' Eve said. 'Roscoe.' She found herself unable to speak further, and it was partly happiness and partly an awakening of something far more complicated. She would be responsible for their wellbeing on the alien shores of England. Plus, they were strangers to Daniel, Eliza and Ellen. These darts of anxiety flew through her mind, but now she beamed at them and at Angus, who wasn't following.

'Gussy,' she said. 'Roscoe's coming to live with you in Netherwood.'

His eyes stretched wide with astonishment. 'You too?' he said to Ruby.

'Naturally,' she said. 'I go where he goes.'

He bounced off the bench and ran in circles around the table, then he stopped by Roscoe and said, 'I can show you *my* house, and t'ponies on Netherwood Common.'

'Where will we swim?' Roscoe said, laughing, but Angus's face fell as he remembered there were no Eden Falls in Netherwood, or anything even vaguely like it.

'There's a town pond,' Eve offered, but she sounded unconvincing.

'Oh well,' Ruby said. 'We're going because it's different, not because it's the same.'

'What about your lovely cottage?'

'It will still be mine and will wait for me, should I need it. Bernard will keep the garden in check.' If he didn't, she thought, the house would be strangled by vines within a year. This was an upsetting image, and she banished it at once.

Eve felt she must speak. There was too much at stake to be anything other than honest. 'Ruby,' she said, 'it's wonderful that you're coming, but—'

'Please,' Ruby said, somehow divining Eve's meaning. 'Don't worry. You feel all our happiness will be in your hands, but you're wrong. Roscoe and I will manage our own destinies. We're simply hitching ourselves to your skirts for a short while.'

'What made you change your mind?'

'I said no without thinking,' Ruby said. 'And then, when

469

I *did* think, I found my mind was far from made up on the matter.'

She smiled briskly, then twisted on her seat and reached behind her, and up, into a mango tree. 'Cut this please, Roscoe,' she said, and pulled on the fruit so that its branch came low enough for Roscoe to cut it loose with a knife. 'Bombay mango,' she said. 'The very best kind.'

'Better pack a few,' Eve said. 'They don't grow where we live.'

But Ruby and Roscoe just laughed, as if they'd already eaten enough mangoes to last a lifetime. 'It will be a fine adventure for us,' Ruby said. 'And it's high time we had one.'

Ruby had already packed two suitcases: surprisingly small for such a long journey, but hers and Roscoe's clothes didn't amount to much. 'We'll go shopping,' Eve said. 'Take you both to Butterfield's. You need more wool in your wardrobe.' At least, she thought, it would still be summer when they arrived.

Silas had to be told, of course, but although Eve had dreaded the moment, he confounded her expectations. 'Well, well,' was all he said. 'I do hope the pair of you know what you're doing.' He showed nothing more than a sort of bewildered concern; Eve was sure that Hugh had already mentioned the plan, giving Silas time to rehearse a reaction.

'Will you manage without Ruby in t'kitchen?' Eve asked. 'I never meant to make things difficult.'

'Didn't you? How kind,' he said. 'We'll be fine. Don't give it another thought. Ruby Donaldsons are ten a penny in Port Antonio.'

She considered his words. 'Don't let that mean spirit get t'better of you,' she said. 'If you try to be kind, you might find you are.'

He gave a short laugh. 'I am what I am. I know the heights I can reach and the depths I can plumb. Better, I think, to know what you're capable of. Then one can never disappoint oneself.'

'You've disappointed me, Silas.'

'But Evie, you're such an idealist. You set yourself up for disappointment. Look at you now: about to set sail with a Jamaican cook and her – my – pickney. What do you imagine will happen? Do you think you can force a happy ending through sheer willpower?'

'I can try.'

'I wish you all the luck in the world.'

'Thank you. Be sure to call in, to see 'ow we're getting on next time you're in town.' She was trying to match his disingenuous cordiality, but it didn't suit her. It was high time she left, she thought; he was a bad influence, even on her.

'I certainly will. And I hope the rest of your family like Ruby as much as you seem to. At any rate, I hope they like her more than Seth does.'

She left him, then, feeling as usual that she had come off worse in yet another battle. He knew exactly how to wound, exactly where to sink the dagger. Seth had been astonished when she had told him about Ruby and Roscoe: astonished, and then furious. His principal concern was a childish one: would either of them be given his room? Eve had almost laughed, but mercifully managed not to.

'Seth, it'll always be your room, whenever you want it,' she said. When they had first moved there, Anna had painted a tree on one wall for him, with a different animal on each bough, and it was quite true that Eve had thought Roscoe might like it. Seth said, 'That's not what I asked. I asked would either of them be given my room?'

'Well, I suppose Roscoe might 'ave it when you're not with us. It's a long time since you've been 'ome, love.'

He had glowered at her. There was so much that she didn't understand. If Roscoe was to be raised – with her help – as an English boy, with an English education and English manners, would Uncle Silas begin to see him differently? That the potential usurper of his position was to be given his childhood bedroom seemed horribly symbolic. He didn't want Roscoe to be raised above his station. He wanted Roscoe exactly where he currently was.

'Don't take them, Mam,' he said, but she didn't understand.

'Don't worry, Seth,' she said. 'All will be well.'

'No it won't.' But because he couldn't explain, she ruffled his hair, kissed his cheek and left to finish her packing.

Eve made her farewells at the hotel, but Scotty, Maxwell and Batista all came to the docks to give the Donaldsons the noisy send-off they deserved. Batista sat down on a pile of grain sacks and sent direct word up to heaven for a safe crossing. Ruby kissed her fat cheeks and found they were wet.

'Don't cry, Batista,' she said, although she was crying too. Batista clutched Ruby's hands. 'Take care chile,' she said. 'Trouble no set like rain.'

'I know it's not, and I will take care.'

'I keep up a prayer fo' you an de pickney.'

'Thank you, Batista.' She found herself grateful now for the old woman's faith; found herself comforted. Then, when Batista released Ruby, Scotty and Maxwell got their hands on her; they each wrapped her in a squeeze and tried to make up for all the times they would have liked to do it but hadn't dared. When Maxwell's hands slid down towards her rear she pushed him away and said, 'Thank you Maxwell, that's enough,' and he said, 'Enough? Me no get started,' and hooted with laughter, which helped, because suddenly the mood became merrier and even Batista's face was transformed by a wide, slow smile at the final goodbye.

The SS *Avonmouth* was basic, but comfortable enough. On the *Cassiopeia* there had been a ballroom with crystal chandeliers and a dining room with walnut furniture and silver candelabra, but Eve didn't miss them and Angus – who had Roscoe – didn't notice. The crossing was uneventful, but then they lost a few days' sailing due to a storm in the Bay of Biscay; the ship holed up in a small port in Northern Spain and they waited miserably for news that the waves had abated and the gales had dropped. Eve worried that the delay meant Daniel couldn't know when the ship would dock. She worried that he'd worry. 'At least we're not caught up in the storm,' Ruby said, looking on the bright side, 'and we won't starve: not on a banana boat.'

The boys were kept busy by the crew, who gave them jobs to do and called it fun. 'They'll be able seamen by the time we dock in Bristol,' the quartermaster said, and it was true that Angus could manage a clove hitch and a slipknot even before they reached Spain, and Roscoe was a regular sight suspended on a boatswain's chair, sanding rust from the metalwork of the ship's high sides. 'The seawater's very corrosive,' he told Eve and his mother with great authority. The two women began to feel quite useless by comparison. 'Should we tell t'captain we can cook?' Eve said. 'Lord no,' said Ruby. 'We won't see daylight again for the duration of the passage.' Instead they stayed out of the way and talked for hours on end about England and Netherwood and Ravenscliffe, Eve all the while trying to convey her love for the place without overdoing it, so that Ruby, when she finally arrived, wouldn't have to hide her disappointment.

They finally sailed into the Royal Edward Dock at Avonmouth three weeks and three days after leaving Port Antonio. Eve was awash with anxiety. As the Bristol Channel narrowed and the ship moved inexorably closer to dry land, she chewed her fingers and wondered what she'd done, and prayed for a warm reception for Ruby, who was so far from everything she knew. Ruby herself stood at the port-side rails and watched the city taking shape. It felt cold, so she had borrowed a shawl from Eve, but this was her only complaint; she shone with a sort of inner excitement and seemed to feel no fear.

'Eve,' she said. 'Look!'

Eve joined her at the rail and followed her line of vision. There were three people on the wharf: three people quite clearly not sailors or stevedores. A man stood with a child on each side of him, one taller than the other but both of them jumping and waving wildly, their voices whipped by the wind and carried to Eve where she stood on the deck.

'The rest of your family,' Ruby said.

Eve fetched Angus, and showed him too. 'Wave,' she said. 'Wave and shout. It's your pa and the girls.'

Suddenly this homecoming felt real. Angus yelled so hard that he went red in the face and Eve joined in, so that then all that could be heard was each other, and she stopped and shushed him because she wanted to hear Eliza and Ellen again. It was wonderful to see them, wonderful to be back. More than wonderful. She felt like a crusader returned from the holy wars: she felt heroic, legendary. She turned to smile at Ruby and share the thrill, but found she had slipped away from the rails and was standing with Roscoe back at the funnel deck, away from view.

'Ruby?' Eve said, and held out her hand, but Ruby just smiled and shook her head. 'This is your moment,' she said. 'Don't worry, we'll follow.'

So after they'd dropped anchor, Eve and Angus descended

the gangplank without them. The girls streamed forwards and they hugged and laughed, and tears poured down their faces. Ellen – stiff, awkward little Ellen – clung on to Eve like a spider monkey, with her legs as well as her arms, and Eliza cried and cried into Eve's neck, although her principal emotion was overwhelming joy. Over the top of Eliza's head Eve looked at Daniel, who had his boy in a bear hug, but was gazing at his wife, waiting his turn. She wriggled free, or at least free enough to move, and she stepped towards him so that he was able to reach with one arm and pull her close. He pressed his lips hard on top of her head and spoke into her hair.

'My God,' he said. 'I thought we'd lost you.' His voice cracked at the memory. She tipped her face up for a kiss and then said, 'I'm so sorry,' which sounded trite and inadequate, but was all she could muster. He shook his head, but couldn't speak.

Ellen released her and said, 'Mam?'

Eve looked down at her and smiled. 'Yes?'

'We've loads to tell you.'

'And we've loads to tell you.' At the edge of her vision she saw Ruby and Roscoe making their way tentatively down the gangplank, like guests late to a party and unsure of their welcome. 'But first,' Eve said, 'there are two very important people that I'd like you to meet.' She looked at them and beckoned them over. Angus trotted across to Roscoe and hung on to his arm, claiming him.

'Roscoe and Ruby,' Angus said to everyone. 'My best friends.'

Ruby held out a slender hand and Daniel took it.

'My name is Ruby Donaldson,' she said. 'I'm so pleased to make your acquaintance.' Behind her, Roscoe risked a cautious smile at the girls. They stared at him until they were told to say hello. If they seemed a little mechanical, a little sluggish with their welcome, it had nothing to do with Roscoe himself. Rather, they saw their little brother's proprietorial fondness for this newcomer and wondered how it had come about, and what exactly it meant for them.

'Ruby saved my life,' Eve said, which was a dramatic statement but seemed to fit the purpose. They all looked at her with new interest, and Ruby didn't protest, because, after all, it was true.

'Come on,' said Daniel. 'There's a place over here where we can wait, while they fetch the luggage.' He moved off the wharf with an arm tight round Eve's waist. Ruby and Roscoe followed, holding hands, and the girls in turn followed them, while Angus weaved recklessly between everyone in an ecstasy of over-excitement.

Eliza watched the slim, strong, straight back of Ruby Donaldson and wondered if she was a dancer. She wondered, too, when she might get the chance to tell her mam about Mr Diaghilev. Ellen, feeling strangely deflated after the tremendous thrill of the wait, wondered why these people were still walking with them. Eve felt the blessed security of Daniel's arm about her waist and wondered how even to begin to tell her story, the story of Jamaica. She wondered, too, how it would end.

But for now, no one said anything, which sometimes happens when there is too much to say.

Chapter 52

On the day of the first Open Garden, Dickie Hoyland came home, unannounced. He arrived inconspicuously with the crowds, which was no one's fault but his own, for forgetting to herald his arrival, but, being Dickie, he took it in his stride. He had never been a demanding fellow and had never expected – or particularly received – any great ceremony at his comings and goings, so he didn't mind at all that it was now at least half an hour after his surprise appearance and the only person who knew he was back was Parkinson. Parkinson was also the only person who knew that Dickie was married. He had on his arm a small, plump, vivacious Italian girl whom he introduced to the butler as 'Antonietta, my lovely wife'.

Since Parkinson had survived the regatta, he now believed he could cope with anything. He didn't even very much mind the townsfolk tramping up the long gravel drive and making free with the outdoor furniture, especially since he happened to know that the bailiff, Mr Blandford, had made a full inventory of statuary and moveables. No: Mr Parkinson had added to his attributes the ability to expect the unexpected. So the fact that young Master Dickie – he was ever thus, in Parkinson's mind – had returned from a three-and-a-half-year absence on the Italian Riviera with a wife, was an entirely manageable revelation. Dickie looked swarthy; with his hair slicked back and darkened by Brilliantine he could pass for an Italian himself. Antonietta, if anything, was paler-skinned than her husband, but her hair was a lavish, shining black and her eyes, which were deep liquid brown, reminded Parkinson of the countess's spaniels. Also, like them, she was frisky: she pouted and giggled, and – he was almost certain – once or twice pinched her husband's posterior.

It was all hands to the pumps, the butler explained. The family was outside for the cricket match. Mrs Powell-Hughes and Mrs Pickersgill were serving cakes in the pavilion. 'Pavilion?' Dickie said. 'Temporary, sir,' Parkinson replied. 'At the top of the south lawns.' He would accompany them, he explained, but regretfully he must remain on duty at the hall in case anyone from the town should misinterpret the invitation. 'Open garden,' he said to Dickie, 'does not mean open house.' Fear of invasion, then, kept him at his post, so Dickie and Antonietta went off together, first of all to startle Mrs Powell-Hughes and eat buns, and then to find a few family members and startle them too. Parkinson watched them bounce off down the steps, heads close, laughing at the marvellous jape of their marriage and surprise appearance, and he allowed himself a brief, indulgent moment of mourning for the gravitas and dignity of Netherwood Hall, which had died with the sixth earl. Then, he took a deep, fortifying breath and braced himself for what remained of the afternoon.

Ruby hadn't wanted to come. It was too soon, she said, and too much. At Ravenscliffe she felt comfortable. It stood alone on the common, and she could sit in the garden and slowly continue the process of adjusting to the surroundings while letting the surroundings adjust to her. She realised what a splash of colour she was in a drab town. The yellows and blues of her Jamaican dresses seemed brighter here, and her skin a darker shade of brown. She had walked with Eve to a shop called the Co-op, and people had put down their shopping the better to stare. Eve had introduced her to the manager, a Mr Everard Holt, who wore a brown shop coat but behaved like a gentleman. They had talked about all the vegetables he didn't stock, and the paltry few that he did. He had never heard of a sweet potato, and found the very idea of one amusing. Mangoes, he said, he *had* heard of, but he believed they were only available in tins, suspended in syrup. She told him about the mango tree by her own little house, and he had marvelled and said, 'Well I never, isn't the world a wonderful place?' But Mr Holt had been the only success: no one else had been brave enough to meet her, which was why she felt it was preferable to confine herself to the small world of Ravenscliffe and its garden, for the present. If a person wandered by, as sometimes happened, they would stare, she would smile and greet them, and they – out of politeness, shock or genuine friendliness, she never knew which – would usually return her greeting. If it took a year or two of meeting people one at a time, so be it. What she couldn't imagine was placing herself in the thick of an event at Netherwood Hall, where her fear was that she would be mistaken for a sideshow.

But Roscoe longed to go, and he wouldn't go without her, so his wishes prevailed. Lilly Pickering, the sour stick of a woman who was paid by Eve and Daniel for doing mysteriously little, had told her not to worry. 'We get all sorts 'ere,' she had said flatly, which seemed a curious sort of encouragement. In the end, Ruby had walked at the centre of a protective cordon, with Anna and Eve on either side and Daniel in front.

Roscoe applied his usual philosophy – which was if he loved the world, the world would love him back – and ran ahead to get there early with Eliza and Ellen, and a protesting Angus pleading with them to slow down. Angus was nostalgic for Jamaica, where he'd had Roscoe to himself. Now Eliza and Ellen knew about Anansi the clever spider too, and Angus wasn't sure this was a good thing.

At the gates Daniel had to leave the three women in order to marshal his gardeners and protect the beds. Anna moved closer to Ruby and tucked an arm into hers.

'Once,' she said, 'Eve walked up this very drive quite alone and asked the earl to invest his money in her business. Before that she'd sold what she cooked to passers-by at her front door.'

Ruby liked Anna. She had an inclusive way about her; she was generous with her time and her friendship. 'In Jamaica, we call such a person a higgler,' she said. 'It's perfectly respectable, although perhaps it doesn't sound it.'

Eve said, 'I was shaking, and 'e made a whole long speech to me and I 'ad no idea what 'e'd said.'

'And now there are four shops,' Anna said.

'No more 'iggling,' said Eve.

Ruby gazed around her as they walked. 'These gardens are wonderful,' she said. 'I wish Bernard could see them.'

'Bernard'd recognise a lot of these plants,' Eve said. '"e's pulled enough of 'em up.' Ruby smiled, so Anna did too, although she didn't follow. Sometimes Ruby and Eve seemed to forget that she hadn't been in Port Antonio with them.

They were making their way to the south lawns, where the cricket match was being held. The New Mill Colliery XI had had an unbeaten season and Amos had taken ninety-one wickets, but he'd continued to allow Lord Netherwood to think he'd had to cobble a team together for the event. Without ever putting words into the earl's mouth he had managed to give him quite the wrong impression, or at least, had let the wrong impression go uncorrected. This amused Amos no end. He knew it wasn't a stunt he could have pulled on the earl's father in his day: probably couldn't have pulled it on his big sister either, who knew pit business like her brother knew the contents of his wine cellar. But Tobias Hoyland had a true aristocrat's blithe spirit and stayed away from the mucky end of his estate's business. This made him fair game, and vulnerable to big hitters and fast bowlers who practised twice a week, whether or not they'd just emerged from a shift at the seam. Amos could hardly wait.

Ruby, Anna and Eve settled on a rug at what was being called, today, the pavilion end, the pavilion being a pretty canvas awning trimmed with fluttering pennants, under which refreshments were being served. People stared at Ruby, which was tiresome, but only to be expected.

'If you'd come with a parrot on your shoulder or an iguana on your arm they would stare too,' Ruby said.

'Just smile,' Anna said. 'And if they don't smile back, stuff them.'

Eve laughed. She felt immeasurably grateful to Anna for immediately including Ruby in their friendship. Anna carried with her the right mix of idealism and pragmatism, so that with her support you might attempt the apparently impossible and make it work. It was Anna who had said, don't explain Ruby's presence in Netherwood, just say she's a good friend from Jamaica. 'Don't mention Silas, and all of that,' had been her advice, 'and before very long she'll be part of the furniture.'

'A very unusual, rather exotic, piece of furniture,' Daniel had said privately to Eve. 'She's welcome here as far as I'm concerned, and so's her wee lad, but I don't think folk'll ever stop staring.' And Eve said nothing, only hoped for the best. Soon she planned to show Ruby her shops: the ones in

481

Netherwood and Barnsley, at least. She saw bammies on the counters, and curry goat, and sweet potato pudding.

The wicket, though recently made, was perfectly prepared, but a perfect wicket is perfect for the batsman, not for the bowler. Amos walked the length of it and saw that it was dry, but not too dry, green, but not too green: ideal batting conditions, but a bowler wishing to take scalps would have to be at his wily best. The earl had billed the match as Lords *v.* Miners, which had raised the hackles among the New Mill boys, and that was no bad thing, thought Amos. Fire in the belly was always a help. Their opposition was an effete-looking lot, he thought: striped blazers and silk cravats, and a collection of shared physical characteristics – long limbs, flushed complexions, aquiline noses – that came from only breeding with their own. They all looked as though they'd have valets to carry their bats. There'd been a big rumpus earlier, a giddy five minutes of braying and backslapping, when Dickie Hoyland, the second son, came jogging out on to the pitch, fresh back from a three-year holiday in Italy. Now he was in flannels too, and was loafing around in front of the pavilion as if he'd never been away.

The captains were tossing a coin to determine which side would bat first; Sam Bamford called heads and lost. The earl, eager to wield the willow, was pleased. He lifted his arm for silence and welcomed the cheerful crowd to the Netherwood Hall Open Garden and Inaugural Cricket Match. There was a ripple of applause.

'I'd like to thank Mr Sykes over there for putting together a team so splendidly at such dashed short notice, and I think it's true to say that what you fellows lack in experience you will more than make up for in enthusiasm.' He paused, expecting another ripple, and was surprised to hear considerable laughter. On he ploughed.

'The Lords won the toss, and although it may seem immodest and my skill as a batsman hardly merits it, I have been prevailed upon to open the innings. So, without further ado, may I say best of luck to everyone, and may the best team win!'

He took off his cap and, looking for the countess in the crowd, he skimmed it deftly through the air so that it landed in her lap, then strode out to the wicket. Thea laughed, and promptly took off her own hat and put on his. Maya, who was sitting next to her, thought she had looked much prettier in the straw bonnet. Thea said, 'Look, how funny, your pop's going to bowl.'

Maya looked anxiously at the pitch. Amos was walking away from the crease so she couldn't see his face.

'Did he look cross?' she said.

'What's that, honey?'

'My dad. Did he look mean?'

Thea chuckled. Maya was such a sweetie. She came out with such funny, unconnected statements.

'I didn't really see, I was admiring my husband. Look, here we go.'

Sam Bamford was fielding at cover point, and as Amos turned, rocked and began his run-up, Sam moved in closer and listened hard for the sound of the bowler's feet on the grass. Sometimes you could hear Amos coming, and on those occasions you knew the batsman might just get the chance to hook the ball over square leg. Other times, his approach was entirely silent; he would come in on his toes, lethal like a speeding arrow, and he might have been barefoot for all the noise he made on the turf. This was such a time. Sam glanced at the earl and thought, You're a split-second away from trouble, my son. He almost pitied him for not understanding that this was a duel; for not being ready.

Amos released the beautiful weight of the ball. He felt it leave his fingers like a smooth, red grenade. He put his heart, soul and the devil into it. He put his thirty years of mining into it, all of his political convictions, his personal loathings, his continued and endless sorrow at the deaths of Arthur Williams, Lew Sylvester, Victor Pickering and countless others who were gone, as well as those whose time had not yet come but certainly would: all of this passion, all of this bitterness, was wound tight and compressed into the seamed leather casing of that ball.

He pitched it short, and it hit the ground then rose high and fast at its target. Tobias had expected the delivery to be wide, or to land sweetly on his bat to be sent sailing to the boundary, and because of this misapprehension he reacted a second too slowly. When the penny did drop he reared up from his batting stance like a startled colt and almost dodged the ball, but it caught him full on the shoulder. The impact threw him off his feet so that he crumpled backwards into the stumps. There was a sharp, communal gasp from the spectators, like at a circus when the trapeze artist falls, and then, together, they held their breath for the outcome.

'I say,' someone said on the pitch. 'If that had been his head, he'd be a goner.'

Amos waited patiently for the ball, and for the dismissed batsman to walk. The earl was on all fours now and Dickie, eager to be of use so soon after his homecoming, sprinted over to help him up. As Tobias rose – unsteady on his feet, green stains on his cream flannels, a bruise the size of a saucer blooming across his left shoulder – he looked at Amos, who smiled grimly and said, 'Beginner's luck.'

Tobias stared into his hostile eyes then, like a man who'd

just seen the future and found it wasn't to his taste, turned and limped disconsolately back to the pavilion, and hoped that, come the Day of Judgment, Amos Sykes would rot in hell.

Amos, wishing much the same thing for the earl, turned and walked in the opposite direction. He would ease off with the next ball. He didn't want to simply skittle them out; there was no sport for the crowd in that. Anyway, he'd made his point; his job was done, for now. There would be other opportunities to shine. He tossed the ball up high into the late summer sky and watched it plummet back down into the cradle of his hand. Then he turned on his heel, ready to face the next man.

Watching this, Ruby wondered if she would grow to like Amos Sykes. He seemed a pugnacious sportsman, although he'd been friendly enough to her so far. When the ball hit the batsman, Anna had gasped and brought a hand to her mouth in shock, and now Ruby could see her looking at Amos with a curious expression of vexation mixed with pride, as if she admired his wildness but wanted him tamed.

She scanned the immediate area for Roscoe, and saw him with Angus and the girls on a flat gravelled walkway, not even watching the cricket. Eliza was dancing to the music in her head and soon, Ruby thought, she would be going away to Paris to live with a chaperone and dance with a distinguished ballet company. Ruby was sad to be losing Eliza so soon after finding her. She was a special girl, with a loving nature and a talent for kindness. If Eliza were her daughter, she didn't think she could bear to let her go. Beside her on the path, but oblivious to her performance, Roscoe sat on the gravel with Ellen and Angus, and Ruby could see from the way he was speaking, and the way that Angus leaned against him in a state of bliss, that he was telling a story. This was how he had captured Ellen's cautious little heart so quickly; he had a fund of Jamaican tales with dark middles and happy endings, and she had found them impossible to resist. Ruby had no worries about Roscoe. He was a chameleon child; he adapted to new places and made them feel like home.

On the cricket pitch, the match seemed to be proceeding in a manner more to everyone's liking. Amos Sykes still had the ball, but he bowled it in such a way that the batsman had half a chance of hitting it. Still, Ruby thought, everyone had seen what he could do and might do again; this made him a powerful man. Anna and Eve, who really weren't interested in cricket, had stopped watching and were chatting about this and that, and Ruby knew that if she wished to be included, she could be. But she was happy for now only to observe, letting her attention wander and her gaze alight where chance took it. There was so much to see, and everything was different from her small, tropical island home: different in ways she hadn't been able to comprehend until she arrived. If she'd sailed to the moon it couldn't be more of a contrast.

'Ruby?'

This was Eve, who had placed a solicitous hand on her shoulder.

'Are you all right? You look a bit sad.'

Ruby considered the question. 'I think perhaps I am a little sad,' she said. 'But that's not to say I'm unhappy.'

Eve moved closer to her on the tartan rug and put an arm around her shoulders. 'Everything will be fine,' she said. 'More than fine.'

Ruby nodded and smiled, to reassure Eve that she believed this too. But truthfully, what Ruby felt was that neither of them knew how fine, or otherwise, the future might be. What she did know was that their journey from Jamaica hadn't ended when they arrived here in Netherwood; rather, it had only just begun.

Bibliography

Bailey, Catherine, *Black Diamonds: The Rise and Fall of an English Dynasty* (Penguin Books, 2008).

Beeton, Isabella, *Mrs Beeton's Household Management* (Wordsworth Reference, 2006).

Carter, Miranda, *The Three Emperors: Three Cousins, Three Empires and the Road to World War One* (Penguin, 2010).

De Courcy, Anne, *1939: The Last Season* (Phoenix, 2003).

Devonshire, Deborah, *Wait for Me!: Memoirs of the Youngest Mitford Sister* (John Murray, 2010).

Donaldson, Enid, *The Real Taste of Jamaica* (Ian Randle, 2000).

Hattersley, Roy, *The Edwardians* (Abacus, 2006).

Hughes, Richard, *A High Wind in Jamaica* (Vintage, 2002).

MacCarthy, Fiona, *Last Curtsey: The End of the Debutantes* (Faber, 2007).

Massie, Robert K., *Nicholas & Alexandra* (Phoenix, 2000).

Phillips, Melanie, *The Ascent of Woman: A History of the Suffragette Movement* (Abacus, 2004).

Pugh, Martin, *The Pankhursts: The History of One Radical Family* (Vintage, 2008).

Rhys, Jean, *Wide Sargasso Sea* (Penguin Classics, 2000).

Sullivan, Caroline, *Classic Jamaican Cooking: Traditional Recipes and Herbal Remedies* (Serif, 2003).

Taylor, Frank, *To Hell with Paradise: A History of the Jamaica Tourist Industry* (University of Pittsburgh Press, 1993)

Thorpe, Andrew, *A History of the British Labour Party* (Palgrave Macmillan, 2008)

Q&A with Jane Sanderson

Jamaica is a brand new setting in the series. Why did you choose to move some of the action there?

It's important – indeed crucial – that a novel holds the author's interest as well as the reader's, and I was ready for a change of scene. I'd done a small amount of research during the writing of *Ravenscliffe* into the banana trade between Bristol and the West Indies, and because of that I knew the tourist trade to Jamaica from England was just starting, at the turn of the twentieth century. This opened up tremendous opportunities for my third novel. The dashing but dastardly Silas Whittam was already well established, and moving some of the action to the Jamaican end of his business empire seemed like a natural progression, as well as an exciting new direction.

Tell us about how you researched the Jamaica of 1909. Were you tempted to make a special visit to the island yourself?

I've come to understand, in the course of writing my novels, that a little information goes a long way. Accurate historical detail is essential for authenticity, but it must be used lightly and I think it's always apparent when the author has let their new-found knowledge of a period run away with them. So although I was making a dramatic move into the unknown, I knew that with the help of a few excellent history books I would be able to paint a picture of Port Antonio by dropping in, fairly sparingly, references to actual places – such as the port and Musgrave Market – and place names – including Spanish Town and Frenchman's Cove. Other books – novels such as *Wide Sargasso Sea* and *A High Wind in Jamaica* – taught me the names of indigenous plants and birds, and introduced me to Jamaican folklore. Lots of people asked if I'd be taking a trip to the island and it would have been terrific, of course, to have done so. But I could learn what I needed to know from my books, and although I've never been to Jamaica I have been to other Caribbean islands, so I know how it feels to be caught in tropical rain and to swelter in that very particular, humid Caribbean heat.

The descriptions of the Jamaican food are mouth-watering. Are you a fan of Caribbean cuisine?
I used to live in Kentish Town, North London, in the late eighties (goodness, that's last century!) and there was a small restaurant just off the high street called Halfway Tree, where you could eat goat curry with rice and peas and a side dish of grilled plantain. That was my first taste of Caribbean cuisine, and I absolutely loved it. Since then, I've had perhaps three or four Caribbean-island holidays, so I've eaten snapper and herring fresh from the sea and tried salt cod fritters for breakfast, and I can confirm that it all tastes even better in a beachside shack with sand on the soles of your feet.

Back in England, the Earl and Countess of Netherwood have something of an open marriage. Do you think this was typical of the time?
In the section of society in which they frolic, their behaviour was not untypical. Edward VII's philandering had set the tone for a sort of aristocratic free-for-all and certainly the king

seemed to be able to help himself to whoever caught his eye, whether or not they were married. However, the fact that Tobias and Thea don't yet have a son makes their behaviour more unusual; letters and diaries from the period make it plain that it fell to the woman to remain faithful to her husband until his heir had been born. I felt that Thea would have no truck with that sort of inequality, and that Tobias – who has never been a particularly possessive type – would also see the injustice in allowing himself dalliances but forbidding them for his wife. As the book progresses, however, both begin to question their choices and are drawn back to one other. This gives me considerable pleasure. For all their flaws, I believe Tobias and Thea make a good couple, and will also be good parents.

What do you think is the biggest difference in the national outlook of 1909 compared to that of 2013?
Having given this question a bit of thought, I ended up seeing a similarity rather than a difference. The concept of the 'home-grown' terrorist is a modern one, coined in response to the influence of Islamic fundamentalism on people born and raised in Britain, but in 1909 there was also a real and growing consciousness among the ruling classes of the enemy within. Revolution was a distinct possibility: the king and his cohorts looked anxiously to Russia (where the 1905 revolution had sent a warning shot to the tsar) because Britain, too, was on the brink of massive political and social change. Lloyd George was railing against privilege, unions across the industries were gaining in strength and number, and the campaign for women's suffrage was growing increasingly violent and vocal. So 1909 was a time when the national outlook was turning away from the Empire and broader international concerns, and inward to the ferment of domestic issues – just as, in a different way, we do today.

Feminism is currently experiencing a huge wave of popularity among the women of today. Do you think this would make the trailblazing Henry happy?

I think Henry is a woman born before her time so yes, she would be extremely happy to see the advances we've made in women's rights. Of course, by the end of *Eden Falls* she has pulled away from the WSPU, following the trauma of her imprisonment. But there's more than one way to be radical, and from the very beginning of the series Henrietta has been an unusually strong woman, with a masculine outlook. Her competence at running the Netherwood estate and her practical preference for riding breeches over traditional skirts single her out as an independent-minded young woman with scant regard for convention.

Which character would be most shocked by how society has progressed?

That would have to be poor Clarissa, the Duchess of Plymouth. Her difficulties would lie not so much with technological advances or changing fashions, but with the breaking down of society's barriers and the blurring of distinctions between the classes. Being a rather apolitical creature, she wouldn't have been troubled by who was or wasn't in government, but as the old feudal hierarchies were dismantled all her certainties would have crumbled to dust. Unlike her offspring, Clarissa isn't adaptable or even particularly resilient. Her strength of character is only skin deep and her sense of self relies on position and privilege. One of the reasons she dislikes Thea so much is that the young American woman has not only breached the defences of the English aristocracy, but seems to feel no particular gratitude at being allowed in. I should add, of course, that Mr Parkinson, the butler, would probably stand shoulder to shoulder with the duchess in condemning the rules – or absence of them – in modern society. Together, they could reminisce about the old days while Parkinson waited on Her Grace's every whim, thereby keeping both of them happy.